OATH OF LOYALTY

Novels by Vince Flynn

The Last Man
Kill Shot
American Assassin
Pursuit of Honor
Extreme Measures
Protect and Defend
Act of Treason
Consent to Kill
Memorial Day
Executive Power
Separation of Power
The Third Option
Transfer of Power
Term Limits

And by Kyle Mills

Enemy at the Gates
Total Power
Lethal Agent
Red War
Enemy of the State
Order to Kill
The Survivor

VINCE FLYNN

OATH OF LOYALTY

A MITCH RAPP NOVEL
BY KYLE MILLS

EMILY BESTLER BOOKS
ATRIA
New York London Toronto Sydney New Delhi

An Imprint of Simon & Schuster, Inc.
1230 Avenue of the Americas
New York, NY 10020

This book is a work of fiction. Any references to historical events, real people, or real places are used fictitiously. Other names, characters, places, and events are products of the author's imagination, and any resemblance to actual events or places or persons living or dead is entirely coincidental.

First Emily Bestler Books/Atria Books hardcover edition September 2022

EMILY BESTLER BOOKS/ATRIA BOOKS and colophon are trademarks of Simon & Schuster, Inc.

For information about special discounts for bulk purchases, please contact Simon & Schuster Special Sales at 1-866-506-1949 or business@simonandschuster.com.

The Simon & Schuster Speakers Bureau can bring authors to your live event. For more information, or to book an event, contact the Simon & Schuster Speakers Bureau at 1-866-248-3049 or visit our website at www.simonspeakers.com.

Manufactured in the United States of America

1 3 5 7 9 10 8 6 4 2

Library of Congress Cataloging-in-Publication Data has been applied for.

ISBN 978-1-9821-6491-1
ISBN 978-1-9821-6493-5 (ebook)

ACKNOWLEDGMENTS

When I took over this series (oh so many years ago) I did it with a lot of trepidation. All completely unwarranted, as it turns out. Not only have I had a terrific time, I've learned a lot from Vince's fans and his amazing team.

So, once again, my sincere thanks to (in no particular order) Kim Mills, Emily Bestler, Sloan Harris, Lara Jones, Simon Lipskar, Dina Williams, David Brown, Ryan Steck, Elaine Mills, and Rod Gregg.

None of it would be possible without you.

At what point then is the approach of danger to be expected? I answer, if it ever reach us, it must spring up amongst us. It cannot come from abroad. If destruction be our lot, we must ourselves be its author and finisher. As a nation of freemen, we must live through all time, or die by suicide.

—ABRAHAM LINCOLN, 1838

PRELUDE

SOUTHWESTERN UGANDA

RAPP nodded, though he doubted the subtle movement would be visible in the moonlight. Mike Nash had managed to get their SUV through the river but then bogged down on the muddy bank only a few yards from dry land. The former Marine was still in the driver's seat, bathed in the glow of the dashboard gauges and dangling a winch remote control through the window.

Beyond that, everything was still. Even the breeze had died, leaving nothing but the hum of insects beneath the idling motor. What little evidence of humanity that existed in this part of Uganda had been left behind a good hour ago when rolling farmland had given way to empty wilderness. Above, the Milky Way was smeared across the sky, creating a false sense of peace and anonymity.

In his younger days, Rapp wouldn't have given his surroundings much thought beyond analyzing their tactical nuances. He'd have obsessed over identifying potential ambushes and escape routes, judging the speed with which he could run across the unpredictable surface, and staying outside the beam of the headlights. Now, though, he could almost trick himself into believing it was a safe moment to take a breath.

"Mitch! What are you doing, man? Irene's waiting."

With no trees available, they were having to use a ground anchor to secure the winch. Rapp looked around and found a patch of dirt soft enough to drive the shovel-like blade into. When the hook was sufficiently buried, he raised a hand and Nash started taking in cable. By the time it went taut, Rapp had retreated another twenty feet into the darkness.

He watched his old friend feather the accelerator while working the remote, breaking the tires' suction while being careful not to put too much pressure on the anchor. Satisfied that Nash would soon have the vehicle back on terra firma, Rapp returned his attention to the sky.

Six weeks ago, Irene Kennedy had asked him to take a job protecting Nicholas Ward, history's first trillionaire. Someone with high-level access to the CIA's mainframe had downloaded sensitive information on him and prompted a desperate mole hunt that only five people in the world were privy to. Since then, the situation had gone steadily downhill. The stolen information had found its way into the hands of the Saudis, who had used it to try to kill Ward, a man whose work in alternative energy threatened to make their oil reserves worthless. Rapp had thwarted their attempt, but in a way that made it appear that the Saudis had succeeded. At that moment, the world believed that Ward was in the hands of one of history's most brutal terrorists and that Rapp, Scott Coleman, and most of his team were dead.

It was an all-or-nothing strategy that had been enough to shake the major economies but not enough to identify their mole. With a little luck, though, that would soon change. Ward was using his international telecommunications holdings to track the burner phones utilized by the mole to communicate with his Saudi masters. It was only a matter of time before he came up with a name.

Without that name, though, they still had no idea how deep the mole was burrowed into the Agency's communications. Because of that, Irene Kennedy had sent Mike Nash to Uganda so that he and Rapp could meet face-to-face in order to coordinate their next move. Simple, low-tech, and secure.

Or so he'd thought.

When Nash arrived, he'd handed over a password-protected tablet that contained a video of Kennedy saying that the plot against Ward went much higher than the Saudi royal family. Apparently, the risks were significant enough that, unknown to Nash, she had come to Uganda to talk to Rapp personally. The video ended with directions to a rendezvous point that was about as close to the middle of nowhere as you could get.

The sound of the SUV's engine grew in volume, and Rapp turned his attention back to the man behind the wheel. He was unquestionably courageous, patriotic, and smart as hell. But was he loyal? Yesterday, that would have been an easy question to answer, but a text Rapp had received a few hours ago made him wonder.

Paranoia? Probably. In fact, almost certainly. But no one had ever died from being too paranoid.

"Which way?" Nash said.

The predicted two hours had been turned into a five-hour ordeal that included two more river crossings and one more opportunity to test the winch. Finally, they'd dead-ended into a paved road.

"Right. We're back on track. This is the same road we turned off of after the gas station."

By the time they passed through a small village that was their last landmark, it was late morning. Rapp reached over and reset the vehicle's odometer. "In twenty-seven point three kilometers there'll be a dirt road on the right. Easy to miss in the dark, but we should be okay now that the sun's up."

According to Kennedy's video, that dirt track would take them to a wooded area too steep and rocky to be useful to the farms that once again surrounded them. A clearing near the middle was where she'd be waiting.

As expected, the turn was obvious, and they began climbing a rough track that penetrated the forest. After a few more hard-won miles, Rapp pointed to a small break in the foliage. "There."

Nash pulled in and stopped. "This is it?"

Rapp responded by opening his door and stepping out. Nash did the same, using a hand to shield his eyes from the sun's glare. The clearing was roughly a hundred yards in diameter and ringed by densely packed trees. The ground rolled a bit, broken by a few rocky outcroppings, but was otherwise unremarkable.

Rapp stayed near the vehicle while Nash walked away from it, finally turning when there was about twenty yards between them.

"Care to tell me what we're doing here, Mitch?"

"We're supposed to meet Irene."

"Irene? What the hell are you talking about?"

Rapp came out from behind the vehicle and began moving away from it. "The message on that tablet was to meet her here."

Nash's expression turned skeptical with just a hint of caution. "I left her looking pretty comfortable in her office, Mitch. And why would she send me if she was planning on coming herself? Is there something you're not telling me?"

Rapp didn't have time to answer before the men appeared from the trees. Three of them, covered head to toe in camo, eyes invisible behind goggles, assault weapons in hand. Their positions were perfect, allowing them to keep their guns trained while avoiding any potential crossfire.

Rapp stopped and watched the way they moved for a moment but didn't reach for the Glock hanging beneath his right arm.

"There are four more in the trees, Mitch—all aiming at your head. Every one of them is a top operator and they know who you are. Even with superior numbers and position, I guarantee they're scared. One twitch from you and everybody's going to start shooting."

Rapp nodded, feeling a flare of rage that quickly dissipated into something much worse. Something that hinted at what he'd experienced when his wife died. A deep sense of loss accompanied by the strange feeling that nothing would ever be the same for him.

"Just keep your hands at your sides and everything will be okay."

"Why do I doubt that, Mike?"

Nash pulled his Colt and backed away another ten feet. He was a bureaucrat now, but not so far from his military roots that he'd feel comfortable putting too much trust in these men to protect him.

"This isn't personal, Mitch."

"How the fuck is this not personal? We've been friends for years. We've fought together. We've bled together. And now I'm standing here waiting to be executed by you. For what? A bunch of Saudi money? Your wife makes more than you can spend."

"Not money, Mitch. And not the Saudis. The president of the United States. It's probably hard for you to wrap your mind around this, but I don't work for you. I don't really even work for Irene. I work for the man elected to the White House."

"So, you sided with a politician? That doesn't make me feel any better."

Nash stiffened. "You think this is what I wanted? Are you fucking kidding me? You can't imagine what I've gone through to try to keep us from ending up here. Ward's people should have died in that first attack. Then it would have been over."

"What's he to you?"

"To me? Nothing. But to the Saudis, a lot. After you rescued Ward's research team, President Cook asked me to get information on him. He said he didn't want Irene to know but I didn't think that much of it. I just figured he was fishing for dirt so he could blackmail Ward into supporting him or something. But then Ward's compound gets attacked and he gets snatched. It didn't take long for me to figure out what I'd gotten myself into."

"But you didn't go to Irene."

"For what? To tell her that with my help, the president of the United States had colluded with a foreign government to get rid of the richest man in history? What would be the point?"

Sadly, he was probably right. Cook had majorities in both houses of Congress and loyalists running the National Security Agency, Secret Service, and Joint Chiefs. The current rumor was that he was about to replace the FBI director with a woman who worshipped him and after that he'd undoubtedly set his sights on the CIA. For all intents and purposes, Cook was now above the law. If he were to start shooting tourists through the White House gate, it was unlikely he'd even get impeached.

Nash started to pace. "The world we've been fighting for is gone, Mitch. We collapsed the Soviet Union and killed damn near every Islamic terrorist who's ever even looked at us sideways. The era of wars between superpowers is over—it has to be or none of us survive. Your friend Nicholas Ward thinks that's going to bring in a golden age. But you know that's bullshit even better than I do. People need hardship. They need something to struggle against. Someone to hate and feel superior to. Without those things they lose their identity and sense of purpose. And they can't handle it. Without a real enemy, they start turning on each other. That video of Irene you just watched? One of the president's people made it in less than a day with software you can get for free online. In another few years, half the videos people see on the Internet will be fake. Served up by right-wing nuts, left-wing nuts, foreign powers, and anyone else with a laptop and a sixth-grade education. If we don't take control of that, we'll end up in a civil war. But instead of the North against the South, it'll be four hundred different factions all swinging in the dark. Flat-earthers. Anti-vaxxers. Nazis. Communists. Antifa. The gluten intolerant—"

"And Cook's going to fix all that."

"I think he has a better shot than most," Nash responded. "He doesn't have any illusions about humanity. He knows that ninety-five percent of people are going to fight tooth and nail against the utopia that all these tech gurus like Nicholas Ward want to force on them. And more important, he understands that they'll drag the other five percent down with them. Cook just wants to give people the leadership they need. He wants to make their lives simple. Focus their energy. Give them something to belong to."

"And that other five percent? I assume they get what they want, too?"

"Yeah. Wealth, power, and a nice tall wall between us and them."

"What a beautiful vision."

Nash let out a bitter laugh. "My entire career has been about fighting for America and the American dream, Mitch. But, at some point, it's time to wake up. At some point, you've got to admit that the monkeys are going to figure out a reason to throw feces at each other. The question is how much of it are you willing to let stick to you. I've spent my entire life trying to save people who don't want to be saved. Now it's time for me to save myself and my family. Twenty years from now, I want my kids to be kicking back in penthouses, not scrounging for scraps and killing each other over every conspiracy theory that comes across Facebook. The job's not stopping al-Qaeda from taking out a few people here and there. Not anymore. Now it's about stopping the mob from destroying themselves and everything people like us have built."

Rapp nodded and looked around at the men holding their weapons on him. "So, what's the plan, Mike? I don't have all day."

"The plan . . ." Nash looked down at the pistol in his hand. "The plan is to clean up as much of your mess as I can."

"My mess?"

"Yeah. Your mess. You made everyone believe that Ward and his people are dead, and they need to stay that way. If they get resurrected, it's going to be inconvenient to a lot of people who don't like being inconvenienced. I assume you've got them stashed somewhere around here with Scott? Tell me where. I'll drive over, have a couple of beers with the guys, and then tonight I'll take care of the problem and drive out before anyone knows what happened. After that, if everyone agrees to keep their mouths shut, they can just walk away."

"And Irene?"

"I can protect her. Cook will make me the new director and he doesn't have any reason to pick a fight. All she has to do is fade into retirement." He paused for a moment, finally pointing an accusatory finger at Rapp. "Like always, the problem is you. You're the part of this shit sandwich everyone's going to choke on."

"And that's why I'll never leave here."

"I don't know. Maybe you do. How about I offer you the deal of the fucking century? You give me your word right now that you'll just let this go. That you'll forget about me, the Cooks, the Saudis, Ward, and all the rest. That you'll go back to the Cape, race your bike, spend time with your new family, and never set foot back in the US. Do that and I'll give you a ride to the airport."

Rapp remained silent.

"Yeah. That's what I thought," Nash said, shaking his head slowly. "But I want to tell you something. I'm going to make you a hero. All the shit you've done that no one knows about? I'm going to tell them. You deserve that."

Rapp walked to a rock outcropping, tracked by the men covering him. He sat and rested his elbows on his knees. "I got an interesting text on the way here."

"I meant to ask you about that."

"Like I told you, Ward's people are still a few weeks out from putting names to the network of burners you were using. But he has put together some of the towers they connected to."

"So?"

"So, he noticed something interesting. That one of those phones connected twice to the same tower I do when I'm at home in Virginia."

Nash's brow furrowed as he tried to make sense of what he'd just heard. Rapp decided to help him out.

"Apparently, Nick Ward's memory is better than mine. I don't recall telling him that the man I was meeting today lived in my neighborhood. But he did."

"I don't understand," Nash said, backing away a few more steps and glancing at his backup to make sure they were all still in position.

"I didn't, either. The video from Irene telling me to meet her in the middle of nowhere. The old password from Belarus that anyone high up enough in the Agency could get hold of. The mole who was too smart for anyone to identify. But then the cell tower put it all together for me."

This time when Nash looked at the men covering Rapp, he did so with the intensity of someone who realized something had gone very wrong. It took only a moment before his body language revealed that he'd figured out what that thing was. It was already over when the men removed their goggles and face coverings.

Nash looked away before he could meet Scott Coleman's eye. Understandable in that Coleman was probably his best friend in the world. Joe Maslick and Bruno McGraw—also present—rated pretty high, too.

"What did you find in the forest?" Rapp asked.

"Seven mercs," Coleman said.

"All dead?"

"All but the one we left alive to interrogate. They were solid operators. Too dangerous to play around with."

Rapp nodded and the silence in the clearing began to stretch out. Finally, he broke it.

"I'm giving you a five-minute head start, Mike. For old times' sake."

Rapp took not-so-careful aim and fired a single round into the trees. The sound of the shot was deafening and the snap of the bullet as it cut through the foliage would be terrifying. Which was the goal.

Thirty minutes into the chase, the grade of the forested slope had increased to probably five percent. Barely noticeable to him, but a significant obstacle for Nash. Things would have been different during his time as a Marine, but those days were long past. He'd largely abandoned his cardio workouts for weightlifting and ballooned to a solid two hundred and ten pounds. Good for stabilizing the damage done to his spine back when he'd still been a man of honor, but not so great for uphill running.

Rapp adjusted his aim a few degrees to the left and fired another round. He'd herd Nash up the incline for as long as possible. Even after years of kissing political ass and polishing desk chairs, the man wasn't to be underestimated.

Rapp started forward again, making some effort to be quiet but not going overboard. The same explosion that damaged Nash's back had also damaged his hearing. It was unlikely that he'd be able to separate the rhythm of human movement from the sound created by the intermittent breeze.

This would be a historically satisfying end for the son of a bitch. Humans had evolved not that far from where they were now with very few physical advantages. They weren't fast. Or strong. They lacked sharp claws or big teeth. Their only talent was an ability to keep going, wearing down prey until they finally stopped, stunned and unable to defend themselves.

Rapp wasn't going to involve himself in hand-to-hand combat with a desperate former Marine who outweighed him by almost forty pounds. No, Nash would end up on his fucking knees—gasping for air and waiting for the bullet that would kill him. Or maybe that wasn't entirely accurate. The truth was that the loyal soldier Rapp had known for so long was already dead. He had been for some time. The bullet would just make it official.

As he weaved through the trees, Rapp couldn't help thinking about how it had happened. He remembered the battles they'd fought, some against America's enemies and others between the two of them. He remembered shouting matches about strategy, tactics, and personnel. He remembered drinking on Nash's deck with Maggie and the kids and teaching their oldest son lacrosse.

Rapp slowed as his white-hot rage faded to dull red.

A few years back, he'd forced Nash to take credit for something Rapp himself had done, turning him into a hero. He'd received the Distinguished Intelligence Cross, the fawning attention of Washington's elites, and an enormous amount of media coverage. The unexpected celebrity had made it impossible for him to continue as a clandestine operative. Through no fault of his own, Nash suddenly found himself shut out of the career he'd spent his life building.

He'd been pissed as hell and, in retrospect, probably with good reason. At the time, Rapp had told himself he'd done it for the man's own good. That he was losing his edge and had a family that needed him. He'd convinced himself that he was protecting his old friend. But was that really his decision to make? And were his motivations really so pure? It had been clear that someone was going to have to take credit for what had been done and Rapp didn't want it to be him. The problem was that he hadn't just fled the spotlight, he'd shoved his friend into it in his place.

Rapp came to a stop, listening to the forest around him for any indication of his target. But there wasn't anything. When properly motivated, Nash could apparently still move his fat ass up a hill.

He started forward again but found that his pace had slowed even more. He thought back to a particularly ugly fight he and Nash had years ago. It ended up with Rapp leaving the man lying on the shoulder of the road.

Now he couldn't even remember what they were arguing about.

He tried to refocus on the task at hand, reminding himself that the penalty for taking Mike Nash for just another manicured bureaucrat could very well be death. But the focus wouldn't come. Only the memories.

The hard-to-face truth was that he'd made Nash the man he was today. He'd sent the Marine to the executive floor kicking and screaming. Once there, what had he expected him to do? Nash always excelled. In school. In sports. In combat. Why wouldn't he examine his new battlefield and calculate how to win on it? Why wouldn't he recognize that Washington was an operating environment that didn't reward loyalty and courage. It rewarded treachery and self-interest.

Adapt or die.

As Rapp slipped through the trees, he reflected on the things Nash had said to him back in that clearing. Was it possible there was a kernel of truth in it? Over the course of their relationship, they'd probably disagreed more than they agreed, but Rapp had always taken the man seriously. Sometimes more seriously than he was willing to admit.

Son of a bitch.

Rapp hated doubt. It was almost as bad as regret on his scale of bullshit wastes of time. But there he was. Walking through the forest wallowing in it. Setting a pace designed to ensure that he never caught his target.

By God, he'd make Nash suffer, though. He'd keep running him up this hill until the forest opened onto farmland and forced the man to double back. He'd keep shooting at random, suspending Nash at the edge of panic. Then, eventually, he'd collect Coleman and the guys and drive away. Nash would stay hidden in the woods for days, starving his ass off, getting chewed on by bugs, and hopefully ingesting an amoeba that would cause truly catastrophic diarrhea. Eventually he'd emerge, filthy, unshaven, and dehydrated. Separated from his Agency support and family. Not knowing who he could trust.

When he finally slipped back to the United States, he'd be Kennedy's problem. Maybe she'd ship him off to surveil a Siberian weather station for the rest of his career. Or shove him in a forgotten warehouse full of Cold War intelligence reports in need of filing. Rapp didn't care as long as he never had to lay eyes on the man again.

The sunlight intensified just ahead, indicating a break in the trees. Rapp turned to skirt its edges before spotting a figure near the middle.

Nash.

He hesitated for a moment, but then moved into a position where he'd be visible but still have reasonable cover. Nash had taken no such precautions. He was out in the open with his gun hanging loosely from his hand.

"You're even slower than I thought," Rapp said.

"I didn't figure there was any hurry. Just putting off the inevitable, right? I'm not going to let you push me up this hill until I drop. I'd like to die with a little more dignity than that. If I'm going down, I'll damn well do it with a shirt free of puke and the crease in my pants still holding."

"Whatever works for you."

"It's been a wild ride, huh, Mitch? The things we've done? The things we've seen? Even if we could talk about it, no one would ever believe it."

Rapp just shrugged.

"I stopped to tell you something. And there's no reason for me to lie anymore, right? So, you should take this seriously. None of this shit matters. Just Claudia, Anna, Irene, and Scott and the guys. That's it. Everyone else is just waiting to stab you in the back. That's what I've learned traveling the world's conference rooms. We all die and, in a few years, no one will remember we even existed. Nothing we do means anything."

"Do you have a point?"

"Yeah. I do. Make peace with the president, Mitch. Even you and Irene can't stand against what's coming. I know you don't want to join him, but at least be smart enough to back away. And while I know you haven't listened to me much over the years, you should think about what I'm telling you. It's good advice."

He raised his sidearm until the barrel was tucked under his chin.

"Mike! No!"

But it was too late. The gun sounded and he collapsed to the forest floor.

CHAPTER 1

WEST OF MANASSAS
VIRGINIA
USA

THE rain just kept coming. In sheets earlier. Then in waves. Now it seemed to go in circles, overwhelming the windshield wipers on Rapp's rental car and swirling in his headlights. Behind, Irene Kennedy was piloting her own SUV, tracking him at a distance of only a few feet. The vague glow of his house started to be discernable through his fogged windshield, but it didn't bring much comfort.

He'd just told Maggie Nash that her husband was dead. The carefully crafted bullshit about his heroics hadn't done much to obscure the fact that she was now a widow with four fatherless kids. Nor had it softened the look in her eyes. The one that said "What the hell was my executive husband with a bad back doing in Uganda? Why is he—like so many others—dead while you just keep on breathing?"

A fair question that he didn't have an answer for.

The modern, vaguely museum-like concept of the house looming ahead had originally been dreamed up by his late wife. Architecturally cutting-edge from the outside while allowing for no-compromises security to be integrated from the foundation up. When first completed, it had felt a little like a bunker. Not that he'd had a problem with that. There was nothing like being surrounded by thousands of tons of concrete to make him sleep at night. With the addition of Claudia, though, it had actually started to feel like a home. The smell of cement and fresh paint had been replaced with that of baking bread, flowers, and coconut shampoo. The hum of the state-of-the-art HVAC had been replaced with Anna's breathless storytelling and the banging of pans.

Now, as he closed in, it transformed back into a bunker. Eight million dollars' worth of dead and empty.

The massive gate opened when he hit a button on his key fob and he kept it depressed to allow Kennedy to tailgate him inside. Additional security lights came on as they pulled up to the front door and jumped out into the rain. A custom-made key got him inside, where he disabled the security system and started a diagnostic. He'd already completed one over his mobile phone but didn't trust it. Anything connected to the Internet could be hacked. The physical system, though, was built into the walls and subverting it would take more than some clever hackers—it'd take jackhammers.

It showed all-clear just as Kennedy entered the vestibule. She held her umbrella outside to shake it before closing the door again. It blocked out most of the sound of the storm, leaving him with the drone of the HVAC again.

"Claudia gave me a list of things she wants me to bring back to Africa," Rapp said. "Why don't you grab a bottle of wine and then meet me upstairs?"

Kennedy nodded silently and started toward the cellar.

"Might as well get a good one," he called as he jogged up the stairs. "I doubt I have much time and I'm not sure I'll ever be back."

In fact, he shouldn't have been there at all. But leaving Kennedy to talk to Maggie alone seemed like the coward's way out. He bore a lot of responsibility for her husband's death and the least he could do was look her in the eye when she got the news.

Rapp entered the master bedroom and used his phone to turn on a white-noise generator that played over hidden Bluetooth speakers. It would obscure any conversation from hidden microphones that were almost certainly not there. Better safe than sorry.

He pulled up the list Claudia had given him and waded into the walk-in closet that he rarely set foot in. The tangle of dresses, shoes, scarfs, and God-knew-what-else at first looked random but upon further examination hinted at some overarching master plan.

He'd still managed to locate precisely none of the things on the list when Kennedy appeared with an open bottle of Bordeaux.

"What's the difference between a heel and a wedge?" Rapp asked.

She poured a couple of glasses and then motioned him out of the closet, taking his phone as he passed. A quick glance at the list on-screen was all she needed to start retrieving things.

"What happened, Mitch?"

"Mike was your mole."

She nodded silently. "Can I assume he was working at the direction of the White House?"

"Yeah."

President Anthony Cook was very different from his predecessors. He was autocratic, ruthless, and had no love for the country he ran or the people who inhabited it. In fact, the opposite seemed to be true. He saw every flaw, every weakness, and had an incredible gift for exploiting them. In his mind, the further he could pit the American people against each other, the more he could control them. His only goals appeared to be basking in the adulation of his followers and the accumulation of power.

In many ways his wife was even worse. She was nowhere near as charismatic, but smarter and more calculating. Combined, they were a force to be reckoned with. If nothing else, Mike Nash had been right on that point.

When Kennedy spoke again, it became clear that she'd been thinking about something that hit a little closer to home.

"Did you kill him?"

"He killed himself."

"Are you speaking figuratively?"

"You mean am I saying that he crossed me and that's as good as suicide? No. He put a gun under his chin and pulled the trigger before I could stop him."

She sagged a bit as some of the tension she was carrying released. He watched for a few seconds as she coiled a belt on top of a chest of drawers.

"What now, Irene?"

She didn't answer immediately but when she did, it was with a phrase he rarely heard from her. "I don't know."

"That's it? You got me into this, remember?"

"Do you mean the mole hunt? Or this life?"

"Both."

"I guess I did. Maybe an apology is in order."

"Nah. We had a pretty good run."

"Have we?" she said, turning toward him. "Because it led here. To this place. To this moment. I recognize now that I've been turning away from the truth, Mitch. For a long time. Maybe for as long as we've known each other."

"What truth?"

"That American democracy is much more delicate than I was willing to admit. I always knew there was a power-hungry ruling class, but I didn't allow myself to see how many people would be willing to kneel in front of it. Maybe freedom just demands too much of the average citizen. Too much personal responsibility. Too many opportunities for failure."

"Right before he died, Mike said we should make peace with the Cooks. That we can't beat them. Or change what's coming."

"It's probably good advice."

"He said that, too."

She carried a neatly folded stack of clothing from the closet and laid it on the bed before returning to her wineglass. Rapp couldn't tell if it was his imagination or if her hand shook a little as she brought it to her lips.

"The role of the CIA is going to change under the Cooks, Mitch. It's going to turn inward. They aren't concerned with outside powers, because they aren't a threat to them. They're much more concerned with internal enemies—political opponents, critics, and eventually the American people. Homeland Security is going to become an organization dedicated entirely to maintaining their power."

"That's a big change that involves a lot of people. Are they going to be able to pull it off?"

"I've given that question a lot of thought and the answer is yes."

"But you're still standing. Sounds like the plan was to put Mike in your chair, but that didn't work out."

"No, it didn't," she said, staring into her wineglass.

"But either way you figure you're done," Rapp prompted.

"No question. I have a lot of public support and some powerful friends inside the Beltway, so the Cooks are moving cautiously. But with the lack of pushback they've gotten on their purge so far, there's no reason for them to hold back."

"And you think it'll be effective," Rapp said.

"Incredibly so. Consider how effective the Stasi was at controlling the citizens in East Germany using only handwritten notes, hardwired listening stations, and black-and-white film. Compare that to high-definition video, social media, and artificial intelligence. The technology to surveil every citizen in America exists today. And not just what they do and say. What they think and feel. It's just a matter of scaling up and putting it in place."

Rapp nodded and folded his arms across his chest. "This isn't what I signed on for, Irene. I was happy to defend my country from outside enemies, but it's not my job to defend it against itself. The fact that the

American people vote for these pieces of shit isn't my problem. But the fact that Cook sent one of my best friends to kill me is."

"You're not having any wine?" Kennedy said, obviously anxious to avoid the issue for just a little longer.

"It probably wouldn't be a good idea."

She smiled bitterly and tipped a little more into her glass. "No. I suppose not."

CHAPTER 2

THE WHITE HOUSE
WASHINGTON, DC
USA

THE experts had once again gotten it wrong.

A briefing from NOAA suggested that the storm would pass harmlessly, with only its edges making landfall. Instead, America's eastern seaboard was being hammered by torrential rain and unseasonably high winds. To the south, a number of major cities were without power and flooding was overwhelming unprepared authorities. The DC area was faring better and, according to those same experts, would continue to do so as the storm weakened. Whether that prediction would prove to be any more accurate than the first one remained to be seen.

Catherine Cook stood silently at the window of her office, watching the trees struggle against the onslaught and listening to the rumble of it through the glass. Not as good a view as those afforded by the windows behind her husband's desk in the Oval Office, but still an extremely interesting perspective. Far different than the one from the office she'd occupied as first lady of California. Or the one she'd had at the hedge fund she once ran.

She'd worked her entire life to get where she was now but had still arrived unprepared for the scale of it. The problems and opportunities of governing California seemed trivial by comparison. And the billions she'd handled during her time in high finance were nothing but rounding errors to the Federal Reserve.

Above it all, though, was the overwhelming sense of opportunity. While many of her colleagues in New York were blind to it, Wall Street's dead end was easy to discern. Once one acquired everything money could buy, it all became a game. A petty competition between people with insecurities that they mistook for ambition and superiority.

Running California had been largely the same. With no access to the national security apparatus, no military, and a limited ability to engage foreign powers, the end of the road had been less obvious, but just as real.

This window was different, though. Despite the driving rain, she could see forever.

She and her husband were the right people in the right place at the right moment in history. They had an opportunity to remake not just America, but everything. The liberty that the free world had enjoyed over the last century was nothing more than an anomaly. A momentary pause between the priests and nobles of antiquity and the politicians and billionaires of the new age. A momentary pause that was coming to its end.

They were entering an era that could be dominated in a different, but much more profound, way than in the past. The acquisition of territory—so important at one time—had become irrelevant. Society's next iteration would be one overseen by a network of loosely allied dictators spread across the globe. The challenge was making sure that it was the American president, and not the leaders of China or Europe, who ushered in that change. And for that to happen, Washington would have to be transformed into a central power that exceeded even Beijing or Moscow. Weakness and compromise could no longer be tolerated.

So many opportunities. But only for those with the courage to take advantage of them.

Boldness in the political arena was not something her husband had ever lacked, but now their operating environment had shifted. And on unfamiliar ground, glimmers of something she'd never seen in him were becoming visible: cowardice.

He had been elected for his charisma, his good looks, and his confidence-inspiring certainty. He could charm, anger, and terrify with an effortlessness that no one in the world could match. Anthony Cook was a lightning rod for human emotion. Whether that turned out to be love or hate was irrelevant. Either way, it dominated everything and everyone that came into his orbit.

Or at least, that's what he had once been. Before they had crossed paths with a meaningless CIA thug named Mitch Rapp.

Catherine turned toward a television depicting the governor of North Carolina walking through the storm that was devastating his state. In normal times, her husband would have been alongside him—looking young and vital, his drenched dress shirt clinging to a muscular torso. He'd have been depicted talking to locals with an expression of deep concern. Unloading trucks. Stacking sandbags. But no more. Virtually all activities that took place outside the gates of the White House had come to a screeching halt. He'd even backed away from the online partisan sniping that kept the American people so entertained. His mind was now focused on one thing and one thing only: countering the perceived threat posed by Mitch Rapp.

She turned back toward the window and after a few moments heard the door open behind her. There was no question as to who it was. Only one person in the world entered her office unannounced.

"I thought you had a meeting with Dick Trenton?" she said without turning.

Trenton was a billionaire donor who reveled in his access to the president and missed no opportunity to sit across from him in the Oval Office.

"I canceled it."

"Why?"

He evaded the question. "Still no word from Mike Nash?"

She let out a long breath but kept facing the window, preferring to look at his hazy image reflected in the glass. "No. But that isn't particularly surprising. He said it would take time."

"But how much time, Cathy? How do we know that he didn't have a change of heart once he reconnected with Rapp and the others?"

"Mike's not an idiot, Tony. He understands where the world is going and the role he can play in it. He's not going to make enemies of us in hopes of getting forgiveness from Mitch Rapp."

"Then maybe Rapp killed him. Like he has everybody else."

She closed her eyes, blocking out the distractions around her. "Mike is a former recon Marine and one of the few people in the world Rapp trusts. More likely, Rapp's already dead and Mike's in the process of getting to Nicholas Ward. Once that's done, we'll replace Kennedy and it's over. No one's going to push back against Mike taking over at the CIA. If anything, he's better liked around Washington than Kennedy. She has a way of making people uncomfortable."

"But can we trust him to stay on the path we're building?"

That was a more difficult question. Nash still had an archaic sense of morality that he couldn't completely break free of. In the end, though, he didn't have to like any of this. For now, it would be enough for him to understand that he had no other options.

"There's nothing we can do about that now," she said. "But there are things we can do about the Chinese making you look weak in the Pacific. And we need to strategize about how to take advantage of the immigration fight that we both know is coming. And then there are your slipping approval—"

There was a quiet knock on the door and a moment later her assistant opened it. "I'm sorry for the interruption, but Stephen Wright just called to say he's on his way here. He wanted me to tell you it's urgent."

Not surprisingly, that got her husband's attention. Wright was the recently installed head of the Secret Service and the man in charge of his all-important physical security.

"When?" Cook said, spinning toward the door a little too eagerly.

"Ten minutes, sir."

Catherine Cook settled into the seating area that dominated the center of the Oval Office. In contrast, her husband chose his normal position behind the modern table that had replaced the Resolute Desk. Constructed of glass, steel, and polished wood, it fit the new décor and was a reminder to all who entered that the past was dead. The battles ahead could be won only by those capable of breaking free of history's limitations.

Cook stood when his Secret Service chief entered, but Catherine remained on the couch. She'd known Wright for almost twenty years and had never seen him looking so haggard. His thick gray hair was still perfectly arranged and his tan improbably even, but there was perspiration gleaming on his forehead and gathering in the lines around his eyes. Not that it was surprising. He was a former judge with no history of running large organizations—government or otherwise. What he did have, though, was a vision of a new world order that was very similar to their own. Further, he was smart, trustworthy, and very much enjoyed the status provided by being a member of their inner circle.

His first task as director had been to begin purging the Secret Service's security detail of anyone with loyalties to either Mitch Rapp or Irene Kennedy. Secondarily, he was augmenting existing security protocols and changing those that Rapp and Kennedy would be familiar enough with to circumvent. Finally, he was quietly overseeing some of the agencies that had not yet been brought under the Cooks' thumb—most notably the FBI.

"What do you have for us?" the president asked.

"My people temporarily lost Irene Kennedy, but then the surveillance team watching Mitch Rapp's neighborhood reacquired her. She went to Mike Nash's house—"

"Is he there?"

"She met someone in the driveway who we couldn't identify because of the weather. They went inside for about forty-five minutes and then drove to Rapp's house. Getting surveillance inside his wall is difficult. Particularly with drones unable to fly."

Cook went silent for a moment, his eyes darting nervously around the office. "Is it him? Is it Rapp?"

"I don't think we need to jump to conclusions," Catherine interjected. "It could just be Mike. He and Kennedy might have business at Rapp's house. They'd certainly have access to it. Mike is probably one of the people who take care of it when it's empty."

Wright just stood there in silence, looking back and forth at them. It was something she'd become accustomed to long ago. They governed very much as a team and people often weren't sure where the power in the room was located.

"It's him," Cook said.

"Tony, we—"

"Don't patronize me, Cathy!" He turned back to Wright. "Is your team ready?"

She felt the hairs stand on the back of her neck. "What team, Tony?"

"Yes, sir. In place and waiting for your authorization."

"Do it."

Wright gave a short nod and rushed from the room. When the door closed, Catherine repeated herself. "What *team,* Tony?"

It was hard to discern whether he was intentionally ignoring her question or just having a hard time tracking on it. "Mike's dead," he said flatly. "And in all likelihood, Rapp tortured him first. If that's the case, he knows everything about our involvement with the Saudis. With Ward. And he knows what we sent Mike to Africa to do. Right now, he and Kennedy are standing in that fortress he built planning their next move."

"You need to calm down, Tony. Even if everything you say is true, we don't know what that next move is. This is our town and our country. Ours. Not theirs."

"I'm not willing to be so dismissive, Cathy. If we let them disappear, they'll reconnect with Coleman and his team. And that's not all. They still have allies all over—"

"If Mike's out of the picture, then Nicholas Ward is probably still alive," she said, trying to stop him before he completely disappeared into the rabbit hole he was heading down. "We're going to have to figure out how to handle that when it becomes public. There's also the problem of no longer having a credible candidate to take over the Agency. Mike was going to be a popular appointment that would provide some cover for the ones that—"

"Politics? Are you really talking about politics while Rapp and Kennedy strategize about how to get to me?"

"I think it's unlikely that's what they're doing. I admit that Rapp isn't one to forgive, but Kennedy calculates everything she does. And a rash move against us isn't going to pencil out to her."

"Tell that to Christine Barnett."

Christine Barnett had been their party's leader before her very unexpected suicide. Conspiracy theories and suspicions abounded, but no one had ever been able to turn up anything that contradicted the official story.

"Speculation, Tony."

"Speculation? Christine thought she was the second coming of Jesus and she was eight points ahead in the polls. Then, right when she's about to get everything she's ever wanted, she kills herself? Don't insult my intelligence. Or your own."

"More reason not to go after Kennedy and Rapp half-cocked, Tony.

Right now, you're in the most secure place on the planet, with a literal army dedicated to your safety. We have the luxury of stepping back and taking a breath."

Another unfamiliar expression flickered across her husband's face. Suspicion?

"That's easy for you to say, Cathy. Rapp's not coming for you. He's coming for me."

CHAPTER 3

WEST OF MANASSAS
VIRGINIA
USA

RAPP'S cell phone began to vibrate and he pulled it from his pocket.

"Problem?" Kennedy asked from inside the closet. She was searching Claudia's drawers for something called an obi belt while polishing off her second glass of wine. It was more than he could remember seeing her drink in their entire relationship. And why not? Neither of their prospects looked particularly sunny. And his had just taken a turn for the worse.

"I just got a breach warning. The power's been cut to the subdivision's main gate."

"I'd hoped you could be on your way before this happened. I imagine the president's anxious to talk to you."

"I'll bet."

"Can I assume you have a plan for something like this?"

He did. The default state of that gate was locked, so cutting the power wasn't going to accomplish much. The incursion team would know that, though, and were probably just using the move as a diversion. In all likelihood, they had people in position all around the property and in the woods behind it. While the specific security measures built into his house weren't widely known, the general level of it was an open secret. They wouldn't want to risk a frontal assault and instead would purposely trigger an alarm in an effort to flush him out. And it was going to work. In the most literal and infuriating way imaginable.

"Yeah," he said at a volume that caused his voice to get swallowed by the room's white-noise generator. "Could you let Claudia know what's happened and put her stuff in FedEx for me?"

"If I'm not in prison," Kennedy said, pouring herself another glass. And not her normal two fingers. If the operators closing in on his property didn't move fast, they'd find her passed out on the sofa.

Rapp scrolled through images from the neighborhood's security cameras, pausing on one that depicted men in tactical gear coming over the southern perimeter fence. Through the rain, it was hard to see detail, but it wasn't necessary. There was no point in trying to get a head count. They looked like swarming ants.

It'd take about seven minutes to reach his property, where they'd dig in. If he didn't make an obvious break for it, they'd lay in an old-fashioned siege. Time, supply lines, and numbers were on their side.

He started for the door but before passing through the hallway he turned back toward Kennedy. "It's been interesting."

She smiled and raised her glass. "That it has."

The rain was really pounding when Rapp stepped outside. If anything, it was coming down harder than when they'd arrived. Even with the powerful security lights, the perimeter wall was just a haze. Puddles had overflowed their customary depressions in the flagstone courtyard and water was rushing toward strategically positioned drains. Once again, he'd gotten lucky. Surveillance drones would be grounded by the weather, and dogs—much more dangerous than humans in these kinds of situations—would be neutralized. He was concerned about the number of men waiting for him in the woods behind his house, though. Was it twenty? Fifty? A hundred? As Kennedy was fond of pointing out, the president of the United States had a lot of resources. Far more than the terrorists and old enemies that the house was designed to turn back.

Rapp was soaked through by the time he reached an island of dense landscaping on the house's west lawn. He fought his way through the foliage, struggling to maintain forward momentum as the branches grabbed at him from all sides. Water was running in a thick stream from the bridge of his nose when he reached the center and dropped to his knees. At least it wasn't cold. Temperatures were still in the high seventies but would drop into the mid-sixties later that night. By that time, though, he'd either be safe and dry or on his way to sunny Guantanamo Bay.

After scooping away a few handfuls of muddy leaves, he found the metal hatch he was looking for. The wheel that opened it was stuck but that was a feature, not a bug. He'd been worried that Anna might happen upon it while searching for the soccer ball that always seemed to get away from her. A little more digging turned up a steel bar that he threaded through the wheel for additional leverage.

Rapp had bitched endlessly about the exorbitant cost of ensuring that his walled property didn't turn into Virginia's largest swimming pool in the rain. About halfway through the excavation, his attitude had done a one-eighty. The engineer working on the project had been more than a little surprised when Rapp suddenly demanded a much larger drainage pipe than necessary. When he'd then insisted that it include an access point big enough for a human to get inside, she'd thought he'd completely lost his mind. In the end, though, as long as the checks cleared no one seemed all that interested in complaining.

It took a little more effort than planned, but he finally freed the latching mechanism and pulled back the cover. Leaning into the hole, he used a red penlight to illuminate the moldy walls of the pipe and the two or so inches of water rushing through its bottom. Fantasizing about twisting Anthony Cook's head off was just enough to motivate him to slip inside and pull the hatch closed behind.

He'd learned to control his claustrophobia, but not the rage he felt at being chased out of his own home. And not by a bunch of ISIS pricks wearing suicide vests or a Russian Spetsnaz team looking to avenge their former leader. No, he was being pursued by the country he'd spent his life defending. Worst-case scenario, maybe even some kids he helped train.

The force of the water and increasing slope of the pipe started to help him along as he inched feetfirst through the confined space. When he reached what he calculated to be the edge of his property, the grade steepened enough to let gravity take over. He could feel himself picking up speed, but in the blackness, it was impossible to tell how much.

It turned out to be more than he bargained for when the pipe finally spit him out about a hundred yards from his property line. He felt himself go airborne, the sensation of the rain again, and finally the impact with the muddy slope. He cartwheeled out of control, finally hanging up in a bush after another twenty-five yards or so. Better than getting stopped by a tree, but still not one of his most graceful or dignified escapes.

He lay there tangled in the branches, completely motionless as he tried to discern whether his reappearance had been noticed. In the end, though, his senses were pretty much useless—overwhelmed by the darkness and crash of the storm. Fortunately, that would go both ways. He'd have had to literally land on a patrol to get picked up.

Rapp waited there for another five minutes before freeing himself from the bush and starting down the mountain. He stayed low, slithering on his stomach, stopping every few seconds to assess. His objective was roughly another four hundred yards downslope and he managed to cross about half of it before the rain started to ease, reducing its effectiveness as cover.

His situation was further complicated by the fact that he was facing an opponent very different from the ones he was accustomed to. The men tracking him were likely military or operators from the Homeland Security branches. Who knew what they'd been told about the mission and the man they were hunting? They would be full of pride and patriotism, willing to do anything to protect their country from the enemies lurking in the shadows. He couldn't in good conscience kill them, but they'd likely be working under somewhat looser terms of engagement.

The next hundred yards went pretty smoothly, though the rain was now turning intermittent. After another couple of minutes, it stopped completely and a hole opened in the overcast. The haze of starlight was just strong enough for Rapp to discern movement to the west. He laid his cheek in the mud and went still, using only his eyes to track a vague silhouette approaching his position. Details became sharper as the distance closed—fatigues, assault rifle, athletic gait despite boots hunting for traction. Even more concerning was the helmet-mounted night-vision gear. Rapp had used a similar setup in an operation about a year ago. The left eye was light amplification and the right thermal. It created an image that was a little disorienting and blurry in detail, but it did a good job of highlighting body heat. The fact that he was caked with mud and there was a tangle of foliage between them would attenuate the effect, but that advantage couldn't be counted on. When being hunted with thermal, it was critical to not allow darkness to make you subconsciously complacent. The trick was to pretend you were wearing a bright orange jumpsuit in broad daylight.

Most of the trees around him had trunks too narrow to provide adequate cover, but there was one about twelve feet away that looked viable. He stayed on his stomach, moving steadily and making it to the tree in question with no fireworks.

Timing was now the issue. Once he came into the man's field of vision, he had to keep his imaginary orange jumpsuit entirely behind the tree. That meant moving around it at the same pace as his pursuer's advance—a trick that had to be done entirely by feel.

After another minute, Rapp had circled a full forty-five degrees around the trunk with no gunshots or shouted calls for backup. It was tempting to stay put long enough for the man to put some distance between them, but he had no idea how many of his comrades were out there or how they were organized. Other teams could be just out of sight, getting ready to move on his position. In this particular scenario, speed gave him a better chance of survival than caution.

He reached the gully he'd been searching for without any more contacts but almost missed what he was looking for. The forest had really taken hold since he'd last been there, causing him to generate more noise than he would have liked penetrating it. Fortunately, the trees around him were still actively dripping, generating a disorienting soundscape that, while not as good as rain, would be enough to cover a little impromptu landscaping.

The hatch he uncovered was similar to the one in his yard, with the exception that it was set up to be easily opened and had a rubber seal to keep it watertight. After slipping in headfirst, he closed it behind him and turned on his penlight. The pipe was a leftover from the construction of the subdivision and significantly larger than the one he'd escaped through. Capped at both ends, it was also quite a bit dryer. Damp and stinking of mold for sure, but at least its eight-foot length was free of standing water.

Rapp's gear was where he'd left it more than a year ago. Fatigues, civilian clothes, an assortment of weapons, cash, and IDs were all sealed in heavy plastic bags. Water and canned food were stacked to one side, but otherwise creature comforts were scarce. A light sleeping bag and waterproof bivvy sack were about it. He'd identified the need for a latrine when he'd created the place, but drilling through the pipe to make one had always been beaten out by other priorities. After a few days, that particular oversight would likely become extremely unpleasant.

CHAPTER 4

THE WHITE HOUSE
WASHINGTON, DC
USA

THREE unfamiliar Secret Service agents ushered Irene Kennedy into the Oval Office and pointed her toward the modern desk that dominated it. She obediently took a position in front of it, examining her reflection in the dark windows behind. It wasn't a pretty sight. Makeup running, soaking wet, and dripping on the president's brand-new oak floor. Virtually nothing of the past—nothing of tradition—remained in the room. And that was probably fitting.

She'd used Rapp's master password to lock down his house while she finished collecting Claudia's things. From his tablet, she'd been able to monitor the teams taking positions outside the wall but none had been in any hurry to come over it. When attacking Mitch Rapp on his home field, caution was very much the better part of valor.

After finishing off another glass of wine and taping up Claudia's box, she'd briefly entertained the idea of just staying. There was probably enough food stored for a year and the wine cellar would last even longer. The government—her government—would eventually sabotage the solar panels, and the diesel backup generators would run dry. At that point, Anthony Cook would order his hesitant men to charge. They'd swarm the property with their automatic weapons and battering rams, and the jig would be up.

After a few hours in front of the fireplace to give Rapp time to carry out his escape plan, the effects of the wine had begun to diminish. And with them, so did the appeal of spending weeks alone in a house under siege. It had been an entertaining fantasy while it lasted, though.

She stood staring at her reflection long enough to create quite a puddle before the Cooks appeared. The president sat behind his desk and dismissed the Secret Service men guarding her. Catherine, interestingly, took up one of their positions. She tended to sit in a chair to the side of her husband's desk or, in more dire circumstances, stood behind his right shoulder. For whatever reason, she seemed content to observe this interaction from a distance. Why? Safety? Perspective? Catherine Cook had a reason for everything she did. It was a trait that she and Kennedy shared and could have potentially become the basis for a functional working relationship. There was no hope of that now, though. In hindsight, maybe it had been naïve to believe there ever was.

"Where is Mitch Rapp?" Cook said, staring directly at her.

"He left the house when your people cut power to the subdivision's gate. After that, I don't know where he went."

"You expect me to believe that?"

"There's no reason for me to know Mitch's escape plan in the event of an attack, nor would I want to. What if I were captured by one of his enemies and questioned?"

She allowed her tone to suggest that she believed that's exactly what had happened.

"Where would he go?"

"Again, I have no idea."

"You're the one who trained him to disappear," Cook said, the volume of his voice rising in step with his frustration.

"Actually, Stan Hurley did. And Stan had a healthy distrust of governments—including his own. I assume that Mitch has safe houses all over the world and a fair number of identities that I don't know anything about. But I couldn't tell you for certain."

"Mike Nash," the president said, seeming to realize that his line of questioning had hit a dead end. But she decided not to let him get away with those two simple words. Not after what he'd done.

"What about him?"

"I want to talk to him."

"I think you've done enough of that."

He extended his index finger and aimed it at her like a gun. In truth it was much more dangerous than that. "You may be useless to me, Irene, but you never struck me as stupid. Just about every ally you thought you had in this town would now slit your throat to stay on my good side. And the ones who wouldn't are on their way out. What legacy are you wanting to leave? And how hard do you want the rest of your life to be?"

He was right. She wasn't stupid. Despite decades of service, she had precious few friends left inside the Beltway. It was a town built around power, and that power now flowed from the man sitting in front of her.

"Mike's dead," she said finally.

Cook's expression went blank. "Rapp murdered him?"

"He committed suicide."

"You expect me to believe that?"

"You didn't leave him much choice," she said, suspecting it was the remaining effects of the wine talking but no longer capable of caring. "You told him to provide you the CIA file on Nicholas Ward so the Saudis could use it to kill him. When you found out you'd failed, you manipulated Mike in a way that left him no option other than to go to Uganda and deal with the situation before we discovered that *he* was the mole we'd been searching—"

Cook's laughter was loud enough to cut her off, but not loud enough to hide a hint of insecurity. He was right to be confident in his position, but overconfidence was an error he wouldn't make. Or, more accurately, an error his wife wouldn't allow him to make.

"Do you have any evidence of that, Irene? Any at all?"

"I don't need evidence, Mr. President. Because this isn't a war I'm interested in fighting. You got this position in a fair election, Mike made the decisions he made of his own free will, and I'm not naïve enough to believe that I could win a confrontation between us."

He stared at her in silence for a long time, but in the end, he seemed to accept her explanation. "But what about Rapp? He's not as smart as you."

"Mitch makes his own decisions."

"And what are we going to do about him?"

She barely managed to stifle a smile—the first one in what seemed like a long time. Cook's conspiratorial tone was so light as to be almost translucent. A test. Maybe not even that. The suggestion of a test. Was Kennedy susceptible to the subtle forces that had twisted Mike Nash? Could Cook look into her soul and find something she wanted? Some weakness that could be used to control her?

No. If that weakness had ever existed, it was gone now. What she'd said about not wanting to fight was true. Perhaps the truest words she'd ever spoken in her time as CIA director.

"I think I can save us some time by telling you that I'm not Mike. You've never done anything to earn my admiration or loyalty, while Mitch has done nothing but. I violently oppose where you and your constituents want to take this country. But I also acknowledge that I'm not in a position to do anything about it."

"Then I guess you know what comes next."

"I do."

"Don't go back to Langley. You won't make it through the gate. Your personal effects will be sent to you."

She turned to leave with no further acknowledgment of him.

"Let this go," she heard Catherine say. "If you do that simple thing, we're willing to send you off with a glowing speech and a Medal of Freedom."

Kennedy opened the door and passed into the outer office like she had on so many occasions before. This time, though, would likely be the last. Her life of service, the battles she'd fought, and the sacrifices she'd made had all come to nothing more than a muddy puddle in front of the president's desk.

CHAPTER 5

WEST OF MANASSAS
VIRGINIA
USA

RAPP activated the light on his watch and looked down at the dial: 10:43 p.m. In one minute, he would be able to commemorate his third day of living in a pipe. It was an arbitrary deadline, but as good as any. He felt around for a can of WD-40 and sprayed some on the hatch's locking mechanism before beginning to slowly twist it. He had no idea what was happening outside, making silence critical. The hope was that he'd emerge into an empty forest, but it was just as likely that he'd find himself surrounded by search parties, dogs, and helicopter-mounted searchlights.

The first quarter of an inch was promising, revealing nothing but darkness beyond. He moved his face close, feeling the cool air against his skin and taking a few gulps of it. Initially, the lack of a latrine had been workable. But after the unexpected failure of one of the plastic bags he'd been using, things had gotten pretty ripe.

Widening the gap a few more inches provided a view of nothing more threatening than trees glowing in weak starlight. Judging by the condition of the ground, the rain must have stopped at least a day ago. The lack of a storm or any appreciable wind would make it easy to hear anything out of the ordinary, so he propped the hatch open and spent the next hour listening.

Satisfied that at least his immediate surroundings were clear, he pushed two liters of water and a vacuum-sealed bag of clothing into the outside world. After crawling after them, he went still again, reexamining his operating environment. Still no sign of any human presence. Skies were dead clear, with temperatures hovering in what he guessed were the low seventies. The search for him had moved on—likely to roads, airports, and friends or family who might harbor him. Anthony Cook would undoubtedly be pulling out all the stops.

Rapp stripped, using the bottled water and some baby wipes to clean off mud, sweat, and the stench of excrement. The process took a little longer than he'd hoped and would have benefited from a Brillo pad and some bleach, but he finally managed to make himself presentable.

The clothes were designed to make him look like a hiker—semitechnical and accompanied by a backpack large enough to carry essentials but not so large that he couldn't move quickly. A subtle pocket had been added to the bottom right that housed his Glock and allowed for an awkward but functional cross draw.

He tossed his dirty clothes and empty containers back through the hatch before closing and covering it with dirt. After another quick check of his surroundings, he started straight downslope. There was a trail that cut across the base of the mountain, mostly used by hunters so vacant this time of year. If Claudia had done her job—and she always did—he'd reach his escape vehicle a half an hour before sunrise. With a little luck, he'd be out of US airspace by early afternoon and back in Africa by tomorrow.

Assuming that's where he wanted to go.

He weaved through the trees, sometimes taking the path of least resistance and other times embarking on random detours. There was no sign he was being tracked, but that didn't mean much. He'd made some formidable enemies over the years: al-Qaeda. ISIS. Half of Congress and two-thirds of the Saudi royalty. But no one quite like the president of the United States. Cook controlled the most powerful military and intelligence apparatus in history as well as the loyalties of world leaders across the globe. In light of that, things were starting to feel pretty lonely.

Of course, he still had Coleman and the guys, but how far did he want to drag them into this shit show? Nicholas Ward had a genuine distaste for the Cooks and enough power that they'd think twice about coming up against him, but there was a limit to the debt he owed Rapp for saving his life.

And, finally, there was Irene Kennedy. A woman who had been there for him since the beginning, but who now had problems that rivaled his own.

It seemed to come down to him, Claudia, and Anna now. But was that fair? He'd made himself so toxic that no one with half a brain would want to stand within a blast radius from him. He'd already been through this with his late wife. And that wasn't a cross that got any lighter with time. Very much to the contrary.

He had bug-out plans formed decades ago and updated every six months. A plastic surgeon in Argentina. Money. Identities. But the secret to a successful disappearing act wasn't the sexy stuff. It was leaving everything behind. Not just friends and family, but in many ways yourself. No more endurance racing. No more security operations of any kind. No travel to places where he'd lived or worked in the past. If he really wanted to get lost and stay lost, he'd have to gain forty pounds, move to Panama, and spend the rest of his life getting drunk on the golf course.

Not a pretty picture, but what was the alternative? Cook would assume that Rapp had killed Mike Nash and that he knew the White House was behind his betrayal. After that, Rapp's reputation would work against him. Cook would assume that they were in a death match. In one corner, the president of the United States backed by the military, Homeland Security, and virtually every intelligence agency on the planet. In the other corner, Mitch Rapp and his Glock 19. Winner take all.

The Ford F-150 was probably five years old, with evidence of its hard life visible even in the predawn twilight. Virginia plates were current, and the filthy bed was scattered with the general detritus of rural life. Most important, it was parked right where it was supposed to be: a rutted dirt road that was all but abandoned during the summer.

The keys were buried beneath a rock near the front bumper and he used them to gain access. After starting the engine, Rapp dug a brand-new satphone from the glove box. Installing the battery, he used an encrypted protocol to connect to Claudia in Cape Town, South Africa.

"Are you all right?" she said by way of greeting.

"Fine."

"Were you in the pipe all this time?"

"Yeah."

"Did you ever install the latrine?"

"Let's not talk about that," he said, accelerating down the road.

"I had to move the plane to its tertiary location. You'll be flying the first leg yourself. The weather looks good and it's an aircraft you're familiar with, but be careful."

He frowned at the thinly veiled—but admittedly deserved—insult to his piloting skills.

"Understood."

"When you get to the second plane, tell the pilot where you want to go. Fair warning: I'm being watched."

It was to be expected. The Cooks would be covering all bases.

"How much effort are they putting into it?"

"One, maybe two people. No electronic surveillance on the property—I'm sweeping regularly—but they probably have some capability outside the walls. I doubt they think you'll show up here. Too obvious."

"Anything else I should know?"

"A mutual friend of ours lost her job."

She was clearly referring to Kennedy but wanted to avoid keywords that the NSA's artificial intelligence might flag for further attention.

"The end of an era," Rapp said, uncertain how to feel about it. Anger? Resignation? The desire to open a good bottle of tequila and toss the cap in the trash?

"True. But it can also be the start of a new one."

CHAPTER 6

THE WHITE HOUSE
WASHINGTON, DC
USA

CATHERINE Cook avoided her normal path across the lawn, staying to the pavement. Temperatures had risen into the eighties, but the grass was still soft from the torrential rains the eastern seaboard had suffered. Most important, though, was that the flooding in the Carolinas had subsided quickly enough to make her husband's lack of interest more a missed opportunity than a weapon for the opposition.

A man with more sensible footwear than her own overtook her to the left, sweating in black tactical clothing behind a German shepherd. He spoke briefly with a group of similarly clad men—these holding assault rifles—before continuing on his way. Manifestations of her husband's increasingly oppressive security.

Outside the gate, traffic was being diverted around recently installed barriers, exacerbating Washington's already significant traffic issues. The additional security personnel were augmented by hastily erected checkpoints and scanner stations, giving points of ingress a distinct airport feel. Further, much of the personnel not directly involved with security had been deemed nonessential and sent home to work until further background checks could be done. She herself had lost a full third of her staff.

Her husband had always been seen as a risk taker. He knew what he wanted and went after it with a level of aggression that was unusual even in her world of high finance. That passion and the destructive impulses that sometimes came with it were what made him so relatable to the common man.

It was also what made them such an effective team. Her dispassionate, analytical nature tended to work as a foil. In the end, their hard-won compromises formed the best of all worlds—carefully calculated strategies wrapped in the messianic flair humanity needed from its leaders.

What she'd missed was that her husband had never been faced with a *physical* threat. The passion that she'd mistaken for strength was turning to terror as he realized that losing to Mitch Rapp wouldn't be the same as a political loss. In politics, there were opportunities even in defeat. Ways to lie, spin, and blame. With Rapp there would be no second chances. His defeated enemies didn't return stronger for the experience. Nor did they come back to fight another day.

To make matters worse, her ability to sway her husband seemed to be slipping. As his paranoia grew, he was increasingly looking to others for counsel. To people who promised him something she couldn't: protection.

Finally, there was the threat posed by Nicholas Ward. He had returned to the public arena the day before, announcing that his death had been faked as part of a strategy to defeat a plot against him. A strategy that hadn't just saved his life, but had allowed Mitch Rapp to wipe out one of the world's most brutal terrorist organizations in the process. The story had hijacked the news cycle so completely that anything short of a war with Iran would be insufficient to get it back.

So, while her husband hid behind his increasingly elaborate security apparatus, the world's first trillionaire was out in public, looking poised, brilliant, and decisive. Worse, he now had the backing of Mitch Rapp and Scott Coleman's organization. With the nearly inevitable addition of Irene Kennedy, he would have more power than most countries.

The fact that Ward was shamelessly taking credit for what had happened in Uganda was telling. He knew that she and her husband had moved against him and was making a show of pushing back. Sending the message that while he preferred to stay out of the spotlight, he understood how to use it as well as anyone.

Of course, the conspiracy theorists were having a field day and their ideas were already beginning to surface in the mainstream media. Ward's paramilitary win in Uganda and subsequent resurrection were being conflated with the increased security at the White House. Elaborate stories about a shadowy war between the billionaire class and the political elite were springing up everywhere. The only variant was which side was good and which evil.

Fortunately, that was something that could be turned to their benefit. The value of Ward's companies had plummeted during his temporary death and the inevitable rebound could be used to generate accusations of profiteering, tax fraud, and stock manipulation.

Even better, Ward's actions in Uganda seemed to have caused the death of numerous minors. The fact that these children were butchers could be glossed over. With a little sleight of hand, they could be portrayed as innocents who could have been rehabilitated if their lives hadn't been snuffed out by Ward in his single-minded pursuit of safety and ever more wealth. With luck, they might even be able to conjure a faint odor of racism.

These were the problems that would be the focus of her imminent meeting with her husband. Just the two of them and their lead political strategist. No distractions, no tangents, and no other considerations. They needed to regain control of the narrative and reestablish Anthony

Cook as the only reliable purveyor of strength, truth, and stability. Because if they didn't do so quickly, everything they'd worked for would collapse. Without a shepherd, the sheep quickly became lost.

"Good afternoon, ma'am."

Catherine gave a nearly imperceptible nod to her husband's secretary as she passed the woman's desk. Her mood darkened when she opened the door to the Oval Office and saw that their political strategist was nowhere to be seen. Apparently he had been replaced by the director of the Secret Service and Darren Hargrave, the man they'd chosen to take Irene Kennedy's place at the helm of the CIA. They were standing close to one another near the room's seating area, speaking to her husband in rushed, muted tones.

The three men gave her barely more attention than she had the secretary outside, but Catherine refused to acknowledge the slight. Instead she took a seat on one of the sofas, examining each of them in turn. It took more focus than she would have liked to hide her deepening concern.

In many ways, Hargrave was Stephen Wright's opposite. The Secret Service director was good-looking, forthright, and a man who made up for his lack of creativity with attention to detail. Hargrave possessed creativity in abundance, but at his core was a backstabbing bastard with a gift for destroying everything and everyone around him. The exception to this was Anthony Cook. For whatever reason, Hargrave was utterly mesmerized by the man. To call him loyal would fall well short of describing his relationship to the president. *Acolyte* might be a better word. Or *disciple*. Hargrave was less interested in gathering power unto himself than basking in the glow of her husband's. He was also almost pathologically jealous, using any opportunity to drive subtle wedges between Cook and anyone else who had his confidence. In fact, Catherine sometimes wondered if Hargrave's wife and children were just a cover. If, in fact, his feelings for her husband went deeper than people suspected.

All this had been quite convenient over the course of their fifteen-year association. Hargrave was a ruthless soldier with boundless devotion and flexible morals. Now, though, he had the potential to become dangerous. She'd monitored him over the years and could already see what was coming. He would carefully stoke her husband's fear, using it to become advisor, confidant, and guardian. Allowed enough free rein, he would set himself up as the only person who really cared while everyone else just wanted to use the president for their own ends.

A few minutes passed before her husband finally looked in her direction. "Rapp's still missing."

"The question is whether he's on the run," Hargrave said, motioning with his head toward the windows. "Or if he's just outside the gate. Waiting."

Catherine watched her husband's expression go slack and couldn't help admiring Hargrave's delivery. Mitch Rapp suddenly felt all but omnipotent. A boogeyman whose menace was made more insidious by his absence than by his presence. An indistinct shadow just beneath the surface of the ocean. A quiet creak in the night.

"What do you think?" she said, turning her attention to Wright. "Is he waiting outside your gate, Steve?"

The Secret Service chief looked at her and then the president, clearly not yet comfortable with his new role. "We're reasonably confident that Scott Coleman and Bruno McGraw are at Nicholas Ward's compound in Uganda, but it's impossible to be a hundred percent certain. Joe Maslick and Irene Kennedy are both at their homes in Virginia and Charlie Wicker is in Wyoming. We have solid surveillance on all three of them. Claudia Dufort, Coleman's logistics chief and Rapp's partner, is at her house in Cape Town with her daughter. Given all that and the level of security here, I don't think an assault on us here would be practical."

"It would be naïve to believe that Coleman and his team are the only people Rapp can turn to," Hargrave pointed out. "I have analysts going over the files on every operation he's ever been involved in, and I can tell you that he has allies everywhere. People whose lives he saved, people who owe him their careers, foreign operatives he's fought with. Even private contractors who will do anything for the right price. You could have men on your security detail right now who have a connection to Rapp that we haven't discovered ye—"

"We've been *extremely* careful selecting the people handling the president's security," Wright interjected, clearly angered by the attack on his competence. "Most are too young to have served with Rapp and the rest have very clear employment histories that never put them in Rapp's or Kennedy's sphere of influence. We've also changed any security protocols . . ."

Catherine tuned out the argument that ensued. She'd been blindsided by the attack on Rapp's house—something that didn't happen often. Her husband hadn't consulted her on the move, either because Hargrave had convinced him not to or because he knew that she'd have objected. It had been a thoughtless act driven by panic and by the sycophants he was surrounding himself with. Foolishness and weakness—traits very much on display in the heated discussion playing out in front of her—tended to be fatal at this level.

"Is Mitch Rapp even a threat?" she interrupted.

The obvious, but apparently unexpected, question caused the room to go silent.

"This isn't your area of expertise," her husband said, turning toward her. "Nor is it mine."

But it apparently *was* the area of expertise of an acting CIA director who, until a week ago, had been their personal lawyer? A Secret Service chief who was still moving into his office? With hindsight, she wasn't surprised that the threat of physical danger would rob her pampered husband of his reason. She was surprised, though, at how quickly and thoroughly the transformation had come about.

"Mitch Rapp loves this country," she said. "He's spent his life defending what he believes are its ideals. You were chosen by the American people and are governing exactly the way you said you would.

Are you sure he wants to assassinate a sitting president and further destabilize a country that's already struggling? And even if he does, any move he makes would put him up against the men and women sworn to protect you. People he knows and admires."

"What do you suggest we do to test that theory?" Hargrave countered. "Have the president make a speech from an open podium in Nebraska? Throw out the first pitch in a stadium full of baseball fans?"

Cook glared at the man, and he averted his eyes. Catherine took a bit of solace in that. Her husband wasn't completely under Hargrave's spell. Not yet. Unfortunately, their former lawyer would come to the same conclusion. He'd retreat for the moment, recalibrating before resuming his slow advance. In a month, would her husband be so quick to put him in his place?

"I don't think we need to descend into the ridiculous," she said. "In the short term, Tony should stay here behind the security the Secret Service has worked so hard to create. We'll use that time to reacquire Rapp, refine our security protocols, and continue to purge people who are loyal to him and Irene Kennedy."

"I agree," Wright said. "I see this as a diminishing threat. Right now, we don't have our systems fully updated and we don't know everyone who owes Rapp or Kennedy. In the coming months, though, we'll sort that out."

"But Rapp knows that, too," Hargrave protested. "He may be the most successful assassin in history. It isn't going to be lost on him that his job gets harder with every day that goes by. If he's going to make a move, it needs to be while there are still cracks that he can slip through."

Cook nodded silently, considering what he'd heard. "We'll reconvene in two days. When we do, I want to know where Rapp is, and I want options."

CHAPTER 7

NEAR FRANSCHHOEK
SOUTH AFRICA

IT always took Rapp a few days to reacquaint himself with driving on the left, and focusing entirely on avoiding a head-on collision felt strangely therapeutic. The long flight to South Africa had been consumed by thoughts of Irene Kennedy, Anthony and Catherine Cook, Mike Nash, and the country he loved but was now struggling to recognize. Setting his mind to the task of not becoming a hood ornament on one of the oncoming farm vehicles allowed him to put everything else aside for a while. To just enjoy the cool breeze coming through the window, the vineyards surrounding him, and the distant mountains glowing under dead clear sky. The United States was now thousands of miles in his rearview mirror. The only question now was, would that be far enough?

He turned onto a gravel road and at the top of the first rise was rewarded with a view that he needed more than he'd realized—the thatch roof of a Cape Dutch home peeking over a tall white wall. Many of the trees around the perimeter had been cut back to improve visibility, leaving the area a bit sparse until the neighbors' vines began. Overall, the property gave the impression of not having changed much over the better part of a century.

In fact, the house included state-of-the-art alarm and surveillance systems as well as some defensive protocols that would impress even the security-obsessed South Africans. At Claudia's insistence, though, it was all cleverly hidden. When they were in America, she subjected herself to his purpose-built bunker. But when she was in South Africa, she got to live in her idyllic turn-of-the-century oasis. Such were the compromises that were so unfamiliar to him but apparently necessary if he wanted to have a life beyond work.

When Rapp pulled through the gate, he was greeted by a now-familiar scene. Two Rhodesian ridgebacks rocketed from around the meticulously whitewashed home, zeroing in on his SUV as Claudia appeared on the front porch. They hit the side of the vehicle hard enough to rock it on its suspension, generating a collage of claw marks that were the reason he'd sprung for the most generous insurance policy Hertz had to offer. There was less growling and salivating than in the past, though. A step in the right direction, but not a big enough one that he would risk getting out before his backup arrived.

It did a moment later in the form of a seven-year-old girl with a tangle of blond hair and a missing incisor. She leapt from the porch and ran toward him, waving excitedly before shouldering past the dogs. Confident he was safe, Rapp opened the door and scooped her up. Aisha and Jambo pawed and barked but didn't seem to want to tear him apart anymore. In fact, they might have actually been excited to see him.

"How's it going, runt?"

"It's going great! Can we go for a ride later? It's still not late. And the weather's really good. Mom doesn't like me taking my bike outside the wall when you're not here. It's so boring to ride around in the yard. We should definitely go out. It won't be dark for hours! And it's supposed to rain tomorrow."

"I don't know. I'm kind of jet-lagged and I'm guessing you're gonna drop the hammer the second we get out on the road."

"I won't! We'll do an easy day! Zone one! Even on the hills."

He grinned as he carried her toward the house. She was already picking up his training jargon.

"If you promise. Recovery pace the whole way."

"I *totally* promise. We'll go hard on Thursday."

They finally reached the stoop and he put her down before giving Claudia a quick kiss. She looked down at her daughter and pointed inside. "I went into your room a few minutes ago and I think you know what I'm about to tell you."

She always spoke French to Anna in hopes of turning her into a native-level speaker. That and the state of the girl's room had become the foundation of a cold war between them. As usual, she got her reply in English.

"It's not that messy. And Mitch just got here!"

"If you want to ride with him later, I suggest you go up there and get to work. Because your butt won't be getting anywhere near that bike seat until everything's back in your closet. And I don't mean just thrown in there, either."

"Fine!" she said angrily and stomped off. Rapp winced. She'd picked that up from him, too. He needed to be a little more careful. What they didn't need was to get a call from school notifying him that she'd kneecapped one of her schoolmates with a cricket bat.

Claudia took him by the hand and led him to a steel reinforced door at the back of the living room. They passed into what had once been a windowless bathroom. The walls were now armored and a metal cabinet full of food and weapons stood where the bathtub had once been. Various electronics were stacked neatly on a shelf next to the sink and below a bank of color monitors. In the center was a tiny table with three folding chairs.

Again, a pale reflection of what he had in the States. Provisions were limited and the space had neither filtered air nor a secure water supply. To the positive, it was soundproof and sturdy enough to hold off even pretty well-equipped attackers for the better part of an hour.

Once the door was firmly shut behind them, Claudia's eyes filled with tears and she threw her arms around him.

"What?"

"I didn't know if we'd ever see you again. With everything that's happened, I thought you might just disappear."

"I considered it," he admitted. "And it's still an option."

She released him and pulled back. "No, it's not."

"Hold judgment until you hear the full story."

They sat, but before he could start, she spoke. "What happened to Mike, Mitch?"

"Maggie didn't tell you?"

Claudia and Maggie Nash had become close friends during their time as neighbors in Virginia and, as a new widow, he assumed that she'd turn to Claudia for support.

"She told me that he saved you and the guys in the jungle. It was a beautiful story. Too beautiful to be true, I think."

"Mike was the mole," Rapp said flatly. "He was working directly for the Cooks."

She brushed a lock of hair from her forehead. The African sun had bleached it noticeably, while darkening her skin an equal amount. The contrast was increasingly obvious, as were the lines at the edges of now-downcast eyes. He knew people called them laugh lines, but in her case that might be a bit optimistic. It was hard not to wonder if their relationship was eating away at her even more than her prior one. Any way you looked at it, it had been a long thirty-five years for her. Sure, many of her problems were self-inflicted, but in his extensive experience, that didn't make them any easier.

"Did you kill him?" she asked finally.

"What difference does it make now?"

"It makes a lot of difference, Mitch. You live with a lot, but Mike's different. If that's something you're going to be carrying around, I want to know about it."

"No. He killed himself. Before I could stop him."

"And that's the truth?"

"Yes."

"I'm . . . I'm sorry, Mitch. I know how close you were."

He shrugged, making sure it looked more casual than it felt. "Everybody dies. And the rest of us move on until it's our turn."

"But move on to where?"

"That's the question. I think it's safe to say that Anthony Cook isn't happy with me."

"And what do you propose we do about that?"

"I'm thinking about asking Irene to try to broker a truce."

Her expression suggested it wasn't what she expected to hear.

"Surprised?"

"A little bit. It seems like an uncharacteristically sensible course of action."

"It's what Mike wanted. What he offered me and I didn't take. If I had, he'd be alive and we'd be a hell of a lot better off."

"But you were angry."

"Hell yes, I was angry. All those years and he turned on me for some piece-of-shit politician he just met. What am—" Rapp caught himself before the bitterness he felt about Nash's betrayal could take hold. Instead, he waved a hand around him, indicating her and the house. "But now I've put myself in a position where sensible is my only option."

"And that's our fault? Mine and Anna's?"

"Fault? No. I made my choices and I don't have any complaints. But you probably should. Anthony Cook is a megalomaniacal nut. And all megalomaniacal nuts have one thing in common: deep down, they're cowards. He's afraid of me. That makes him dangerous."

"Having him as an enemy," Claudia said, speaking deliberately, "is less than ideal."

"That's one way of putting it. The bottom line is that if he isn't willing to let this go, I've got problems. And if we stay together, you do, too."

"We've had this conversation so many times, I feel like we should record it and just play it back to each other once a year."

"I hear what you're saying, Claudia, but this isn't some terrorist looking to make a name for himself. There could be a Reaper drone circling us right now. And when the government here complains about the new crater in their wine country, he'd say they were targeting an al-Qaeda cell, then spread around enough money to make the whole thing go away."

"Like I said, it's not ideal," she admitted. "But you still have friends. Irene, Scott, and the guys. If he drops a bomb on us, they'd react. And that's not a group you start a war with lightly."

"I don't—"

"I'm not done."

He fell silent.

"This is our life, Mitch. We consciously decided to gather all our skeletons and combine them in one closet."

"Kind of a crowded closet, though, isn't it?"

"Yes. But it is what it is. You can't keep seeing this family as a temporary accommodation that can be unraveled every time something bad happens. We're in this together. We're stronger that way. We have to be."

He considered that for almost a minute before speaking again. "Then where do we stand?"

"Like I told you on the phone, we're being watched by at least one operative, probably two. I assume they also have our everyday phones and unencrypted Internet traffic."

"So the Cooks know I'm here."

"No question. Irene, Joe, and Wick are in the US and all are also under surveillance. Bruno and Scott are in Uganda at Nicholas Ward's compound, so they're probably clear for now. The US doesn't have much intelligence infrastructure there and, as you know, it's a fortress."

Rapp nodded. "Then for now, we run with this strategy. As long as me and the guys are in plain sight, Cook doesn't have much to worry about. Maybe we can turn down the heat on this thing."

"A gesture of good faith," she said.

He smiled. "More likely an easy target."

Rapp stepped out onto the porch, squinting at the dogs rushing him from the east. This time he didn't call in his prepubescent bodyguard, instead glaring intensely at them. Their speed faltered and both stopped a few feet away, content to eye him from that distance. After a few seconds he stepped forward and gave each of their heads a good scratching. When he pulled a phone from his pocket and started walking, they fell in behind.

The Samsung was an off-the-shelf model with no special security and connected via Claudia's family plan. He rarely used it because it was too easily compromised, but in this case that was what he was hoping for. After selecting a name from his contacts, it seemed like it rang for an abnormally long time before being picked up.

"Sunning yourself?" he said.

"Actually, I was outside doing a little gardening."

"Did you say gardening?"

"You sound surprised."

"No. Not at all. It sounds like retirement's agreeing with you."

"Retirement," she said. "Is that what we've decided to call it?"

"Based on what I've been seeing on the news, yeah. The Cooks aren't exactly singing your praises, but they're being cordial."

"I imagine that the first lady has convinced her husband there's no profit in a war between us. That the best thing for them is to just let me fade away."

Rapp shaded his eyes and watched the sun glint off the broken glass that topped the wall. Dust from the surrounding vineyards was creating a haze over the mountains as the wind started to kick up. He wondered if it would be enough to dampen Anna's enthusiasm for a bike ride.

"What about a war with me, Irene? Do they see a profit in that?"

There was a long pause before she answered. "There's no question that the president sees you as a threat. Right now the resources of the US government are focused almost entirely on his personal security."

"I don't know much about politics, but that doesn't seem like a winning strategy. People don't elect a president to spend four years hiding under a desk."

"I imagine his campaign advisors would agree. But what about you? What are your thoughts on this?"

He took a seat on a stone bench, leaning back against the perimeter wall as the dogs dropped into the grass at his feet. They didn't stay long, though. Anna appeared in the front door and started toward the outbuilding where the athletic gear was kept. She laughed as they danced around her, trying to smack them on their noses, but every time proving to be just a fraction too slow. He watched her in silence as she crossed the lawn. A reminder that he had no choice but to ignore every instinct he'd developed over the years. Mitch Rapp the family man. The peacemaker. The fount of reason and compromise. It was hard not to laugh.

"I want a truce. Can you broker it?"

When Kennedy responded, she didn't bother to hide her relief. "I'll call Catherine this morning and see what I can do."

CHAPTER 8

CIA HEADQUARTERS
LANGLEY, VIRGINIA
USA

EVERYTHING looked familiar but, like so many things in Langley, it was an illusion. In fact, nothing was the same. The organization she'd spent so many years shaping was gone. The ideas, values, and beliefs it was built on had been cast aside with terrifying speed and ease.

Irene Kennedy was wearing a visitor's badge and being led through the building by a nervous young woman she'd never seen before. Catherine Cook had refused her request for a face-to-face meeting and instead insisted that Kennedy go through Darren Hargrave, the man who had replaced her. She assumed that it was a reminder from the president that she was now persona non grata in Washington. Catherine Cook likely would have preferred to handle this herself. It was a meeting that had the potential to define her husband's time in office and the first lady was too smart to trust it to a man as unstable as Hargrave.

The reaction of the people she passed was interesting in its predictability. A few—old acquaintances close to retirement—stopped to exchange veiled words about what was happening to the organization and country. Most, though, just averted their eyes and scurried away.

In the alternate universe that was the nation's capital, one was either in power or invisible. It was an adjustment that many influential people never managed to make, causing them to spend the rest of their lives begging for scraps. Kennedy, on the other hand, had always looked forward to the day she would leave it all behind. Obviously, this wasn't the way she'd imagined that exit, but it had its advantages. A clean break with no entanglements that could arrest her momentum.

Mitch Rapp's philosophy was even more unusual. His preference would have been to go through life without anyone in Washington ever knowing he existed. Paradoxically, he'd accomplished too much to make that possible.

And now here she was, not asking for the gratitude he was owed or the recognition he deserved. Nor for compensation for the endless list of injuries he'd accumulated or the personal losses. Only that he be allowed to live out his life in peace. After everything he had done, that was the best he could hope for.

They entered the elevator and rose to the seventh floor. When Kennedy stepped out, she found the same décor but all new faces. Expected, but still disorienting. Old colleagues had warned her that Hargrave had little interest in the Agency's operations throughout the world and was focused entirely on eradicating her influence from the organization. Talented veterans were being demoted, forced into retirement, or moved to remote posts, only to be replaced by people she would have never dreamed of putting in positions of responsibility.

After only a week under Hargrave's leadership, her prediction was coming true. The CIA's focus was moving from protecting the country to protecting the Cooks.

She was pointed to a chair in what had been her outer office and told to wait. It would be a while, she suspected. A petty power play that so many in Washington couldn't resist. Yet another reminder of her newly minted insignificance.

Kennedy pulled a tablet from her bag and opened the book she was reading. Incredibly, it contained nothing at all about geopolitics, economics, or military strategy. Instead, it was a memoir by a woman who had moved to Italy to renovate an old house. Kennedy had bought it in hardback when it was first released but had been forced to donate it unread to the library when she'd run out of bookshelf space. Now she was a third of the way through the electronic version and enjoying herself immensely.

"Ma'am?"

Kennedy looked up at Hargrave's assistant. "Yes?"

"Electronic devices are prohibited."

She smiled and went back to reading.

"You're up, Irene."

Almost forty-five minutes after her arrival, Darren Hargrave finally appeared in what was now his doorway. Kennedy powered down her tablet and stood, but instead of waiting to shake her hand, he disappeared back into his office. She collected her things and entered, closing the door only to find him already stationed behind his desk.

Of course, all her personal belongings were gone. As promised, they'd been delivered by courier the day after her dismissal. The artwork, most of which had been on loan, was also missing, replaced with myriad eight-by-ten photos of Hargrave posing with other people. Not unusual. Washington's denizens loved to hang pictures of themselves hobnobbing with the rich and powerful. Upon closer inspection, though, she noticed that Hargrave's taste was a bit more specific. Every single picture—and there were more than she could count without being obvious—featured Anthony Cook. Also interesting was that there was no third person in any of them.

"Sit," he said, motioning to a chair in front of his desk.

She did, ignoring the fact that the command was delivered with the tone someone would normally use to address a dog.

"Catherine told me I should take this meeting, so here we are. Now, what is it I can do for you?"

"I assume that by now you know Mitch is in Africa?"

He just glared at her. A man like Hargrave would take that as a veiled insult. A reminder that he'd failed both to capture Rapp at his home in Virginia and to prevent him from leaving the country. In fact, she had no such intention. While she had a strong distaste for her successor, she couldn't blame him for his lack of success. If she'd been charged with capturing Mitch Rapp, she wouldn't have fared any better.

"Why would I care?" he shot back and then immediately seemed to recognize the idiocy of the response.

"It appears that the president is concerned that Mitch might want to do him harm. I'm here to convince you that's not the case."

He laughed. "I'm told that you're a persuasive woman, Irene. But I'm not an idiot."

"Neither is Mitch. He recognizes that the president was within his rights to ask Mike Nash to provide him with information from the CIA database and that he was free to do as he saw fit with that information."

"There's more than that, though, isn't there, Irene? Nash didn't go to Uganda just to talk."

"Mike could have walked away at any time. The fact that he didn't was his own decision."

"I'll ask you again, Irene. What do you want?"

"A truce."

He studied her silently for a few seconds. "Terms?"

"None. He wants to be left alone. If the president doesn't make any moves against him, he'll show the same restraint."

"So, the great and terrible Mitch Rapp is just going to turn the other cheek, huh?"

"He's not as volatile as people make him out to be, Director Hargrave. And he has a family now."

Her successor considered that for a few moments. "Well, he might not have terms, but I think we would."

"Such as?"

"That he and his people stay in plain sight and none of them ever set foot in the United States again."

"When you say 'his people,' who are you referring to?"

"Scott Coleman and his team."

"Impossible. They have lives here and nothing to do with the relationship between Mitch and the president. The government certainly has the ability to watch them when they're on American soil, but it's a waste of time and resources. Even if Mitch wanted to harm Anthony Cook—which he very much does not—he'd be reluctant to involve the people close to him."

"What about Rapp, then?"

She let out a long breath. "I imagine I can convince him to stay out of the US as long as the Cooks are in power. As far as being in plain sight, he'd likely agree to not actively try to evade surveillance. If your people were to lose him for whatever reason, they could just call and he could tell them where he is. Also, I think it would be reasonable to allow him a three-month window to wind down his affairs here."

"No way in hell. Let his girlfriend deal with it."

Once again, Kennedy found herself disoriented by what was happening. Without Mitch Rapp, there likely wouldn't even be an America. After a domestic terrorist brought down the country's power grid, it had been he who'd captured the man and figured out how to get the electricity flowing again. In the absence of that, America would have collapsed into hunger, cold, and violence. Anthony Cook had admitted as much in a recent meeting.

"I'll have to ask him," Kennedy said finally. "But I think he'll agree."

"Then I'll do the same with Tony."

She reached for the bag next to her chair and stood. "Thank you."

He pulled a file folder from a stack to his left, refusing to further acknowledge her.

CHAPTER 9

NEAR FRANSCHHOEK
SOUTH AFRICA

RAPP glanced at the heart rate monitor on his handlebars and saw a number that was a little concerning. One hundred and eighty-three. The big-screen TV in front of him depicted his avatar surrounded by other cyclists on a dead flat road. The video game allowed him to connect his bike trainer to real-time races that drew competitors from around the globe. This one had started fairly slow, but at the thirty-mile mark, a small group that included a few young pros had broken away. In a moment of temporary insanity, he'd decided to go with them.

His training program—a document that he generally treated as having been delivered on stone tablets—had him scheduled for a hundred miles at a moderate heart rate of one hundred and thirty-five. Going out on the open road where he could be easily taken out by a rifle shot or even a car, though, hadn't seemed like a great idea. So, while this virtual race wasn't ideal, it was a lot healthier than numbing his anger and frustration with whatever he could find at the back of the liquor cabinet.

The simulated road steepened, and the trainer increased its resistance in response. Rapp shifted and stood, sweat cascading to the floor despite the outbuilding's bay doors being thrown open to the sixty-degree air outside.

One hundred and eighty-seven beats per minute.

On-screen, a kid who rode for a Belgian team came around him and went up the road. No one was crazy enough to try to follow. Rapp was still carrying too much weight in his shoulders and chest to even consider it. And then there were the years. Every one of them harder than he cared to remember. Instead, he stayed in the middle of the chase group as the pace took its toll and it began shedding riders.

One hundred and ninety-one beats per minute.

There had been a time when that number wouldn't have been all that alarming. Now, though, he had to recognize that if the pace got much harder, a sixty-two-kilo kid riding in his basement in Antwerp might do what so many before him had tried: kill Mitch Rapp.

His lungs felt like they were full of battery acid and the pain in his legs had numbed in a way that suggested they were going to shut down pretty soon. Less than half a minute to the top of the climb. He just had to hang on for thirty more seconds.

One hundred and ninety-three beats per minute. His coach was going to read him the riot act when she saw this data file. Maybe he could get Marcus Dumond to hack into it and forge a nice six-hour endurance ride.

The Metallica blaring over his earbuds was suddenly replaced by an old-fashioned ringtone. Irene Kennedy's number appeared on the phone attached to his bars, but neither that nor the fact that his peripheral vision was starting to go blank was enough to make him give up. Leaning forward and closing his eyes, he sprinted for the summit. Only when the group started down the other side did he pick up.

"Yeah," he panted as riders flowed around him and disappeared up the road.

"Mitch? Are you all right?"

He rested his arms and forehead on his handlebars. “I will be.”

“Do you have time to talk?”

“Yeah. Go ahead.”

“I spoke with Darren Hargrave about you yesterday and he called back this morning to tell me that the Cooks have agreed to the terms I set out.”

Rapp stumbled off his bike and dropped to the cold stone floor. “What . . . What terms?”

“That you stay in plain sight and don’t return to the US while they’re in power.”

He used a towel to wipe the sweat from his face. “I can live with that. You never know. Maybe he’ll lose the next election.”

“That’s certainly my hope, but I don’t think it’s something you should count on. There’s a good chance that he’ll serve all eight years. And I think there’s also a reasonable chance that his wife will win the nomination after he’s done.”

“So, potentially sixteen years.”

“Yes. Assuming they don’t find a way to extend.”

“That seems far-fetched.”

“Underestimating them would be a mistake.”

The number sixteen seemed kind of abstract until he realized that Anna could realistically have children of her own before he set foot back in his country. And he’d be nearly eligible for Social Security.

“What’s that get me in return?”

“I think we can expect continued surveillance on you, Scott, and his key people but beyond that, the Cooks forget you ever existed.”

“Do you believe him?”

“Here’s what I can tell you. Right now, he’s scared. The Secret Service is restructuring his security in a way that’s designed specifically to stop an assassination attempt by you. Once that’s done and some time passes with you abiding by your side of the agreement, he should feel significantly safer. At that point, you’ll probably be fine.”

“Probably?”

"I'm not going to lie to you, Mitch. Anthony Cook is a man motivated by power and dominance over others. You know his type as well as I do. The question is whether that need is more powerful than his survival instinct."

The number she'd called from was encrypted but not one of their highly secure protocols. It was possible the NSA was listening, but he was beyond caring.

"I see that as leaving me with three options."

"Three?" Kennedy said. "Do tell."

"One, I could try to take him out. But it'd be a heavy lift and guaranteed to come back and bite me in the ass."

"I agree. What's your second option?"

"I disappear. Pack up tonight, slip out of here, and spend the rest of my life under the radar."

"I see a lot of drawbacks to that plan, Mitch. If you drop out of sight, he's going to think it's to come after him. The entire world's going to be hunting you. Let's talk about option three."

"That's the simple one. I take him at his word. My life here isn't anything to complain about. I can get back into racing, heal up, and, if I get bored, I can do some jobs with Scott."

"I don't want to sound like I'm backing you into a corner, Mitch, but I think that's the only viable way forward. It's possible that Cook won't be able to let this go, but I'm leaning in the direction of him just wanting it behind him. And I can almost guarantee the first lady does."

"Okay. You've convinced me. But before I agree, I need to talk to Scott and the guys. They're going to end up under surveillance and at least for a while there's going to be a risk to them bunching up. The opportunity to take them out in something that looks like an op gone wrong might be too tempting for Cook. But if they're okay with it, then we have a deal."

CHAPTER 10

THE WHITE HOUSE
WASHINGTON, DC
USA

"I JUST got a call from Irene Kennedy," Darren Hargrave said. "Rapp's agreed to our terms."

President Anthony Cook scanned the Oval Office, settling first on the concerned expression of Stephen Wright and then on the more enigmatic one of the first lady. With everyone else standing near the middle of the room, she'd chosen a place on one of the sofas.

It appeared that his wife had finally come up against a problem her brilliant mind couldn't solve. Her fatal flaw had always been her belief that other people—at least to some degree—were slaves to the same cold logic that ruled her existence. In fact, nothing could be further from the truth. The average human's mind was a tidal wave of contradictory emotions unbounded by intellect or calculation. Love, hate, fear, greed, lust—all fighting for dominance, advancing and retreating, controlling and justifying every action and reaction.

While her advice was perhaps valuable when dealing with someone like Irene Kennedy, she was completely lost where a man like Mitch Rapp was concerned. He was smarter and better trained than most but ruled by the same urges and passions. Cook, unlike his wife, understood those impulses because he, too, felt them. It was what fueled his popularity, making him relatable to the average voter. It was also what allowed him to understand the threat that Mitch Rapp posed in a way his wife never could.

Or was it more than that? He'd been dreaming of the presidency almost all his life, but it was she who had shown him that it didn't have to be an end in and of itself. That it could be a stepping-stone. With her eyes locked entirely on that prize, though, was he becoming just another cog in her machine? Losing the next election would be devastating to her achieving her goals. On the other hand, his death would be only a speed bump. One she could use to propel herself into the presidency. A few years earlier than they'd planned, of course, but she could recalibrate. Catherine Cook could always recalibrate.

"Do you trust him?" Cook said finally.

Hargrave laughed. "Are you kidding? The way he sees it, you sent one of his best friends to kill him. And I don't think anyone's dumb enough to buy the story of Nash's suicide. Rapp tortured him to death like he does all his enemies."

Cook felt a vague wave of nausea wash over him at the man's words, but didn't let it show. "So he offers the truce in an effort to buy time."

"It's exactly what I expected, sir. He needs to keep us off him so he can figure out how to make his move before we get your security fully up to speed."

"My understanding is that we're now tracking everyone in his inner circle," Catherine interjected.

Hargrave shrugged. "We still don't have reliable surveillance on Scott Coleman, but we believe that he's still at Ward's compound in Uganda. Bruno McGraw recently turned up in Greece and our people there are watching him. But again, none of this is a surprise. While it's true that they're all in plain sight, they're also separated from one another in Europe, Virginia, South Africa, and Wyoming. At best, he's making it impossible for us to take them all out in one operation. At worst, he's putting them in position to come at us from too many directions for us to handle. And at this point in our preparation, it'll likely work. These aren't a bunch of amateurs or fanatics. We're talking about the team that's assassinated everyone from the head of ISIS to the president of Russia to Christine Barnett."

Cook turned toward his Secret Service director before the first lady could mount a counterargument. "Steve?"

"We're making steady progress and every day our ship gets tighter. But are we ready for a concerted attack by someone like Mitch Rapp? No."

Cook nodded slowly. Despite the people in his office and the millions of devotees around the country, he felt increasingly isolated.

"I agree," he said finally. "The fact that Rapp and his people are suddenly so visible and spread out seems like a trick to me. I wonder if he's not trying to get us focused in the wrong direction. Like Darren said in our last meeting, Scott Coleman and his men aren't the only Rapp loyalists out there. We have no idea what kind of plans he could be making with operatives we don't know anything about."

"Our thoughts exactly," Hargrave said. "I have teams going through the Agency's database looking for the exact kinds of people you're talking about. We're already at more than a hundred, about half of whom are foreign. And let's not forget that Rapp is wealthy in his own right and that his brother is a billionaire. With those kinds of resources, he could hire a contractor or series of contractors that he has no traceable relationship with. All he'd have to do is provide them with a plan and access."

"And what do you propose to do about that?" Catherine said from her position on the sofa. "You already tried to get to him at his house and failed. Why is it you're so reluctant to consider the possibility that he's willing to let this go? Mitch Rapp is a cold-blooded killer, but he's never been someone who's hidden behind lies and deception. If he wants someone dead, he's not coy about it."

"Your point?" the president said.

"My point is that if you go after him again, you'd better succeed. Because if you don't there won't be any more negotiations or truces. It's going to be him or us."

"Him or *me,*" Cook corrected. "I'm the one in his crosshairs, Catherine. Not you. Not Darren. Not Steve. *Me.*"

She refused to look away. "More the reason to proceed with caution, don't you think?"

"Absolutely," Hargrave said, a barely perceptible smile playing at his lips. Cook recognized the expression. He knew something everyone else didn't.

"What've you got, Darren?"

"Well, obviously, we have to agree to his offer of a truce. After that we can't be seen going on the offensive. But that doesn't mean someone else can't."

"I'm in no mood for your drama today," Cook said. "Spit it out."

The CIA chief's smile broadened. "Like I said, we've been going through all of the CIA's classified files on Rapp and the people he's come into contact with over the years. Surprisingly, his most interesting relationship turns out to be with a contract killer named Louis Gould."

"Gould?" Cook said. "I was briefed on him and his wife at some point. If I remember right, they're both dead. They have been for a while."

"Louis is definitely dead. Killed by Mitch Rapp's mentor. His wife, though, is a different story. You can't imagine how much effort has been expended creating the impression that she's dead and wiping all references to that effort from the Agency's databases. In fact, they did such a thorough job, it left a number of loose ends. Holes that only someone looking very carefully would notice."

"Why do we care?" Catherine said, not bothering to hide her increasing irritation.

"There were no photographs of Claudia Gould left in our database, but the Mossad managed to put their hands on one." He reached into his pocket and pulled out a grainy photo of a young woman sitting at what looked like a European café.

"May I present to you Mitch Rapp's girlfriend, Claudia Dufort."

Cook took the picture and examined it. "Are you sure of this?"

"One hundred percent."

"Interesting," Stephen Wright said. "But how does it help us?"

"Claudia Gould wasn't just Louis's wife; she handled all the research and logistics for his operations. And as a full partner, she made a lot of enemies. That's why it was necessary for her to disappear. And while the Agency doesn't have much information on her life as Claudia Dufort, we have a great deal of information on her and her husband's activities in years past. That includes a pretty solid list of people she's crossed. What if one of those people were to find out that she isn't dead? That, in fact, she's living the good life in South Africa?"

Cook thought about that for a moment. "They'd go after *her,* not Rapp. And if we're careful about how we share the information, there'd be no reason for him to think we had anything to do with it."

"Exactly," Hargrave said. "At that point, our worst-case scenario is that Rapp stops an attack on her and becomes consumed by the fear that word about her being alive has hit the street. Or maybe he fails and then becomes consumed with guilt and the idea of exacting revenge."

Cook nodded slowly. "Either way, we get some breathing room to consolidate my security."

"Exactly."

"You said that's our worst-case scenario. What's best case?"

"That he takes a bullet for her or her daughter and ends up as collateral damage. If that happens, all our problems are solved."

Catherine Cook watched Hargrave and Wright file out of the Oval Office and then turned her attention to her husband. He looked tired. Uncertain. Instead of exuding strength, he seemed to be hiding weakness. It was a subtle change, but one the American people had a sharp nose for. Once it took hold in their subconscious, their reverence for their president would transform into loathing. Without ever knowing why, they'd turn away from him in favor of someone who could give them what they needed.

Her husband met her eye. "What?"

"How much security will be enough, Tony? What will it take for you to say you're safe from Mitch Rapp and his people? How long will it take? And will safety only be here in the prison you've created for yourself? Or one day will you be able to go back out into the country you're supposed to be ruling? Because the press and your constituents are already starting to notice. While Nicholas Ward is going head-to-head with African terrorists, you're hiding behind your desk."

As expected—and intended—his anger flared. "We control Congress, we control most of the government agencies that mean anything, and I've proven I have got the power to get people elected or tossed out on their—"

"All of which can disappear overnight, Tony. You know that as well as I do. We've seen it happen to other politicians and to think we're immune could be fatal. Look, I agree that we need to take precautions and increase your security, but at some point there needs to be an end to it. We need to have a plan with concrete, measurable goals. And when we achieve them, we need to move on."

"Suddenly you're a security expert?"

"Suddenly Darren is?" she retorted. "He's a manipulative psychopath who's obsessed with you. And that made him easy to use, but I sense that you're not in the driver's seat anymore."

"He's loyal, Cathy. That's a rare thing in this town. Maybe rarer than I thought."

She wasn't sure if that was aimed at her, but now wasn't the time to try to find out. "He cares about you the way a parasite cares about its host, Tony. He wants to feed off of you. To bump everyone else out of your orbit and be the only one left. Mitch Rapp is the best thing that ever happened to him. There'll always be a new angle, a new threat that only he can protect you from. Think about it, Tony. How many people has Darren Hargrave destroyed over the years we've know him? How many careers has he ended? Don't fall into this trap. Please."

Cook turned toward the windows and gazed through them at the lights beyond. "I'm not being played by Darren, Cathy. I understand him better than anyone. Better than he understands himself. Without me, he ceases to exist. The orbit analogy you used is a good one. I'm the sun to him. If I'm killed, everything goes dark."

"I never thought I'd say this to you, Tony, but you're being naïve. Darren's the most dangerous person in the world to you. He can't give this truce a chance because if it works, he becomes just another Washington player. You've shown him a path to possessing you and he'll risk everything—including your life and his own—to get that prize."

With his back still to her, Cook began slowly shaking his head. "Everyone else in this town has a plan B. Right now, they need me to maintain their power. But if I were gone, they'd just move on to the next in line or maybe even find a way to use my absence to better their position. But Darren doesn't have a plan B. He doesn't want to be president. Or a senator. Or even the director of the CIA. He just wants to feel my gratitude. And my love."

CHAPTER 11

NEAR FRANSCHHOEK
SOUTH AFRICA

RAPP dug into a drawer and finally located the item he was searching for: a Safariland level II vest. While it wouldn't stop much, it was fairly comfortable and better than nothing. He put it on over a mesh tank top and then covered it all with a dull green sweatshirt. Matching shorts and shoes broke with the current fashion of brightly colored running clothing but would help camouflage him if his trail run didn't go as planned. And if things really went south, he had a Glock 30 and spare mag in his fanny pack.

It had been two weeks since his truce with the Cooks had been finalized. In that time, he hadn't ventured beyond the walls of Claudia's property. It had been a surprisingly relaxing break that allowed him to sort out some neglected aspects of his life and finally put the finishing touches on his home gym. Still, he couldn't hide forever. At some point he'd have to stick his head back out into the world and see if the Cooks tried to take it off.

That day was today.

He planned to have Claudia drive him to the northeast edge of a local trail system and then three hours later a cab would be waiting for him on the southwest side. At last count, the American team watching him had swelled to three people, but none looked like shooters. And even if he was wrong about that, they'd have a hard time setting up a last-minute ambush in a public recreation area. Not hard enough that he was willing to leave the vest and gun at home, though.

Rapp selected a CamelBak from his collection and was filling it in the bathroom sink when AC/DC's "Back in Black" began playing over his cell phone. It was connected to the house's security and each subsystem had its own ringtone. That particular song related to the motion sensors on the private road leading to their gate. It was Sunday, so no mail or deliveries were scheduled, though that didn't necessarily mean anything. His new life made it impossible to control variables the way he was used to. Playdates, neighbors dropping by, and livestock wandering off nearby farms were a constant problem. If it weren't for the Cooks, he'd have probably muted that particular alarm during daylight hours.

He grabbed the phone off the counter and connected to the appropriate surveillance cameras. What he saw wasn't a lost cow or vineyard worker looking for a spot to take a break. Instead he was met with the image of two late-model SUVs driving fast toward his gate. Likely rentals, but that didn't tell him anything about who was inside other than that they weren't local. It would probably turn out to be nothing, but the speed at which they were traveling made him uncomfortable.

"Anna!" he shouted, running out into the hallway.

"In my room, Mitch."

He found her sitting at her desk, arranging stuffed animals instead of finishing the homework she'd been putting off all weekend.

"Come on," he said, holding out a hand. "Downstairs."

"Why? What—"

He grabbed her by the arm and dragged her off her chair. "Let's go!"

When they reached the steps, he scooped her under one arm and took them three at a time.

"Claudia!"

"Living room," she called back, and he felt a wave of relief. Thanks to the overcast and cool temperatures, she wasn't outside screwing with her landscaping.

"Safe room! Now!"

"What is it?" he heard her say as he pulled open the steel-core door and tossed the squirming girl inside. They'd trained for this, and Claudia passed by without waiting for an answer. Rapp stuffed his phone in the zipper pocket of his sweatshirt and used some duct tape he found in a drawer to secure a Bluetooth earbud. A moment later he picked up a call from Claudia.

"The monitors are coming online. One SUV is stopped in front of the gate and another is skidding in behind it. No other potential threats visible."

Skidding to a stop wasn't a maneuver common to FedEx contractors or even the alcoholic relatives of their next-door neighbor. The chances of this being a false alarm were fading fast.

"The passenger of the lead SUV is stepping out. He looks . . . I'd swear Latino. Lots of tattoos, no obvious weapons, but he's got something in his hand. Okay . . . He's taping it to the latch. It's got to be an explosive."

Her voice betrayed nothing—no fear, doubt, or hesitance. Sometimes it was easy to forget, but when she needed to be, Claudia Gould was a consummate professional.

"It's going to work," Rapp said in an equally businesslike tone. "That isn't the Virginia gate."

In fact, it was just a simple set of iron bars with a standard locking mechanism and retail hinges. Once the bolt was defeated, the only thing holding it shut would be the flimsy machinery that allowed them to open and close it by remote control.

He was temped to go to the windows, but resisted. Claudia had high-definition audio-video of the house and grounds, as well as control over every relevant electronic system. No reason to put himself in harm's way until it was absolutely necessary.

"Should I activate the alarm, Mitch?"

It was connected to a private armed response company that would dispatch someone and notify the police. In the end, though, they would just add to the unpredictability of the situation. At best they'd get in his way and at worst they'd get themselves killed.

"Negative," he said. "Not unless I go down."

The muffled sound of an explosion reached him as he entered the kitchen and opened a drawer in the granite island. It was on full-extension slides but stopped three-quarters into its travel. A hard yank broke the piece of wood blocking it, revealing a Glock 19 and two spare magazines at the back. He had similar stashes all over the house, but none were as accessible as he would have liked. The price of living with a seven-year-old.

"They're using one of the SUVs to push through the gate and—"

He heard Anna say something unintelligible. Whatever it was got an immediate response from her mother. "Get back down on the floor and shut your mouth!"

Not surprisingly, barely audible sobs ensued.

"It's okay," Rapp said calmly. "One step at a time. Are they through yet?"

"Yes. One man on foot. He's holding a pistol but I can't see what kind. The others are still in the vehicles. One driving toward the front door, the other toward the east wall."

What happened next wasn't hard to predict.

"The dogs are coming around from the back, Mitch. Anna! Stay under the table and keep your head down! It's going to be okay."

Rapp jogged into the living room but stayed near the back wall. The sound of revving engines was followed by rapid firing from what sounded like a single weapon. He moved to a position where he could see what was happening through the westernmost living room window. The shooting went silent when Aisha and Jambo collided with the man. He lost his grip on his weapon and was relegated to trying to fight them off with bare hands. A few moments later, Rapp's concerns about Anna's dogs being more bark than bite were laid to rest. Their muzzles were stained red and their victim was no longer a threat.

"The one on foot looks to be out of the fight," Claudia said. "Men are getting out of both vehicles."

"Can you give me a head count? I can't see from my position."

"Not yet," she said. "The dogs are going after the car along the wall."

Rapp moved right until that vehicle came into view. Both animals hit their targets: the first two men out of the SUV's driver-side doors. Both intruders were thrown back and both went down, one firing reflexively but not hitting anything. The smaller of the two dogs was the smartest. She went straight for the throat and started shaking the man by it.

The other had her target by the arm. He seemed to have panicked to the point that he'd forgotten the purpose of guns and instead of shooting was using his as an ineffectual club.

"I've got the vehicle by the wall in view," Rapp said. "Talk to me about the other one."

"Stand by . . . Okay. They're out. Five men in total."

All were out of the east one as well. The remaining two men had wisely exited the other side and were coming around the front and back. The fact that the dogs were now more or less stationary made them easy targets. They went down in a hail of bullets, but not until after leaving two men dead and one injured. The odds against Rapp had been significantly reduced but, at the same time, a number of questions had been raised. Most important, who were these assholes? Not pros. They seemed more like a group of drug cartel enforcers he'd once faced in California.

"Ten men in all." Claudia's voice over his earpiece again. "Two are down; one is still active but with a wounded left arm. Both dogs are down."

Anna's voice rose up, but again she was cut off by her mother. "*I told you to stay down and shut your mouth!*" This time Anna's sobs rose to the level of outright bawling.

"The three men from the east vehicle are going around that side of the house," Claudia said, her tone returning to one of confidence-inspiring serenity. "The injured one is bleeding badly but not doing anything about it. Armed with a pistol. The other two have assault rifles. All the men from the other vehicle look like they're going to come through the front door. Two more assault rifles, the other three have handguns. No body armor is obvious, but they could have light vests under their clothes. One is wearing a tactical belt with pouches that look like they might contain grenades. It's possible that the men going around back are equipped with explosives, too, but I don't have the angle to confirm it."

"What's the status of the interior doors?"

"Most are open, but I've locked all of them. If you close them, they'll stay that way."

Fortunately, the old house was cut up into a lot of individual rooms—compartmentalized in a way that favored a single man against a larger force. Rapp started through the ground floor, pulling doors shut as he went. With Claudia's help, he'd be able to enter any room he wanted, but his attackers would find themselves relegated largely to tight hallways, landings, and the main living area.

Another advantage he had was understanding the materials that made up the house's interior. Some doors were just wood, but others had bullet-resistant cores. Similarly, some walls were made up of studs and insulation, others original stone, and still others were reinforced with ballistic fiberglass. All were subtly color coded so he didn't have to remember which was which in the heat of battle. Add a few Kevlar-reinforced pieces of furniture, and that's what he had to work with. Nowhere near the standard of his house in the US, but not the end of the world, either.

"Two men out front have broken off and are going around the west side of the house. That will make five in the back, one injured. The three in the front are spreading out. One toward the door, one toward the first dining room window, and the remaining one with an assault rifle toward the first living room window. The man at the front door is talking, probably into a throat mike. They're coordinating and he looks like he's in charge."

All the windows were barred—nothing fancy but not trivial to get through. Even with explosives it would be low percentage. Bars tended not to have enough surface area to absorb much force and the exterior walls they were set into were stone. The front and rear doors were the best bet for access, though also not trivial. Both were steel core with multiple dead bolts and reinforced hinges. An insufficiently powerful explosive would be more apt to jam them than open them.

"Unlock the front door," Rapp said.

"Understood. Unlocking the front door. Okay, they look like they're going to break the front windows. I think you can count on some fireworks, but you should be fine where you're standing. The men in back are placing something that looks like a charge on the door."

Rapp moved to a position behind the entryway staircase, giving him a view into the living room in one direction and the dining room in the other. He put his back against the wall, staying in the middle to give him maximum protection from any potential explosions.

"Get ready for the windows. The man at the door is reaching for the handle."

The sound of shattering glass was followed by the creak of the front door opening. A moment later a blast from the back shook the house.

"The back door is gone and so is part of the wall. The front door is open and the front windows are broken. No one's coming in the back yet. There's a lot of smoke and some fire. Do you want me to turn on the sprinklers?"

"Not unless it gets out of control. Let's limit their vision and ability to breathe as much as we can."

"Understood. The men out back seem to be arguing about who's going in first."

That suggested they weren't complete idiots. Once they got past the mudroom, they were going to find a smoke-filled hallway lined with locked doors and sealed off from the main house by another.

"The man I suspect is in charge is preparing to come through the front door, Mitch. Handgun only. His back is against the exterior wall to your left and he's looking around the jamb. Okay. He's in. Looking toward you and up the stairs. Turning right . . . He's focused on the living room. Now!"

Rapp moved along the wall far enough to bring the man into view. A single round hit him in the left temple and splattered the wall with brain tissue, blood, and bone shards. Rapp retreated again.

"The man at the dining room window is shouting at the man at the living room window," she said, though he could hear them from his position. Spanish.

"They don't seem to know what to do. Two men entering the back while the other three stay outside. There's still a lot of smoke but the fire seems to be going out on its own."

"Roger that."

Rapp started easing left, but then dropped to the tile floor when Claudia came on again.

"Grenade coming in through the living room window!"

The blast threw a heavy credenza across the room and he saw it shatter against the wall. Great if their target was the big-screen TV that had become the family's *Grand Theft Auto* battlefield, but otherwise a waste of a perfectly good explosive. Again, he asked himself who these pricks were. If this was the best the Cooks could come up with, US spec ops had really gone to shit.

"It's still hard for me to see clearly into the rear hallway, but the two men appear to have reached the door at the end. The two men out front are moving toward the still-open door. I think one has a grenade in his hand but no other explosive is visible. If you move now, you can just make it."

He leapt to his feet and sprinted across the entryway, slamming the front door and then retreating to his former position. A grenade wouldn't be enough to penetrate unless the blast could be concentrated. They might be able to use their vehicle for that purpose but, frankly, they didn't seem that clever.

"Am I clear to go into the living room?"

"Yes. They've stopped along the wall. The door slamming seems to have surprised them."

"Give me the exact position of the one closest to me," he said as he moved forward. The sofa was smoldering to his left, but no open flames were visible.

"Maybe one meter to the east of the porch. The other one's in a similar position on the west side. They're facing each other with their shoulders maybe half a meter from the house. The men at the back look like they might be setting a charge on the door leading to the main part of the house. If it's as powerful as the first one, they'll have full access after it's detonated."

He didn't respond, instead taking a position in front of the broken window. Because of the angle, it was impossible to see the men near the porch, but the closest would be less than ten feet away. He could hear them speaking unintelligibly as he slipped the gun through the bars. Aiming based on Claudia's description, he emptied his magazine and then immediately ran for the dining room, slapping in a fresh one as he went.

"One hit! The man's down, but I can't tell how badly he's injured. The other is backing along the wall, shooting toward the window you fired from. Two meters from the first dining room window, staying close to the wall. One meter, still focused on the living room window, not looking behind him."

Rapp stayed near the back of the dining room, counting on the relative gloom and increasing haze from the burning couch to obscure him. His target came even with the window a moment later, still shooting at nothing, oblivious to everything else around him.

The bars and what remained of the glass made the shot tricky, so

Rapp lined it up carefully. A gentle squeeze of the trigger sent a round just behind the man's left eye, snapping his head around before he disappeared from sight.

"He's down!" Claudia said over his earpiece. "Dead or dying. The men in the hallway are retreating. I think they're going to blow the door, so stay clear. The man on the east side of the porch isn't dead and he's trying to get to his feet."

Rapp strode to the window and peered through. Sure enough, the man had made it to all fours. He looked up just in time to see the muzzle flash that killed him.

"You have no more threats at the front of the house. Still five in the back. All outside now. The injured one is still bleeding but steady on his feet. The sofa fire is getting pretty serious. Can I put it out?"

"Go ahead," Rapp said, hearing the living room sprinklers activate before using a finger to plug his open ear in anticipation of what was to come. He didn't have to wait long. Again, the house shook, but this time the tremor was accompanied by smoke and vaporized plaster billowing through the first floor.

"The door is down," she said unnecessarily. "All five men are still outside, two with their backs to the east side of the door. Three in the same position on the west side. None are moving yet. The hall camera's still functional but there's too much smoke and dust for me to see anything."

Hesitating was a mistake on the assault team's part. If all five had immediately charged up that corridor with the lead man's gun blazing, Rapp would have had serious problems. Instead he was able to make it to the closet at the back of the living room unchallenged. The quiet click of Claudia unlocking it sounded as he reached for the knob. Inside, a 3M respirator was dangling from a hanger and he put it on before turning his attention to the Benelli M4 shotgun above the jamb. The wooden hooks securing it to the wall didn't have a release mechanism and it took almost his full weight to break them. Yet another safety precaution designed with Anna in mind.

"One man's entered the hallway," Claudia said as Rapp moved toward it. "Two covering him. One more entering. They're moving slowly at an interval of about one meter, but it's still hard to see."

Rapp took a position next to the opening, listening to the men coughing inside. Their eyes would be burning and watering even worse than his. That, combined with the still-dense smoke in the corridor, would make them virtually blind.

"All five are in the hallway now, Mitch. Crouched and moving slowly. The lead is probably three meters from you."

He gave a thumbs-up that she would be able to see on camera

"The lead man is now one and a half meters from you."

Rapp swung his shotgun around the jamb and pulled the trigger. The double-aught ammunition hit his target in the upper chest, dropping him.

By the time his team returned fire, Rapp had pulled well back from the opening again.

Six down, four to go.

"The new lead is roughly three meters back, on one knee, dead center of the hall," Claudia said, though he was barely able to make out her words over the gunfire. "His pistol is out of ammunition and he's reaching into a pocket for what I assume is another magazine. The man in second position is about a meter behind, firing over him with an assault rifle. The remaining two are holding the same intervals, staying low, and not shooting."

The accuracy of her account was easily confirmed by the pattern of bullet holes being stitched across the back of the staircase about four feet up. Rapp dropped to one shoulder on the tile floor and once again brought the shotgun to bear. Through the smoke, he saw the new point man insert a fresh magazine into his weapon. The blast from Rapp's shotgun took the right side of his head off before he could use it. The man behind adjusted his aim toward the muzzle flash but Rapp had already pulled back. The rounds ricocheted off the floor and pounded the back of the stairs.

"Seven down," Claudia said over the gunfire. "Three remaining. One in the hallway shooting at you. He's backing up and looks like he might be going for the kitchen. The other two are back outside against the wall to the west."

She would have locked the door to the kitchen, but if he recalled correctly, it wasn't reinforced. The sound of splintering wood that became audible a moment later confirmed that.

"He's through," Claudia said. "The men out back are holding their position, shouting at each other."

Rapp pushed himself to his feet but didn't make any further move. The man in the kitchen had no other way out. The glass door leading into the yard was barred, as were the windows. But that wasn't necessarily a bad tactical position. Rapp wasn't anxious to go into the hallway with those two men out back. There was no telling when they might regain their nerve.

The answer to that question came from Claudia a moment later. "The men outside are going for the front. One around the east side of the house and one the west. The man in the kitchen is uninjured and crouched behind the north side of the island. I'm sorry, but that's where I keep my Le Creuset."

Those were the extremely heavy enameled pots she favored. They made a hell of a beef bourguignon but would also provide good cover to anyone taking refuge behind them. The other side was full of random cooking utensils that wouldn't stop much.

Rapp started down the hallway, sliding along the wall until he reached the broken kitchen door. The smoke had cleared enough to provide decent visibility, but it was still burning the hell out of his eyes.

"I've unlocked all the doors in the hallway if you need them. The position of the man in the kitchen is unchanged. The two men going around the house just reached its edges. Both are stopping to see if it's clear to come around. The front door's still locked and undamaged. There's no easy way for them to get inside."

Rapp signaled to the hallway camera that he'd understood, then swung the shotgun around the doorjamb and fired over the granite countertop. The move generated a lot of noise and showered plaster down on the man's position. Rapp then emptied the weapon into the Le Creuset side of the cabinet before switching to the Glock 30 in his fanny pack.

The next few rounds were aimed at the floor near the front edge of the island. It stood about five inches above the tile on stainless steel legs.

"It's working!" Claudia said over his earpiece. "He's moving to the other side!"

In fact, the man went one step further, stretching an arm beneath the island to shoot in the general direction of the door. The onslaught posed no real threat to Rapp, but it did give him a better idea of his opponent's position. Now clear of Claudia's iron pots, he presented a viable target. Rapp fired a pattern of five rounds into the back of the cabinet. The sound of shattering glass, wood, and ceramics was accompanied by an agonized shout.

"At least one hit," Claudia said. "But I can't tell how bad—"

Rapp was already sprinting across the kitchen floor, replacing his magazine as he went. He leapt onto the island, sliding partway across it before using his free hand to grab the edge and arrest his momentum. That position allowed him to hang a hand over the back and fire five rounds in what he calculated was the general direction of his target.

"He's dropped his weapon!" Claudia shouted over his earpiece.

Rapp pushed himself forward far enough to see that the man had been hit in the shoulder and stomach. A round to the top of his head finished the job.

"What's going on out front?" he said after stripping off the respirator and sliding back onto the floor.

"Both men are in the vehicle that was by the door and are on their way to the gate."

"Understood," he said, jogging into the entry and grabbing Claudia's car keys off a hook. She buzzed him out the front door and he used the fob to remote-start her SUV as he ran across the empty courtyard.

"Grab Anna and come to the front," he said, sliding behind the wheel and backing the vehicle to the front patio. He threw open the driver's-side door and climbed between the seats into the back just as Claudia appeared.

She was carrying Anna, using one hand to keep her face buried in her shoulder. Not particularly efficient—the girl was getting too heavy for her mother—but effective at keeping her from seeing the damage and bodies he'd left behind.

Claudia dropped her into the driver's seat and then shoved her onto the passenger-side floorboard.

"Don't move!" she said, climbing in and accelerating toward the gate. Anna did as she was told, huddling on the floorboard, sobbing.

Rapp had considered just staying put and calling the cops, but without knowing exactly what they were up against, he'd discarded the idea. Even if the Cooks had decided the truce wasn't working for them, they'd shy away from ordering a running fight through South Africa's wine country.

He leaned into the SUV's cargo area, using a hidden button to open a hatch in the floor. It originally contained a little extra storage and tools for tire changes, but the armoring company had made some modifications. The tools were now under the chassis and the shallow space was filled with foam cut to hold an HK416 assault rifle, two Glock 19s, and numerous spare magazines.

"Hold on!" Claudia shouted. She swerved, clipping something with the left edge of the vehicle's brush guard. Anna squealed in terror and Rapp was thrown backward hard enough to wedge him between the front passenger seats. When he glanced over, Claudia's face was a mask of calm concentration. She'd taken a number of evasive driving courses over the years and was frankly pretty good at it.

They skidded dangerously close to an irrigation ditch, but she managed to finesse their way to safety while he freed himself from the seats. The vehicle they'd collided with was the one that had disappeared through their gate a few minutes earlier. Apparently the two men inside had found their courage and pulled into the vines to ambush them. Like their earlier plan, though, it hadn't gone particularly well. Their right quarter panel was trashed and looked like it was rubbing the tire as they pursued.

The chance of them catching Claudia in the supercharged tank she was piloting was pretty much zero, but still he reached for the HK.

"Slow down."

"We can outrun them, Mitch."

"I want to ask a few questions."

She hesitated—undoubtedly because Anna was in the car—but in the end did as he asked. The gap between them began to close as the man in the passenger seat wrestled an assault rifle through his open window. At the same time, Claudia pushed the button that opened the SUV's rear window.

Rapp fired a couple of controlled bursts in the direction of the driver. The upgraded suspension he'd paid through the nose for turned out to be worth the money, and he managed a twelve-inch grouping despite the rough road surface. It was hard to see through the glare coming off what was left of the windshield, but the driver seemed to have taken a number of rounds to the neck and face. The vehicle drifted right as the man now leaning through the passenger window tried to grab the wheel. He couldn't commit to dropping his weapon, though, and the delay cost him. The tire that was rubbing the fender hit the edge of the ditch and blew. That was enough to eject the passenger through the window and roll the vehicle.

"Stop!" Rapp shouted, watching the man somersault through the air and into the vines.

Claudia skidded to a halt, and he stepped out into a cloud of dust. A quick examination of the wrecked vehicle confirmed that the driver was dead and that fire danger was low.

The second man was a little more challenging to locate, having torn through various rows before landing. Rapp followed the damage, doubting the man's survival more with each step.

An ornate cowboy boot became visible in some wire used to support the plants, providing a little hope. That hope faded when Rapp discovered that while the boot still contained a foot and lower leg, the rest of its owner was still MIA.

He retrieved his phone, disconnecting the still-open line to Claudia before dialing another number. Scott Coleman answered just as Rapp arrived back at the road and began running toward the idling SUV.

"Hey. How's the good life?"

"Not what I was hoping for. I need an extraction for three people."

"Shit . . . Where are you?"

"About a quarter mile from my front gate in Claudia's SUV."

"Injuries?"

"None."

"Got it. Get lost for about fifteen minutes and I'll call you back with a time and location."

CHAPTER 12

Over Southwestern Uganda

THE emerald carpet rolling hundreds of feet beneath Rapp's feet was comfortingly familiar, as was the rotor wash lashing him through the chopper's open door. Less familiar was the little girl sitting next to him. He'd fashioned a harness for her out of webbing and connected it to the fuselage. Despite sitting in the doorway with her feet dangling in space, there was no fear visible through the hair whipping across her face. Only anger and sorrow.

Helicopter rides like these always helped him think. Time with nothing to do but watch the world pass by and ponder the inevitability of it. Whether Anna would have the same reaction remained to be seen. She'd undoubtedly witnessed at least some of what he'd done from her position in the safe room and it was clear that she knew her dogs were gone. How would she deal with it?

The sun hit the horizon, splashing orange across the undulating landscape and causing the temperature to drop. He wrapped an arm around the shoulders of the girl next to him but she didn't seem to notice. Rapp followed her gaze toward the deepening colors, trying to focus his mind on the question of what the hell had just happened.

It was clear that the men who had attacked Claudia's house weren't members of an elite American team or even professional mercs. Based on the tattoos, the Spanish, and the way they handled themselves, he'd guess Latin American cartel enforcers.

At first blush, it seemed like a strange group for the Cooks to recruit, but the more he thought about it, the more it made sense. One of their disciples was now running the DEA, giving them access to cartel leadership. How hard would it be to offer a few favors in return for help with a little problem they had in Cape Town? Maybe the quiet release of some people from prison. Or the promise to look the other way on certain large shipments. Then, once Rapp was dead, they could use an unsanctioned operation he'd carried out against the Esparza Cartel to make it look like he'd involved himself in the drug trade. Very tidy. The Cooks continued to live up to their reputation. But not for much longer if he had anything to do with it.

By the time they began their descent, Anna was asleep with her head on her mother's lap. The landscape below had been a nearly uniform black for the last half an hour, but now something that looked like a single point of light was visible to the north. Nicholas Ward had constructed a mountaintop compound in that remote area of Uganda and, despite being the wealthiest man in history, spent a lot of time there. His excuse was that he had a pet research project nearby, but it was more than that. Like Claudia's house in South Africa, it had the benefit of feeling cut off from the real world. A world that, against all reason, was becoming more dangerous and unpredictable as humanity progressed. The enlightened age that technology and democracy were supposed to usher in seemed to have been canceled.

Their pilot homed in on the light and a few minutes later they touched down on a concrete pad tastefully executed to look like flagstone. Rapp disconnected himself from his safety line and retrieved

Anna. She was dead to the world—the impenetrable sleep of a seven-year-old who had a lot to escape.

They climbed out of the aircraft and headed for a shadowy figure at the edge of the ring of light.

"We've got you set up in your normal bungalow," Scott Coleman said. "Is everybody okay?"

"Yeah," Rapp responded, diverting toward a wooden walkway to the east. Dim lanterns set into the ground came on as they walked, illuminating the path. They turned off it after about a hundred and fifty yards, taking a similar walkway to a small building tucked away in the trees. The woodstove in the living area was lit, illuminating a modern interior through the two-story glass façade. Claudia slid the door back and Rapp laid Anna on a sofa that had been pulled out into a bed. The compact kitchen looked like it had been recently stocked and there was an ice bucket bristling with beers on the counter.

"We've got clothes for both of you in the loft as well as a couple of secure laptops connected to the compound's network," Coleman said. "Let me know if there's anything I forgot and I'll get it over to you tomorrow when the staff gets up."

Claudia walked over and hugged the former SEAL. "It's good to see you, Scott."

"You, too. I'm sorry about the circumstances."

"Why don't you get settled in," Rapp said, grabbing a couple of beers from the bucket and heading toward the open door. "Scott and I have a few things to talk about."

They stepped outside and Rapp scanned the sky, searching the stars for movement that might indicate an aircraft. Coleman seemed to read his mind.

"The Ugandans have created a fifty-mile no-fly zone around the place. We have solid radar coverage and pretty sophisticated surface-to-air capability. The terrain, combined with the perimeter wall, would stop a Panzer division. Cameras and sensors out in the forest are state-of-the-art."

"Personnel?"

"A contingent of fifteen top-notch operators and we can theoretically get air support from the Ugandans inside of thirty minutes. We also just finished mounting miniguns with overlapping fields of fire on the walls. They're controlled remotely with some really slick new software. You should check it out when you get a chance."

"Escape routes?"

"Four by land and we have three choppers."

Rapp handed him one of the beers and took a pull from his own. A little over a month ago, Nicholas Ward had financed a wildly successful operation against a paramilitary cult terrorizing western Uganda. He also provided a lot of jobs, financed NGOs, and built hospitals and schools. Not to mention quietly funneling millions into the Swiss bank accounts of key government officials. While Ward could be a bit of a Boy Scout, he understood how the world worked. You didn't make a trillion dollars over the course of sixty-one years without knowing how shit got done.

"So, you feel good about security?"

"Who's the enemy?"

"What if I said Anthony Cook?"

Coleman smiled and shook his head slowly. "Look, Mitch, this may be the most well-protected private installation on the planet, but against stealth bombers? No."

"Is Ward here?" Rapp said, changing the subject. "I've been seeing him all over the news."

"No, he's in the States. His sudden resurrection has been kind of complicated. The press is selling a lot of papers by pitting him against the Cooks, and the SEC is threatening to come after him for securities fraud."

"Is he pissed?"

Coleman drained some of his beer and shook his head. "Nah. He knows he'd be dead if it weren't for you. And having a trillion bucks makes you kind of above the law. Having said that, I think he's interested in defusing the situation if he can. No one wants a fight with the White House."

"Unless you can't avoid it," Rapp said. "Do you think the Cooks can get to the government here?"

"Irene says no. The Ugandan president is smart enough to know they'll use him and then hang him out to dry. Nick, on the other hand, is a straight-up guy with a genuine interest in the country."

"How sure of that is she?"

Coleman pointed with the neck of his bottle. "You should ask her yourself. She's staying two bungalows down."

"She's here? Now?"

"Yeah."

"Why?"

"Depends on who you ask. Nick thinks he's in the process of hiring her and she thinks she's on vacation. Not sure which one of them will come out on top."

CHAPTER 13

RAPP woke the moment the sun penetrated the bungalow's glass front. Claudia had pushed him to the far right of the bed in order to make space for Anna, who had crawled in sometime after midnight. Normally he wouldn't have been particularly tolerant of spending the night teetering on the edge of the mattress, but he was willing to make an exception in this case. If curling up next to her mother could help Anna recover from what had happened, a fall or two onto the wood floor would be a small price to pay.

When the powerful rays made it to within a few inches of him, he untangled himself from the duvet and walked silently to the closet. It opened on well-oiled hinges and he dug out some clothes before descending a spiral staircase in his boxer shorts.

There was a French press on the counter, but with the open floor plan, he'd wake up the whole house trying to find a pan to heat water. Instead he pulled on his jeans and a sweatshirt before slipping through the front door.

Outside, the air was still and crisp. The scent of flowering plants was overwhelming and the only rustle in the surrounding trees came from birds perched in them. Nicholas Ward had spent untold millions creating this mountaintop haven and, as usual, he'd succeeded wildly. The fact that, the day before, Rapp had been in a battle that left Claudia's house trashed and ten men dead seemed like a hallucination. Someone else might have almost been able to convince themselves it hadn't happened. Unfortunately, wishful thinking wasn't one of his gifts.

Rapp stepped into a pair of flip-flops and walked along the pathway that ran in front of the bungalows. He found what he was looking for two units down. Irene Kennedy had never been much of a sleeper and, while not a coffee drinker, she was never without her stash of highly caffeinated tea.

She was sitting in front of a fire pit lit against the morning chill. An oversized porcelain cup was keeping her hands warm and she took a sip of the steaming liquid before nodding toward a go-cup on the table next to her.

"That one's yours."

"I hate being predictable," he said, picking it up. Not tea, as it turned out. A nice French roast.

Rapp dropped into an Adirondack chair and propped his feet on the edge of the fire pit. In front of him, the smoke rose in a perfect column toward a crystalline sky.

"How have you been?" she said after almost a minute of silence. "Anything interesting going on?"

He laughed, but couldn't bring himself to tackle the subject without a little more caffeine. "Nothing comes to mind. You?"

"Relaxing for the first time in years. Catching up on some reading. That kind of thing."

"Nice place to do it."

"Nick's been very generous."

"Really? He doesn't want anything in return?"

"Oh, he's trying to hire me, of course."

"And?"

"I'm pretending to be dense and not notice."

"Is that fooling him?"

"No."

"Is it something you're considering?"

"I'd be lying if I said I didn't find the idea intriguing. He actually might be capable of reshaping the world in a way that governments can't anymore. After a career spent putting out one fire after another, something like this might be exactly what I need."

"And it might provide some cover. He's got more money and political clout than most countries."

"Maybe. But the opposite could be true, too. Going to work for him isn't exactly fading away into a think tank or teaching position. It might make the problems between him and the Cooks worse."

Rapp had known her long enough to know that her last sentence was crafted to nudge him into acknowledging the elephants in the room. Anthony and Catherine Cook.

"There's a pot on in the kitchen," she said, giving him an unexpected reprieve. "Why don't you get a refill?"

He stood and went inside, discovering that it wasn't a reprieve at all. Next to the coffee maker was a printout of an article from the *Cape Times*. It included a picture of Claudia's courtyard taken through her damaged gate. An ambulance was parked out front and two men were loading a sheet-covered body into it. The word *bloodbath* was used multiple times in the write-up, but details were sketchy. The names of the property owners had been omitted, stating only that they were missing. The number of casualties was listed as "up to twelve," and an unnamed police department source was quoted as saying none appeared to be local. The last paragraph was dedicated to requesting that anyone with pertinent information step forward.

He filled his cup and returned to his position in front of the fire pit.

"Accurate?" Kennedy said, referring to the article.

"Only ten casualties unless you count the dogs. *Definitely* not local. I'd swear they were Latino. Maybe mercs, but if so, somebody didn't get their money's worth."

"And who is that somebody?"

"We both know the answer to that."

"You have a lot of enemies, Mitch. The Cooks are only two of them. And they have the resources to do something more effective and less likely to end up on the front page of the newspaper."

"Maybe. Or maybe not. They're not omnipotent. Not yet anyway. They can't just send Delta. I know too many of those guys and it'd be a little obvious to have an American spec ops team shoot up the South African wine country. Better to find someone more arm's-length. Someone no one can trace to them."

"I admit that what you're saying is plausible, but we need more than a gut feeling to go to war with the president of the United States. It'd be devastating for them, for you, and for the country."

"This is more than a gut feeling, Irene. You don't think it's a little strange that right after you negotiate a truce with that ass-kissing piece of shit Darren Hargrave, an out-of-town hit squad shows up at the house of Mitch Burhan, a retired American Army officer?"

"Again, I'm not saying you're wrong, but the pieces don't completely fit for me," she said. "For instance, why nonlocals? With all the gangs in South Africa, why not pick one of them? It'd be less suspicious, and they'd have more experience operating locally."

"Maybe."

"Look, I understand that you've been attacked in your home twice in three weeks. And this last time with Claudia and Anna involved. But if you start an open conflict with the Cooks, there's no going back. Even if you . . ." Her voice faltered. "I have a hard time even saying this out loud. Even if you manage to assassinate the president of the United States, you're destined to lose. You'll never get your life back. Or any life at all, really. You'll live out whatever years you have left alone and on the run."

"Your point?"

"It's safe here and Nick will let you stay as long as you like. It's going to take some time, but let me try to find out what's happening. I might not be the director of the CIA anymore, but I still have contacts who can help."

"And if we find out that the Cooks are behind it?"

She let out a long breath. "Then we'll retool. But very, very carefully."

Rapp walked slowly along the path back to his bungalow, still unsure of his next move. His time with Kennedy hadn't provided as much clarity as he'd hoped. Maybe the smart thing to do was just keep walking. To penetrate the jungle and never be seen again.

When he arrived at the junction leading to Claudia and Anna, he stopped. Straight ahead, the perimeter fence was visible in the distance. Through the trees to his left, Claudia was sitting on the porch, oblivious to everything but the laptop in front of her.

He looked at the way her hair flowed from beneath her knit hat. At the flushed cheeks and dark eyes partially obscured by glasses she used for reading.

She was one of the most impressive—and complicated—people he'd ever met. A loving mother and loyal partner, but also the ex-wife and former accomplice of one of history's most successful private assassins. Strictly speaking, she had never been the one who pulled the trigger, but that was a fine distinction he'd left behind long ago. Like him, she'd spent years living by the sword and one day she might die by it. They'd both made that choice and they both accepted it for what it was.

But Anna had no say in any of this. She'd been born in a hole, and he couldn't help feeling that he was shoveling dirt down on top of her. He'd done a pretty good job maintaining the illusion that he could guarantee her safety and provide her the life she deserved, but that had just imploded. It was time to move on. But not by slinking over the fence. That was the coward's way out.

He could feel the cold sweat on his forehead as he started toward the bungalow. Despite the sound of his footsteps on the boardwalk,

Claudia remained intent on the computer screen. Or maybe it wasn't the screen at all. Maybe she just couldn't bring herself to look at him because she'd come to the same conclusion.

He hoped so. It would be so much cleaner.

"Can we talk?" he said, taking a seat across the table from her.

That was enough to get her to meet his eye, but not enough to prompt her to speak. She wasn't going to make it easy on him. Story of his life.

"This was too close, Claudia. You could have been killed. Anna could have been killed. And even though she wasn't, what's this going to do to her? She saw at least some of what happened and hasn't said a word to me since. Is she afraid of me now? Why wouldn't she be?"

Claudia just stared at him, seeming almost catatonic. Finally, she blinked. "Please stop."

"Look, I know we just had this conversation and that we've had it more times than we can count. But this is the last."

"Mitch, please. Stop."

There was something in her tone that made him fall silent. This wasn't a conversation either one of them wanted to have, but it seemed like more than that. There was something he wasn't seeing.

"What?"

She turned the laptop toward him. The screen depicted a high-resolution image of the dead man in her entryway. She zoomed in to highlight a tattoo that covered the left side of his neck, rising all the way to his jawline. It consisted of three letters intertwined with skulls and roses.

"Those aren't your enemies, Mitch. They're mine."

CHAPTER 14

THE WHITE HOUSE
WASHINGTON, DC
USA

"SUBTLE," Catherine Cook said as soon as Darren Hargrave closed the Oval Office door. "The Cape Town media is already calling it the Franschhoek Bloodbath and saying that the owners of the house are missing. Can I assume that Rapp killed all your people and escaped?"

"They weren't my people," Hargrave said, sounding less defensive than she would have guessed. He was becoming increasingly confident in his position. Maybe too confident, but it would be a mistake to count on that.

"This was a hit team sent by Gustavo Marroqui," Hargrave continued. "A Guatemalan gang leader who Louis and Claudia Gould have a very ugly history with. A similar team showed up at a house they were living in in Bosnia a few years ago but they were tipped off and managed to escape. It's completely credible that Marroqui could have discovered that she's alive and it's absolutely certain that if he did, he'd move against her. Like Mitch Rapp, Gustavo Marroqui isn't a man to let things go."

Catherine took a chair in the Oval Office's seating area while her husband seemed content to spectate from behind his desk.

"So, this is your definition of a success?" she asked.

"One hundred percent," Hargrave replied. "We always knew that the chances of a bunch of Guatemalan gang members succeeding against Mitch Rapp were low, but it doesn't matter. We accomplished exactly what we set out to do. It won't take Rapp long to figure out these were people from Claudia's past and not his. When he does, he's going to have no choice but to go after Marroqui—a man who even the CIA can't locate and who virtually owns the Guatemalan government. That leaves Rapp—and likely his people—consumed with something that has nothing to do with the president."

"You don't think that the timing of this is going to seem a little suspicious to Rapp and Kennedy?"

"I'm sure Irene will acknowledge the possibility that we discovered Claudia Gould's identity and leaked it to Marroqui. But is she going to let Rapp go to war with America over that possibility? With no evidence at all? I seriously doubt it."

"What about the police investigation? The South Africans—"

"Cathy . . ." her husband said in a tone that suggested her battle was lost. She fell silent, but Hargrave smelled blood and decided to push.

"The South Africans have probably already figured out where the dead men came from. It's literally tattooed onto their skin. But, again, that has no downside to us. In fact, it might lead them to think that Rapp's involved in the Latin American drug trade. If that's the case, it could motivate them to start looking deeper into his identity or even deport him. Both of those things would just increase the turmoil in his life and make him even less likely to move against us."

His explanation ended with an arrogant smile that her husband wouldn't be able to see from his position.

It had been a significant skirmish in the escalating war between them and there was no question that he'd won. While she suspected that his machinations involving Rapp were dangerous and unnecessary, there was no denying that his little plot had worked. In the unlikely event that Rapp didn't intend to honor his truce, any vendetta he was planning would now have to wait. Gustavo Marroqui wouldn't stop until Claudia Gould was dead.

"Where is he?" Catherine said, wanting to wipe the smug grin off Hargrave's face. "One of the benefits of having Rapp in Franschhoek was that we could keep him under surveillance."

"We believe he's at Nicholas Ward's compound in Uganda along with Kennedy and Scott Coleman."

"You believe?"

"Our people tracked him to a private airstrip where he, Claudia, and her daughter got on a private jet. They landed at the Entebbe airport and then drove into Kampala, where we lost them. Based on satellite images, though, a helicopter landed at Ward's compound not long after. I think it's reasonable to believe he was on it."

"If all of them are together there, does that provide an opportunity?" President Cook asked.

"For God's sake, Tony," Catherine said, but no one seemed to hear.

"At this point, I don't think so, sir. The security at Ward's camp is extraordinary. Obviously, we're capable of taking them out but hiding our involvement would be impossible. A much more viable strategy would be to go after Rapp in Guatemala. He's eventually going to have to go there and it's not his normal operating environment. Once he's in-country, he'll be vulnerable to our operatives or maybe just to Marroqui. If we leak who he is and his objective to the right government officials, he's going to find Guatemala a very dangerous place."

"But even if he manages to kill Marroqui, it's going to take time," the president said. "By then, my security upgrades will be in place and we'll have purged everyone loyal to Rapp and Kennedy from the government."

"Yes, sir. At that point, we'll be in a much stronger position."

Catherine sank a little deeper into the cushion behind her. Hargrave would never concede that security was sufficient. In fact, she wondered if he was really even going to put people in Guatemala. If Mitch Rapp were ever killed, the threat to her husband—and his dependence on Hargrave—would disappear.

CHAPTER 15

SOUTHWESTERN UGANDA

WITH her customary efficiency, Claudia had already compiled a shockingly detailed briefing on the criminal organization run by Gustavo Marroqui. Drugs, prostitution, murder for hire, human trafficking, pornography—largely the child variety—and government corruption were only the tip of the iceberg. If it was illegal, Marroqui had his hand in it. He was estimated to be worth a good quarter of a billion dollars, but Rapp wouldn't be surprised if he still shoplifted in convenience stores.

The Guatemalan's outfit encompassed no fewer than thirty interrelated street gangs in addition to the more elite group that he surrounded himself with. He'd spent years in a bloody battle for the domination of his country and that was a big part of what had made it the murder capital of the world. Now, though, he'd more or less won. For sure, MS-13 continued to be a significant force, but their territory was being chipped away, leaving them to fight other, even more marginalized gangs for Marroqui's scraps.

Rapp flipped to the last page of the report and skimmed the rest of its contents. The takeaway was that the situation was worse than he thought. And not by a small amount. Going after Marroqui in Guatemala in some ways would be harder than moving against Anthony Cook in Washington. Assassinating a president would be a clean, sophisticated operation. Professional operators, split-second timing, cutting-edge equipment. Taking down Marroqui on his home turf was something completely different. Most likely a blood-soaked clusterfuck.

He tossed the folder onto the table and couldn't help allowing a smile to play at his lips. In a tree next to him, a brightly colored bird was singing its heart out. The sky was still cloudless and the temperatures had risen into the low seventies. A breeze was blowing from the north, bringing with it the scent of the rain forest.

Fuck, he felt better.

The weight of what happened in South Africa had been too heavy for even him to carry—something he hadn't realized until Kennedy lifted it off him. Rapp was still suspicious that the Cooks could be behind what happened, but she'd made a strong case against that theory. While it was certainly possible that Darren Hargrave had discovered Claudia's true identity and notified Marroqui, it wasn't the most likely scenario. The truth was that Claudia still used her old contacts in the criminal world from time to time. Obviously, she leaned toward people she trusted, but crooks were crooks. None were particularly reliable partners, and it would take only one slip for it to get out that she was alive.

Despite not being entirely convinced, Rapp was willing to tentatively proceed under the assumption that the timing of this was just an unfortunate coincidence. And if that was the case, then all this was *Claudia's* fault. It was something she didn't seem to see the humor in, but he was enjoying the hell out of it.

In all likelihood, the broken-record conversation Claudia was so tired of having would never have to come up again. What she'd said last time was right. They both had skeletons in their closets and when one inevitably crawled out, they were better off together than apart. The battle at the house had demonstrated their effectiveness as a team in a very visceral way, but it went further than that. With Kennedy out of the Agency and likely looking to pursue a cushy private-sector job, he was cut off from the intelligence and logistic resources he counted on to operate. Claudia's considerable talents in that realm would go a long way to fill the gap. Conversely, the death of her husband had left her without any reliable operational capability—a void he was highly qualified to fill.

The door to the bungalow opened and Anna appeared. She stopped short of the threshold, contemplating him intensely in her Powerpuff Girls pajamas. Rapp found himself similarly frozen. What did she see? The man who had done what was necessary to keep her safe? Or a butcher who had calmly executed ten men while she watched in high definition?

Finally, she started toward him. The relief he felt when she climbed into his lap was surprisingly intense. Strange that not long ago, he'd have been doing everything in his power to hand her back to her mother.

She leaned her head against his chest but remained silent. Unquestionably, as the adult, it was his responsibility to say something comforting. Maybe even profound. But what? Should he explain how the world worked and his unique part in it to a seven-year-old? Or was it better to just pretend none of it had ever happened? Kids had short attention spans, right? And home invasions weren't exactly unheard-of in South Africa. Even at her age, she'd have heard stories from classmates. In a few days, this would already be a hundred miles in her rearview mirror. Right?

"You want me to make you some breakfast?" he said, missing profound by a fair margin, but perhaps grazing comforting.

"No. Mom's doing it. She said she's going to bring it out."

"What's she making?"

"Not, like, eggs and ham or anything. Like yogurt and fruit."

She fell silent and he let it stretch out for almost a minute before speaking.

"I'm sorry about what happened. I didn't want to hurt those men. But I didn't have a choice if I wanted to protect you and your mom."

"You didn't protect Aisha and Jambo."

The dogs. It wasn't a response he was prepared for. She didn't seem bothered by the fact that he'd killed those men. She was bothered by the fact that he hadn't killed them fast enough.

"I couldn't get to them in time. But they got their shots in before they went down."

"Mitch!" came the cautioning voice of Claudia from inside the bungalow. Apparently, she was eavesdropping.

It was too late, though. Anna looked up at him with a slightly curled upper lip and a gleam in her eye that made him a little queasy. He remembered her father having the same expression when he thought he'd had Stan Hurley dead to rights. Just a few moments before Hurley ripped his throat out.

Footsteps became audible on the path behind him and he craned his neck to see Scott Coleman approaching. The former SEAL gave the top of Anna's head a quick rub before dropping into a chair.

"How you doing, kiddo?"

"They killed Aisha and Jambo."

"Yeah, I heard. I'm really sorry. But they loved you and wanted to protect you. They were happy to die doing it."

"How do you know?"

"Because Mitch and I would have been."

Rapp felt a pang of jealousy. Coleman was a natural. He never got nervous around her. Never felt the need to calculate every word that came out of his mouth. Back home in Virginia, they'd go out and work in the subdivision's makeshift farm for hours, chatting away about nothing. No awkward silences. No misunderstandings or uncomfortable blank stares.

Rapp treated his relationship with her like a minefield that, with enough calm forethought, could be safely navigated. Coleman had no such bias. He knew that sometimes an explosion was necessary.

She stared at the man for a moment and then suddenly burst into tears. Rapp felt his teeth clench as she pressed tighter against him, but Coleman just commandeered his coffee and watched impassively.

She normally calmed down pretty quickly but it wasn't the case this time. When her sobs turned into convulsive wails, Rapp tried holding her tighter. Then patting her back. But nothing worked. Finally, Claudia came out with breakfast and a rescue.

She managed to peel the girl off Rapp and led her into the house while the two men watched. When the door closed behind them, Coleman began slowly shaking his head.

"Gustavo Marroqui. You lucky bastard. I can't believe you're off the hook."

"Are you done?"

"I am," Irene Kennedy said. "Thank you. Everything was delicious as usual."

Claudia moved everyone's plates to a table next to the outdoor sofa. They'd eaten in silence, but now it was time to talk business—something she didn't seem anxious to do. It wasn't surprising. While she never made excuses about her previous life, she only discussed it when absolutely necessary. And even then, she spoke as if she were telling half-remembered stories about an acquaintance.

"Years ago, Louis was . . ." Her voice faltered and she glanced back at the bungalow to make sure Anna was closed up inside. "Louis and *I* were contracted to kill Gustavo's older brother, Alvaro, who was running their operation at the time."

"By whom?" Kennedy asked.

"There were a lot of buffers, but I assume it was the Guatemalan government. Alvaro was amassing a lot of power and bringing various gangs into his organization. It went counter to the government's policy of playing the different factions against each other to keep them weak."

"And you were successful?" Coleman said.

"Yes. But the politicians didn't get the result they expected."

Kennedy sighed quietly. "It's the same mistake made over and over again. Never get rid of someone unless you're certain their replacement isn't worse."

"And Gustavo isn't just worse, he's *the* worst, right?" Coleman said. "Isn't he the guy who dismembers people's entire families, sews them back together with pig parts, and leaves them around town like sculptures?"

"Yes," Claudia said, staring at the table in front of her.

"That's the kind of thing that gets you what you want in a place like Guatemala," Rapp said.

"And it's what's kept him alive when so many people—including me—want him dead," Kennedy said. "It's an easy choice for government and law enforcement officials there. Go along with him and receive millions in bribes, or have your family end up as a modern art installation."

"So, you've looked into getting rid of him?" Rapp asked.

"I looked into helping *Guatemala* get rid of him. But it's impossible to tell where he starts and the government ends."

"And that makes him hard to find," Rapp said.

"Virtually impossible," Kennedy said. "Very few people know where he is and those people are one hundred percent loyal—either because they're part of his organization or because they're afraid of him."

"Well, virtually impossible or not, we've got to track him down. How do we do it?"

Coleman leaned back in his chair and folded his arms across his chest. "With difficulty. Even if we could just roll down to Guatemala and find people who know where he is, how are we going to get that information? They know they're being watched. And given the repercussions to their families of turning on him, they're going to hold out for a while—even under pretty harsh questioning."

"Giving Marroqui time to change location," Rapp said.

"Right."

"There's no question that this is a two-part operation," Kennedy said. "The first is finding the man. Until then, at least Claudia's out of reach."

"But we can't spend the next five years here," Claudia said. "And it could literally take that long to succeed where half the world's intelligence agencies have failed."

Rapp let out a long breath. "Maybe not."

"Meaning what?" Kennedy asked.

"I met a guy in Mexico a while back who might be able to help us."

"Who?" Kennedy asked.

"Damian Losa."

"You *met* Damian Losa?" Claudia said, stunned. "Personally?"

"Who's Damian Losa?" Coleman asked.

"A Latin American businessman with a fairly diverse portfolio," Kennedy responded. "Mostly narcotics and arms trafficking, but also a significant number of legal and quasi-legal activities throughout the world."

"Have you ever had any dealings with him?" Rapp asked.

"No. But some of my counterparts have. I understand that he can be surprisingly reasonable when his interests are being served. In a way, he's a much more powerful, much wealthier, and much smarter version of Gustavo Marroqui. That's given him a somewhat protected status where the world's intelligence agencies are concerned. As embarrassed as I am to say it, sometimes a person like him can be useful."

"Having met him, I'd agree with that assessment," Rapp said. "He comes off as the Hyde to Nick Ward's Jekyll."

"Actually, that's probably a more apt comparison," Kennedy conceded.

"So, you think he'd know where Marroqui is?" Coleman asked.

Rapp shrugged. "If anyone does, it'd be him."

"Would he tell you?"

"I don't know. We got along okay. In fact, he tried to hire me."

"No," Claudia said, speaking in a tone firm enough for everyone to turn toward her. "Asking for Losa's help would be a mistake. He might come off as very slick and professional, but let's not lose sight of what he is."

"And what's that?" Rapp said.

"A man you don't want to owe."

"I'm not disagreeing with you, but I don't see that we have a lot of choices. Other options?"

"We could form a private intelligence team and put them on the ground in Guatemala," Claudia said. "Nick could probably lend some technological resources. Given time, we might be able to find him."

"Yeah, but how much time?" Rapp said.

"A year," she admitted. "Maybe more."

"Maybe never," he said, pulling out his phone. "Whatever the risks are, there are rewards, too. If we can take out someone like Marroqui—particularly if we do it fast—it's going to send a clear message to anyone else out there who might have heard rumors that you're alive."

They all watched nervously as he searched for the stored number and then sent a brief text.

"Don't look so worried," he said, putting the phone on the table. "It's been a long time. I doubt he'll even ans—"

His phone started ringing. The number on-screen was the one he'd just texted.

"I stand corrected," Rapp said and then picked up. "Thanks for getting in touch."

"I have to admit that I'm surprised to hear from you," Damian

Losa said with an accent that straddled British and Ricardo Montalbán. "I heard you'd found a place in Nicholas Ward's organization and that Irene Kennedy is likely to follow."

"You're well informed."

"I keep up with the gossip. Now, what is it that I can do for you, Mitch?"

"I'd like a location on Gustavo Marroqui."

There was a brief pause over the line. "I read that a group of Guatemalans attacked a family in South Africa a few days ago. The owner of the house executed all of them and then disappeared with his wife and young daughter. Might you know something about that?"

"I might."

"I'm not aware of you ever having had dealings with Gustavo."

"I haven't."

"Then how did we get here, Mitch?"

"Does it matter?"

"I've survived this long because I don't make decisions without all the information available. If you think I'm going to get involved in something I don't understand, you've misjudged me."

Inconvenient, but not exactly unexpected.

"What I'm about to tell you doesn't go any further than us."

"You have my word."

"He wasn't after me. He was after the woman I live with."

Rapp heard the tapping of a few keys on the other end of the line. "One Claudia Dufort."

"Her real last name is Gould."

This time the pause over the line was longer. It finally ended in laughter. "Claudia Gould? You have strange taste in women, Mitch."

"Will you help?"

"At the risk of sounding mercenary, what's in it for me?"

"I'll owe you one," Rapp said, finding it difficult not to choke on the words.

It didn't take long for Losa to make a decision. "Give me twenty-four hours and I'll have my assistant text you the coordinates you're looking for."

Rapp disconnected the call. "He says we'll have a location by this time tomorrow."

"That easy?" Coleman said.

Rapp shook his head. "I think that one's probably going to come back to bite me. But for now, yeah. That easy. Can I assume you're up for a quick trip to Guatemala?"

The former SEAL smiled. "Anything for a good piña colada."

CHAPTER 16

GUATEMALA CITY
GUATEMALA

IF anything could be said about Claudia, it was that she had friends in low places.

Rapp was sitting in the rotting backseat of an SUV that sounded like it was going to rattle itself apart. The driver was navigating a mix of asphalt and dirt that snaked through a slum on the outskirts of Guatemala City. In addition to the men in front, two more were crammed in on either side of him. All were a good twenty years younger than he, and all were covered in tattoos identifying them as members of Mara Salvatrucha. Better known as MS-13.

The notorious gang was being increasingly outmaneuvered by Gustavo Marroqui's superior organization and penetration into the highest echelons of the local government. Also advantageous was the indirect support he enjoyed from the United States and other countries whose politicians benefited from being associated with the battle against the most infamous gang in the world. There was nothing like photos of dead MS-13 members to divert people's attention from Marroqui's growing power in Latin America.

The enemy of my enemy is my friend. It wasn't an adage that had worked out so well for Rapp in the past. But there was always a first time.

He reached across the shirtless man next to him and rolled the window down a couple of inches. The stench of sweat—some his own—was getting overwhelming.

The flow of cool air was an improvement despite carrying a hint of sewage, diesel, and decay from the cinder-block buildings around them. Corrugated walls and roofs were illuminated in the headlights, some painted with graffiti, others with rust. The flash of colorful clothing drying on lines occasionally caught his eye, but most of this part of the city was dark. Electrical poles slung with wires were plentiful, but the lights on them were either burned out or intentionally broken. With its deteriorating position in Guatemala, MS-13 had adopted a strategy that was unusual for them—a low profile. The operations once carried out with purposeful impunity were now going underground. The arrogance of young men capable of incredible violence had been attenuated by the realization that someone else out there was capable of even more.

In a way, it felt familiar. The Taliban were the masters of intimidation, but when the US military was around, they tended to keep their mouths shut and crawl back in their holes. Unfortunately, that was where the familiarity ended. Rapp knew virtually nothing about the country or city he was in, didn't speak the language, and had no support from either the Guatemalan government or US intelligence assets working in-country. And while MS-13 wasn't the first strange bedfellow in his career, he wasn't normally this reliant on them. For all intents and purposes, he was now an honorary member. The failure or success of this mission turned on how reliable his new allies proved to be.

The man to his left cracked opened a beer and Rapp watched him drain it in one long pull. By his count, that was the eighth since they'd picked him up thirty minutes ago. Not exactly confidence inspiring and one of the reasons that Scott Coleman was operating independently with a different MS-13 faction. It was the best thing they could come up with to spread the risk.

Rapp checked the screen on his phone but found nothing from the former SEAL. Slightly worrying, but not yet panic-inducing. Coleman was actually the one doing the heavy lifting in this particular operation, and it made sense that he'd be off-line.

Damian Losa had identified Marroqui's current location as a heavily fortified and well-protected mountaintop in the southern part of the country. Ironically, it wasn't much different than the one Nick Ward had set up in Uganda and was probably damn near as secure. No roads came within fifteen miles of it, the terrain was extremely rugged, and the entire thing was surrounded by a heavily guarded concrete wall. What it lacked, though, was Ward's antiaircraft capability. At least that was the hope.

As popular as Rapp was in Uganda for dealing with their terrorism problem, Coleman was even more popular in Latvia for helping them deal with an incursion by the Russians. That made it relatively easy for him to get on the phone with their generals and quietly order up some military-grade weaponry. Add to the mix a few professional smugglers and they'd soon be in possession of an item that would send a clear warning to anyone else out there with a grudge against Claudia Gould.

The driver turned into a tarp-covered gap between two houses and slowed. The makeshift tunnel was steep—probably a ten percent grade—and went on for longer than Rapp would have thought possible. Eventually they came to a large graffiti-covered door that was rolled back by an armed guard. They passed through a number of similar doors before coming to a parking area covered with still more corrugated metal and containing maybe ten other cars. By then the vague thumping that Rapp noted when they'd entered the tunnel had turned into deafening Spanish rap music. To what he calculated to be the north, colored lights swirled through a gap in the wall.

Three of his new companions wandered off when they got out of the car, but the driver motioned for him to follow. They slipped through the gap and Rapp found himself in a similarly covered enclosure probably a hundred feet square. The people packed into it were roughly split between men similar to the ones he'd arrived with and young, attractive women. Likely selected for those very features from a local population not really in a position to argue.

The dancing crowd parted for him and his guide, eyeing them as they passed. The building had been kludged together from debris but was accented with opulent flourishes. A Ferrari that looked like it had never been driven was parked on a platform in the middle. A marble fountain sprayed water from Italian-looking sculptures. A well-stocked bar that would have been at home in a Monaco casino dominated the far wall. Things people bought when their criminal enterprise generated a lot of cash, but not many opportunities to spend it.

They finally arrived in an area that had booths reminiscent of a high-end nightclub. Rapp was led to a corner seating area that contained a number of men in their thirties along with the youngest, prettiest, and most scantily dressed of the women in the room. On the table was a silver tray filled with shots and lines of what might or might not have been cocaine. His escort peeled off, but it was clear that Rapp was to continue forward and present himself for inspection.

When he got within a few feet, a man approached from the right. He was wearing a silk shirt completely unbuttoned to reveal an impressive set of pecs and an even more impressive set of tattoos. He started screaming in Spanish and then shoved Rapp with enough force to make him stumble backward into the dancing mass of humanity behind. The man at the back of the booth—clearly the one in charge—made no move to interfere.

Not an ideal situation. In total, there were at least fifty intoxicated gang members in the room, he had no backup, and, worse, he needed their help. Beating this asshole to a bloody pulp wasn't going to go anywhere good. But neither was bowing down to him. In the end, it was a situation that needed to be handled diplomatically.

Not exactly his forte, but it was never too late to learn.

The man reached out to shove him again and Rapp grabbed his thumb. A hard jerk combined with a foot sweep put him down on the back of his shaved head. He was dazed, but instead of taking advantage of that to finish him off, Rapp adjusted his grip and pulled him back to his feet. Laughing, Rapp grabbed a couple of shots from the tray, handed one to the confused man in front of him, and slammed back the other. It went down like battery acid.

The man stood frozen with the glass in his hand as Rapp became aware that the dancing had stopped and everyone in the room was watching. All this prick had to do was drink the shot. If he did that, everyone would save face and they'd both survive. If not, things were going to get interesting.

The seconds seemed to tick by at a comically slow pace. One . . . Two . . . Three . . .

The man laughed and swallowed his drink, slapping Rapp on the shoulder and pointing to the booth. Two girls slid out to give him space and the people on the dance floor went back to grinding, drinking, and whatever the hell else it was they were doing.

"I'm told you're someone who backs his mouth up with action," the man at the back said with a perfect American accent. Probably one of the many MS-13 members who had grown up in Los Angeles and then been deported.

Rapp just nodded.

That seemed to satisfy him and he pointed toward the lines of powder on the tray in front of them. Close up, they had a grayish color and strange granular quality.

"What is it?" Rapp asked.

"A proprietary blend."

If there was one thing Rapp had learned over the years, it was to run from anything described as a proprietary blend or a delicacy. That wasn't an option, though. It was clearly another test.

He leaned forward, closed off one nostril with an index finger, and discovered that, whatever it was, it kicked like a fucking mule. He temporarily lost his sense of up and down, tilting to the left far enough that the girl next to him had to push him back upright. A hard shake of his head left hair pasted across his sweat-soaked face. When he tried to speak, he discovered his tongue was numb enough to give his words a thick drawl.

"That's good shit."

Rapp was sliding along the wall, staying as far away from the dancing mass as he could. His fifth beer was in hand and the alcohol was just now starting to calm the jitters he'd gotten from whatever it was that he'd put up his nose. The edges of the building were dotted with various seating options, and he zeroed in on one that looked like a cushion-strewn queen-sized bed. There were already two girls lounging on it, but they were small enough to leave plenty of room. Neither protested when he collapsed in the space between them. The chances of him sleeping that night were precisely zero, so he just stared up into the spotlights playing over the crowd.

He wasn't sure how long he lay there before his phone began to vibrate in his pocket. Two minutes? Two hours? Enough time that the girls had fallen asleep and were now curled up to the sides of him. He moved one of their legs and fished out the phone, inserting a set of wired earbuds in an attempt to deaden the music.

"Go ahead!" he shouted, holding the cord mike close to his mouth.

"You gonna live to see sunrise?" Scott Coleman said.

"Sixty-forty. You?"

"A woman who people seem to be afraid of has taken me under her wing. I don't know what I'm going to have to do to pay for the protection, though."

"I'm sure you can handle it."

"I dunno. She outweighs me by about fifty pounds and half her face is inked to look like a skull. Something about a split personality, I think. My Spanish is pretty marginal."

"What's the word on our package?"

"It came into Puerto Barrios a few hours ago. Last report I got was that it sailed through customs and is on a truck coming our way. Should make it with time to spare."

"And our plane?"

"It's ready and waiting for our instructions. I don't want to name the airstrip until the last minute, though. You never know who's listening."

"Roger that. I'll see you tomorrow. And in the meantime, watch your ass."

"I don't have to. Clarita's doing it for me. Seriously. Right now. Staring right at it."

Rapp disconnected the call.

CHAPTER 17

THROUGH heavily tinted windows, Rapp could see that the poverty-stricken slum had given way to a middle-class shopping area. It wasn't yet dark at six thirty in the evening, but there was enough traffic to make their improvised motorcade blend in. He scanned the pedestrian-filled sidewalks and then looked past them to the outlines of volcanic peaks on the city's outskirts. He'd finally managed to get to sleep when the party died down around eleven a.m. Despite what had seemed like a seven-hour coma, he still felt like he'd been rolled down the side of a mountain. It had crossed his mind to ask his host exactly what he'd snorted, but then decided he really didn't want to know.

On the bright side, his performance the night before seemed to have moved him up in the pecking order. He was traveling in the same vehicle he'd arrived in, but this time he rated the front passenger seat. Behind the wheel was Carlos, the man he'd put on his ass the night before. The young Guatemalan wasn't holding any grudges, chatting away in amicable but virtually incomprehensible English. The expensive clothes had disappeared, replaced by a pair of grimy jeans, running shoes, and a completely bare torso. Through the tattoos, Rapp could see an impressive road map of bullet holes, knife wounds, and burns. There was no question that the man had been in a lot of fights in his twenty-odd years, but based on the number of scars he'd accumulated, he might not have won any.

Rapp was scheduled to rendezvous with Scott Coleman at a drug runner airstrip a little less than two hours away. In theory, the weapon they'd requested from the Latvians would be there along with the plane designated to transport it. Whether that was really going to materialize, though, was hard to say. MS-13 wasn't exactly known for its operational precision, and he hadn't been able to reach the former SEAL since they'd talked the night before.

At that point Rapp calculated the chances of successfully dealing with Gustavo Marroqui at around even money. When the sound of multiple automatic rifles erupted a few minutes later, he had to revise his estimate down to less than ten percent.

Their lead car was taking fire from two vehicles parked on either side of the street, causing it to stop short as civilians scattered in every direction. Rapp pulled his Glock from the holster beneath his right arm and instinctively twisted around in his seat. As expected, their chase car started taking fire a moment later, this time from three men who had appeared in storefronts.

The two men in the backseat of Rapp's SUV rolled down their windows, shouldered their assault rifles, and started firing. They didn't have an angle, though, making their effort little more than an exercise in wasting ammo and endangering civilians.

"Stop shooting!" Rapp yelled.

They either didn't hear or didn't understand. Carlos accelerated and Rapp turned to face forward as the vehicle hopped the curb. "That's not an exit!" he shouted as the Guatemalan aimed at a too-narrow gap between shops and parked cars. Like his companions, though, he seemed uninterested in Rapp's thoughts on the matter.

Fuck this.

Rapp threw his door open and jumped out, managing to stay on his feet as his momentum slammed him into the side of a water cooler delivery truck he'd identified moments before. The impact intensified his pounding headache but significantly improved his tactical situation. Metal and concrete weren't as effective at stopping bullets as most people believed, but water could usually be counted on.

The roar of machine gun fire started to falter as the shooters in front expended their ammunition and were forced into clumsy reloads. Carlos discovered too late that Rapp had been right about the size of the gap he was going for and swerved, shattering the glass façade of one store and crashing into the next.

The ground clearance of the water truck was high enough that Rapp was able to roll under it and come out on the street between it and a car that had been abandoned by its terrified occupant. When he did, he spotted three of the forward shooters, now concentrating their fresh magazines on Carlos's immobile vehicle. Behind, Carlos's men were trapped in the chase car, staying low, taking fire from all angles. Strangely, no one seemed to be paying any attention to Rapp. Why was a mystery, but no point in looking a gift horse in the mouth.

He rose to one knee and took careful aim. His first round hit one of the shooters out front in the head and his second penetrated another man's side just below the shoulder. Both collapsed and Rapp moved around to the front of the truck. The third man didn't seem to have any idea that something had happened to his companions and was fully invested in spraying Carlos's vehicle on full auto. One of the men in the backseat had almost made it out but was now lying facedown on the asphalt with one foot tangled in a seat belt. Neither Carlos nor the other man who had been in the backseat was visible and Rapp assumed they'd escaped into the shoe store the vehicle was partially parked in.

The remaining shooter at the front seemed to come to the same conclusion and stopped firing, running in a direction that would take him past Carlos's SUV and give him a shot at anyone behind it.

Rapp broke cover and scooped up a fallen AK-47, firing a controlled burst at the running man. To his surprise, he missed—punching a hole in the wall of a clothing store to the man's left. Judging by the tight pattern he left, it was clear that it wasn't his aim but instead the combination of a banged-up sight and a shit weapon. Apparently, these men's work tended to be of the close-up variety.

Before he had time to compensate for the poor setup, the man had cleared the front bumper of the SUV and was adjusting his aim toward someone behind it. This time Rapp fired on instinct. It wasn't particularly clean, but one of the rounds impacted the man's forearm with enough force to cause him to lose his grip on his weapon.

Rapp sprinted across the street, staying low as the shooters focused on their chase car started to take notice of him. He made it back to the cover of the water truck and fired around it at three approaching men. He hit one before exhausting his magazine, prompting the others to seek cover. Out of the corner of his eye, he saw Carlos appear from behind his vehicle, but instead of picking up a weapon and coming to Rapp's aid, he started kicking wildly at something out of sight on the ground. Almost certainly the man Rapp had shot. Carlos's right arm was hanging limp and it was coated with blood flowing from a wound in his biceps. If he survived, he'd have a nice addition to his scar collection.

The two remaining shooters had split up and were trying to get position on them. Rapp ran toward Carlos, who was still focused on the unconscious man at his feet. He let out a stream of Spanish expletives as Rapp grabbed him and dragged him deeper into the store. It was devoid of both customers and employees, which suggested a rear exit. Rapp snatched a couple of shirts from a rack and led Carlos into the back room, where he shoved him against a wall.

"Listen to me," he said as he tore the sleeve off one of the shirts and began winding it around the man's wound. "We've got to keep moving. If they know I'm here, it's not just those six guys. It's going to be fifty."

The man looked confused as Rapp tied off the makeshift bandage. He assumed that it was the language barrier, but when he started to repeat himself more slowly, Carlos spoke over him.

"No is you, tío. The man you kill is my asshole cousin." He grinned and slapped Rapp on the shoulder. "He does this always."

Rapp wiped away as much blood as he could and then helped the Guatemalan into a clean shirt. The shaved head and tattoos were never going to allow him to blend into polite society, but it was better than nothing. They found the rear exit and Rapp pushed Carlos through before using a fire extinguisher to smash the door's inner handle. With a little luck that would slow down any pursuit.

The alley went on farther than expected, crossing multiple streets as it led east. The first few were emptied of people, but the sound of the gunfight could only carry so far. By the time they'd covered five blocks, city life had returned to normal.

"Can you drive?" Rapp asked as they joined a group of pedestrians waiting to cross the street.

"No problem" came the less-than-convincing reply. Blood was dripping from the cuff of his shirt and the people around them were starting to back away. When the light turned red, traffic came to a stop. The car in front would be easiest to take, but Rapp was fairly certain it had a manual transmission that would be impossible for Carlos to operate. The second in line was a late-model Hyundai sedan, which would have been fine, but the windows were rolled up and the woman inside was eyeing them suspiciously. Undoubtedly locked up tight.

The third vehicle turned out to be what they were after: a well-cared-for Toyota Yaris. The only person visible inside was the driver—an oblivious young man holding a cigarette out the open window.

Rapp angled right, keeping a casual pace and taking advantage of the fact that he'd look like a tourist to most people. The man in the car was so focused on smoking and the music blaring from his radio that he didn't see Rapp until he found himself being dragged from the vehicle and onto the pavement. The kid looked like he was going to fight, but his motivation faltered when he saw Rapp's bloody, tattooed companion. In the end, he wisely decided to run for the relative safety of the sidewalk.

Rapp slid across the hood and got in the passenger side while Carlos struggled to squeeze behind the wheel. The light changed and the two cars in front left a little rubber during their escape. Behind, a few horn blasts rose up and a siren sounded somewhere in the distance.

A moment later they were accelerating smoothly up the road.

It seemed like the correct turn, but GPS instructions were open to interpretation in this part of rural Guatemala. Rapp steered the Yaris up a steep dirt track and slowed to less than ten miles per hour. The vehicle he'd carjacked wasn't exactly ideal, but he managed to coax it along without snapping an axle or flatting. Another minor miracle to add to the fact that the local cops had never managed to mount a pursuit.

Forty minutes later, he found what he was looking for at the top of the climb: a Cessna turboprop that had been optimized for hauling narcotics. The pilot was standing just beyond the reach of the headlights, illuminated only by the glow of the cigarette in his mouth. According to Claudia, he was one of the best—a prodigy behind the yoke and a man who had spent decades calmly battling darkness, storms, and the DEA.

Rapp stepped out of the car and into the cool mountain air. Light rains had passed intermittently overhead during the drive, but at the moment only the humidity remained.

"Benjamín?"

The man nodded. "Mitch?"

Rapp went around the back of the plane and approached, pointing to the cigarette between the Guatemalan's lips. He pulled out a pack and shook one out before retrieving a lighter. Rapp cupped his hand around it, closing his eyes against the flame.

"Is there something wrong with your friend?" Benjamín said, pointing to Carlos slumped in the passenger seat of the car.

"I think he might be dead."

"What?"

"He was bleeding pretty bad and hasn't said anything for a while."

He seemed uncertain that he was picking up the nuance of Rapp's English.

"Should we . . . Should we do something?"

Rapp took a light drag on the Marlboro. He wasn't really a smoker, but over the years he'd discovered that it was a surprisingly effective bonding exercise. Not to mention a pretty functional way to kill time.

"Nah."

Another twenty minutes passed before the dull glow of headlights became visible to the west. Rapp raised a hand to shield his eyes from the approaching Ford F-350's roll bar–mounted LEDs, lowering it again when the vehicle turned one hundred and eighty degrees. Both he and the pilot started forward as the driver maneuvered the pickup's bed into a position next to the plane's open cargo door.

The wooden crate in the back was significantly larger than Rapp expected, hanging over the open tailgate and rising a good two feet above the box sides. A hydraulic crane had been mounted to the bed and its cargo hook swung lazily as Scott Coleman cut the lights and stepped out.

"You look like shit," he said as he approached.

"I feel like shit," Rapp responded. "How'd your night with Carlita go?"

"I don't want to talk about it."

"Then why don't we talk about that?" Rapp said, pointing to the truck.

"Nice, huh?"

"Not exactly compact."

"Maybe it's just a lot of packing material," Coleman said, digging around in the truck and coming up with a couple of crowbars. "Let's find out."

It took a fair amount of effort, but they finally got the crate broken down. What they were left with was a tube about ten feet long and a little over a foot in diameter. The front was covered in a clear glass dome with stabilizer fins just behind. At the other end were significantly larger guidance fins and markings that identified it as Soviet in origin.

"I said I was looking to take out a house, Scott. Not a town."

"We're not sure if Marroqui has antiaircraft capability, so I figured we'd drop something from high up. The problem is that if you're going to do that, you need guidance. This was the smallest thing the Latvians had lying around that's got the right mix of features. Besides, you said you wanted to make a statement, right? Well, nothing says 'fuck you' like eleven hundred pounds of fuel-air explosive."

Rapp nodded in the darkness. The man had a point.

CHAPTER 18

"Too much or just enough?" Scott Coleman shouted over the gale blowing through the turboprop's open door. They were cruising at twelve thousand feet above a black, uninhabited landscape. As forecasted, the clouds were continuing to dissipate, giving way to patches of hazy stars. A few dim red lights illuminated what had once been the passenger area of the aircraft but was now a stripped-down cargo hold.

The former SEAL had just finished taping protective foam to the bomb's tail fins in a configuration that would protect them as they went through the door but then be torn off by the wind as it fell. The operation was more art than science, though. The Soviets had designed the weapon to be released by a mechanism somewhat more sophisticated than two guys chucking it out the side of a smuggling plane.

"Looks okay to me!" Rapp shouted back.

Coleman gave him the thumbs-up and walked over to a console fitted with a joystick, a monitor, and a disconcerting amount of Cyrillic writing. The bomb had a camera in the nose cone that could be used to find and lock on to a target. Once that was done, the fins—hopefully undamaged from their exit and no longer covered in padding—would take over.

A yet-unanswered question was whether Marroqui followed blackout protocols at night. While modern weapons would have infrared, starlight, laser, and whatever other overpriced systems defense contractors could come up with, this relic relied entirely on black-and-white video with the resolution of an *I Love Lucy* rerun. Fortunately, what Soviet engineers lacked in finesse they tended to make up for with brute force. Pinpoint accuracy wasn't really necessary for this beast.

Their pilot appeared from the cockpit and raised a fist—the signal that they were five minutes from their target and that he was going to bring them to their operational altitude of twenty-five thousand feet. Rapp put on an oxygen mask and attached the bottle to his belt. Coleman did the same and they tied off to a couple of lines that would allow them to reach the open door but not fall through it.

The sensation of gravity intensified as they started their climb. Rapp put on a down jacket and goggles and then slid forward on his stomach until the rope attached to his harness went tight. Even through his headset, the roar of the engines and wind was deafening as he hung his head into space. No sign of anything on the ground, but based on the lack of stars, it seemed likely that they were passing through one of the intermittent clouds.

To his right, Coleman was messing with the video console, occasionally glancing at the rather rough Google translation of the instructions. Rapp focused on him for a moment, regretting all the times he'd taken the geeks at Langley for granted. Their abilities with languages, computers, and a hundred other things had saved his ass more times than he cared to remember. If they didn't end up crashing into the side of a mountain or vaporizing themselves with their new Soviet toy, maybe he'd send donuts.

"You got anything?" Coleman shouted over his earphones.

"Not yet."

The plane's interior lights flickered, suggesting they'd reached twenty-five thousand feet. Rapp continued to search the ground, finally picking up something in his light-sensitive peripheral vision.

"Benjamín. Do you see that?"

"Sí! Right where the coordinates you gave me said it would be."

The plane continued on course as the dim glow intensified. After another minute or so, it resolved into lights forming a rough circle in the sea of darkness. Not surprising. To the degree Marroqui expected trouble, he'd reasonably assume it would come from the ground. Based on that, security floods on his perimeter made a lot of sense. At least they had until he'd sent a hit squad to the South African wine country.

"One minute!" their pilot said.

Rapp and Coleman took positions on either side of the bomb. It was too long to point directly at the open door, but it was more or less angled in that direction.

"Get ready . . . On my mark . . . Now!"

The plane banked hard, tilting down on the door side to provide a gravity assist as they started pushing the weapon. Even with the incline, it was heavy as hell. Progress was slower than expected, right up to the moment that the nose cleared the aircraft's fuselage. Despite the fact that they'd slowed to barely above stall speed, the wind caught the front fins and spun the weapon like it was made of papier-mâché. It hit Coleman about calf height, knocking him down and fouling his safety line in one of the rear fins.

Rapp dove on top of him as the line went taut, pulling a switchblade from his pocket and snapping it open. In the end, though, it was unnecessary. The fin cut through the line before they could be dragged out and the bomb disappeared into the darkness. Suddenly free of its weight, the plane jerked back to level and their pilot throttled up. Rapp lifted Coleman and dragged him toward the video console, starting a silent countdown in his mind. Approximately thirty seconds to impact.

The former SEAL's nose was pouring blood and he looked dazed, but with Rapp's help he managed to get his hands on the joystick. At first, the screen was dark.

Twenty-five seconds . . .

Coleman manipulated the stick and a moment later the image of Marroqui's security lights appeared.

"Twenty seconds to impact!" Rapp shouted.

Coleman brought the crosshairs into the middle of the circle and depressed a button. Words appeared on-screen that Rapp assumed confirmed a target lock and Coleman's legs collapsed beneath him. He tied the man off with what was left of his safety line and started for the door but was blinded by a powerful flash before he could close it.

The old Soviet piece of shit had actually worked.

He dropped to his stomach and slid toward the edge of the door again. The aftermath of their attack wasn't exactly subtle. The small ring of electric light had been replaced by a raging fire probably twenty times the diameter.

He'd wanted to make a statement and it looked like he'd succeeded. They'd blown the entire top of the mountain off.

CHAPTER 19

THE WHITE HOUSE
WASHINGTON, DC
USA

ACTING CIA director Darren Hargrave strode past the president's assistant, feeling the same sense of euphoria he always did. No, that wasn't true. It had become even more powerful. More intoxicating.

The office had been completely transformed both in a literal and figurative sense. When he'd first started doing legal work for the Cooks so many years ago, their political aspirations were little more than dreams. Whispers. But Anthony's potential was impossible to ignore. He combined the alpha quality of Teddy Roosevelt with John F. Kennedy's good looks and FDR's uncanny ability to exude strength and compassion simultaneously. To that he added the understanding that the constraints holding his power in check were imaginary. A faded dream of men long dead.

Cook was finally where he was meant to be. And as CIA director, Hargrave was in a position to keep him there for four years, eight years, and beyond. He'd always known that Cook would lead him to greatness, but the reality had now exceeded even his wildest expectations.

He opened the door to the Oval Office, not bothering to ask permission or to wait for his arrival to be announced. Cook was alone, sitting at his desk, speaking on the phone. A rare opportunity for a private audience. His wife—the demon whispering in his ear—was in Ohio trying to cover for her husband's increasingly obvious absence from public life.

Cook finally put down the phone, focusing his attention on Hargrave but not offering any kind of greeting. It wasn't a surprising reaction. He'd undoubtedly read the CIA's preliminary report about the recent disturbance in Guatemala.

"What you sent me wasn't worth the paper it was printed on," the president said finally. "Just a bunch of speculation from corrupt Guatemalan politicians."

"It literally happened only a few hours ago and in an extremely remote part of the country. We're learning more every minute."

"Learning more," Cook said, his stare intensifying in a way that was equal parts thrilling and terrifying. "Over the course of a few days, Mitch Rapp seems to have done something the combined intelligence agencies of the world couldn't: kill Gustavo Marroqui. And not only that, he also managed to vaporize the mountain the man lived on."

"I'll remind you that that's not proven, sir. Marroqui's made a lot of enemies and—"

"Are you suggesting this was done by rival gang?" Cook said angrily. "Marroqui has that country in his pocket. No one's even come close to making an attempt on him in years. Now, a week after he attacks Mitch Rapp, his compound and everything within a half a mile of it goes up in a pillar of fire?"

"I agree that it's a remote possibility," Hargrave said, backing down. "A much more likely scenario is that Rapp managed to get hold of a military-grade weapon and either smuggle it into Marroqui's compound or drop it from a plane."

"So now it's possible that Rapp has access to military-grade weapons," Cook said, pressing his palms against his temples.

"It's possible," Hargrave conceded. "But that's useful information as we continue to adapt your security."

"I thought you had people in Guatemala. That you were going to deal with him there."

"Intercepting him was always a long shot, sir. Carrying out operations from the shadows is what he does and, let's be honest, he does it well. Further, he has Irene Kennedy, who knows our capabilities around the world better than anyone, and Claudia Gould, who's likely to have extensive contacts in Guatemala's criminal underground."

Cook continued to massage his temples for a moment before leaning back in his chair. "Where is he now?"

"We don't know, sir. But we do have surveillance on most of his team. Joe Maslick, Bruno McGraw, and Charlie Wicker."

"You mean the three men he *didn't* need in order to kill someone who had nearly as much security as I do and lived in a country that Rapp's never operated in?"

It infuriated Hargrave that a meaningless enforcer like Mitch Rapp had the power to affect a man as great as Anthony Cook, but he reminded himself that good could come from it. Only through adversity would the president learn to differentiate those who truly cared for him from the leeches who swarmed around him.

"Yes, sir, but—"

"There are no buts, Darren. That could have been me. It *can* be me. For all we know, he's sitting in rural Maryland right now programming a guided missile to come through my window. What good are your security measures against that? And what good are your excuses going to be to me when there's nothing left of the White House but a crater?"

"He wouldn't do that. There'd be too much collateral damage."

"You have no idea what a man like Mitch Rapp would or wouldn't do."

"Yes, sir. Obviously, we're including this new intelligence to our comprehensive review of your security. Right now, we're looking at expanding the restricted airspace around you, reducing exceptions for things like traffic and news aircraft, and building a more robust intercept capability. While I still think it's an unlikely strategy for Rapp to pursue because of the number of innocent lives that would be lost, it is something we have the technology to counter."

"Eventually."

"Steady progress is being made, sir, but I'll admit that Rapp was able to neutralize the Marroqui threat faster than expected. But Claudia Gould has more than one enemy. If the Guatemalans found out about her, I don't think it would be a stretch to expect other people from her past to have stumbled on the same information."

"Even if that's true, Rapp made it pretty clear what happens to people who come after her. People are going to take that into account and reevaluate whether a little revenge is worth losing their life."

"She has a pretty colorful past, Mr. President. Some of her enemies aren't easily intimidated."

"And you could tip another one off."

Hargrave gave a short nod.

"Do you think it'll buy us the time we need?"

"It's impossible to say for certain, sir, but I think so. And even if it doesn't, it'll certainly get us closer. Every hour he's distracted puts us in a stronger position."

"And once everything's in place?"

"Then, of course, we'll start moving toward a more permanent solution to the problem. Mitch Rapp is an extremely experienced operator with a lot of support, but he's just a man. Difficult to kill? Yes. He's proved that over and over. But impossible? Hardly."

CHAPTER 20

NEAR FRANSCHHOEK
SOUTH AFRICA

CYRAH Jafari couldn't help but admire her surroundings. She'd arrived in South Africa about a week ago and had spent the time familiarizing herself with the Franschhoek area. The entire Western Cape was stunning, but this road was particularly special. It was unpaved but well maintained and bordered on either side by vines. Beyond, a series of verdant hills gradually morphed into majestic, stony peaks. Even with dark sunglasses, she was forced to squint through the sun pouring through the windshield.

The property she was searching for turned out to be accurately represented by the photos she'd seen—a clean white wall that blocked everything from view except the gray thatch roof peeking above. As she got closer, a corrugated metal gate became visible, but it had been made clear that she wasn't to approach. Instead, she searched to the east for the narrow track that had been described to her.

It appeared after another hundred meters and she eased the car right, making sure not to kick up dust that would be visible from a distance. The path through the vines led to a shed containing agricultural equipment, with just enough space remaining for her to squeeze into.

She stepped out and, after locking the door, used the side mirror to check her appearance. The sunglasses and a knit hat left little more than dimpled cheeks and full lips visible. The coat she'd put on to combat the chilly temperatures was formless in a vaguely stylish way—a description that also fit a pair of loose-fitting jeans.

Her most memorable features—eyes, hair, and athletic figure—were well concealed, but in a far less rigid way than they had been growing up in Iran. At thirty-five, she still possessed what most people would describe as innocent beauty—a relentless cuteness that was difficult to escape with Western styles of dress. There was something about the anonymity of a Muslim upbringing that could in many ways feel comforting. Safe. A lie, of course, but not always an unpleasant one. As long as she was the one in control of it.

Cyrah shouldered a canvas purse and started back up the dirt track on foot. She was in danger of being late.

The damaged gate had originally consisted of open iron bars but they were now sheathed in metal to shield against prying eyes. It had been pulled back just enough to let her pass through, but that fact had been camouflaged by an empty police cruiser pulled up just in front. Based on the information she'd been given, the property was unoccupied and had been since the attack. As had been widely reported by the media, the owners miraculously overcame a ten-man Guatemalan hit squad and escaped to parts still unknown.

When she was only a few meters from the gate, a Caucasian man wearing the uniform of a low-level police official appeared in the gap. His deep-set eyes and thin beard fit the description Cyrah had been given by the woman who'd set up this meeting.

Officer Michael Pistorius made no effort at a greeting, instead eyeing her silently before starting across the courtyard. She followed, but at a pace that allowed her to take in her surroundings. The house was traditional Cape Dutch—white, with a central porch and a row of first-floor windows that had been partially covered with plywood. Four dormers with glass intact hinted at a second story and added interest to the steeply sloping roof. The grounds were a combination of well-tended grass, gravel, and flagstone, with an abundance of flowering plants. To the east was a sizable freestanding building with bay doors firmly closed.

"Hurry! We don't have much time," Pistorius said, using a key to open the front door.

Cyrah nodded and passed into the house's dim interior. The extensive damage was immediately evident, as was a puddle of dried blood outlined in blue tape on the entryway floor.

"You have my money?" he said, making a show of his distaste for her.

"Of course." She dug a stack of cash from her purse and handed it to him.

"What about your phone?"

"Turned off as we agreed."

"Let me see."

She fished it from her pocket and showed him the dark screen.

"No pictures," he reminded her. "And any specific details you want to print in your article have to be approved by me."

She shrugged. "I always protect my sources. The people I work for are more interested in blood and sensationalism than fact checking."

"And who are those people exactly?"

Another shrug. "Whoever's willing to pay the most."

He motioned with his head toward the living area. "Don't touch anything."

"Can I use my flashlight app if I promise—"

She fell silent when he pulled a light from his belt and offered it to her.

The damage was indeed impressive. A sideboard was shattered on the floor, white walls had been darkened by smoke, and the sofa had been partially consumed by fire, revealing what appeared to be layers of Kevlar. Some walls had been penetrated, while others were intact. Not unusual for an old house—original walls were often constructed of stone or brick while newer partitions would be made from plasterboard. That didn't seem to be the case here, though. There was no coherent architectural pattern and eventually she found a gouge big enough to confirm the presence of ballistic material.

"He had hidden weapons, too," Pistorius said. "A lot of them."

"Really?" she responded, shining the flashlight at the molding near the ceiling. There was something about it that had been bothering her and now she knew what it was. The paint was color coded to indicate the strength of the walls. It wouldn't have been obvious in normal light, but the powerful LED beam exaggerated the different shades where the corners met.

"You have eight more minutes," Pistorius said, looking increasingly nervous.

"My understanding is that there's a safe room?"

He nodded and motioned for her to follow.

It wasn't particularly elaborate—basically the best that could be retrofitted into the space. A bank of monitors were undoubtedly fed by hidden cameras covering every room from at least one angle. Redundant communications and network equipment was equally sophisticated, including controls for what appeared to be remote door locks.

It seemed almost certain that Mitch Burhan—a former Green Beret—had been fed real-time information on his enemies' movements from this room. Combined with a truly extraordinary amount of nerve and skill, he'd managed to take down eight heavily armed killers here and two more on the road. Even with his training and background, no small feat.

"Can I go upstairs?"

On the second floor, there was enough sun coming through the windows to make the flashlight unnecessary and she gave it back to

Pistorius. The layout was fairly simple—a master bedroom with an en suite bathroom, a second bedroom set up for guests, and a room that was obviously the home of seven-year-old Anna. The latter two shared a bathroom in the hall.

The fight had clearly not reached that level and there was no appreciable damage. Cyrah entered the closet and reached for a drawer but her police shadow immediately protested.

"What are you doing?"

"Just looking for some personal details. These kinds of stories are about human interest. People want to know who these people are. How they—"

"No," he said firmly. "I told you not to touch anything and I meant it. You have three more minutes."

"If it's a matter of money—"

"Two minutes fifty-five seconds."

She knew men like him and recognized that nothing short of a claw hammer against his skull was going to change his mind. Tempting, but not practical.

She finished her tour of the second floor and then descended again. There was a mangled door lying on the tile behind the entry and she looked down a hallway that led to an exit covered with plywood. Based on the limited damage to the front of the house, this is where the main incursion had likely happened. But it was tight, favoring a single man against a larger force.

"Thirty seconds."

She would have liked to see the kitchen, but instead headed back toward the front door. There was nothing to be learned there. In the end, the visit had probably been a net negative. She'd revealed her existence to a dishonest policeman and accomplished little beyond confirming what she already knew: the family had been expecting trouble and were prepared for it. What she hadn't fully understood—fully internalized—was how dangerous the owners of this house were.

Claudia in particular piqued her interest and admiration. When those men attacked, she'd gathered her daughter, entered the safe room, and then calmly directed Burhan in his battle.

A formidable woman. It was going to be a shame to kill her.

Cyrah glanced in her rearview mirror but saw only the dirt road and mountains. Pistorius was likely securing the house in a way that would hide the fact that he'd allowed a visit by someone he believed to be a reporter.

When her vehicle reached the paved rural highway, she used her phone to send a code that would let her colleagues know that she was clear. It took longer than normal to get confirmation that the message had been received, but she wasn't surprised. Her associates didn't share her enthusiasm for this job and used every opportunity to subtly remind her of that.

Not that there was any need. She understood their position completely. They'd already had an extremely successful year, completing four assassinations in its first half. An Asian political hopeful, a European playboy, an aging Qatari billionaire, and a cheating husband who had underestimated both his wife's vindictiveness and her resourcefulness. That had netted them just under seven million euros after expenses, which, split three ways, had allowed her to increase her holdings by more than two million euros.

One of her colleagues wanted to take the rest of the year off for additional training, technology upgrades, and to do a detailed analysis of the few mistakes made during the year's operations. The other wanted to do all those things plus cherry-pick a few easy jobs. Since their fee was set, there was no incentive to take on anything dangerous or complicated. In their minds, easy money was better than hard money.

The logic was unassailable, but life wasn't about logic. It was about living. It was about excitement, challenge, and adrenaline. It was about finding one's boundaries and pushing through them. Discovering what one was capable of and what one wasn't.

As her associates' caution came to feel more and more like a straitjacket, Cyrah began escaping it through personal pursuits. Rock climbing. Bungee jumping. Cave diving. They helped fill the empty part in her soul, but not in a way that was particularly satisfying. Nothing could match the thrill of the hunt and it made little sense for her to risk her life for free when she could do it for significant profit.

So, when they'd received the dossier on Claudia Gould, Cyrah had jumped. Not only because Claudia had been half of one of history's most successful private contracting teams, but also because of the series of events the attack on the Franschhoek house had unleashed. The fact that Claudia and her partner had been able to defeat Gustavo Marroqui's hit squad was impressive, but nothing compared to what followed. Over the course of just nine days, they'd not only located Marroqui, but killed him. And not with a gunshot or by paying off some disgruntled associate. No, they'd annihilated the entire top of the mountain he'd lived on.

Claudia Gould was not only an incredibly dangerous woman; she was also a woman with style. Someone with the courage to say that she was not to be crossed and then vigorously support that statement through action.

Cyrah felt a dull pulse of excitement at the realization that she wasn't safe. No matter how careful she was, no matter how well crafted her plans, there was no way to fully protect herself from Claudia Gould. And anyone arrogant enough to think they could would likely end up like Gustavo Marroqui.

CHAPTER 21

NEAR FRANSCHHOEK
SOUTH AFRICA

THE weather had turned cold, barely above forty degrees Fahrenheit, with heavy clouds rolling in the night before. The rows of vines on either side of the muddy road Rapp was driving down seemed particularly still as they disappeared into a hazy distance.

It had taken him and Coleman a full two weeks to get out of Guatemala. The death of Gustavo Marroqui had been a far more significant event than they anticipated. The government had descended into chaos as corrupt politicians lost their cover. Gang warfare erupted throughout the country and someone at MS-13 had provided the authorities with his description. So, with no backup, grade school Spanish, and dwindling cash reserves, they'd had to get out on their own. The day they'd finally made it across the border to El Salvador had been one of the happiest of his life.

Rapp looked up through the sunroof but didn't see anything beyond overcast. Despite that, it was certain that he was being watched. He'd booked his flight from Central America under the name Mitch

Burhan and made no secret of renting the car at the Cape Town airport. There was no question that he'd been reacquired, as had Scott Coleman when he'd transited through Entebbe on his way back to Nick Ward's compound.

With that, Rapp and his core team would all be accounted for again. He'd agreed to stay in plain sight, and it was in his best interest to live up to that agreement at this point. He was still suspicious that Cook wasn't actually abiding by the terms of their truce, but for now it made sense to pretend. Blowing things up at this point would open another battlefront that he wasn't prepared to deal with. Better to leave that war for later. Or, with a little luck, never.

The gate leading to Claudia's house was pulled closed and covered in corrugated metal. Rapp slowed the car to a crawl but kept driving. There was no point in going out in the rain when he could let the front bumper do the work.

Once inside the courtyard, he pulled up to the porch and stepped out. Police tape was fluttering in the wind, and he pulled it off before opening the door. A quick test of a light switch suggested the power was out—likely shut down at the main to prevent any nicked wires from catching fire. The bodies were gone but he could still smell death beneath what he assumed was a punctured sewer line.

Pretty much everything in the living room was a loss. Tape outlines remained on the tile and there was water damage on the ceiling that was starting to mold. Walls were in equally bad shape, some having taken fire in addition to the explosives. Even worse was Claudia's beloved artwork.

He continued into the kitchen and found it in somewhat better condition. Based on the stain on the floor, the freezer had melted. Maybe it was that and not sewage causing the smell, but he didn't open it to find out. Instead, he grabbed a bag of tortilla chips and a warm Coke from the pantry. After righting a stool stained with dried blood, he sat at the pockmarked island and dug in.

Clearly, this wasn't a job for a gallon of spackle and some paint.

It was the domain of an architect and full construction crew. The whole bottom floor was a gut job, which would be expensive and time consuming—particularly if their insurance didn't cover Guatemalan hit squads. On the other hand, it would allow Claudia to add the modern touches she was always going on about and him to install a more integrated security system.

Or maybe their time in South Africa was over. The shit that had gone down there could have put them back on the radar of their long list of enemies. Probably better to keep their distance for a while and handle renovations over the Internet. Then, when the work was done, they could decide whether it was viable to move back in or if they should just put the property on the market and disappear.

Usually that kind of vanishing act was the answer when you were up against a wall, but he questioned whether it was even an option anymore. First, the level of discipline and attention to detail it demanded would likely prove impossible for a girl Anna's age. Second, dropping off the face of the earth would violate the terms of his truce with Anthony Cook and any armistice they might or might not have would be right down the toilet.

After thirty minutes, he'd gone through two soft drinks and the entire bag of Africa's answer to Doritos but come to no conclusions. In truth, soul-searching wasn't his reason for being there, but it seemed like a good use of the downtime. Likely, it wouldn't last.

He slid off the stool and was going to go upstairs to see if there was any damage but then spotted a police vehicle creeping through the gate. He examined it through a rare unbroken window and then started for the entryway.

Even after three weeks, the press couldn't let go of the Franschhoek Bloodbath, with much of the continued interest being generated by the fact that the house's owners were still unaccounted for. If they ever had a hope of returning, he needed to quiet this thing down and get on the right side of the law.

"Afternoon!" Rapp called to the man stepping from the cruiser. He was alone, probably five inches taller than Rapp, with a shaved head and impeccable uniform.

"I'm Thato Gumede," he said through a pleasant African accent. "Do I have the pleasure of addressing Mitch Burhan?"

"In the flesh," Rapp said, keeping his tone lighter than the circumstances probably warranted. What he didn't need right now was to get hauled off to an interrogation room. "Is it just you?"

The man stopped in the grass about ten feet away. It was no longer raining, and he seemed to judge it a safe distance.

"After what happened here, I didn't think that backup would do me much good."

Rapp wasn't sure how to respond so he didn't.

"May I ask where your partner and her daughter are?"

"In a safe place."

The man nodded. He didn't look stupid and clearly wanted to keep this situation on as even a keel as possible. It was a significant relief. If some cowboy had showed up looking to throw his weight around, things could have deteriorated pretty quickly.

"Can you prove this?"

"Absolutely. Before you leave, let me give you our attorney's card. She can get you anything you need, including scheduling a Zoom call with Claudia and Anna."

They were represented by one of the most prestigious firms in the country—something that would hopefully enhance what little credibility he had left. Blowing away a bunch of Latino gangbangers in the hoity-toity South African wine country wasn't a great way to ingratiate yourself with your adopted country.

"So, what happened here, Mr. Burhan?"

Rapp sat in one of the slingback chairs on the porch and invited Gumede to do the same. He politely refused, preferring to stand in the wet grass than get any closer.

"All three of us were home when two SUVs came through the gate and ten armed men attacked us."

"But they were all killed in the attempt."

"Yes."

"By you."

"Yes."

"Alone. There was no one else here?"

"No one except Claudia and Anna."

"Captain Mitchell Burhan," Gumede said, beginning to recite the elaborate identity Rapp had created to establish his South African residency. "Former Green Beret. Honorably discharged from the military after serving in various combat zones, most notably Afghanistan."

"That's me."

"After you left the military, you went to work for a little-known security company. What did you do there?"

"Personal protection, mostly. Some private clients but primarily American diplomats traveling in the Middle East."

"Are you now going to tell me that one of those diplomats or private clients caused you to anger Gustavo Marroqui?"

Rapp suppressed a smile. This guy thought he knew exactly what he was dealing with, and he was so close to being right that there was no reason to fight it.

"I've made a lot of enemies over the years. Sometimes it's hard to remember them all."

"But they're fresh enough in your mind to be prepared for them. South African homes are known for their security, but yours takes that to another level."

"Hope for the best but prepare for the worst."

"I live by the same adage, Mr. Burhan, but this still seems extreme for a retired soldier and bodyguard. A mix of bulletproof and non-bulletproof walls, at least twelve hidden weapons, Kevlar in various pieces of furniture. A safe room with overlapping video coverage and remote-controlled door locks. Impressive."

"Thank you."

"But even with all that . . ." Gumede continued. "Defeating ten men like you did. It seems extraordinary even for a Green Beret."

"A little skill. A little luck. A couple of damn fine dogs. And, frankly, opponents who weren't exactly the cream of the crop."

Gumede changed the subject with a suddenness designed to disorient him. "Have you read the reports about Gustavo Marroqui's assassination? Apparently by some kind of high explosive. Possibly dropped from a plane."

"I think I might have seen something about it on CNN," Rapp said in a tone meant to make it clear that he'd personally gone down to Guatemala and blown that motherfucker into the stratosphere.

"I see," Gumede said, making it equally clear that he'd picked up the subtext. "I understand that men like you often go to work for other types of government agencies after you retire from special forces. Ones that have"—his voice faded for a moment—"broader missions."

"Sometimes."

Again, the African nodded thoughtfully, clearly considering how far he wanted to insert himself into this. "I've made a number of official inquiries about you to the American government and they've been very forthcoming with superficial information. But when I try to dig deeper, I run into an extremely polite wall of red tape."

"Bureaucrats," Rapp said sympathetically. "What are you gonna do?"

"What indeed. And the bureaucrats here don't seem to want to make any more of this unfortunate incident than necessary. They see it as a clear example of self-defense and believe the courts would do the same."

"Very sensible on their part."

"More cowardly than sensible, I think. In the end, though, pursuing this further is bad for their reputations, bad for tourism, and has the potential to cause diplomatic headaches they don't want to deal with."

"Problem solved, then."

"May I speak plainly, Mr. Burhan?"

"I'd prefer you did."

"I think you're a sociopath and cold-blooded killer. And while I believe you used those traits in the service of your government, I also think that at some point you got involved in the drug trade. Now, whether that was for the benefit of your Central Intelligence Agency or for your own bank account, I can't say. And it doesn't matter, because I'm wise enough to know there's nothing I can do about it."

Rapp leaned forward, resting his elbows against his knees. He couldn't help liking this asshole. If the world had about a billion more of him, Rapp would have had a lot quieter career.

"I appreciate your honesty, Officer. So let me return the courtesy. I am not, nor have I ever been, involved in the drug trade for my own account. Further, whatever I've done in the past is just that: in the past. My goal now is to live out a peaceful retirement. And as inconvenient as this kind of thing is to you, it's a hell of a lot more inconvenient to me. But, as you've noticed, it's being taken care of."

CHAPTER 22

A SECTION of ceiling completely gave way and Rapp barely managed to avoid it coming down on his head. He dropped the pry bar he'd been using and caught what he could in a strategically placed wheelbarrow. Despite having turned off the water to most of the house, some of the plaster was still wet enough to stick to the antique tile floor Claudia loved so much. The rest enveloped him in a cloud that he could smell through the mask that wouldn't fully seal against his beard.

He pushed the wheelbarrow through the haze to the front door. An improvised ramp allowed him to avoid the porch steps and he continued across the grass to a large dumpster near the perimeter wall. Once there, he pulled off his mask and used a shovel to begin transferring the debris.

Finally, he stepped back, shading his eyes against the sun and taking a moment to survey his progress. The gate was unrepaired and still covered with corrugated metal that was pretty effective in deterring press photographers and general curiosity seekers. Of course, they could still use drones, but he hadn't seen any yet. If that changed, he had a twelve-gauge by the door.

The freezer was cleaned out, as was the damage to the sewage line, which had taken care of the worst of the odors. An electrician had tested as much of the wiring as was practical and cut off any questionable circuits at the breaker box. That had left much of the ground floor without power, but with the creative use of extension cords, he could run the refrigerator, microwave, work lights, and basic power tools. Though not all at the same time.

Most of the furniture and artwork from the first floor had found a new home at the dump. Later that week, a moving van was scheduled to take the rest of their belongings to a secure storage unit outside of Cape Town. Then the place would be ready to hand over to the architect Claudia had coming to meet with him.

After that, he wasn't sure. Doing a proper job of renovating the house would take at least six months and after that their tentative plan was to return. By then, the press would have moved on, any rumors about Claudia that might have taken hold in criminal circles would have died down, and his truce with the White House would be worn in.

What could possibly go wrong?

The phone in his pocket began to vibrate and he pulled off his work gloves to dig it out.

"Are things still on track?" Claudia said when he picked up.

"More or less. I'm going to have to scramble to get everything ready for the movers, but it's doable. The boxes and packing supplies are supposed to be delivered today."

"It's a lot, Mitch. Are you sure you don't want me to come and help? Scott's back and between him and Irene, they can handle Anna."

"No. I've got this. Stop worrying."

"I'm not worrying. But this is my fault and I'm sitting around the pool while you live in a house with no power and a leaking toilet."

"I'm sure you'll find a way to make it up to me," he said. "How are things going on your end? Have you found us somewhere to live yet?"

"No, but I'll have some options for you to look at when you get back. Obviously, everything has its pros and cons. Do we get lost in a big city like Paris, London, or Istanbul? Or do we want to disappear into something more rural? There are some nice places in Asia, but I'm leaning more toward Latin America. I'd like Anna to learn a little Spanish, which wouldn't be hard with her foundation in French. And while I admire her devotion to Afrikaans, I'm not sure it's going to be that useful in the long run."

"What about my Alaska idea?"

He'd read that it was possible to just get off a train in the middle of nowhere and claim some acreage. They could build a cabin next to a lake and turn off the world for a while. Hunt. Fish. It'd be good for the kid to get some survival skills under her belt.

"I'm ignoring it."

Her tone suggested that pressing the issue would be futile, so he changed the subject.

"How's Anna doing?"

"Better. She can't get enough of the pool, and Scott's taking her on a gorilla safari tomorrow. But she misses her friends. I'd like to fly in Ahmale, but we're not very popular with the other parents right now."

"Have you talked to her about the fact that we can't come back for a while?"

"No. I think it's too soon. She's resilient, but I want her to bounce back a little more before she has to face that. Also, I think it would be better if you were here when we deliver the news. Not that I'm trying to push any of this off on you, but we need to present a united front. Is that okay?"

His phone began vibrating again and he glanced down at the letters on the screen.

GAz.

They were ones he thought he'd never see again and, more important, they were ones he'd never *wanted* to see again. Grisha Azarov was a Russian assassin he'd come up against a while back in Saudi Arabia. At the time, the man had been pretty much at the top of the food chain. He'd nearly killed Coleman in Pakistan and when Rapp finally faced off against him, it hadn't been pretty. Rapp had come out the victor, but that victory involved being blown off an oil rig and having to extinguish his burning hair in a sand dune.

In the end, though, Rapp had decided there was no reason to kill the man. His attacks weren't personal—they'd been carried out at the orders of the Russian government. With his former masters dead, Azarov's only interests were anonymity and a Californian surf instructor he'd met. Last he'd heard, the Russian had married, gained twenty-five pounds, and developed a fondness for high-quality weed.

"Are you still there?" Claudia said.

"Yeah."

"Can I take your silence to mean you think I should handle Anna on my own?"

"No. I agree that it's better if we both do it." The letters continued to pulse on-screen. Relentless, like the man they represented had once been. "Listen, I've got a call coming in. Can we continue this later?"

"Sure."

She disconnected and he picked up the other line. "Problem?"

"Not for me," came the accented response. "For you."

From most people, that would have sounded like a threat. But not from Azarov. He wasn't the type.

"What are we talking about?"

"I recently received a dossier on one of my old email accounts. It contains a significant amount of information on Claudia. The fact that she's really Louis Gould's former wife, her current alias, a photo, her address in South Africa, a description of her car, the places she shops, Anna's school . . . You get the point."

"Do you know where it came from?"

"An anonymous Gmail account. I imagine untraceable."

"What's the offer?"

"None. Just a single line asking me if I would be interested in taking her out. My assumption is that whoever sent this is counting on me holding a grudge against her for a run-in I had with her husband years ago. He caused me a lot of problems with Moscow and I had every intention of killing him. But he slipped through my fingers and then your friend Stan Hurley beat me to it."

"When did the message come in?"

"Maybe three weeks ago?"

Rapp's jaw clenched. "How many days exactly?"

There was a short pause before the Russian spoke again. "Nineteen."

"*Shit,*" Rapp muttered, counting backward. That was the day after he'd killed Gustavo Marroqui. Someone with serious intelligence capability had taken note of the fact that the Guatemalan had been neutralized and moved down the list of Claudia's enemies. Any hope that the attack on the house was a coincidence or bad luck had just imploded. This had Darren Hargrave's name written all over it. And that boot-licking son of a bitch didn't take a dump without Anthony Cook's blessing.

"I didn't want to get involved, Mitch. But Cara made the point that if our positions were reversed, you'd pick up the phone. It took a while, but this morning, I decided she was right."

"Did you respond to the message?"

"I'm sorry. I told them no."

"Same day that you got it?"

"Yes."

A string of curse words in no fewer than five languages went through Rapp's mind, but this time he kept his mouth shut. If Azarov had remained silent as to whether he was interested, it could have bought some time. But with a hard no, Hargrave would have already moved on to the next person who wanted Claudia dead.

"There's nothing to apologize for, Grisha. I appreciate the call. If you ever need anything, I'll remember you made it."

"I'll forward you the dossier. Good luck. To both of you."

The line went dead.

Rapp grabbed the handles of the empty wheelbarrow and sent it careening across the grass. "Fuck!"

CHAPTER 23

SOUTHWESTERN UGANDA

THE sun was up, but still low on the horizon when the chopper landed. Rapp jumped down to Nicholas Ward's helipad with a duffel slung over one shoulder. Claudia and Anna were looking on from a safe distance and the young girl raised her arms as he approached. Rapp took the hint and scooped her up as the aircraft lifted off again.

"I didn't think you were ever coming back. We're going to see gorillas! Do you want to come? I bet there's room still. It's a big truck and we rented like the whole thing."

"Sounds fun, but I'm going to have to skip this one. I've got some work to do."

"Mom says she's going to see if Ahmale can come next weekend. Nick isn't ever even here and he says we can use his pool anytime we want. He works even more than you. I saw him on TV yesterday. He's really boring when he's on it. Not like in real life."

"Anna, Mitch has been dealing with the house all week and traveling all night," Claudia said. "The least you could do is walk yourself."

She rolled her eyes and wriggled from his grip.

"In fact, why don't you run ahead and make Mitch your special cereal. He hasn't had breakfast yet."

Anna perked up at that. Apparently she'd learned to create quite a concoction out of muesli, milk, yogurt, and local fruit—typically served in a coconut shell that leaked. Claudia waited until she'd disappeared up the trail before taking a position blocking his path.

"Why are you here, Mitch? You weren't due for a few more days and you're supposed to be meeting with our architect."

He pulled out his phone, retrieved the dossier Grisha Azarov had sent, and handed it to her. She scrolled for a few seconds, the blood draining from her face.

"This is not good. . . . Not good at all."

Irene Kennedy finished going through Azarov's email and then handed the phone to Scott Coleman so he could do the same. They were sitting across from Rapp and Claudia in the shadow cast by their bungalow. Everyone remained silent while the former SEAL studied the dossier and then tossed the cell on the table.

"I only see one explanation for this," Rapp said.

"I know," Kennedy said. "But I think it's too soon to come to any hard conclusions."

"Seriously?"

"Look, I eradicated all the information about falsifying Claudia's death and creating her new identity from the CIA's database. In fact, we went so far as to have Marcus create a worm to find and delete any reference to it."

Whenever Kennedy resorted to stating the obvious, it was in an effort to give herself time to think. Rapp knew that, but his anger had reached the point that he wasn't willing to play along.

"There's no way to eradicate that many files that's even close to clean, Irene. Even if Marcus's worm worked perfectly, that just replaces one set of problems with another. You end up with incomplete narratives, references that don't go anywhere, and reports that don't make sense. And that's ignoring the fact that a lot of the people who helped us make her disappear still work at the Agency. Sure, we picked ones we could trust, but where do their loyalties lie now? I hope you know, because after what happened with Mike, I sure as hell don't."

"No system is foolproof," she admitted.

"And this is just the kind of sleazy, backstabbing operation that Darren Hargrave would come up with."

"It also makes sense that Grisha would be high on his list," Kennedy conceded. "The information about his run-in with Louis is well documented in the CIA's database but your relationship with him isn't. That information was so sensitive that we never recorded anything about it. There was never a file to delete."

"Hargrave is a scumbag, but you've got to give him credit," Coleman said. "This was a slick move. If Mitch really was going after the president, his window's closing as they harden their security. This allows them to tie Mitch up without implicating themselves. Maybe even get him killed."

"Look," Kennedy said in the soothing tone she tended to adopt when things were blowing up. "I agree that there's a good chance that Darren Hargrave is behind this. But whether it's been done with Cook's knowledge is—"

"Come *on*," Rapp interrupted. "Hargrave is so far up the president's ass, Cook can taste his hair spray. He—"

"*Be that as it may*," Kennedy said, wrestling back control of the conversation, "we need to understand what we're dealing with and what our options are. Rushing into a war with the president of the United States isn't going to go well."

"I completely disagree," Scott Coleman said, and everyone immediately turned toward him. He had a deep respect for—and more than a little fear of—Irene Kennedy. Rapp couldn't remember him ever taking a strong stance against one of her positions.

"These assholes aren't going to just go after Mitch and let me and the guys off the hook. If they don't kill us outright, they'll figure out a way to arrest us for treason or murder and put on some big show trial. We aren't exactly a bunch of nuns. We've all done some things that might not look so good in the news cycle. I say we go after those motherfuckers. We kill Cook, his creepy-ass wife, and then we throw Darren Hargrave in a wood chipper. Before they can close the gates around themselves."

A stunned silence enveloped the table for a few moments before Kennedy broke it. "I understand that there's a clock ticking, Scott. I can hear it just as clearly as everyone else. But we need to make sure there are no other options."

"And if there aren't?"

"Then we can't make the same mistake they did and miss. We have to have a clear idea of what we're doing and how we can be absolutely sure they *all* end up in the wood chipper."

The former SEAL leaned back in his chair again. "I can live with that."

"In the meantime," Kennedy continued, "I think it makes sense to understand who could potentially move against Claudia and neutralize them before they become a threat. Maybe even use them to our advantage."

The sun crept to the edge of the table and Rapp looked up at the sky. It was hard not to think about the similarities between his situation and that of Gustavo Marroqui. The difference was that his enemies didn't need to chuck a Soviet surplus bomb out of a narcotics plane. They could fly over in a B-2 and drop something state-of-the-art.

Claudia dug an uncharacteristically crumpled piece of paper from her jeans and unfolded it on the table. She seemed less put out by the situation than the rest of them and Rapp suspected he knew why. This was no longer her fault. That millstone was back around his own neck.

"I've made a list of people who might still be motivated to kill me and have the ability to do it."

"How many?" Rapp said.

"Six."

Fewer than he'd expected. Her husband had been a sociopathic bastard, but there was no denying the skills. He wasn't a man to leave a lot of enemies behind.

"Names?"

"Malthe Kierkegaard, Oren Avraham, Earnst Lang, Aat Rueng, Josef Svoboda, and Enzo Ruiz."

Coleman let out a low whistle. "Not to be negative, but there are some people on there you don't want coming after you."

"Could be worse," Rapp said. "Let's start at the beginning. Malthe Kierkegaard."

Coleman shook his head. "There wasn't any money on offer in that email to Grisha. Kiki wouldn't step on a cockroach without a guaranteed payday. It costs a hundred grand just to get him to consider taking a job. Don't ask me how I know."

"Agreed," Kennedy said. "But we need to contact him and tell him to let us know if anyone sends him that dossier. Also, we need to make it clear that he should respond by saying that he's going to do the job. That'll buy us time and maybe even help us find the person who sent it. Easy work and tell him we'll pay him whatever he wants."

"No problem, I'll handle it."

"Who was next?" Rapp said.

"Oren Avraham."

"He's dead," Kennedy said.

"Really?" Rapp responded. "I hadn't heard that. Are you're sure?"

She nodded. "Bottom of the Indian Ocean."

"Well, there you go. Next?"

"Earnst Lang."

"Didn't you use one of his offshore companies to finance an op a few years ago?" Coleman asked.

"Yes," Kennedy confirmed. "It was something the CIA couldn't have a connection to."

"Can you still get to him?" Rapp asked.

She pulled out her phone and scrolled through the contacts before setting the audio to speaker. It only rang twice before being picked up.

"Is this a joke?" came the German-accented voice.

"No, it's really me, Earnst."

"Why?" he said suspiciously. "I haven't done anything that would cause you problems. And I heard you were fired."

"It's not what you've done, it's what you might do. Have you received any interesting anonymous emails lately?"

"I have no idea what you're talking about."

"You're sure?"

"Of course I'm sure."

"Okay, then. It's possible that you're going to get a dossier on a woman you don't much care for—her name, photo, address, habits—everything you'd need to exact a little revenge."

"So?"

"So, I'd be disappointed if something happened to her."

"Why don't you government people ever speak plainly? What you mean is that if I make a move, you'll send that psychopath Mitch Rapp to kill me."

"I'm sorry. Force of habit. Yes. That's exactly what I'm going to do."

"Not really a problem for me because I can't think of a single woman in the world that I hate enough to bother killing."

"I'll remember you said that. Also, if you do get a dossier like the one I'm talking about, I need you to say you're going to act on it and call me immediately."

When he spoke again, Lang had turned back into the businessman he'd always been. "I'm hearing you asking for a lot of favors, Dr. Kennedy."

She winced and Rapp understood how she felt. How many markers were they going to leave around the world before all this was over? It was worth killing Cook just for that.

"I'm hearing the same thing, Earnst."

"In that case, I'd be very happy to help. Just like I imagine you will be if I ever need it."

She disconnected the call. "Next?"

"Aat Rueng," Claudia said.

"Who's that?" Rapp said.

"A midsized Thai gangster. Last I heard, he was being squeezed by a number of other gangs and had lost a lot of his influence. I can contact him directly. It'll cost some money and a little groveling, but he'll back off. After that, we have Josef Svoboda."

"I hate that prick," Coleman groaned. "He gives the business a bad name."

Rapp nodded in agreement. The man was talented, but also extremely public. An army of lawyers and greased politicians allowed him to stay one step ahead of Interpol and live like a rock star. Last Rapp had heard, he'd bought a stake in a nightclub in Prague. Svoboda patterned himself after Hollywood's image of a hit man—five-thousand-dollar suits, Italian sports cars, arm candy. He reportedly drank martinis and actually had the balls to order them shaken, not stirred.

"How'd you piss him off?" Rapp said.

"He and Louis were double booked on a job and Louis got the upper hand. Svoboda came off looking incompetent and cowardly and thought he could regain some face by retaliating. The problem for him was that, while he's not actually incompetent, he definitely *is* cowardly. He knew he wasn't likely to survive a confrontation with Louis but I'm a softer target."

"Can we use that?" Rapp asked.

"I doubt it," Kennedy said. "While it's true that he doesn't like to put himself at risk, he's unpredictable. I don't think we can count on threats because we can't be confident that he'll act in his own best interest."

"Then can we just kill him?" Rapp asked.

Coleman was quick to answer. "I'll handle it."

"Another problem solved. Was there anyone else?"

"Only one," Claudia said. "Enzo Ruiz."

"Never heard of him."

"He's a Spanish drug runner who worked the routes from North Africa."

"Another drug trafficker," Rapp sighed.

"They have a lot of money and want a lot of people dead," Claudia explained. "This was early in Louis's career, and he actually botched the job. Ruiz was the target and he survived being shot. It left him partially paralyzed, though, and his kids forced him out of the business."

"I remember this," Kennedy said. "Part of a war between Spanish gangs and ones based in Morocco."

"It was during that war, yes. But what no one knows is that his children hired us and used the dispute with the Moroccans as cover. In any event, Louis was going to finish the job, but they told us to stand down and paid us in full. Apparently, they despised their father and loved the idea of seeing him powerless and wasting away."

"How old is this guy?" Rapp asked.

Claudia considered the question for a moment. "Around ninety?"

"So, a partially paralyzed ninety-year-old who was put out to pasture by his own family? What am I missing? How is this guy a threat?"

"He's not just *a* threat, he's the most dangerous," Claudia said. "Ruiz is an extremely sadistic, violent man who blames me and Louis for what he's become. Also, he isn't as out to pasture as his children think. He still controls a fair number of hidden accounts and is surprisingly well versed in the use of the Internet. People say he's built quite an online criminal empire, though I've never done anything to confirm those reports."

"He'll be hard to reason with," Kennedy pointed out. "We don't have anything he wants, and a man in his position isn't going to be easy to intimidate."

"I'll pay him a visit while Scott's in the Czech Republic dealing with Svoboda," Rapp said, turning to the former SEAL. "Scott, make it look like an accident. We don't know how accurate the Cooks' list of Claudia's enemies is and we don't want them to catch on to the fact that we're neutralizing them. Better to string them along as long as we can."

"No problem."

Rapp glanced around the table. "Anything else?"

When no one spoke up, he stood. "Then let's get to work."

CHAPTER 24

GIRONA
SPAIN

THE chatting of a couple of mountain bikers became audible on the dirt road behind and Rapp moved aside to let them pass. Girona, Spain, was one of the cycling capitals of the world—a beautiful city and a popular place for pros to train in the off-season. He was tempted to have Claudia put it on her list of potential temporary homes, but that was impossible. As he got fitter, he'd start getting noticed and that was pretty much the opposite of their goal. Barcelona might not be a bad choice, though. It was only a half-hour train ride, and he wouldn't mind joining Anna in learning Spanish. It seemed to be coming up in his life more and more.

But for now, he needed to focus on the task at hand.

The Guatemalan strategy of go big or go home wasn't going to work here. Enzo Ruiz needed to be interrogated, making dropping a bomb on him impractical. It would also likely be frowned upon by the European authorities. Quiet in and quiet out was the mission. The question was how to best get that done.

Claudia's extensive research had turned up a number of complications. To the positive, the former drug runner's house was only moderately protected—relying on an ancient stone wall and a few guards to keep out undesirables. Further, the man himself was not only in his nineties, but reportedly confined to a wheelchair. Not exactly the terror of southern Spain he'd once been. To the negative, his modest security team weren't coked-up psychopaths but instead legitimate salaried guards. And as such, all were completely off-limits.

Climbing the wall and then getting to Ruiz's second-floor room would be fairly easy but the habits of his security people had been randomized by the fact that there was really no viable threat to the man. They mostly just wandered around, talking, smoking, and screwing with their phones. With no pattern, the chance of him being spotted was too high.

In light of all that, a more direct approach was warranted.

Rapp turned onto a quieter dirt road and walked past a low stacked-stone fence. In ruins now, it had never been meant to do much more than keep the goats in and likely hadn't seen any maintenance in over a century. After another two hundred yards, Rapp crested a hill and saw the massive farmhouse he was looking for. Situated in the middle of a field and framed by a heavily treed hill behind, it and the wall that surrounded it were completely monochromatic—constructed of the same reddish brown local stone. A few tiny windows were visible on the top floor and the roof had a deep bow, further confirming its ancient origins.

The iron gate was elaborately wrought and provided a good view of the courtyard through widely spaced bars. Inside, there was no sign of activity at all. It was four in the afternoon and temperatures were in the nineties, likely driving everyone into the cooler interior. Or was it siesta? Rapp could never remember what time that started and ended.

There was a call button next to the gate, so he pressed it. A moment later, a man appeared in the house's front door and began walking unhurriedly toward him. He spoke in unintelligible Catalan, but seemed largely unconcerned. The Walther P99 on his hip came off as an afterthought.

"I'm here to see Enzo Ruiz," Rapp said in English.

He seemed to understand the name but nothing else. A quick wave of the hand suggested that Rapp should wait while he went back to the house to find someone with better English skills. Still unconcerned, he lit a cigarette as he ambled off. It was a good five minutes before the next man appeared, matching his colleague's complete lack of urgency as he approached the gate.

"Can I help you?"

Heavily accented but easily understandable.

"I'd like to talk to Enzo Ruiz."

"There is no one here called this."

"Why don't you go inside and make sure. Tell him Mitch Rapp is standing at his gate."

His bored expression gained a hint of suspicion, but no recognition. This guy was probably a former cop who would have no reason to know who Mitch Rapp was. That name circulated in darker places. Places that his boss had spent his life.

After a moment's hesitance, he headed back to the house. This time the delay was long enough that Rapp started to worry that they were smuggling the old man out the back.

Finally, he reappeared. "Señor Ruiz would be pleased to meet with you. Are you armed?"

"Yes."

"You can leave your weapon with me."

"No."

This time he was only gone for about three minutes. When he reappeared, his concern over Rapp's gun had vanished. Not surprising. The most dangerous enemy someone like Ruiz had was boredom, not assassins. When Claudia said his family had put him out to pasture, she was speaking literally. The man who had reinvented drug running from North Africa and spent his youth with people prostrated before him now lived in the middle of a field protected by a few sleepy guards.

"Please follow."

Rapp did, lagging a bit as they entered the house. Simple layout. The steps to the second floor were built into the wall with no railing and made of the same stone as everything else. It would be possible to jump from the top of them and land on a table that looked like it could take the weight of a dump truck. Then it was a straight run to the front door with no cover. Not that any of that would likely be necessary, but best to be prepared.

The door they passed through was at the end of a narrow hallway on the second floor. It led to a large room with a single window on the north side. Furniture was a weird mix of ancient wood and the plastic and stainless steel of various medical machines. A hospital bed set up in the center dominated, making the wheelchair-bound man by the wall seem even smaller than he was.

Ruiz slurred something in Spanish and the guard left, closing the ill-fitting door behind him. His red-rimmed eyes had a yellowish hue beneath a wrinkled scalp still holding on to a few clumps of white hair. Time didn't care about Ruiz's time as an enforcer for Spain's dictatorship. Or the fact that he'd managed to beat the Africans at their own brutal game. Or even about the immense fortune he'd amassed. Kings, peasants, killers, and victims. Everyone ended up in the same place eventually.

"Mitch Rapp," the man said. Based on those two words, his English was excellent. According to Claudia, he'd had a British mistress in the seventies and British nannies had raised his kids. "What is your interest in Claudia Gould?"

Rapp tried not to react to the Spaniard's words, but still Ruiz managed to pick up on his surprise.

"It's a curse," Ruiz explained. "Most men's minds weaken along with their bodies. Mine's gotten stronger."

"Then why don't you tell me?"

Ruiz used a joystick to bring the chair around to fully face his new opponent. A smile played at his chapped lips. "Gustavo Marroqui sent men to her house in South Africa to kill her. But, because he's a moron, he sent other morons to do the job. You were the man who executed them and then you destroyed the entire mountaintop he lived on." The Spaniard hacked out a laugh. "You live up to your reputation, Mr. Rapp. Or do you prefer Mr. Burhan now?"

He clearly loved having the upper hand. It was a sensation he probably hadn't experienced in years. But he wasn't clairvoyant. More likely he'd already had the pieces to the puzzle and Rapp's appearance just showed him how to put them together.

"So you got the email. The dossier on her," Rapp said.

Another smile, this time wide enough to reveal teeth stained by the better part of a century of smoking.

"I did."

"When?"

"You haven't answered my question."

"My interest in her is personal."

He nodded slowly. "That was the only logical conclusion I could come to, but I found it hard to believe. Weren't she and her husband responsible for your wife's death?"

"Yes."

"Then you and I should want the same thing."

"And yet we don't."

"You're a much more complicated man than I would have thought, Mr. Rapp."

"Now you answer my question."

"What question? Oh, yes. The dossier. Some three weeks ago."

"And what did you do with it?"

Ruiz pushed himself into a slightly more upright position. "What a strange surprise life has given me. This morning I was resigned to sit here staring out the window like I do every day. And now I have Mitch Rapp in front of me with hat in hand."

"That's not a hat, Enzo. It's a gun."

Again, he choked out a laugh. "As useless as tits on a bull. Isn't that what you Americans say?"

"How do you figure?"

"Death didn't scare me when I had something to live for. It certainly doesn't now. But maybe you're thinking you can use torture to extract the information you want. Look at me. How long do you think I'd last before my heart gave out? So, now you're considering threatening my family. Do you think I'm some kind of idiot? Do you think I don't know it was them? That they were the ones who hired Louis Gould to kill me and then, when he failed, left me here to rot? If you do decide to kill them, please bring them here and do it in front of me. I'd love to watch."

The old bastard was right. But he was also a simple creature with even simpler needs. He wanted dominance over others. In Rapp's extensive experience, there were only two ways to deal with the Enzo Ruizes of the world: kill them or give them what they want. And since the former wasn't going to get him very far, Rapp had no choice but to choose the latter.

"You're holding all the cards," he admitted. "What do you want?"

It was a question that had already been answered, really. And while Rapp wasn't particularly happy about whacking Ruiz's kids, they weren't exactly innocent bystanders.

"It's not what I want, Mr. Rapp. It's what I *don't* want. I don't want to die of old age sitting in this chair. That's not a fitting end for a man like me."

"What's that have to do with me?" Rapp said, not sure anymore where this was going.

"I want to be killed by the world's most infamous assassin."

Rapp just stood there.

"Not what you expected?"

"I figured you'd want me to go after your kids."

The old man nodded. "It's tempting. And a few years ago, that probably would have been my request. But I made them what they are. They're my legacy. They're the reason I won't be forgotten."

"Well, then you and I have no problem, Enzo. I'd be happy to kill you."

Ruiz seemed unwilling to take the statement at face value. "But what I'm going to tell you isn't what you want to hear. It's going to make you angry."

"Even more reason for me to twist your head off."

"Even more reason for you to leave me to rot," the Spaniard countered.

"If you know anything about me, you know I'm a man of my word."

That seemed to satisfy him. But only barely.

"Unknown to my children, I still dabble in the business online. It's what keeps me sane. The file came in on an email account I use for one of those businesses. From a Gmail account."

"Whose Gmail account?"

"I have no idea. Besides the file, there was just a brief message asking me if I would be interested in killing her."

"And you said?"

"I said yes, of course."

"What else?"

He shrugged weakly. "I've contacted that Gmail account on a few occasions since, but received no response."

"Have you done anything about this?"

"About killing her?"

"Yes. About killing her."

"We still have a deal, correct?"

"I said we do, Enzo. And to be completely honest, I was planning on killing you anyway."

The Spaniard seemed to want to smile again but caught himself. Clearly, he'd done something Rapp was going to be extremely pissed-off about. But what?

"I sent the document to Legion. He accepted the job and I have paid in full."

Rapp waited for more but apparently that was the punch line. "Call him off."

The Spaniard looked perplexed. "I can't call him off."

"Can't or won't?"

His confusion deepened. "Is it possible that you aren't familiar with Legion?"

Rapp shook his head. He didn't have much interest in the new generation of private contractors unless they were careless enough to get in his way. Most weren't. The rest were dead.

Once again, Ruiz found himself in the driver's seat. He straightened a bit more, clearly having the time of his life. "Legion is a completely new kind of killer. He has an anonymous email address that very few know of. If you want someone eliminated, you create your own anonymous email account and send him information on the proposed hit. If he agrees, you send two million euros in bitcoin. After that, both email accounts are deleted."

"So how do you get in touch with him if you change your mind?"

"You don't. Legion doesn't know who I am, and I don't know who he is. We have no way to contact each other. Once the contract is accepted and payment is made, the target is as good as dead."

"So, you just sent two million euros into cyberspace with no guarantees? That seems a little trusting. What if he screws up? Or just walks with your money?"

"Then it will be the end of his business. Word spreads quickly in the circles I run in. Similar, I imagine, to your network. But it's never happened. Legion never fails."

"There's got to be some mechanism for canceling."

The smile appeared again. It shook a bit, possibly because Ruiz hadn't used those particular muscles in years. "Not that I or anyone else knows of. But even if I could call him off, that wasn't part of my deal with you. I gave you the information you asked for and the fact that Claudia Gould will soon be dead has no bearing on anything."

Rapp sighed quietly and pointed to a laptop built into a swing-arm attached to Ruiz's wheelchair. "So, you deleted all the emails related to this?"

"The ones to Legion. That's the agreement. But not the others. Why would I?"

So you don't get caught contracting a hit, Rapp thought, but then saw the error in his logic. What did this geriatric piece of shit care? If the Spanish authorities put him in prison, he'd probably be running the place inside of two weeks.

"Print them out."

Instead of refusing, he did so with as much glee as a man like him could conjure. He'd called down the wrath of God on the woman Mitch Rapp loved and there was nothing Rapp could do about it. To a man like him that was heroin.

Sheets of paper started coming out of a printer near the foot of the bed and Rapp scanned them before shoving them in his back pocket. There was a hand towel hanging on one of the rails and he took it, walking around the back of Ruiz's chair and clamping it over his mouth and nose.

The Spaniard fought for one last time in a life filled with violence. Rapp focused on keeping the towel in place with as little pressure as possible and preventing the old man from banging up his flailing arms. While it would be pretty clear what had happened there, best to keep the physical evidence to a minimum.

As Ruiz himself had predicted, he didn't last long. Rapp kept the towel in place for another thirty seconds after the man had gone limp, just to make sure. When he finally pulled it away he saw that the old bastard had died with a smile on his face.

Rapp descended the stairs and found the English-speaking guard standing in the entry hall.

"What's your name?"

"Alexandre Fabre."

Rapp handed him a sticky note with a name and phone number scrawled across it.

"Do you know who that is?"

"Jordi Cardenas? Of course. He is the director of our intelligence services."

"And an old friend of mine. If you should have any problems that you think might have something to do with me, that should be the first number you call. His assistant will put you right through."

He was understandably confused but pulled out his wallet and put the piece of paper safely inside.

CHAPTER 25

NORTH OF CAPE TOWN
SOUTH AFRICA

THE trail became steep enough that Cyrah Jafari had to use her hands for balance as she continued upward. The area was a rock-climbing destination that had faded in popularity due to frequent car break-ins and then been abandoned entirely after a deadly mugging.

That was two years ago, but the parking area was still there, well out of sight of the highway. Disused trails were still passable with some effort and the views were spectacular. A solid workout after too many days of inactivity and a perfect location for what she had to do.

The path flattened but also narrowed, tracking a bulging cliff face on one side and a hundred-meter drop-off on the other. Skies were uncharacteristically gray and she found herself looking into them often, calculating the chance of rain. Climbing down was always harder than climbing up and wet surfaces would add a little excitement to what was scheduled to be a tedious day.

Another half hour took her to a summit of sorts—the top of a tall cliff that still had steel climbing anchors glued into it. The views were intermittently obscured by mist, but with that came an enhanced sense of anonymity. The very thing she was there seeking.

Cyrah wasn't really worried that she was being actively watched, but casual surveillance was an increasing problem in the modern world. Shared networks, Google, security cameras, and a hundred other things constantly conspired against the oppressive secrecy that her operation was built on. That secrecy, combined with a one hundred percent success rate, was what allowed her and her people to operate in a completely new way. One that their competition lacked both the skill and creativity to emulate.

She dropped her light backpack and sat with legs dangling over the cliff. After watching the swirling fog for a few moments, she dug out a phone. It had been purchased on the black market in China and at the moment lacked both a battery and SIM card. Cyrah installed both and waited for it to capture a mobile network. As promised by her out-of-date guidebook, signal strength was excellent.

The proprietary Internet calling app had numerous layers of security but she finally managed to navigate to a waiting area. A chirp sounded when her two colleagues entered and she put in a wired headset.

"Everyone is well?"

The voices that responded had been making her smile for almost fifteen years now. To call them sisters would trivialize their relationship. Sisters shared parents and an upbringing but that was nothing compared to what they'd been through together. What they'd escaped together.

"The weapon used in the Guatemala attack was likely dropped from a plane and was unquestionably military in origin." Nasrin's voice was steady as always. A woman of logic and control. "Further, the house in Franschhoek is still being watched by a three-man team. American and very professional. There's no doubt they saw you."

"No doubt," Cyrah responded, unconcerned. The Americans watching Claudia Gould's house would see exactly what had been presented to them—a low-level policeman making a little extra cash helping a reporter.

"At this point, I think we can be certain that Mitch Burhan is still connected to the US government," Yasmin chimed in. She was the group's most empathetic member. A creative who was sometimes hard to keep on track but who understood people and was a fountain of improbable ideas that almost always ended up working.

"Why are we wasting our time on this?" Cyrah asked.

"A reminder that we shouldn't have taken this job," Nasrin snapped.

"We only take work that everyone votes for. And that's what happened."

"Because we were afraid you'd kill yourself swimming through one of those caves," Yasmin said.

"Or expose us all by getting arrested driving one of your sports cars at three times the speed limit," Nasrin added. Her fears were largely unfounded, though. Cyrah was the one who was exposed. The one who pulled the trigger. The other two could disappear in a matter of hours, leaving barely a trace that they'd ever existed.

"Were we able to track Burhan?" Cyrah said, unwilling to rehash this argument.

"No," Nasrin said. "We have limited resources on the ground in Africa and we weren't expecting him to leave. By all appearances, he wasn't expecting it, either."

"How so?"

"He had a meeting with his architect in two days' time that's now been canceled. He also canceled the moving van that was scheduled to move items from the house to a storage unit he rented."

"The question is whether he'll return. Has anything been rescheduled? I see him as our best chance of finding Claudia."

"Nothing that we're aware of," Nasrin said. "We're following their architect, contractors, law firm, realtors, and every other person or organization they might need to work with. Up to the moment he left, it had been a productive strategy. While we hadn't gotten anything actionable yet, it seemed only a matter of time. It was reasonable to expect regular communication with the people they hired, meetings, payments, and the like. Potentially even physical inspections that Claudia might want to be directly involved in. And all of that would have to be scheduled ahead of time."

"Something had to have happened in order to make him leave so unexpectedly," Cyrah said. "Do we have any idea what?"

"Not at this point," Yasmin replied. "But we're working on it."

"What about the police?" Cyrah continued. "How did his meeting with Thato Gumede go?"

"Quite well, apparently. Our informants say that the police have no interest in charging Burhan with a crime. He has a right to defend himself and based on what happened in Latin America, they've come to the same conclusion we have about his involvement with America's clandestine services."

"But his identity is still checking out?"

"Yes, but that doesn't mean anything. So does Claudia's and we know it's false. Again, it's hard not to see the hand of the American government in this."

"Agreed. But they have a weakness."

"The daughter," Yasmin said.

"Precisely. Have you found anything useful on her?"

"We're putting together a list of her friends and we're already looking into Ahmale Okoro, who appears to be her closest. Young girls' phones tend to have light security, and they often misplace them. Some also play online video games with each other. It'll take a little time, but there's a good chance we can follow these kinds of connections to Anna."

"I wonder if they'll commit such a careless error."

"Children are hard to control," Nasrin said. "But I agree. I'm less confident in that approach than Yasmin. One thing we're working on is penetrating the communications of the American team watching him. But their level of professionalism makes it no small task. Also, it appears that they were as surprised by his departure as we were."

"Any indication that they know where he went or when he'll return?" Cyrah asked.

"None."

"It's a thread we can pull—but only with great care. We don't want to risk revealing ourselves to the American government. In the end, I think we have to resign ourselves to this taking a while."

"We have money and time," Yasmin said. "That gives us the luxury of being methodical. If it takes six months, it takes six months."

Cyrah nodded, gazing out over the empty landscape below. "Then as they say, the ball is in your court. Get me a location on Claudia so I can go to work."

"But you're not going to get bored in the meantime, right?" Nasrin said. "You're not going to start shark diving or hunting leopards with your bare hands . . ."

Cyrah smiled and shut down the connection before removing the SIM card and battery. The former she destroyed with the flame from a lighter and the latter went over the side of the cliff. A fist-sized rock was enough to deal with the handset and she'd randomly scatter the debris as she descended.

Then what? Perhaps a drink in her rented apartment? Not something she did often, but a pleasure forbidden to her in her youth might be a nice way to finish the day. Yet another reminder of how far she'd come.

The voices became audible when Cyrah was still more than a hundred meters away, echoing off the stone. Not English or Afrikaans, but one of the country's tribal languages.

Out of force of habit, Cyrah had already been moving quietly, but now she slowed and went entirely silent. It was a skill she'd learned avoiding her abusive father and one that even her male instructors had begrudgingly acknowledged.

In truth, she'd done everything well, excelling at every test she was given. Speed, endurance, intelligence, courage. But above all, her ability to remain calm under pressure. Even her greatest weakness, physical power, was far better than anyone would guess of a woman who stood only one hundred and sixty centimeters and weighed barely fifty-six kilograms. It was a disconnect between expectation and reality that proved quite useful. But not one she'd ever had an opportunity to leverage in the service of her country.

The relatively liberal Iranian president had started the program with the idea of creating a division of women spies and saboteurs that would be so unexpected as to be invisible to their Israeli opponents. He'd recruited young women from a wide swath of society. In her case, the police, but also universities, intelligence agencies, and the sciences. Of course, most washed out quickly, but she and a few others held on. At the end of their training only she and two others—Nasrin and Yasmin—remained.

But there were to be no clandestine infiltrations into enemy territory. No glorious operations that thwarted their enemies and proved the value of their gender. In the endless push-pull between the civilian government, religious leaders, and military, the president had been forced to turn the program over to the Republican Guard. Predictably, they'd immediately replaced her instructors with the cruelest and most misogynistic men they could find.

The night before what was to be her graduation, the director of the program had come into her quarters and violently raped her. He explained that it was an experience that she'd need to be prepared for if she were ever captured. Nasrin and Yasmin, she discovered later, had suffered the same fate.

Despite the humiliation and considerable injuries, all three of them had gotten up that morning, dressed, and made their way to the ceremony that would welcome them into Iran's most secretive intelligence organization. They'd stood at attention outside their commander's office for hours before one of his people told them that the program had been canceled and that they'd been reassigned to the typing pool.

The typing pool. Who knew such things even existed in this day and age? Or maybe they didn't and one had been created especially for them. Because being raped wasn't sufficiently humiliating.

Sadly for their new commander, his new typists had learned their lessons too well. The last hour of his life had been extraordinarily painful, ending only when she severed his penis and slowly choked him to death with it. After that, it was just a matter of using his computer credentials to transfer money into foreign accounts they'd opened and create safe passage out of the country.

Shortly thereafter, Legion was born.

The trail widened and Cyrah crouched, moving to a vantage point above the clearing where she'd parked her rental car. The guidebook's warnings about criminal activity turned out to be prescient. Her assumption had been that when the climbing community had abandoned the area, so would the men who made it so undesirable. Never underestimate the persistence of the criminal element. She of all people should have known that.

It appeared that her problem consisted of only two men, both wearing jeans and ragged T-shirts. Both were also wearing flip-flops despite the cool temperatures, but they still looked capable of moving quickly. They'd arrived in a dilapidated white van streaked with rust. Neither seemed to be armed.

As was wise in the area, she'd left the car unlocked and the glove box open to demonstrate that there was nothing in it to steal. Despite this, the two men had decided to perform a thorough search. Not really a problem for her as long as they finished it quickly and moved on. If not, it might become necessary to take action.

Cyrah retrieved a SIG Sauer P226 from her pack and screwed on an Octane 9 silencer. Sighting over it, she tracked one of the men as he started back toward the van. His companion, meanwhile, opened her vehicle's hood.

There was a deep glow in the cloud layer to the west and hazy shadows were stretching themselves across the clearing. The impending darkness would probably discourage anyone else from coming up there that evening, though it was far from certain. These two had. The question now was, what to do about it?

As was so often the case in life, there were no good options. She could sit there and let the men strip her car, which would inevitably lead to significant contact with the police and endless problems with Avis. Her cover and passport would likely survive additional scrutiny, but it would all be very public, time consuming, and could affect her ability to quickly leave the country if necessary. On the other hand, dealing with the situation in a more aggressive manner involved its own risks and irritations.

Which to choose?

When the man at the van reappeared with a lug wrench in one hand and a box brimming with other tools in the other, she took careful aim and squeezed off a single round. The SIG bucked, and the silencer produced enough sound to make the man hovering over the engine look up. The metallic rattle of his companion dropping the box distracted him and he turned toward the sound. Cyrah waited for him to present an optimal target before squeezing off another round. He immediately crumpled, disappearing behind the front bumper.

It took five minutes of downclimbing to arrive at the clearing and when she did, she winced in the waning light. Both shots were perfect, leaving neat holes dead center of mass in both men. It looked like exactly what it was—the work of an anal-retentive professional assassin. Minimal ammo, minimal mess, maximum efficiency. Force of habit and, in retrospect, not what she was after.

Cyrah emptied her magazine at random into the two men but was still unsatisfied with the effect. She needed to leave absolutely no doubt that this was the result of gang rivalry or a turf war. If someone somehow found evidence of a doe-eyed, dimpled young woman being in the area, the very thought that she might be involved would have to be laughable.

She went to the back of the van and looked at the clutter of car parts, old furniture, and landscaping equipment. A rusty ax was resting on one of the wheel wells and she picked it up, testing the weight of it in her hands. They said that diamonds were a girl's best friend but in some cases a sharp, heavy blade was just as good.

Cyrah took off her pack and set it down. There was a liter of water in it, still untouched due to the cool temperatures. Plenty for an impromptu, if somewhat frigid, bath. She put a fresh magazine in the gun just in case someone came upon her and then began to strip. When she was completely nude and her clothes were neatly folded on a rock, she picked up the ax and headed for the closest corpse. Something was playing at the back of her mind as she walked. A vague memory from a documentary she'd once watched about an American woman from Victorian times.

What was her name?

It came to her as she stopped in front of the shirtless man and raised the blade. Lizzie Borden. That was it. A formidable woman, ahead of her time.

CHAPTER 26

THE WHITE HOUSE
WASHINGTON, DC
USA

DARREN Hargrave took his customary seat next to the president while Stephen Wright, the Secret Service director, settled in across the coffee table. Sam Hutchinson, the administration's chief political strategist, kept a little more distance but, interestingly, not as much as Catherine. There were too many people in the meeting for her to completely retreat, but still she'd selected the chair farthest from her husband. The farthest from the power, Hargrave noted with a smile.

"So, the main venue will only seat a couple hundred people," Hutchinson continued. "All enthusiastic supporters who'll give the room a lot of energy."

"And the rest?" Cook asked.

"Another ten thousand in various locations around DC and the country. All wearing these." He handed the president a pair of virtual reality goggles. "They'll allow every person, no matter where they are, to feel like they're three rows back from you onstage."

"So, you're saying this is different than just watching on a screen."

"There's no comparison. If they turn their heads, they'll see the sides of the auditorium you're in. If they look behind them, they'll see what looks like a very exclusive and intimate crowd. I guarantee you that everyone will one hundred percent feel like they're there."

Cook seemed skeptical as he handed the unit back. "I understand that it's the best we can do for now, but I'm not sure about it in the long run. Politics has always been an in-person business."

"I understand, sir, but trust me when I tell you that we're only scratching the surface of this technology. It has the potential to actually *enhance* your ability to connect with your constituents. In the future, we'll be able to digitally map your face to an actor's. That'll allow for virtual appearances at much smaller venues than you'd normally have time for. It'll make your supporters feel like they have personal access to you."

"It also has a lot of potential with regard to security," Wright interjected. "We can set up these appearances to make it hard for people to know where you really are. For instance, you could have an actor doing a live appearance from Camp David when you're really here."

"It seems like those are the kinds of games that could leak to the press."

"It's possible, but we think the risks are low," Hutchinson said. "The technology is so good that even experts can't spot it with any certainty. Plus, we could just say that we're using artificial backgrounds at the request of the Secret Service. I don't think anyone's going to begrudge you that."

"There are going to be pictures of the crowds," Catherine pointed out. "Thousands of people in virtual reality goggles. It's going to look like nineteen-fifties science fiction."

"I understand what you're saying, ma'am, but I think it's going to go over really well with the younger demographic. Polls show that they're counting on technology to solve pretty much all their problems. Depicting the president as someone who's mastered it is going to be a net positive. Particularly as the older, lower-tech demographic dies off."

"Okay," Cook said, starting to lose interest in the subject. "We're going to try it and see how things go. If it's a disaster, we'll rethink. Thank you, Sam."

The man stood and nodded respectfully before retreating from the office. The president waited for him to close the door before speaking again.

"Are you sure you can secure this event, Steve?"

"Yes, sir. We're still purging people connected to Kennedy and Rapp, but we'll have enough loyalists to cover it. And no one's going to know which of the local venues you're going to appear at until the last minute, which makes coordinating an attack all but impossible. Particularly by someone with limited manpower."

"That said, it's my understanding that we're still not certain of Rapp's or Coleman's locations."

"Coleman just reappeared at his house in Greece, and we have people watching him," Hargrave said. "Rapp flew to Nicholas Ward's compound in Uganda after he left South Africa and as far as we know, he's been there ever since."

"As far as we know," Cook repeated. "Remember that one of the terms of our truce with him is that he stays in plain sight."

"Yes, sir. I agree that the time he spends at Ward's camp is problematic. We need to agree to some reasonable surveillance protocols, but with everything that's happening, it made sense not to push. In another day or two, though, I think it'll be reasonable to insist."

"Okay," Cook said. "Steve, unless you've got anything else, I'm going to let you go. I know you've got a lot on your plate."

"Thank you, sir."

Again, the president waited for the door to fully close before he spoke. "I'm not happy, Darren."

"Why not, sir?"

"Enzo Ruiz."

"Ruiz was extremely ill and in his nineties, sir. He died in the middle of the day, surrounded by guards who all agree his heart finally gave out. An initial review by medical examiners has confirmed that."

"But without having reliable eyes on Rapp, there's no way to prove that he wasn't responsible. It's possible that he slipped out of Ward's compound, flew to Spain, interrogated Ruiz, and found out about the dossier we sent."

"Anything's *possible,*" Hargrave agreed. "But plausible? What you're talking about here is that, based on an attack by Gustavo Marroqui, Rapp's embarked on a campaign of wiping out Claudia Gould's enemies. Then he just walked into a guarded compound and extracted information from a brutal drug lord who wouldn't survive any kind of coercion. And if that's not far-fetched enough, he then killed the man in a way that fooled both his security detail and the authorities."

Cook leaned back and crossed his arms over his chest. "I agree that it's improbable, Darren. But I want to make sure we're not taking anything for granted. Where Rapp is concerned, getting complacent isn't an option."

Hargrave nodded silently, reluctant to respond with anything more. In fact, Rapp's involvement in Enzo Ruiz's death wasn't as far-fetched as he was making it out to be. Initial reports were coming in that another one of Claudia's enemies—a Czech assassin named Josef Svoboda—had died in what was being called an accident by authorities. It was a worrying coincidence, but not one that the president needed to know about at this point. It would only make the situation more stressful and could shake his trust in the CIA. That was something that had to be prevented at all costs. The spell his wife had cast on him was weakening but not yet broken. She couldn't be allowed information like this while she was still strong enough to weaponize it.

"But your plan seems to be falling apart," the first lady said. "It revolves around keeping Rapp off balance and focused elsewhere. How does the Legion contract accomplish that if he doesn't know anything about it?"

Hargrave grinned. “Actually, the situation couldn’t be more perfect.”

Watching the subtle change in the woman’s expression and body language was like electricity running up his spine. Her normal condescension and disgust had become tinged with fear. She knew that her ability to use her husband for her own ends was slipping away. That Anthony Cook was finally starting to see her for what she was.

“Perfect?” the president said. “How?”

“We’ll warn Rapp that we picked up chatter about Legion being contracted to kill Claudia Gould. It works on every level for us. Not only does it appear to be an act of good faith on our part—”

“But it puts him in panic mode,” Cook said, finishing Hargrave’s thought. “Now he’s not facing a bunch of incompetent cartel enforcers. He’s facing one of the most successful and relentless killers in the world.”

“Exactly. And after Claudia dies—which she almost certainly will—Rapp will spend the rest of his life trying to find Legion and exact revenge. Then, at some point during all that, he’ll make himself vulnerable and we’ll put an end to this once and for all.”

With Hargrave finally gone, Catherine was alone in the Oval Office with her husband. She watched him pace and, for one of the first times in her life, had no idea what he was thinking. Every day she became more convinced that he was misjudging Mitch Rapp on virtually every level. Most notably the belief that he hadn’t intended to live up to their truce, but more crucially that he was an easily manipulated thug fueled by instinct and rage. A man like that would have been dead a long time ago.

She was also concerned that Hargrave was downplaying the possibility that Rapp had discovered the existence of the dossier on Claudia Gould. How hard would it be for Claudia to identify and locate her surviving enemies? Once done, Rapp could either kill—like he perhaps had done with Enzo Ruiz—or subvert them with threats. While these kinds of people might have a heightened thirst for revenge, they possessed an equally heightened survival instinct. Defying Mitch Rapp wasn't the path to a long life.

Finally, the idea of Rapp becoming obsessed with Legion after Claudia's death seemed overly optimistic. Would a man like him even give Legion a second thought? There was nothing personal there—just a business providing a service for payment. Much more likely, Rapp would focus his substantial energy and resources on finding out who had written the check. Technically Enzo Ruiz, but would he be satisfied with that? Or would he be motivated to look deeper?

She squinted into the sunlight coming through the windows and the figure moving through it. Her husband wasn't a brilliant man in the normal sense, but he'd also never been a stupid one. Along with his gift for connecting with the common man, he'd always had a natural intuition for who to trust, who to subvert, and who to destroy. Now he seemed to be hanging on Darren Hargrave's every word. He'd become so desperate for protection against Mitch Rapp that he'd actually convinced himself that Hargrave was capable of providing it.

Could a man who had become defined by doubt and fear win a second term in the White House? Realistically, they needed four full terms to achieve the kind of power necessary to perpetuate it indefinitely. Losing would be the end of everything they'd dreamed of.

"Things aren't going well," she said finally.

"We'll find Rapp."

"I'm not talking about him, Tony. I'm talking about your poll numbers. You look weak and ineffective. We didn't run on an ambitious legislative platform. We ran on the force of your personality. Your ability to make your constituents feel like they have power and a voice. The longer you stay behind these walls, the more that fades."

"I know you're not impressed with what Sam's setting up, but I think it's a step in the right direction."

"I concede the point. But it can't be the *only* step. You're not even engaged in social media anymore. You're leaving it to people who don't have the authority to put out anything but bland government-speak. Your gift is understanding what people want and giving it to them. You can't let your fear of Mitch Rapp cause you to lose that. We've got a couple of potentially strong opponents in the next elec—"

"I can't win if I'm dead."

"You think Rapp can't control his impulses, but I think he can. What would happen if he just went to ground and stayed there? I'm afraid you'd run down to the White House's bunker and huddle there until you lose the election. Then he'd have you right where he wants you. If Rapp really is after you—and at this point you and Darren may have made that a certainty—your only defense is your ability to stay in power."

He stopped pacing and glared down at her. "If he does manage to get to me, I imagine you'll end up behind my desk."

She couldn't tell if it was an accusation or just an observation. Either way it was a rather obvious and banal statement that didn't merit a response. His assassination would almost certainly be an event powerful enough to ride into the White House. The much more difficult problem was if he survived to lose the next election.

If her husband insisted on destroying himself, was she obligated to go down with him? To give up everything she'd worked for because of his cowardice and miscalculation? Their relationship was largely one of convenience and shared vision. Each of them had a unique role to play in realizing that vision. Could he still be counted on to play his part? How ironic that she was now concerned that the president of the United States could become an obstacle to the accumulation of power.

"That's not the plan, Tony. And you're not going to die. For now at least, you have more security than anyone in history. Mitch Rapp is a talented killer, but he's not an avenging angel. He can't walk through walls or be in two places at once."

Cook didn't respond, instead turning his back to her and staring through the window.

CHAPTER 27

SOUTHWESTERN UGANDA

RAPP stepped off the chopper, shouldering his duffel and running crouched through the swirling dust. Claudia was visible, standing at a safe distance in the dawn light, but no one else was in evidence.

As the aircraft lifted off behind him, Rapp couldn't help wondering how much longer Nick Ward was going to let them use his Ugandan compound. Right now, he was in the US dealing with various lawsuits and SEC inquiries relating to the measures they'd taken to keep him alive. When he returned, though, he might not be interested in standing so close to people targeted by a president who already despised him.

"I read that Enzo Ruiz recently died of natural causes," Claudia said as he approached.

"Sad, isn't it?"

"Do you have any exposure there that I need to deal with?"

"No. Jordi Cardenas is taking care of the witnesses and investigators. There's not much reason for anyone to kick up dust over this. What about Svoboda?"

"You didn't see?" she said, pulling out her phone and scrolling for a moment before handing it to him.

The screen depicted the front page of some tabloid written in Czech. Nearly the whole thing was taken up by a full-color photo of a man hanging from his neck in what looked like a posh hotel suite. His face was purple, and he was naked except for a pair of boxer shorts still hanging on his ankles. A little strategic blurring had been done in an unsuccessful effort to make the image a little less lurid.

"Erotic asphyxiation?" Rapp said, handing the phone back.

"Scott thought it was fitting."

It was hard to argue the point. "Cops?"

"No. Everyone's so happy he's gone, the police have already categorized his death as an accident and closed the case."

"Where's everybody now?"

"Scott's at his place in Greece. Bruno moved on to New Zealand to go fishing. Wick's at his house in Wyoming and Mas is at home in Virginia."

Rapp didn't particularly like having his forces so spread out, but under the circumstances it was marginally better than bunching them up.

"What about Irene? Is she still here?"

"She is."

"Can you ask her to come by the bungalow? We need to talk."

The expansive front deck was still in shade, clinging to the morning cold. Anna was asleep inside, though, so Rapp built a fire in the pit and pulled a few chairs up to it. Claudia appeared in the doorway with two cups of steaming coffee just as Irene started up their flagstone path with her customary cup of tea. Rapp gave her a kiss on the cheek before pointing her to a chair.

"It seems that everything's gone smoothly," she said, scooting a little closer to the flames.

"Ruiz is dead, but it didn't solve as many problems as we hoped,"

Rapp said, handing her the emails the old man had printed. He watched as she leafed through them, her mouth tightening in a way that would have been invisible to anyone who hadn't known her for decades. He could decipher the expression easily, though. The shit had now officially hit the fan.

Kennedy let them fall to the ground and just stared straight ahead, seeming to forget everything around her. It appeared that he was the only one who didn't bother to follow the new generation of private contractors. For everyone else, the word *Legion* hit like a set of brass knuckles.

She finally removed her reading glasses and rubbed at her eyes with a thumb and index finger. "I don't think there's any reason to mince words here. This is a worst-case scenario for us. Not only because of Legion's reputation, but because we can now pretty much guarantee that the dossier won't go to any of the people we've subverted."

Claudia nodded. "Once Legion is contracted, he never stops. If the Cooks wanted to put me in jeopardy and keep Mitch occupied, they've now officially accomplished that."

"Irene," Rapp said. "Can you trace those emails?"

"Impossible. Legion is a little like Gustavo Marroqui. Every intelligence agency in the world has tried to get to them and we've all failed."

"Them?"

"Our best guess is that it's a team. I'd say three people. Two wouldn't be sufficient to have carried out the assassinations we suspect them of and with four it becomes hard to maintain the level of secrecy they count on."

"So, Ruiz was telling the truth. They really are ghosts."

"Until I read those emails a minute ago, I couldn't have said with one hundred percent certainty that Legion even existed. Their hits always look like accidents or natural causes, and they're done so well that it's possible they are."

"So that's it? That's all we've got?"

"I think we can make some assumptions that go a little further.

Like I said, it's probably not an individual but a small team. Well trained to the degree that it's almost certain they worked for a government at some point."

"Maybe they still do," Rapp said.

"It's unlikely because of the diversity of the people we suspect they've killed. Criminals, financial people, a few political operatives with nothing in common . . ."

"If they were trained by a government, it narrows things down," Rapp said. "Probably not any of the ones we regularly work with. My front-runners would be the Russians or Iranians. The Chinese and North Koreans could train somebody to this level, but it's harder to imagine them losing control. The Syrians come to mind, too, but I'd say it's a long shot."

"Speculation," Claudia said. "And vague speculation at that."

"Agreed," Rapp said. "How do we get something actionable?"

The question was met with silence. Finally, Kennedy stood. "Let me think about this. We'll reconvene later this afternoon. In the meantime, maybe it would make sense to review the security measures here."

"Agreed," Rapp said. "Scott set us up for more conventional attacks and it sounds like that's not Legion's MO."

Kennedy reached over and gave Claudia's hand a squeeze before starting back for her bungalow. When she disappeared behind the trees, Claudia suddenly stood and announced that she needed to go for a walk.

"Do you want me to go with you?"

"No. Thank you, but I need some time to think."

And with that, Rapp found himself alone.

More than thirty minutes passed before Claudia returned to find him exactly where she'd left him. Anna was still asleep and there wasn't much to do other than sit and think—mostly about spectacularly painful ways to kill Anthony Cook. But they were just fantasies. Say what you will about the man, his twisted plan was working. Rapp had neither time nor resources to expend on him. His entire world had narrowed to one objective and one objective only: neutralizing the threat posed by Legion.

She stopped a few feet away, backlit by the morning sun. Rapp squinted up at her, seeing an expression of resolve that overwhelmed the glint of tears drying on her cheeks.

"I have some things to say, Mitch, and I need you to let me say them without interrupting."

He nodded silently.

"I'm as good as dead."

Rapp immediately tried to back out of their arrangement, opening his mouth to protest before being silenced by her raised hand.

"Even if I stay here, Legion will eventually get to me. Maybe it will take a year. Maybe it'll take ten. Or maybe they're excavating beneath us right now so that next time it rains, I'll die in a mudslide. And I know you'd do anything to protect me, but even you can't kill what you can't see."

She took in a breath and let it out. It was dead steady.

"Second, I know you blame yourself for this. But you shouldn't. Every day I've woken up after what happened to your wife . . ." Her voice faltered for a moment. "Every one of those days has been a gift. I finally found the love of my life in you, and I've gotten to spend time with Anna that I didn't deserve."

She took a seat across from him, preferring to look into the flames than to meet his eye. "Now, on to more practical things. The good news is that there's never any collateral damage in Legion operations. So, you and Anna are safe. The problem is that while we still might not have proof solid enough for Irene, we both know that the Cooks are behind this. We also know they aren't going to let it go. Their security will never be perfect, so they know they'll never be safe until you're dead." A tear ran down her face, leaving a fresh streak among the faded ones. "If something happened to me, I'd decided to leave Anna with you. You've become such a good father and you need something to keep you busy in your old age. The truth is, you need her as much as she needs you. But now that's impossible. And I'm not sure Irene or Scott are in a much safer position than you are."

"Claudia . . ." Rapp started, but again she silenced him.

"The only person who makes sense is Maggie Nash. A woman who already has four kids and who was recently widowed because her husband thought you were going to kill him." She let out a choking laugh. "Quite a business we've chosen, isn't it?"

"Can I speak now?"

"Yes."

"You're talking like you just got diagnosed with pancreatic cancer."

"No. People survive pancreatic cancer. No one's ever survived Legion."

"No one's ever survived me, either. Irene's going to figure out how to find these assholes and I'm going to put a bullet in them. After that, I'm going see Anthony Cook off in a big state funeral."

She pulled out a tissue and dabbed at her eyes. "And Maggie?"

Rapp adjusted uncomfortably in his chair. Uncertainty wasn't a sensation he was particularly accustomed to, but despite what many people might have thought, neither was arrogance. It would be stupid not to consider the possibility that this was the battle that would finally kill him. "I agree that it might not be a bad idea for us to talk to her. Just in case."

She nodded. "One last thing."

"What?"

"I want to leave here. I want us to put together new identities and I want to show Anna the world in the time I have left with her."

"Claudia . . ."

"Promise me."

He leaned back in the Adirondack chair and let out a long breath. What could he do? "Fine. I promise."

CHAPTER 28

RAPP slowed his stroke to the point that he was in danger of sinking to the bottom of the pool. Anna pulled even with him a couple of seconds later, making up for her lack of technique with flailing determination. They reached the other side together, and Rapp used his superior reach to touch the tile edge just before her. She put her arms up on the deck, panting wildly as he pushed himself up and sat.

"You almost got me."

She clearly wanted to agree but couldn't get in enough air.

The sun was dropping toward the horizon, creating drawn-out shadows as the light passed through Nicholas Ward's house. It was a strange building, with exterior walls made of wood louvers that, when open, turned the structure into something akin to a fenced patio. Rapp looked through it, past the industrial kitchen and stylish furniture to the mountains beyond.

"Your arms are too long!" Anna said, finally capable of lodging her protest. "You barely even have to swim to get across."

"A poor craftsman blames her tools."

"I don't even know what that means."

He pointed. "Do another lap. Let's see what you've got."

She took a few more seconds to catch her breath and then pushed off defiantly.

"Stop lifting your head all the way out of the water!" Rapp shouted. "Just turn it to the side when you want to breathe!"

She did her best to comply, and he paid just enough attention to make sure she didn't drown. The remainder of his mind turned to Claudia. Would she have been so anxious to get together with him if she'd known he'd end up in a death match with the president of the United States? Of course she'd say yes, but would she really mean it? In many ways, Claudia behaved like she owed him a blood debt for her involvement in the death of his wife. And now it looked like she might end up paying it.

He could kill Enzo Ruiz, Josef Svoboda, and every other enemy she'd ever made. He could take out the president or sacrifice himself to remove the object of Cook's obsession. But none of it would matter. With Legion, the fuse had been lit.

"*Mitch!*" Anna said, punching one of the legs he had submerged in the water.

He hadn't been fully conscious of the fact that she'd successfully completed her lap of the pool.

"What?"

"Are you okay?"

"Sure. Why?"

"You look sad."

He glanced at his watch. "I'm not sad, I'm late. We've got to go."

"Can I stay? Just for a little longer?"

He looked down at her and frowned.

"Come, on, Mitch. I promise I won't get in the pool without you here. I'm just going to sit in one of the chairs till I'm dry and stuff."

"You promise you won't get in the pool?"

She grinned. "One hundred percent!"

"Okay, then."

He lifted her out and handed her one of the towels rolled up next to him.

"Can I have one of Mr. Ward's root beers?"

He thought about it for a moment. "One. But that's it. If he comes home and his fridge is empty, you're going to be in serious trouble."

"He can afford more," she grumbled.

"Anna . . ."

"Sorry."

"And what else are you not going to do when you're inside?"

"Sit on his furniture in my swimsuit."

He stood. "Exactly."

"Where's Anna?" Claudia said as he approached, still drying his hair with a towel. Kennedy was already present, sitting in the shadow of the bungalow to escape the afternoon heat. The fact that there were no snacks or drinks confirmed his impression that Claudia was hanging on by a thread.

"She wanted one of Nick's root beers."

"But she's not going to get in the pool."

"I made her promise," he said, sitting next to her and tossing the towel on the stoop. "Have we come up with anything?"

Neither of them responded.

"What?"

"I've thought through some options," Kennedy said, "but there's something we should talk about first."

"And that is?"

"About an hour ago, I got a call from Darren Hargrave."

"Why?"

"Two reasons. First, he wants to set up a system for confirming your presence here. Second, he wanted to warn you that the Agency's picked up chatter about Legion being hired to kill Claudia."

Rapp kept his expression impassive, wondering silently what Kennedy would make of this. She had an understandable bias against going to war with the democracy she'd served so long. Would that affect her judgment? If so, it would be a first, but they were living in a world of firsts right now.

"It was the call I was hoping I'd never receive," she continued. "Hargrave doesn't know that Grisha contacted you or that you visited Ruiz. In light of that, it was in his best interest to tell you about the Legion threat."

"Because if I'm not fighting Legion, I have time to spend on his boss. Plus, it makes him look like he's on my side. Once again, credit where credit's due. If it weren't for Grisha, we might have even fallen for it. Smart play."

"Yes," she said, sounding a little defeated. "Smart."

"So, am I right in saying that you no longer have any doubts about the Cooks' involvement in all this?"

"There's no other credible explanation," she admitted.

"Then I think we should deal with them. Cook's security isn't getting any lighter as time goes on."

"I think we need to take care of Legion first," Kennedy said. "After that, we can discuss the Cooks."

"Are you telling me you've figured out a way?"

"Maybe."

Rapp waved her on. "I'm listening."

"You're not going to like it."

"I'm guessing you're right. But let's hear it anyway."

"Okay. What we need to focus on is that we have an advantage that no one else ever has."

"What's that?" Claudia asked.

"We know Legion's coming."

"No," Rapp said, shaking his head. "I already know where you're going with this. We're not using Claudia as bait."

"That's my decision," Claudia shot back. "Not yours."

"It's no one's decision," Kennedy said. "Exposing you isn't going to be necessary."

"Then what?" Rapp said.

Kennedy handed him her tablet. It contained the picture of Claudia included in the dossier sent to Grisha Azarov and Enzo Ruiz. She was quite a bit younger, sitting at what looked like a Paris café wearing sunglasses and a scarf that covered part of her chin. It had been taken in less-than-ideal conditions, leaving it slightly grainy.

"I'm still not following you," Rapp said.

"It's not a very good picture," Kennedy pointed out.

"But they included my address and a detailed analysis of my daily habits," Claudia said. "I mean, it's always nice to have multiple high-res shots, but in this case, it's not really necessary."

Kennedy pulled a single piece of paper from the pocket of her jacket. On it was printed an equally distant and grainy shot of Claudia wearing the same sunglasses and scarf, but this time standing in front of a brick wall.

"That's not me," Claudia said.

Rapp leaned forward. Upon closer inspection, she was right. This woman was thinner, with higher cheekbones and blond strands visible around where Claudia's hair had been photoshopped on. There was something familiar about the partially obscured face and when he realized what it was, he shoved the picture back in Kennedy's direction.

"No way in hell."

"Who is she?" Claudia asked.

Kennedy seemed reluctant to say the name aloud, so Rapp was forced to do it for her. "Sadie Hansen. Also, Sadie Griffith. And Hanna Larson. And Hailey Tolstoy. Have I missed any?"

"At least five," Kennedy said.

Sadie was a young, beautiful psychopath who also suffered from manic depression, possibly a touch of Asperger's, and a compulsion for shoplifting. On the other hand, she also had the best situational awareness Rapp had ever seen and seemed impervious to fear or panic. But more in a suicidal way than a courageous one.

Sadie was a British national recruited and quickly abandoned by MI6. The Agency picked her up a while back over Rapp's objections, but then he'd had to eat crow when she'd proved critical to resolving a devastating attack on America's power grid. Kennedy was fond of saying she was no worse than her other, even more infamous, recruit: an angry kid with no appreciable skills named Mitch Rapp.

"Sadie's an inch taller and about five pounds lighter," Kennedy said. "Right now, her hair's longer and blond but it's about the same texture so that's an easy fix. So are her skin tone and eye color. Plus, she's good at accents."

"Probably because she's schizophrenic," Rapp said.

"The medication's done wonders."

He let out a long breath. "So, let me get this straight. You're proposing that Sadie and I go back to the house in South Africa, and we use her to draw in Legion."

Kennedy nodded. "Also, we bring in Bebe as your new live-in help."

Bebe Kincaid was yet another misfit—a former FBI agent with an honest-to-God photographic memory. That, combined with the fact that she was overweight, middle-aged, and blessed with extraordinarily unmemorable features, had made her the best surveillance operative in the business. The problem? Her inability to forget made it increasingly difficult for her to differentiate recent memories from distant ones. And that was driving her slowly insane.

"So, we keep Sadie inside the walls and let Bebe go out," Rapp said.

"Exactly. If anyone's watching you, she can be counted on to notice."

"What about Anna?" Rapp asked.

"She'd stay here with Claudia. Based on the state of the house, it's perfectly reasonable that you wouldn't bring her back with you. The idea is that you'd be working on getting renovations started. Not really a safe or healthy environment for a girl her age."

Claudia, who had been uncharacteristically quiet during this, finally spoke up. “No. I don’t want someone standing in for me. What if she gets killed?”

“Then Legion moves on,” Rapp said. “We still have a lot of problems, but at least one’s off the table.”

“That seems callous, even for you,” Claudia said.

He shrugged. “It’s just Sadie. I doubt she’d care.”

“No reason to speculate,” Kennedy said. “We can ask her. In fact, Claudia, why don’t you do it? Give her a full reading of the risks and ask her if she wants the job. She’s a private contractor, so if she doesn’t, she can say no. If she does, she can name her price.”

CHAPTER 29

Cape Town International Airport
Cape Town
South Africa

RAPP stood with his back against the wall of the arrival hall, studying the people flowing past. Some were meeting loved ones, others went straight for the doors, and still others were collecting around the rental car agencies. So far, he'd only noted a single familiar face—one of the American surveillance operatives keeping tabs on him. Infuriating, but likely harmless in the short term.

Legion, on the other hand, wasn't so benign. It was almost certain that they'd had someone watching him since his return home, but who? One of their team? Members of a local gang? A legit private eye? There was no way to know, but he'd be surprised if they made a move that day. The chances of them going for something like an improvised rifle shot were around zero. Making their assassinations come off as accidental or natural was a big part of their secrecy protocol.

He'd been back for three days, removing remaining rubble, getting the rest of the plumbing and electricity rigged to work, and buying up a patchwork of furniture from local showrooms. The last thing on his list was to get the annoying rattle out of the dishwasher. He suspected it was a bullet being thrown around by the spray arms but so far hadn't been able to locate it.

The house still wasn't pretty, but it was livable, and getting better by the hour. Bebe Kincaid had settled into one of the guest bedrooms the day before and was unleashing the full force of her OCD on the place. Surfaces were being scrubbed, holes were being spackled, and hastily purchased knickknacks were being put into place with the aid of her personal ruler.

Rapp frowned as he continued to study the airport through dark sunglasses. Not only was he about to be living with two of the craziest people he'd ever met, but they were crazy in exactly opposite ways. One wandered indifferently through combat situations that she forgot about the next day. The other traveled with her own measuring devices and remembered everything.

He pulled his phone from his pocket and pretended to scroll through the screen. After a few more minutes, he spotted Sadie in the flow of people coming from baggage claim. He didn't react immediately, instead evaluating her in his peripheral vision.

She was wearing the same style and brand of sunglasses that Claudia had bought a few months before. Her hair was exactly the right cut and color but much of it was hidden beneath a floppy straw hat. Her loose-fitting dress wasn't familiar but definitely reflected Claudia's style—a subtle red that descended to midcalf before meeting a pair of leather boots. Even more interesting was the fact that Sadie's face had filled out enough to hide her sharp cheekbones. From what he'd been told, it wasn't makeup; it was the result of a crash diet of six Big Macs a day with accompanying fries and milkshakes.

The overall effect was incredible. With twenty yards of distance still between them he had no criticisms of her appearance and only minor ones relating to the way she moved—something Legion would have no way to gauge. It was so good that he was starting to feel a glimmer of hope that this could actually work.

Rapp made a show of spotting her and pushed himself off the wall. A moment later they were in a warm embrace and he was taking charge of her rolling suitcase. It seemed crazy, but she even smelled like Claudia.

They walked through the doors and into the sun, Sadie nuzzling his shoulder in a way that would make it impossible for anyone watching to get a full view of her features. She chatted amiably as they walked to the parking area, speaking with a French accent that was virtually identical to Claudia's. He responded appropriately, asking vague questions about Anna's well-being and detailing his progress on the house.

If Legion saw through this, they were a hell of a lot more observant than he was.

Cyrah Jafari was behind the wheel of her rental car two rows from where Mitch Burhan had parked his recently repaired armored SUV. Following him there without being seen was a trivial matter because she didn't have to follow him per se. All she had to do was follow the team of Americans that hounded his every step. Why they were so interested was still a mystery. None had the look of operators, making them poor choices to move against or protect him. They appeared to be content to just spectate.

The police had publicly stated that no charges were being brought against Burhan and with predictable misogyny, made the assumption that the Guatemalans had been after him and not Claudia. What could a pretty little Frenchwoman possibly have done to anger a Central American drug lord? Surely she was an irrelevant bystander, someone whose role was limited to stifling her tearful screams while her man protected her.

Which, admittedly, he'd done with disturbing competence. As was always the case with Claudia Gould, she'd chosen wisely. Finding someone both willing and capable of dealing with her past wouldn't be easy.

Cyrah sank a little deeper in the leather seat and let out a long breath. So many unknowns. In reality, too many. But she could feel the blood pumping through her veins and the intoxicating trickle of adrenaline mixing with it.

One of Burhan's watchers suddenly scurried from his position at the front of the airport and Cyrah focused on the doors. A moment later the trickle of adrenaline turned into a flood.

It was her.

The return of Burhan, the flurry of activity at the house, and the appearance of a middle-aged woman who seemed to be some kind of servant had been encouraging, but far from conclusive. With Marroqui neutralized, the hope had been that Claudia would feel safe enough to return and take control of the renovations of her home. On the other hand, the fact that Legion had been contracted suggested that Marroqui wasn't the only person looking to settle an old score with her. Would she be aware of that? Apparently not.

Cyrah followed them with her eyes as they made their way across the parking lot. Claudia looked quite lovely in a dusty red dress, leather boots, and straw hat. Her companion was equally attractive—vaguely Arab-looking with long hair, a neatly trimmed beard, and an athletic gait.

There was a barely perceptible bulge beneath his arm, marking him as armed and left-handed. Claudia stayed to his right so as not to interfere if the weapon should become necessary. He was taking in everything around them, whereas she seemed oblivious to her surroundings. Clearly, Claudia Gould had found a man she believed she could trust.

Sadly, the girl, Anna, was still missing. Caring for a child tended to cause people to drop their guard. Having said that, it was hard to complain. Over the course of the last few days, the situation had gone from unproductive boredom to rather promising. Claudia was within reach and the as-yet-unidentified servant seemed to work and run errands on a predictable schedule.

Cyrah smiled and turned the key in the ignition. Finally, something they could work with.

The gate was more or less functioning again and Rapp pushed a button on his key chain to start it grinding slowly open. Cleaning products were neatly lined up inside the wall, suggesting that Bebe was still hard at it. Sadie had remained in character the entire drive, expressing her relief that the Guatemalans were dealt with, throwing out ideas about the house renovations, and lamenting Anna's absence.

As they pulled in, Bebe appeared on the front porch, her short gray hair hidden under a bandana and broom in hand. She leaned it carefully against the wall and walked across the recently mowed lawn to greet them.

"It's so nice to meet you," Sadie said, smiling warmly and offering a hand. Her already amazing accent seemed to improve every time she opened her mouth. "Thank you so much for coming to help us. I know these aren't ideal conditions but I'm certain we can get things back on track."

"It's nice to meet you, too, Claudia. And don't worry. I like a challenge."

Sadie put a hand on her back and began ushering her toward the house. "Why don't you give me a tour of the damage and tell me a little more about yourself? Mitch has hardly said a word. You know how he can be. Or if you don't, you will soon."

He was about to return to the SUV for Sadie's suitcase, when Bebe glanced back at him and mouthed, "Wow."

Wow indeed.

CHAPTER 30

NORTH OF CAPE TOWN
SOUTH AFRICA

CYRAH Jafari glanced at the odometer and confirmed that she was now ten kilometers from the nearest paved road. The land around her was largely flat and covered with low, dusty foliage. Roughly two hundred meters to the east, a shallow canyon dropped to a river that provided enough water for tightly packed trees to replace the brush.

The rain against her windshield was light but starting to create a layer of mud on the dirt track. If she stayed out there too long, the nondescript hatchback might have problems getting her back to civilization. A good excuse to keep the conference quick and efficient.

Deeming the location sufficiently remote, she shut down the engine and stepped out into the mist. This time she limited herself to a range of no more than ten meters from her vehicle. What she didn't need was to replicate the disastrous spectacle of her last staff meeting. While the mutilation of those two men had been immediately blamed on gang violence, involving herself in their deaths had been a careless mistake. And she wasn't in the business of making mistakes—careless or otherwise.

With her communications application active and a wired headset inserted in her ear, she scanned the empty landscape and waited. Her two colleagues would be in similarly remote locations, but she had no idea where—not even what continent. With modern technology there was no need for the others to be physically present during an operation. That was her role, and hers alone.

A tone sounded and she was connected a few moments later.

"Everyone is well?"

Affirmatives all around in the precise wording they'd agreed upon. Any deviation would signal a problem and result in them going to ground until contact could be safely reestablished. Likely never.

"With our recent stroke of luck, can I assume you've made some progress?"

"Some," Nasrin said. "But I can't help wondering *why* they've returned."

"Meaning what?"

"Meaning that Burhan had stabilized the house and looked to be preparing to move their things to a storage unit before he unexpectedly disappeared. Now, suddenly they're not only back, but back with a servant."

"It seems likely that Claudia decided she wanted to take a more hands-on role in repairing the place," Cyrah said. "It's perfectly livable—particularly the second floor. And with the Guatemalan threat neutralized, why not?"

"Then why didn't they bring back the daughter?"

"Because she's traumatized by what happened there? Because the ground floor is still badly damaged? Because she'd be underfoot with what they have to do? Your distaste for this mission is making you overly suspicious, Nasrin."

"And your passion for it is making you incautious."

"Then between the two of you, we're exactly where we need to be," Yasmin interjected. Always the peacemaker.

"I'm going to say this one more time, though I shouldn't have to," Cyrah said. "We've taken the contract and we've been paid. Our decision has been made. What we need to concentrate on now is the fact that Claudia Gould is within reach. For how long, we don't know. What we do know is that the sooner this gets done, the sooner we can move on."

Silence reigned for a few seconds before Nasrin broke it. "They don't appear to be planning on leaving anytime soon. The furniture has been replaced—though haphazardly. We're continuing to monitor everyone they've contracted to work on the renovation as well as people and organizations that might be called upon later."

"Are there opportunities there?" Cyrah asked.

"I'm skeptical that they'll need much construction help in the short term. In the event that they do, it will be for random repairs. Work with the architect will be more predictable because meetings will be necessary—likely not all at the house. Their architect's office has very little security and it's also possible that they'll go to places with sample construction materials. We've identified all the companies the firm works with and should be able to get prior warning if appointments are made. Also, once the work starts in earnest, they'll have to move back out."

"Construction site accident?" Cyrah mused but then decided to move on. "What about Anna? Have we made any progress?"

"We managed to get hold of her best friend's phone long enough to load spyware," Yasmin said. "That's given us access to all her comms and social media accounts. She communicates with Anna primarily via WhatsApp. Thus far no actionable information."

"And there's no way to track where she's transmitting from?" Cyrah asked.

"No. It's well hidden."

"Again, suggesting they still sense some threat," Nasrin said.

"Of course they do," Cyrah responded. "Gustavo Marroqui isn't the only enemy Claudia left behind and her partner may have similar problems. I wouldn't expect them to just leave the girl with a babysitter down the street."

"The sarcasm isn't helpful," Yasmin pointed out.

Cyrah sighed quietly and pulled up her hood against the intensifying rain. "I'm sorry. What I meant to say is that if we could find her, maybe it would be possible to injure her in some kind of accident. If so, I think we could expect her mother to come to her without much thought to security."

"No collateral damage."

"No collateral damage," Cyrah agreed. "But at her age, things like broken bones heal quickly and don't leave any permanent damage. Let's try to keep thinking creatively on that front but for now move on to the servant."

"Bebe Davis," Nasrin said. "We haven't had time to do in-depth research, but based on a search of the Internet, she's never been married, has no children, and has had a fairly varied work history. Primary school teacher, realtor, bookkeeper, librarian. Before taking this position, she seemed to be between jobs. She lives in a modest home with no mortgage and drives a fifteen-year-old Subaru, suggesting she doesn't have many expenses."

"Interesting that she would accept a job based in a foreign country. Particularly under the circumstances," Cyrah said.

"We agree," Yasmin responded. "It might suggest a past relationship with either Claudia or Burhan."

"Can we use that to potentially learn more about them? I'm particularly interested in Burhan and whether he's who he says he is."

"Only if we send someone to investigate on the ground," Nasrin replied. "At this point, I'm not sure it's worth the risk. We know he's dangerous and probably connected to the CIA. I'm not sure additional information would change anything."

"Okay. Is there any other way we can use her?"

"Possibly," Yasmin said. "Obviously, the downside to her being there is that Claudia is going to leave the house less. The assumption is that Bebe will be doing much of the shopping, errands, and the like. Having said that, based on what we've seen, she's very much a creature of habit. She lives her life on a strict schedule to the point that suggests compulsiveness. If that turns out to be the case, it could present some interesting opportunities."

"All right," Cyrah said. "We remain in data-gathering and planning mode, but the situation has definitely taken a turn in the right direction. Let me know if there's anything you need from me. Until then, I'm going to pull back."

They disconnected and Cyrah began searching for a jagged rock large enough to break apart the phone. After spending a little extra effort on the SIM card, she scattered the individual pieces in the brush.

Over the short time Legion had been operational, they'd used everything from apparent heart attacks to private plane crashes to complete their contracts. Their most creative moment thus far was death by stampede. A Russian oligarch obsessed with the American Old West had created a massive cattle ranch in Belarus and liked to walk alone through his herd. Unfortunately, this was a shockingly safe activity. She'd had to hide among the irritatingly docile creatures, hit him in the skull with a weapon built in the shape of a cow hoof, and then coax them with food to walk over him. And that turned out to be the easy part. Actually starting the stampede that was necessary to make it look natural had been the real challenge. As it turned out, his cows had an extraordinary tolerance for being shot with a pellet rifle. The ones she'd experimented on in Finland had been quite a bit more skittish. How was she to know there was variation between breeds?

Even compared to her foray into bovine psychology, though, this operation was hopelessly complex. The deadly Mitch Burhan with his likely connections to the Central Intelligence Agency. The cunning Claudia Gould. The presence of the American surveillance team. Everywhere she looked, there were threats.

The mist had condensed to the point that Cyrah was starting to hear the muffled slap of individual drops. She folded her arms across her chest, looking out across the lonely plain. Whatever happened with Claudia Gould, there wouldn't be many more days like this one. Yasmin was already making subtle hints that she wanted out. The draw of a normal life—husband, children, friends—was powerful to her. It always had been.

And on the day she logged off, so would Legion. Cyrah would find herself alone for the first time in her life. Unmoored from the sisters she loved, the challenges she craved, and the excitement she had become addicted to.

What then?

CHAPTER 31

NEAR FRANSCHHOEK
SOUTH AFRICA

RAPP followed the new woman of the house to their safe room and joined Bebe inside. Some construction materials had found their way under the table, but everyone still managed to sit. Sadie was close enough that her shoulder pressed against Rapp's and she patted him on the leg affectionately. Scooting away wasn't an option because there was nowhere to go.

"I've swept the entire house," Bebe started, her fleshy body squeezed into the facing chair. "It's clean. My guess is that Legion and the Americans didn't expect you to come back. The place is a disaster."

Sadie stiffened and responded in the French accent that never slipped. "That seems kind of negative."

She was doing a good job of filling out a pair of Claudia's jeans with the weight she'd gained. They were a little short, but the flowing white blouse she'd found in the closet fit perfectly.

"I don't think Bebe meant—" Rapp started, but she cut him off.

"It may not look like much now, but when the renovations are done, it's going to be amazing."

Bebe's brow furrowed, but she didn't otherwise acknowledge that the woman had spoken. "As you know, this room is soundproof at conversational levels, and I've disconnected all the electronics from their power sources. Also, I installed new secure hardware for the network and changed all the passwords. I think it's unlikely anyone could have tapped in, but better safe than sorry. The bottom line is that I'm confident we can talk freely in here."

Rapp nodded. "Where Legion is concerned, there are no precautions I consider overkill. We don't understand their capabilities, resources, or operating history. Irene's pretty comfortable attributing four hits to them, but it's almost certain there are more. These aren't people who come at you with guns blazing. They're people who release a shark when you're swimming in the ocean or swap out your blood pressure medication for sugar pills and wait for you to have a stroke. Even with our eyes wide open, there's a good chance we won't see them coming."

"They're *incredible,*" Sadie said. "No pattern at all. Everything they do is bespoke. Tailored perfectly to their target. And the fact that they can use double-blind protocols for anonymity is proof. How good do you have to be to get people to send two million euros to an anonymous email account that will be shut down the day the money's transferred?"

She sounded more like a fangirl than a target, but Rapp let it go. Sadie was Sadie and there was nothing anyone—including him—could do about it.

"So, what I want to do," Rapp continued, "is turn this thing around. There's a lot of experience in this room. If the three of us had been hired to get to Claudia, how would we do it?"

"Are we assuming that it can't look like a hit and there can't be any collateral damage?" Bebe said.

"Those seem to be the parameters Legion works under."

"Not easy, then. The obvious thing would be to use the crime problem around here as cover. Attacking the house again would be a stretch. Maybe a carjacking? And haven't I read something about people randomly throwing cinder blocks off freeway overpasses? I mean it's not exactly elegant, but in the context of South Africa it wouldn't generate a lot of questions."

"Too low percentage," Sadie said. "Particularly with the armored SUV. A carjacker would need an RPG and how do you aim a cinder block well enough to guarantee a kill? Plus, it just feels wrong for them. Too heavy-handed. What about the water supply? Are there any common diseases or contaminants around here? Even if it didn't kill me, it could create an emergency that would force us to improvise."

"All the water goes through a filtration system that's inside the house and still fully functional. It'd have to be taken off-line for that kind of an attack to be feasible."

"Okay, maybe not," Sadie conceded. "But what about the air-conditioning units? I once rigged an HVAC system at a hotel and pumped carbon monoxide through an open window. It killed the target's wife, too, though." She turned thoughtful for a moment. "But I think his kid survived. I can't remember."

"They're outside the house, but still inside the wall," Rapp said, recalling that the kid in fact had not survived. "And we're trying to avoid collateral damage."

"Are you a hundred percent sure that rule's still in play?" Bebe asked. "After what you did to the Guatemalans, you might have lost innocent bystander status. If I were them, I'd break my rule and do you at the same time. The last thing in the world I'd want is to spend the rest of my life waiting for you to drop a Soviet surplus bomb on my house."

"I'm not a hundred percent sure," Rapp admitted. "But we have central climate control so that means you die, too."

"Inconvenient, but not insurmountable," Sadie said. "Run the gas and when everyone's unconscious, short out the unit. After that, all you have to do is stroll in with a tank of carbon monoxide and a face mask. Claudia dies and everyone else makes a full recovery."

"You mean *you* die and everyone else makes a full recovery," Bebe said, but Sadie ignored her.

"You could even make it look like undiagnosed damage from the gunfight."

"Complicated," Rapp said.

"Yeah, but there's no easy way to get to Claudia. And that's what Legion does, right? Complicated?"

"Okay. You've convinced me. Bebe, I've got carbon monoxide detectors in the house, but they're just ones I bought from the hardware store. I don't even know if they work anymore. Can you install some hidden ones that we can count on?"

She jotted a note on the legal pad in front of her. "Consider it done."

"Next?"

"We talked about creating an emergency to get Claudia outside the gate where she's vulnerable," Sadie said. "But what about your vulnerability? I know you've been staying off the roads lately, but I've read about people stringing wires and creating other kinds of traps on trails. I'm not sure it happens here but it does in the US and Britain. If you got badly hurt, I'd come running."

"I'm going to avoid putting myself at risk until this is resolved. No mountain biking, trail running, or climbing."

"What about Bebe?"

"Unpredictable," Rapp said. "I might respond to that, not you."

"To me, Anna's the weakest link," Bebe said. "Any problem with her creates a panicked response in her mother, who would then ignore her own safety to get to her as quickly as possible."

"Agreed," Rapp said. "We're letting Anna communicate in a limited way with her friends but obscuring her location. I think we should assume that, at a minimum, Legion's already compromised her best friend's phone. Can we use that to maneuver them into making a play?"

"I'd be pretty focused on Anna if I were them," Bebe said, lining up her collection of pencils to the right of her pad.

"So, we let them find her," Sadie proposed. "They injure her and I bolt out of here in a way that looks panicked but is actually carefully controlled. When Legion make their move, we take them out."

"I hear what you're saying," Rapp said, "but putting Anna in harm's way is a hard no."

"I think your judgment's clouded," Sadie said. "Getting hurt is better than losing your mother, right? And there's no way they're going to kill her. A dead daughter lacks urgency. I mean, why would Claudia even leave the house? More likely you'd just have someone bring the body back for burial, right? I'd go for a really visceral and painful injury. Not so bad that she'd end up in a coma, though. Something that would keep her awake, suffering, and calling for her mother. Bad burns? Or what about an animal attack? Do they have chimpanzees in Uganda? I saw a news report once about a woman who got charged by one. It bit her face right o—"

Rapp held out a hand, silencing her. The images were causing a constriction in his chest that was starting to feel vaguely dangerous. "Let's back-burner this for the moment. I think we can do better."

Sadie just shrugged.

"What do you have in mind?" Bebe said.

"No big moves that could be noticeable. We'll let you create an extremely predictable routine and see if you can identify anyone watching you. You're better at that than anyone and they won't be prepared for someone who's incapable of forgetting a face. In the meantime, we need to figure out how to create an opportunity for Legion and funnel them into it. Maybe through Bebe, maybe through the architect or construction people. Even Anna's not completely off the table as long as we can be sure they never get anywhere near her. We've got to put ourselves in a position where we don't just have the ability to predict their moves, we have the ability to control them. Because without a face or a name, that's the only way we're going to identify them. Remember, they have no idea we know they're out there. That gives us an edge."

"What about me?" Sadie said. "What's my role?"

"For now? Staying out of sight inside the wall. You've got Claudia down pretty well, but you're not her twin. If Legion figures out we've pulled a switch, this whole thing is blown."

"That's it?" she said, folding her arms and staring straight forward. "So, endless boredom."

"But since you're the target, boredom is good," Bebe pointed out.

"Not if I die of it."

Rapp grabbed his pillow off the bed, tossing it and a blanket onto the sofa beneath the window. The house's master bedroom was large enough that Claudia had put a sectional in one corner. Until now, it had largely served to cause arguments about him using it as a receptacle for laundry.

With no strong sense of Legion's surveillance capability, it made sense to keep things as natural as possible. Unfortunately, that precluded him moving into the guest bedroom. With Guatemala, the new housekeeper, and the sudden reappearance of Claudia, there was already too much unusual activity. Not that he thought Legion could be spooked in the normal sense of the word, but they could be made more cautious. And what he didn't need was for this to turn into an endless staring contest.

The only light in the room was coming from the partially open door to the bathroom. Rapp used the tenuous illumination to pour a small glass of bourbon. He dropped onto the sofa and put his feet on the coffee table before taking a cautious sip. While the idea of dulling his senses became more appealing with every minute Sadie was in the house, it wasn't in the cards. When all this was over, though, he promised himself a proper binge.

The shower was running, and he watched the steam flow into the room. It swirled hypnotically, as though it was trying to reveal something to him. But what? Any way he looked at it, there wasn't much time left. Every year his world felt like it got a little smaller. Maybe that was just the way things went as people aged. For him, though, it didn't have anything to do with fear. More like a tighter focus on what was important. And at this point the list was pretty short. One: kill Legion. Two: get rid of the Cooks. Three: find a sustainable way forward.

He heard the shower go off and a moment later Sadie appeared in the doorway. She was backlit but he could see that she'd removed her brown contacts, revealing bright, strangely dead blue eyes. Her naked body was still wet enough to glisten, highlighting a series of long, thin scars next to her meticulously groomed pubic area. Unquestionably self-inflicted.

"What's that?" she said, pointing to the pillow next to him. The French accent was fully part of her now.

"I was planning on sleeping in here. It'll look more natural."

"Even more natural in the bed. And I can personally guarantee it'll be more comfortable than the sofa."

He mentally reeled through a list of potential responses. Everything with her was a delicate balancing act. Finally, he affected a grin. "With Legion after you, I'd rather keep a little distance between us."

She ran a hand through her wet hair but didn't move from her position in the doorway. "You're not going to let me have any fun at all, are you?"

CHAPTER 32

FRANSCHHOEK
SOUTH AFRICA

THE words *safe room* had taken on a completely new meaning. Rapp was closed up in his, sitting with a cold beer in his hand and two more in a bucket of ice near his feet. He'd repurposed one of the security monitors as a television and was tuned into a mountain bike race. The audio didn't work for some reason, but it didn't matter. In fact, the quiet was welcome.

Outside the locked door lurked his increasingly chaotic world. That morning, he'd gone out to his gym and discovered that Bebe had rearranged all his tools by color. And based on the dull whine barely audible through the walls, she was now brandishing her new favorite weapon: his Shop-Vac.

More pronounced than the sound was the smell of a soufflé baking in the oven. When he'd gone to the kitchen for the beer, Sadie had accused him of clomping around like a drunken horse, speculating that it was going to cause a catastrophic failure in her dessert. He'd beat a hasty, light-footed retreat.

She was losing herself in the role more and more every day, making it impossible to know who he was talking to. Clues were visible only in her eyes, partially obscured by brown contacts. He seemed to be dealing with a hybrid now—a pendulum that swung in an ever-narrowing band.

Rapp glanced at his phone, noting the time. He was surprised at how much he was looking forward to his upcoming call. Not the most cheerful subject matter, but still a brush with some much-needed sanity. He was starting to feel like an orderly in an asylum. Or maybe he was just another inmate. Either way, the sensation was becoming more overwhelming with every passing day.

The encrypted line began to ring at precisely the agreed-upon time and he picked up.

"Go ahead."

"How are you? Are things going okay?" Claudia said. The voice was disturbingly similar to Sadie's.

"Everything's good. You?"

"Fine. I'm getting a little break. Levi took Anna to patrol the grounds."

Levi Mizrah was a former Israeli operator who Rapp had known for years. He was in charge of the compound's security now that Coleman had relocated to his house in Greece.

"What about Irene? She's gone, right?"

"Yes. To Europe to meet with some former colleagues. And I think Nick is on his way to Brussels to see her."

"Why? Are they still going around about whether she's going to take a job with him?"

"Is that a joke?" Claudia said, sounding a bit confused.

"What do you mean?"

"Well, at this point, I think it's pretty clear that their interest in each other is more than just professional."

He didn't immediately respond. Kennedy had once been married, but he never thought of her in those terms. Since they'd known one another, her personal life had largely been swallowed by the Agency. Apparently, unemployed and with her son in college, she had time for other things. Why not a relationship? If anyone deserved a little happiness, it was her.

"Okay. I guess I missed that."

"In your defense, at this point it just seems like another negotiation. All relationships are complicated, but this one—assuming anything comes of it—is a whole other level. The richest man in history and the former director of the CIA. That would be quite a union."

The understatement of the century. "Where do we stand with Legion?"

"Irene's tried to contact them but none of the email addresses they're suspected of using in the past are active. We don't anticipate them issuing another until . . ." Her voice faded for a moment. "Until this job's done. She's also talked with her contacts around the world and no one knows any more than the Agency. We're still assuming that Legion was trained by a government but have no idea which one. Irene has good back channels in Russia and Syria, and she's reasonably convinced they didn't come from there. But that doesn't help much."

He heard some banging and then Anna shouting. "Is that Mitch? Hey, Mitch! I was just on patrol!" Claudia put her on speaker so she could speak at a normal level. "When are you coming back?"

"Should be pretty soon."

"We ought to come there instead. I miss my friends at school. And I can't talk to Ahmale. Just text and Mom erases half the stuff I say."

"She's a difficult woman."

"I know! Right? And then Ahmale lost her phone. But she found it like the next day. Her parents were really mad. It was a brand-new iPhone. They're superexpensive you know. Like ten thousand rand. And she— Hey! Wait! I'm not done talking!"

"Yes you are," he heard Claudia say. "Now go start your schoolwork. I'll be up in a few minutes to help you."

"Bye!" she yelled.

"Okay, I'm back, Mitch. Where were we?"

"Ahmale lost her phone and then found it the next day?"

"I thought the same thing. We should assume that Legion was behind it and that they now have spyware installed."

"Maybe it's something we can use?"

"Maybe. Let me know if you want to go in that direction. In the meantime, how's the house project going?"

"The architects are working on some initial ideas, but that doesn't really involve anything hands-on. I'm sure Legion has access to all their communications and that they're watching every contractor and construction supplier as well as moving and rental companies. Again, a lot of opportunities to flush them out, but not without putting Sadie at risk."

"Bebe hasn't noticed anything?"

"Just the American surveillance team."

"You can't let anything happen to Sadie," Claudia stressed. "It's not her job to die for my mistakes. How is she holding up?"

A potentially loaded question. The fact that he was living in such close quarters with a woman someone once dubbed *Victoria's Secret Agent* likely wasn't sitting well with her.

"She'll be fine. Nothing ever happens to people like her. What about the Cook issue?"

"I haven't spent much time on it. Irene wants to take point."

"Meaning she wants to do nothing."

"For now."

"Yeah, but what if now is our chance? I'm not saying that we should make a move, but it's possible that we could somehow subvert his security upgrades while they're in process. Maybe create a hole or get someone inside? This might be the time to lay a little groundwork. If we don't ever use it, fine. But it'd be nice to know it's there."

"You should talk to her, not me," Claudia said, sounding uncharacteristically hesitant.

"Whose side are you on here?"

"The side that ends with you alive, Mitch. This is a big step. Sometimes you just have to put your trust in someone else. Seriously, tell me another person in the world you'd rather have working on this. Me? No. Scott? No. You? God, no. As you're fond of saying, take the win. For now, just take the win."

"I don't know, Claudia. Irene has a strong bias here. Are we missing an opportunity? With the right preparation, anyone can be killed."

"Maybe you should put Sadie on it."

He let out a long breath, but not so loud that she'd hear. He didn't want to talk about Sadie. He wanted to spend a few minutes with his mind clear of her soufflé, the fact that she got off on cutting herself, her increasing despondency over her separation from Anna—a girl she'd never met . . .

"She's nuts, Claudia. And I don't mean a little bit off. I mean batshit insane. But she's convincing. And that's what we need."

"Talented, dangerous, and beautiful. What did Liz Dawson call her?"

Here it came.

"Victoria's Secret Agent?"

"Please tell me we're not having this conversation," Rapp said.

There was a long pause over the line. "We're not."

"Then can we return to my other problem?"

"So, you're *not* just going to take the win?"

"I'm considering it."

"Fine. Cook is doing a hybrid physical-virtual event in two days. It seems like this is the direction they're going in to give him maximum exposure to his constituents while at the same time giving him minimum exposure to you."

"So, you *are* paying attention."

"Of course I am. I'm not trying to take options off the table, Mitch. I'm just trying to manage them."

"And?"

“What I’m seeing isn’t encouraging. There are three potential sites, all heavily secured. The audience will be brought in on buses, but which venue is being used will only be known less than an hour before.”

“But he’s actually going to be at one of them personally. He’s leaving the White House.”

“Yes. But we don’t know when or how or where exactly. Also—and I’m not exaggerating when I say it—this could literally be the most secure event in history. What we need to do here is sit back, watch, and get some insight into where their security protocols are headed.”

“You said you don’t know exactly where he’s going to appear. That there are three possible venues.”

“Correct.”

“Are all of them in the DC area?”

“Yes.”

“And you’re telling me that all our guys are being watched.”

“Physical, electronic, drone . . . They’re completely locked down. Why?”

He smiled. “No reason.”

CHAPTER 33

BEBE Kincaid looked down sadly at the towel in her hand, knowing it was the last dry one in the house. The night before, a nicked pipe had given way and by the time they'd woken, a minor disaster was in the offing. Mitch had shut off the water and cleared most of it using a huge squeegee attached to a rake handle. After he'd left for the plumbing supply store, she'd attacked the problem with rags and now the floor was dry. The problem was that the grout was coated with a pasty haze of plaster.

The haphazard staining thwarted her every effort at cleaning and distorted the perfect grid effect created by the tile. Nothing lined up anymore. Nothing was consistent. What if it was permanent? What would they do then?

She knelt and began scrubbing again, ignoring the arthritis in her shoulder until it became intense enough to overshadow her panic about the floor. Finally, she sat back on her heels and counted the way her therapist had taught her.

One, two, three . . . It doesn't matter. Four, five, six. It's just a floor.

Seven, eight, nine. I could buy grout cleaner and a stiffer brush. Ten, eleven, twelve. That would do it. That would fix it.

It was 10:44 a.m., sixteen minutes before her scheduled departure time. She went back to her room and cleaned up, changing into newly pressed clothing and then walking back down the stairs on rubber-soled shoes. Grocery bags were hung by the front door, making it possible for her to escape without having to go anywhere near Sadie's kitchen.

At eleven sharp, she was behind the wheel of Claudia's armored SUV, engine started and bags folded neatly in the passenger seat. The sense of relief she felt once outside the gate was always welcome. The house became more oppressive every day. More hopeless. She wondered if this was what it had been like centuries ago when a castle came under siege. Knowing that time was on your opponent's side and that eventually yours would run out.

She glanced at the speedometer, confirming that she was traveling at exactly forty kilometers per hour, before squinting into the rearview mirror. Instead of the house's perimeter wall receding into the distance, though, she saw someone rising from the SUV's cargo area. Panic seized her and she slammed a foot on the brake pedal, causing the vehicle to fishtail despite its sophisticated antilock system.

"It's me!" she heard the woman shout. Her French accent was unmistakable.

Bebe lifted her foot off the brake and regained control, heart pounding wildly in her chest. Sadie tossed a straw hat onto the dashboard and then rolled gracefully over the seat. A moment later she was settling onto the bags in the front passenger side.

"What . . . What are you doing?" Bebe stammered.

"Coming shopping with you," Sadie replied, pulling the seat belt across her and clicking it into place. "I thought you might need some help."

"Mitch said you have to stay at the house."

"I haven't set foot outside those walls in a week. I feel like a prisoner and it's going to start looking suspicious to anyone watching. I can't stay in there forever."

Bebe examined the woman in her peripheral vision, taking in the constantly improving package. Her weight had stabilized at a point that exactly mimicked Claudia's and she now filled out her clothes almost perfectly. Today she'd selected a pair of jeans, a printed tunic, and oversize sunglasses that were currently in fashion.

"I should take you back. I can still get to the store on time if I hurry."

"Don't take me back. There's something I need to talk to you about."

Bebe gripped the wheel a little tighter, unsure what to do. Mitch was going to be furious if he found out she'd taken Sadie to the grocery store. What would he do? Certainly nothing violent. This woman, on the other hand, was more of a wild card. Suffering from various mental illnesses herself, Bebe was sympathetic to people struggling with inner demons. But Sadie needed a serious intervention. Preferably one that included a small, well-padded room. There was no telling what could happen if she or her growing delusions were challenged. The threat of Legion was starting to seem trivial compared to the fact that Sadie Hansen had access to sharp objects.

"Okay," Bebe heard herself say. "What?"

Sadie smiled warmly. Claudia's smile.

"Have you noticed anything weird about Mitch lately?"

They pulled out onto the paved road. "What do you mean?"

Sadie seemed a little uncomfortable, turning away and looking through the side window. "It's a little personal."

"Then we probably shouldn't talk about it," Bebe said hopefully. "You should go directly to him."

Sadie ignored her. "It's just that . . . Well, he won't touch me. He's been sleeping on the sofa, and it's one excuse after another. Now he says it's his back. But I'm starting to wonder if there's really anything wrong with it. He's never been like this before. Has he said anything to you? Is he mad at me for some reason and just doesn't want to tell me?"

Bebe tried to stay focused on the road but couldn't help noticing that Sadie's eyes had taken on a glassy look. Was she going to cry? Over Mitch's coldness to her? His coldness to Claudia? Which of the two women was in the car with her?

"He's under a lot of pressure," Bebe said finally. "He blames himself for all this. And he misses Anna."

Sadie nodded and contemplated the floorboard. "Me, too. But what matters is that we know she's safe."

"You should stay in the car," Bebe said as she pulled into her customary space on the eastern edge of the parking lot.

"No, I'll come in and help you."

"Mitch is already going to kill us. Let's not make it worse."

"Do you always do what Mitch says?"

"Yes."

"Well, I don't," she said, eyes narrowing in a way that Claudia's never did. A fleeting glimpse of the real person behind them? Assuming there was one.

Bebe took three deep breaths and then used her shoulder to open the heavy door. Her only option was to get this over with as quickly as possible. "Take the bags. And don't forget your hat."

Sadie trailed her as they hustled across the lot and through the doors of the store. Shopping was simple because there was virtually no variation in their diet. Bebe had a vegetable and grain bowl three times a day with only slight modifications to distinguish breakfast, lunch, and dinner. Mitch and Sadie had a full ham, egg, and potato breakfast every morning and grilled chicken for lunch. Their dinners rotated on a seven-day schedule. Tonight was Mitch's favorite: steak, baked potato, and Caesar salad.

"I'll push the cart," Sadie said, grabbing one from where they were lined up. "What's first?"

"Lettuce," Bebe responded, walking past a flower display to the vegetable aisle. They were going to be okay, she told herself. There was no way Legion would be able to anticipate Sadie coming out that day. They were planners. The chances that they'd make some half-cocked move were precisely zero.

Zero, zero, zero . . .

When they came to the romaine, Sadie reached for one. Bebe moved to block her, carefully tearing off the canned food section from her list.

"Why don't you take the cart and get this stuff?" she said, figuring the woman couldn't mess up the assignment too badly.

As Bebe watched her retreat toward the back of the store, she took the opportunity to scan the faces of the people Sadie passed. All the employees were familiar, as were two of the customers—both long-term residents of the area.

She turned back to the lettuce, putting on a plastic glove and sorting through the heads until she found a uniformly shaped one with unblemished leaves. Once selected, she carefully placed it in a bag and set course for the meat counter.

About halfway down the aisle, a ping from her phone caused her to stop. She retrieved it and reluctantly looked down at the text. Apparently, Mitch had finished his errands and was back home.

Where the hell is she?

Nerves caused Bebe to type a lengthier response than he was probably looking for.

She's with me. I swear it's not my fault. There was nothing I could do.

Almost thirty seconds went by before she got a two-word answer.

I know.

When they pulled through the gate, Mitch was standing on the grass waiting. Bebe swung around to put the passenger door closest to him and maintain as much distance as possible. He looked like he was going to dismember someone and throw their body parts on a bonfire—an act he'd probably actually carried out at some point in his life.

"What the *fuck*?" he said when Sadie stepped out with a bag of groceries. Bebe exited her side and made a subtle slashing motion across her throat. This woman was holding on by a very thin thread.

"Don't you dare talk to me like that," Sadie responded.

"I told you to stay inside the walls. Were those instructions too complicated for you?"

"Do you ever think of me, Mitch? Or do you just think of yourself? I'm bored. And I'm lonely. And I can't even cook to relax because we eat the same things day in and day out!"

"What the hell are you talking ab—"

"Do you think another woman would put up with this?" she said, her voice rising in volume. "With *you*? Well, then you should go find her!"

She burst into tears and ran into the house, leaving him standing at the edge of the lawn. Bebe walked cautiously up to him. "You should tell her you're sorry."

He put a hand on his face and wiped slowly down it before stalking toward his gym.

CHAPTER 34

WEST OF MANASSAS
VIRGINIA
USA

JOE Maslick shouldered a tactical backpack and stepped out onto his porch. After pulling the door shut, he squinted up at the sky—a recently formed habit that made him feel like he'd gone from fighting terrorists to joining their ranks. Somewhere up there, just out of sight, was a camera drone. Physical surveillance started just outside the subdivision's gate. Two-man teams working around the clock in eight-hour shifts. The electronic side of the operation was harder to detect, but at the very least his main phone and Internet were compromised.

He'd been serving his country since he'd turned eighteen and that piece of shit Anthony Cook was making him feel like a criminal. A traitor. Which is why when Rapp had called on an encrypted line and asked him if he wanted to make the situation worse, Maslick had jumped at the chance. Not smart, for sure, but the Cooks could pucker up and kiss his ass. And not on the cheek, either. Right down the fucking middle.

He tossed the pack in the bed of his pickup and slid behind the wheel. As he drove through the neighborhood, it felt like a graveyard full of overpriced mausoleums. Mike Nash was dead. Scott Coleman was in Greece. Bruno was in New Zealand, and Wick had gone home to Wyoming. Finally, there was Rapp, who was in South Africa waiting for the shit to hit the fan with no backup other than Bebe Kincaid and that mental defective Sadie Hansen.

Where the hell was all this going? He agreed that bunching up could create an irresistible target, but how long would they have to stay scattered across the world? There was a good chance that Anthony Cook would win reelection and, according to Dr. Kennedy, a decent chance his wife would follow. Did that mean the next time he got together with his boys, he'd have gray hair and a walker? Because of a fucking politician? Not on his watch.

The Nashes' house appeared on the left and it was hard not to look away. Maslick had promised to take their son Rory skeet shooting later in the week and tomorrow morning he needed to install a gate on their deck so Maggie didn't have to worry about Chucky falling down the steps. After what had happened, they were now the responsibility of the village. Unfortunately, the village right now was just him and a few old guys who'd been badasses in their day but now weren't good for much more than drinking beer and criticizing his construction abilities.

What the hell was happening to his country? Mike Nash had been one of his closest friends. America's motto was quickly turning from *E Pluribus Unum* to *every man for himself.* Families were being torn apart. Lifelong friendships were ending. No one believed in anything real anymore. No one would acknowledge that they owed America a debt—not the other way around.

And now here he was, right in the middle of the shit storm. If it hadn't been for the military, Scott, and Mitch, he'd probably be working at the gas station down the street from where he'd grown up. Instead, he'd met some of the most impressive people in the world and traveled to more countries than he could count. Thanks to them, he was behind the wheel of a ninety-thousand-dollar pickup and living in a mansion.

The radio was turned up just high enough for the news to be comprehensible over noise from the truck's oversize tires. Maslick normally refused to listen to this kind of political garbage but acknowledged that there were a lot of people who ate it up. What was it about his fellow citizens that made them go to rallies and cheer like Jesus Christ himself had walked out onstage? What did they think these assholes were going to do for them? Why would anyone give a shit that Anthony Cook hadn't made a personal appearance in weeks or months or whatever? What was he going to say that he hadn't said a hundred times before?

The announcer became more breathless as the pivotal moment drew closer. The moment that the great Anthony Cook would finally return to the spotlight and bless everyone with his presence. Two more minutes. One more minute. Thirty seconds until he came onstage and made every one of his constituents rich, good-looking, and fulfilled. Fifteen more seconds before he led everyone straight to the fucking promised land.

When the crowd erupted, Maslick looked for somewhere to pull over. The rural road between his home and Washington, DC, was pretty much abandoned, with dense forest on either side. His dashboard suggested that temperatures were hovering in the nineties but he didn't search for shade, instead selecting a wide spot with no tree cover.

He jumped out and leaned into the truck's bed, sliding a Nemesis Valkyrie sniper rifle from beneath a tarp and strapping it to the side of his pack. The sound of a motor reached him from the west, but when the vehicle appeared over a low rise, he saw that it wasn't one of the cars used by the surveillance teams hounding him. Another minute passed before the blue Nissan Murano he was waiting for appeared. When it did, he shouldered the pack, turned in a way that would make the rifle obvious, and then darted into the woods.

President Cook walked briskly across the stage, displaying the strength and energy his supporters had come to expect of him. To *need* of him. He took a position behind the lectern and raised his hands in the air, drinking in the adulation of the people packed into the small venue.

Cook lowered his arms in a call for quiet, but his followers didn't obey. Instead, the volume of their cheers increased. This was what made all his sacrifices worthwhile—the almost religious devotion of his supporters. The knowledge that they would believe anything he told them. Do anything he told them. They'd destroy themselves and everything around them to feel the sense of power and belonging only he could give them. *He* was America. Not Mitch Rapp. Not Irene Kennedy. *Him.*

The crowd finally calmed down and he began to speak, moving his gaze smoothly from teleprompter to teleprompter. It would provide the illusion of making eye contact with every person in the audience as well as those scattered throughout the country watching through VR technology. The speech itself wasn't anything special—largely attacks on his political opponents and a healthy dose of flattery for his followers. Public policy was unimportant in modern politics—too remote and complicated to create a connection between leaders and the led. Identity and tribal affiliation were what mattered now.

Out of the corner of his eye, Cook noticed some kind of disturbance offstage. He tried to keep reading his lines but began to falter as the commotion grew. When five Secret Service agents began charging him, he took a hesitant step back. A moment later they had completely surrounded him and he was being pulled toward the exit. Stumbling with feet barely touching the ground, he could hear the screams of his audience, increasingly muffled as he was dragged down a narrow concrete corridor.

When they entered the underground parking area, he saw his limousine speeding toward one of the exits amid an escort of black Yukons. The civilian vehicles crowding the garage were all on the move as well, their screeching tires echoing throughout the space as they abandoned it. He was shoved into the back of a nondescript Ford Explorer and two Secret Service men climbed in on either side of him. The driver joined the fray, melding with the decoys and finally exiting the parking garage to the south.

"What?" Cook finally managed to get out. "What happened?"

The head of his security detail twisted around in the front passenger seat. "Joe Maslick evaded our surveillance on his way to Washington, sir. And when he did, he was carrying a sniper rifle."

CHAPTER 35

WEST OF MANASSAS
VIRGINIA
USA

THE sun was down, but temperatures were holding in the high eighties. Joe Maslick, now outfitted in Bermuda shorts and a Hawaiian shirt, was in his backyard with a beer in one hand and a spatula in the other. The grill was flaming up around his burger a bit, but better to cook it fast.

His plan when he'd woken up that morning had been pretty mundane. Hit Home Depot to pick up some lumber for Maggie's gate and then get some ribs on the smoker. Maybe extend a last-minute dinner invitation to Skip McMahon. The retired FBI agent was full of entertaining stories and there was at least a fifty-fifty chance he'd drink too much and fall asleep in his barbecue sauce. Always good for a laugh.

But then Rapp had called with his cryptic request.

Hey, Mas. Would you mind driving toward DC about an hour or so before the president's rally? Then, when he goes onstage, park your truck by the side of the road and run into the forest with a sniper rifle?

Why?

No reason.

What forest?

Don't care.

How long do I have to stay out there?

I dunno. Half an hour?

Not that it was the strangest request Rapp had ever made of him. That prize would probably go to the time he'd handed him a suitcase full of cash and told him to purchase—then temporarily manage—a brothel outside of Fez, Morocco.

In retrospect, not the worst job he'd ever had. Not by a long shot.

He grabbed another beer from the refrigerator next to his grill before carefully arranging lettuce, tomato, and a roasted green chili on a bun he'd just finished toasting. After putting a slice of cheddar on the patty, he drained the can in one long pull and went in for another.

The cheese was barely starting to melt when he heard a hum overhead. Apparently, the surveillance drone operator was no longer under orders to be subtle. It slowed to a hover over the patio, turned on a spotlight, and focused it on him. Maslick put his spatula down and raised the middle finger of his newly freed hand.

The clock was ticking.

He slid his burger onto the patty and began wolfing it down. A little rarer than he liked, but he ground his own steak, so not bad. The cheddar still had a little tooth, though. And in his haste, he'd completely forgotten the onion slices lying on his kitchen counter.

As Rapp had predicted, the sound of cars roaring up his driveway became audible a few moments later. He kept cramming the burger in his mouth as men armed with assault rifles approached from both sides of the house. The exact models were impossible to discern in the semidarkness but that was less important than the fact that they were all pointed in his direction.

"Put your hands where I can see them!" someone shouted.

Maslick jammed the rest of his dinner in his mouth and then

obeyed the command. When he spoke, the burger made his words nearly unintelligible.

"What seems to be the problem, Officer?"

Catherine Cook was clicking through the news channels in the White House residence, stopping whenever she saw a video of her husband being dragged offstage. It had been hours ago, but the clips were still saturating every media outlet from cable television to Twitter to Facebook. She hit the pause button a split second before the lead Secret Service man reached him, and took in how small he looked. How frightened and weak.

Apparently, he had been taken directly to one of the new fortified locations that Rapp and Kennedy knew nothing about and was now on his way back to the White House.

For what it was worth.

She lowered herself into a chair, staring silently at that frozen image until the door opened. Her husband walked across the wood floor and stopped behind her. He didn't seem to have anything to say. But she did.

"You can steal, Tony. You can lie. Cheat. You can even pursue policies that destroy the lives of your own constituents." She pointed to the screen. "What you *can't* do, is look like *that*."

"Sam's already working on a story about an operation I'm carrying out against ISIS. We're going to say that we received information that they were planning an attack. Darren's feeding the FBI disinformation about an Egyptian immigrant studying at Georgetown. They're going to pick him up tomorrow. It'll have more impact if we can put a face on it."

Again, she pointed to the TV. "You *have* put a face on it, Tony. That's going to be your next opponent's campaign poster."

"Joe Maslick—"

"I heard," she interrupted. "How far from that venue was he? Still an hour? With traffic an hour and a half? What exactly was the threat again?"

"You have no idea," Cook responded defensively. "Killing is all Mitch Rapp and his people do. We can't afford to take chances."

She held up an eight-by-ten photo depicting Joe Maslick flipping off a surveillance drone. "He's toying with you, Tony. How much more obvious could it be? He wanted to make a fool out of you and to make you pull back from the public even more. What Rapp wants is for you to lose the next election. Because once you're out of the White House, you're defenseless."

"I—"

"He *knows,* Tony. I don't know how, but he knows about the dossier. Probably from Enzo Ruiz, but it doesn't matter. Mitch Rapp just sent you a message. The truce is off. And if Legion manages to kill Claudia Gould, there's nothing he won't do to see you dead."

"She and Rapp are back at the house in South Africa with limited security. Darren thinks they're trying to draw Legion in. We need to quit screwing around and deal with him."

She laughed. "We *did* deal with him. We agreed to a truce. And he was going to abide by it. All you had to do was nothing. But you couldn't help yourself."

"So now you trust Mitch Rapp?"

"I trust him to pursue his own self-interest and the interests of his country. He'd have understood that what we were offering was a good deal. And if not, Kennedy would have convinced him."

"I disagree," her husband said coldly.

"What now, then? Do we take another run at Rapp and hope it goes better this time? Scott Coleman? Irene? What about the hundreds of other people who owe Rapp their lives?"

"We already have Maslick."

"For God's sake, Tony. Let him go. He's a war hero who hasn't broken any laws. Right now, Irene Kennedy is sitting around figuring out how to leak this to the press in the most damaging way possible."

Cook finally came around and sat on a sofa in front of her. "Lately all I hear out of you is criticism. That I'm a coward. That I'm an idiot. That I'm being played. What I don't hear is solutions."

"I gave you the solution!" she snapped. "You threw it away. And now you're going to sit there and try to shift the blame? I'm not one of your adoring cult members, Tony. Don't treat me like one."

He leaned back, putting as much distance between them as he could without appearing to retreat. When he spoke again, his tone was more respectful. "You always have a plan B, Catherine."

"Not this time. Trying to take out Rapp and his people would have a high probability of failure and a level of political backlash that even we wouldn't be able to withstand. And reaching out to him and trying to reestablish our truce is impossible because he has no reason to trust us."

"Then what?"

She let out a long breath. "I see only one path. That you rely on your security and go back to your political life."

He stiffened. "That sounds like a recipe for my death."

"Maybe," she admitted. "But losing the White House definitely is."

CHAPTER 36

NEAR FRANSCHHOEK
SOUTH AFRICA

RAPP finished his last set of pull-ups and dropped from the bar hanging in front of his gym's sparkling clean windows. Bebe's endless cleaning and straightening did have its benefits. On the other hand, he still hadn't figured out her latest tool organization protocols and couldn't find an entire category of wrenches. Asking her would be the logical solution but would lead to an intricate explanation that he didn't want to listen to. Besides, it was a problem that shrunk to insignificance when compared with the one standing right in front of him.

When Sadie had first arrived, she'd trained hard—primarily with free weights and intense interval sessions on the treadmill. She'd seemed dedicated to her fitness level—for good reason in her line of work—but also used the time to blank out whatever the hell it was that went on in that beautiful head of hers.

Now, though, there were no more heavy dead lifts or steep sprints. To the degree she exercised at all, it was just a few graceful yoga moves in Claudia's stylish athleisure wear. Occasionally, when performing a gymnastic act that Claudia would be completely incapable of, her eyes would harden behind the brown contacts obscuring them. Those glimpses of the real Sadie Hansen, though, were becoming more fleeting.

Today she wasn't there to exercise, but instead to feed the newest addition to their misfit household—a collection of white mice contained in individual wire cages. He noted that each hair in her ponytail seemed to have been groomed individually, and that she was wearing a well-coordinated collection of Claudia's gardening clothes. Somehow she made the ensemble look more like a new fashion trend than something one would wear to mow the lawn.

He stared at her from behind for a while, but when she looked like she was about to finish, he jumped back on the bar. Any excuse to keep their interactions to a minimum.

Not that he was doing a particularly good job of it. The night before, she'd come out of the bathroom and sat naked in front of him on the bed. Instead of making a pass, she'd stared at him with Claudia's eyes and apologized for going to the store without telling him. From his position on the sofa, he'd done the same—saying that he was sorry for "overreacting," and chalking it up to how important she was to both him and Anna. At that, she'd stood, kissed him gently on the forehead, and slipped beneath the covers.

So now, instead of tolerating her mental problems, he was feeding them. But what choice did he have? Legion was still out there and the wheels were falling off this operation at an ever-increasing rate. The more Sadie transformed into Claudia, the more afraid Bebe became of her. To the point that she'd actually cut back on her relentless cleaning in favor of sequestering herself in her room.

And they weren't the only problem. A critical skill for staying alive in this business was being able to honestly evaluate your own psychological condition. His was deteriorating. He was cooped up here with no idea when or from what direction Legion was going to attack and trying to manage two teammates who were far from the squared-away operators who normally backed him up. He occasionally found himself lying awake at night, fantasizing about Legion succeeding. With Sadie dead, the job would be done and he, Claudia, and Anna could disappear into a new life and identity. Obviously, the Cook issue would still be hanging out there, but he'd burn that bridge when he got to it.

How twisted was that? While Sadie might not care much about whether she lived or died, he had an obligation to every member of his team. Crazy or not, Sadie was his responsibility. Why was he having to remind himself of that? He'd always worried about his body going, but maybe that wasn't the problem. Maybe he was getting soft in the head.

Rapp dropped off the bar, turning reluctantly. The afternoon feeding was done and Sadie was looking right at him.

"You seem lost in thought, Mitch."

"Do I?"

She nodded. "What about?"

"My back," he lied.

At first, his imaginary bad back had been a joke that they'd both more or less been in on—a way to clarify that their relationship was all business without putting too fine a point on it. Now, though, it had taken its place in the alternate reality they were spinning.

"Still bothering you?"

"Yeah. I've been laying off it, but I think it's getting worse."

"You should let me rub it for you."

"Thanks, but it's a disk. Won't help. If it doesn't get better soon, I might try a cycle of prednisone. But that's a last resort. I've popped way too many of those in my lifetime."

He reached for the bar and made a show of using it to stretch his spine. She walked behind him and wrapped her arms around his stomach, leaning a cheek against his back. He'd been ready for it and managed not to stiffen.

"You're not as young as you used to be, Mitch. But you always bounce back. Once all this is over, you can finish getting in shape and do your big race. Anna can't wait to stand by the side of the trail and cheer you on. Who knows, maybe one day you two will do it together."

The phone he'd left on his workbench began to ring and she released him so he could pick up.

"Hello?" he said and then mouthed "Irene" as Sadie continued to stare enigmatically at him.

She broke into a smile and mouthed back, "Say hi."

Rapp made a beeline for the door, the sense of relief surprisingly powerful as he exited into the yard. Kennedy still hadn't said anything, though, and he thought he might have lost the connection.

"Irene? Are you there?"

"How exactly did you think that would be productive?" she said, undoubtedly referring to the little prank he'd had Joe Maslick pull.

"Not productive," Rapp said. "Just fun."

"You made the Secret Service drag him out of a public appearance. Why in God's name would you throw gas on this fire, Mitch? Particularly in your current situation."

"Too much slinking around, Irene. I don't like it. Now everyone's on the same page."

"You just basically told him the war between you is back on."

"It was never off. And not only that, he didn't come after me, he came after Claudia. I won't tolerate that kind of behavior."

"Before we had some room to maneuver. Now we have nothing."

"Maybe. But now Cook's even more scared. And he's all over TV looking like the punk we both know he is."

"Are you sure you want him this scared? Are you sure you want the president of the United States backed into a corner?"

"Yeah, Irene. I do. And you know why? Because *I'm* scared and backed into a corner. I'm afraid I've missed something that's going to get Sadie killed. I'm afraid Cook's going to grow a pair and come after you and the guys individually. I'm afraid he's going to decide his administration can deal with the blowback from vaporizing Nick's compound. And there's nothing I can do about any of that right now. But what I *can* do is make sure he feels my breath down the back of his fucking neck."

It was a long time before she responded. "Do you want to know what I see, Mitch?"

"Probably not, but I figure you're going to tell me anyway."

"I see two wounded predators eyeing each other over a dead gazelle."

"Yeah? Well, let's see who ends up getting to eat."

CHAPTER 37

NORTH OF CAPE TOWN
SOUTH AFRICA

"WE'VE continued to monitor Ahmale Okoro's communications with Anna, but we haven't been able to glean any useful information. It's likely that she's being censored. The fact that she never lets anything slip about her location seems far-fetched otherwise," Nasrin said over the encrypted line.

"IP address?" Cyrah said.

"Hidden."

She was walking along a dirt track similar to the last one, but this time with clear skies and temperatures hovering around seventeen degrees Celsius. The dry, rolling landscape was empty in every direction, making her and the car she'd parked fifty meters back the only indication of human existence. She adjusted her headset to minimize the wind noise before speaking again.

"What about Morocco?"

Claudia Gould had flown to Cape Town on a commercial flight originating in the African nation and there was no indication it was a connection. More likely, she had been hiding out there and if that was the case, it was plausible that Anna still was.

"Nothing actionable. We found a vacation rental in Marrakesh that she might have stayed in and had it searched but, as expected, there wasn't anything to be found."

"I think we have to agree that this is becoming increasingly suspicious," Yasmin interjected cautiously. "Why is the girl so well hidden if Claudia believes the attack on her was just the result of her history with Gustavo Marroqui? Clearly that problem has been solved. The separation must be difficult, and the house is set up for a long-term stay now. You yourself said the entire upper floor was undamaged."

"That's true," Cyrah admitted.

"And Claudia never leaves the compound. Not to go to her gym, shop, visit friends . . ."

"She's only been back ten days and they're busy working on plans for the renovation. Also, I suspect their friends might be a little wary of them after what just happened. This doesn't seem all that surprising to me."

"Nothing does anymore," Nasrin commented.

"I'm not getting dragged into another debate about this. And what you're saying isn't even accurate, is it? Claudia left to go to the store three days ago."

"Your single-mindedness is what makes you capable of what you do," Yasmin said, her caution growing further. "But we're concerned that it's becoming an obsession. Or worse, a frenzy. You seem to have taken the attitude that you'd rather die than fail."

"We're not going to fail," Cyrah said, feeling a spark of anger in the pit of her stomach. This was a coordinated attack. The two of them had been rehearsing it.

"Set your ego and adrenaline addiction aside for a moment," Nasrin said. "Are you completely blind to the possibility that they suspect someone—maybe even us—is hunting Claudia? That she's willing to put herself out as bait, but unwilling to endanger her daughter?"

"How would they know?" Cyrah said before she could stop herself. The statement was absurd and only went to support Nasrin's position that she'd lost her professional objectivity.

"How would they know?" came the inevitable retort. "This is one of the first risks we identified when we created our protocols. Because we have no idea who we're working for, we can't monitor if they talk too much or if they've been compromised."

"And the risk is even more inherent in this operation," Yasmin said, picking up the thought. "We have a man who is probably former CIA and who still has significant capabilities. It wouldn't be difficult for Claudia to put together a list of her surviving enemies and for him to find them."

Cyrah turned back toward her vehicle. "Can I assume it wouldn't be difficult for you to generate that same list?"

"It would not," Nasrin said.

"Can I further assume that you've done it?"

"We have."

"And?"

"Two of the people on it have died in the past two and a half weeks."

"Details?" Cyrah said.

"Josef Svoboda, who you're familiar with, died apparently of erotic asphyxiation."

"The surprising thing there is that it didn't happen sooner."

"And Enzo Ruiz purportedly died of a heart attack."

"Who is that?"

"A former Spanish drug smuggler."

"Was he at risk for a heart attack?"

There was a long pause before Nasrin answered. "He was in his nineties and in a wheelchair."

Cyrah laughed. "Nineties?"

"I'm not sure what you're laughing about," Nasrin shot back. "Including Marroqui, *three* of Claudia Gould's former enemies have died over an improbably short period of time. Are you really willing to ignore that?"

"Yes," Cyrah said simply. "I acknowledge the possibility you're right but if we walk away from this, it's the end for us. I agree that we need to be even more cautious than usual, but I'm not ready to be done. I suppose that the question now is whether I continue on my own or whether I continue with your support."

"That isn't the question," Yasmin said. "Of course you have our support."

"We're not in danger," Nasrin said. "Only you are. And, as you say, if we pull out, you'll continue—something we believe will end with you either dead or captured. And if not, it's only a short delay in your sprint toward the inevitable."

"Very poetic."

"You're our sister and we don't want harm to come to you—self-inflicted or otherwise," Yasmin said. "But you need to understand that if we manage to bring this operation to a successful conclusion, the two of us will be exercising more discretion about what jobs we take going forward."

Cyrah decided to ignore the threat. "*Can* we bring it to a successful conclusion?"

Nasrin's sigh was audible even over the hiss of the strengthening breeze. "We may have found a way."

"Explain."

"There are no predictable deliveries to the house—just sporadic drop-offs of what appear to be construction materials from a wide variety of sources. An architect has been engaged, but all their communications thus far are electronic. Physical drawings and meetings about these kinds of things aren't as frequent as they once were."

"But?" Cyrah said. She was passing her car for the second time in their conversation and didn't want to stay out there for any longer than necessary.

"The key may be in their diet. Based on what's being purchased at the grocery store, it doesn't vary at all."

"How can we use that?"

"The opportunity is with the servant," Yasmin said. "She's extremely compulsive in her behavior, which makes her predictable in all things. What we're interested in, though, is one narrow facet of that compulsiveness. Specifically, how she selects romaine lettuce."

CHAPTER 38

FRANSCHHOEK
SOUTH AFRICA

BEBE Kincaid committed to one more loop of the parking lot. Despite the fact that the store wasn't particularly busy, someone had taken her customary space along the eastern edge. How long would the vile parking space thief be inside? Maybe they were just getting something quick. Should she wait? Keep driving around until . . .

One, two, three, it doesn't matter. Four, five, six, it's just a parking lot.

She backed into a space that provided just as good a view of the area and pretended to look at her phone as she scanned through the windshield. There were a few customers visible, only one of whom she'd seen before—an old woman with a cane that seemed to cause more problems than it solved.

The American surveillance team had kept tabs on her for a little over a week, but now seemed to have lost interest. And why wouldn't they? No one in this world knew or cared that she existed. No one but Mitch, Claudia, Scott, and his men.

In her younger years, she had been the FBI's most valued surveillance asset. Later, as her mental state deteriorated, she'd become a liability. Her husband—a wonderful man—had finally been forced to leave as she began to combat her issues with ever-more-compulsive behavior. Her friends had drifted away for the same reason. Finally, the Bureau had forced her into early retirement. If Mitch Rapp hadn't offered her the job with Coleman's company, she didn't know what she would have done.

After three deep breaths, Bebe finally stepped out of the vehicle and started toward the store. After selecting a cart, she pretended to browse the vegetable department, but really focused on the people around her. Whoever Legion were, they were good. Anyone she'd seen more than once on her journeys outside the walls had been confirmed as a longtime local or tourist with a background that checked out.

She used her customary dispenser to get a plastic glove but was forced to pause on her way to the romaine lettuce. A young woman she'd never seen before was standing in front of the display. Probably early thirties, Middle Eastern descent, pretty in a pixyish kind of way. Bebe filed her face away—she was incapable of doing otherwise—and waited for her to move on before approaching the display.

She used her gloved hand to pick through what turned out to be an extremely disappointing selection. The situation took a turn for the better when she dug down a layer and spotted some crisp leaves peeking through. A moment later, she was holding a head blessed with beautiful sheen and graced by leaves that undulated in uniform waves along their length. After easing it into a bag, she started in the direction of the meat counter.

CHAPTER 39

NEAR FRANSCHHOEK
SOUTH AFRICA

BEBE Kincaid paced in front of the gate, her sneakers barely making a sound against the flagstones. She was sweating profusely despite the cold temperatures and her lack of a jacket. The house behind her was completely dark, adhering to Rapp's blackout protocols and forcing her to count on the starlight to keep her from tripping.

She was counting silently to herself, trying to quiet her mind. At 2,312, it still hadn't done the job. She felt terrified and alone. The first sensation was well justified, but the second probably less so. Legion was out there. Waiting. Maybe in the vines. Maybe just on the other side of the wall.

A motor became audible in the distance, and she looked down at the security camera feed on her phone. Nothing for a few seconds and then the glare of headlights followed by the vague outline of an ambulance. They tended not to run their emergency lights in an effort to not attract attention. And at this time of night, there was little traffic to contend with anyway.

Bebe swiped to another app and used it to open the gate. A few moments later, she waved the vehicle inside and jogged along behind as it went for the front door.

"What's happening?" the woman who stepped from the passenger side asked. She was in her early forties, with dusty blond hair and a heavy South African accent. Based on a thorough investigation of the paramedics serving the area, Bebe immediately recognized her as Aileen De Jager. Originally from Durban, she'd been on the job for more than a decade.

"They're upstairs," Bebe said. "Both of them are really sick. You have to hurry."

The driver jumped out and went straight to the back of the ambulance. His profile flashed in the light bouncing off the house, allowing Bebe to identify him as Gatik Patel—an eight-year veteran. She managed to relax just a bit. Not Legion. Not yet.

They were both extremely professional, getting the gurney up the stairs without even bumping a wall and then following Bebe into the master bedroom. The acrid smell of vomit preceded their entry, but neither seemed to notice. They headed straight for Sadie, who was sprawled motionless on the bed in a stained sleepshirt. Rapp was still moving, dry-heaving over the toilet clad only in sweatpants. Beneath a patchwork of scars, his sharply defined muscles contracted a few more times before he finally slid to the floor.

"Let's get him first," De Jager said, pointing to the bathroom. "Then we can come back for the woman."

The quiet ping brought Cyrah Jafari fully awake. She retrieved a cell phone from the nightstand and looked down at a three-letter text onscreen. A paradoxical mix of excitement and calm overtook her, and she savored it as she walked barefoot to the kitchen. The endgame was finally in play.

She took the SIM card out of the phone and put it in the microwave. Dull sparks lit up the room as she wrapped the handset in a dish towel and smashed it with a kitchen hammer. When the level of destruction was satisfactory, she retrieved another phone, loaded another SIM, and turned it on.

A proprietary app streamed video time-stamped seventeen minutes ago. It had been taken by a drone operated by Nasrin from some unknown location—likely the other side of the world.

An ambulance was visible in the glare of its lights splashing against a whitewashed Cape Dutch house. The front door was open, but the angle made it impossible to see inside. She fast-forwarded to a moment when two paramedics rolled a gurney onto the porch. Mitch Burhan was motionless on it, his bearded face the only thing extending beyond the sheet covering him. He was slipped efficiently into the back of the vehicle before the two responders grabbed a stretcher and headed back inside.

When they reappeared again, it was with Claudia Gould. She appeared to be in equally bad shape, the lower half of her face darkened by what was presumably vomit. Cyrah's lips curved into a smile that faltered when Bebe Davis appeared. She looked completely healthy as she began a frantic, hand-waving exchange with the female paramedic. Finally, she retreated inside and the ambulance headed toward the open gate.

It had worked. Her instructors would have undoubtedly praised Allah at this moment, but she praised her team. The lettuce had been laced with a substance that mimicked the symptoms of food poisoning and it had done its work on their primary targets. The hope had been that Davis would also be affected but the possibility that she ate separately from her masters was something they'd considered. Inconvenient, but hardly devastating.

The older woman appeared on the porch again, now wearing a coat and proceeding to Claudia's SUV at a waddling jog. A moment later, she was through the gate and accelerating in pursuit of the ambulance.

Cyrah shut down the phone and pulled the SIM card, repeating her worn-in destruction ritual. When finished, she went back into her room and pulled a series of large plastic bags from beneath the bed. Each was scrawled with three letters, and she selected the one that corresponded to the text she'd received. They represented the hospital that would be the ambulance's destination and inside were the appropriate scrubs and IDs, as well as a clipboard containing documents with the correct letterhead.

She dressed and then rolled down her waistband, using tape to secure a ceramic knife that would be invisible to metal detectors. In the kitchen, she unlocked a small medical-grade refrigerator and retrieved a syringe contained in a slimline plastic case. After taping it in a similar position on the other side of her abdomen, she put on a long coat and headed for the door.

Cyrah waited in the hospital's parking lot until two ambulances arrived simultaneously and entered through the glass doors in the ensuing chaos. Navigation to the information desk was done with the help of a schematic she'd memorized.

"What can I do for you?" the woman behind it said amiably. She seemed uninterested in Cyrah's identification badge or the fact that most of her face was covered by a surgical mask.

"I'm looking for Mitch Burhan," she said. "He was admitted around three a.m."

The woman turned to her computer screen, needing only a few seconds to retrieve the data. "Suspected food poisoning. Tests have been done, but it looks like they're still waiting for results. Room four twenty-eight."

Cyrah flipped a page on her clipboard. "It says he came in with a Claudia Dufort. Similar condition."

The woman moved her mouse around on the pad next to her. "Right. Dufort. She's here, but no labs on her yet, either."

"Are they in the same room?"

"No. She's in four thirty-two."

Cyrah smiled warmly through her mask. "Thanks."

• • •

The elevator let her out on the fourth floor, and she took a left, passing another information desk as well as a small waiting room. Scanning lazily across it, she searched for any sign of Bebe Davis. Nothing. It seemed unlikely that she'd be in the room with Claudia, but it wasn't impossible. The question was what to do if she was. Come back later or ask her to leave and move forward with the operation? Normally, the former would be the obvious strategy, but with the compulsive behavior the woman demonstrated, it was possible she'd stay by Gould's bed until she was released.

When Cyrah turned the next corner, her question was answered. Davis was standing at the far end of the passage talking on her phone. She glanced up from the screen, fixing on Cyrah for a moment, and then started in her direction. They nodded absently at one another as they passed and then the American woman disappeared down another hallway.

It was a closer brush than Cyrah would have liked, but hardly worth worrying about. The only time Davis had seen her was the day she'd planted the tainted head of lettuce at the grocery store. And then, only in profile and only for a few seconds. It was unlikely the woman would remember her under the best of circumstances, but with protective glasses, a mask, and a bandana to cover her hair, it would be impossible.

Room 432 was easily found, and Cyrah peered through the glass portal set into the door. The lights inside were off, but there was just enough illumination to see. Claudia Gould was lying on the only bed in the room, elevated into a partially seated position with an IV running into her left arm. The gurney she'd presumably been brought in on was still in the corner. Probably because it was covered in various bodily fluids and would need cleaning before being put back into use.

Satisfied by what she saw, Cyrah pushed through the door and closed it behind her before retrieving the syringe from her waistband. She'd prefer to do this in darkness, but it didn't fit with the role she was playing. A nurse checking on a patient would do so with the overheads lit.

She located the switch and flipped it, but nothing happened.

Her hesitation lasted probably less than a tenth of a second, but it was enough time to remember her arrogance. Her dismissiveness when her sisters raised their concerns about this mission. Her thirst for excitement and success.

She started to spin and was unsurprised when a hand clamped around her wrist. She dropped her clipboard and went for the knife taped to her stomach but then felt the bite of something penetrating her thigh.

An arm wrapped around her, powerful enough to make it hard to breathe, but she still managed to get her fingers around the blade. They'd already gone numb, though, and she could feel her legs melting beneath her. An overwhelming sensation of warmth and weightlessness was the last thing she remembered.

Rapp lowered the woman to the ground and picked up the knife and syringe she'd dropped. By the time he'd stashed them in the pocket of his paramedic uniform, Sadie was out of bed and out of her hospital gown. She threw it and it hit him in the back of the head, hanging around his shoulders as he stripped the unconscious woman on the floor.

He almost had the gown on her when Sadie, dressed in a matching paramedic uniform, wheeled the gurney up. They lifted the woman onto it and pulled a sheet up to her neck.

"My god," Sadie said, looking into her serene face. "She's so . . . cute."

Not a particularly relevant observation, but undeniably accurate. Iranian if Rapp had to guess—a nationality that fit pretty well with the profile they'd worked up. Other than that, all he could say for sure was that she was in her thirties and had a thin, athletic build that made her heavier than she looked. Not someone you'd take for one of the most successful killers of her generation. More like the new kindergarten teacher who got all the husbands to suddenly take interest in student conferences.

Rapp shoved her clothes and the clipboard she'd been carrying under the sheet and then hung another from the side of the gurney. It contained the appropriate hospital transfer paperwork in the unlikely event someone stopped them.

"Ready?"

Sadie nodded and he confirmed that the corridor was clear before they wheeled the gurney out. At a natural pace, it took them about a minute to make the elevator and another five to reach the rear exit. An ambulance was waiting, and they put the woman in the back with Sadie climbing in behind.

CHAPTER 40

CYRAH Jafari opened her eyes to a gloom that for a moment made her think she was still at the hospital. As her surroundings and memories sharpened, though, it became clear that wasn't the case. With her strength beginning to return, she tried to get into a sitting position but failed.

Letting her head loll to the left, she saw that her arm was straight, secured at a right angle to her body by tape wound around her biceps, forearm, and wrist. A moment later, she confirmed that her right arm had suffered the same fate. An attempt to move her bare feet from what felt like rough-hewn planks produced nothing beyond the sensation of something cutting into her ankles.

She returned her head to a neutral position and stared at the dark ceiling. A metal bar bisected her view, confusing her for a moment but then providing the clue she'd been searching for. A weight bench. She was secured to a weight bench.

In some distant land, Nasrin would be shaking her head angrily. In another, Yasmin would be quietly sobbing. Cyrah had always known she wasn't destined to die of old age, but she'd hoped to celebrate her fortieth birthday. Why that particular milestone? She had no idea. It was just lodged in her mind for some reason.

Fully conscious now, she lifted her head as far as she could, looking down her naked body and beyond. What little illumination existed in the room was thanks to slivers of sunlight finding their way through a set of double doors. There was a workbench to her left and the tools it contained—some unrecognizable—didn't bode well for her. She'd been thoroughly trained in what it was like to be interrogated, but there were limits to what even her former commander could do. Whoever was responsible for securing her there had no such limits. And in the end, there would be no revenge like last time. Only a very welcome death.

She closed her eyes and tried to think. The bench was made of heavy steel and felt like it was anchored to the floor. Her ankles were secured tightly—almost certainly with zip ties. The tape holding her arms in multiple places was thick and black. Probably the Gorilla brand that she herself favored for its stickiness and strength. Nothing sharp anywhere near her and even if there was, she couldn't move much more than her head.

With no real hope of escape, she went back to studying what could optimistically be referred to as her operating environment. A pink bicycle with colorful streamers coming from the handlebars immediately captured her attention because it seemed so out of place. After a moment's thought, though, she realized that it was Anna's. This was the outbuilding next to Claudia Gould's house.

With nothing else to see, Cyrah closed her eyes. When she was a child, she'd had a similar, if somewhat more dilapidated, bicycle her uncle had bought her. She'd loved the sense of freedom it had given her and remembered how resentful she'd been when her father had finally taken it from her. When she'd finally become old enough that such freedoms were forbidden.

No matter what happened in the coming days—or even weeks—she had few regrets. She'd risen above what the men in her country had imposed on her. She'd freely chosen this path and the responsibility was hers and hers alone.

Cyrah didn't know how long she lay there, but by the time the door opened and the overhead lights came on, her teeth were on the verge of chattering. She felt the warmth flow in with the sun, focusing on how it felt against her skin and glowed beyond her closed eyelids. A memory to turn to while she was enduring what was to come.

"I know you're awake." A male voice. Two sets of footfalls, though. She listened to what sounded like him pulling a chair up next to her. Something was placed on her stomach just below her navel, but she didn't know what. Small. Light. Maybe plastic. Some kind of torture device? She'd soon find out.

"Open your eyes."

With no compelling reason not to, she obeyed. Mitch Burhan was leaning over her, perched in a folding chair that had been leaned against the wall. Work jeans and an old T-shirt emblazoned with the word *Specialized* instead of the expected leather apron and rubber gloves. He looked up and down her body with a somewhat enigmatic frown. Not angry or sadistic. If she had to describe it, she'd say it carried a deep sense of irritation.

Claudia was visible over his shoulder. She was leaning against the workbench twirling a screwdriver deftly in her left hand. Her expression was even more enigmatic and unexpected. Dead, but with a gleam in her eye that suggested . . . lust. For what? Her? Blood? Both? It was then that she realized something else. Claudia Gould was right-handed.

Cyrah returned her gaze to the ceiling, now blazing with LED light. The man hovering over her seemed to read her mind and answered the question consuming it.

"She's in Uganda with Anna."

He leaned back and crossed his legs, bringing a black cowboy boot into Cyrah's field of vision. "Now, why don't you tell me about yourself?"

She'd been taught to remain silent during questioning. Anything she said would be used against her by the people on the other side. The ones still capable of coherent thought. The ones who weren't suffering.

"I don't like interrogations," he said when she didn't answer. "Don't make me turn this into one."

The woman at the back suddenly raised a hand as though she were a schoolgirl trying to get her teacher's attention. "I'll work on her."

The accent was British, not French.

Burhan twisted around and glared at her. She lowered her hand and went back to twirling the tool. When he faced forward again, his irritation had deepened and Cyrah's calm had started to crack. If they were playing good cop/bad cop, they were doing an excellent job of it. After hearing only a few words, she was entirely focused on not being left alone with that woman.

"My name is Cyrah Jafari."

There was no reason not to speak, she reminded herself. This wasn't for God or country. It wasn't even for her sisters, who were in no danger from anything she could say. Her silence was nothing but a vestige of her training. And pride.

"Iranian?"

"Yes. I was part of a special unit that trained women to infiltrate Israel."

"But you decided to bug out and go private."

"The program was shut down by the new administration. My commander, after teaching me one last lesson, decided my place was in the typing pool."

"I'll bet the typing pool sounds pretty good right now."

"No," she said after a few seconds' thought. "It still doesn't."

He folded his arms and stared down at her for probably thirty seconds. "I have to hand it to you. If there was a magazine called *Leafy Greens Monthly,* that head of lettuce would be a centerfold."

"Thank you. I trimmed it by hand. The secret, though, is in the wax. That's what gives it the satiny appearance under the lights. My compliments on making your servant's compulsions seem so real."

"No, she's really like that. You have no idea how many ways a silverware drawer can be arranged."

Cyrah smiled sadly and he reached over, tapping the thing on her stomach.

"What's in here?"

She lifted her head and saw the syringe that had been destined for Claudia. "*E. coli* bacteria along with a heavy dose of the toxin they produce."

"Isn't that what was on the lettuce?"

"No. Too unpredictable. That was a non-lethal synthetic poison I mixed with the wax so it couldn't be washed off. Undetectable by normal methods and it tends to act within a very narrow time frame. We did put bacteria on various other heads of lettuce from that supplier, though. You'll start to see people in the area fall ill over the next few days, but not fatally. It would have covered Claudia's death."

"Very thorough."

"Thank you. May I ask how you knew?"

"We don't eat anything Bebe buys from the store. Our food came in on one of the early construction supply trucks." He pointed and she managed to crane her neck far enough to see a set of mouse cages.

"We've been testing everything she brings in. None of the mice would touch that lettuce. The food poisoning angle seemed obvious at that point."

"Yes," Cyrah responded quietly. "I suppose so. Obvious."

"But you didn't do all this yourself."

"No."

"How many more?"

"Two."

"Names?"

"Nasrin Pour and Yasmin Housseini."

"Where are they?"

"I have no idea."

He took the syringe from her abdomen and turned it thoughtfully in his hands. "That's the wrong answer."

"But you know it's the truth. Our operation is built entirely on secrecy. I never know where they are. And now that I haven't checked in, they've run."

"But you have a way of reconnecting with them."

"Of course. But again, they'd never reveal their locations to me. In any event, they're no threat to you. Even if they were to decide that they want revenge—which they have no reason to—they aren't operators. They're analysts. If you have contacts in Iranian intelligence, you can confirm this."

He started playing with the syringe again and she knew what he was thinking. That she would have a way to warn them if he forced her to initiate contact. And, of course, he was right.

Finally, he twisted around and looked at the woman by the workbench again. "Brunch?"

Rapp exited through the kitchen door with both a nice meal and some time to think under his belt. The thrill of the operation, combined with having Cyrah Jafari taped naked to a weight bench, had been enough to drag Sadie back into reality. He'd thought his problems with her were more or less solved until the act of preparing food kicked her right back into Claudia mode. Her desire to go medieval on the Iranian had now been overpowered by her desire to create a celebratory meal fit for a French king. Bebe, who was back from returning the ambulance, had closed herself up in her room again. Probably sitting on the edge of her bed with bags packed.

Rapp opened the door to the shed and snapped on the lights again. The woman didn't react at all and he stopped at the base of the weight bench, looking down at her. She stared defiantly into the bright light, teeth chattering and skin covered in goose bumps. He couldn't help being intrigued by what he saw. She was tough, well trained, and extraordinarily creative. But the main thing he got from her was drive. This was a woman who knew what she wanted out of life and was either going to get it or die trying.

"What happened to the guy who taught you that last lesson and put you in the typing pool?"

"I cut off his genitals and choked him to death with them."

"Harsh."

"We had history."

He grabbed a paint-spattered drop cloth and threw it over her before sitting again.

"So, what now, Cyrah?"

"I'd be grateful if you just killed me. Everything I've told you is the truth and I don't know any more."

"You wouldn't rather I just let you go?"

"That's not possible. You suspect that I'd just try to finish what I started. Legion is built on success. A single failure would cause it to collapse."

"Because the person who took out the contract would spread around that you'd run off with his money and not done the job."

"Yes."

"You were hired by a man named Enzo Ruiz. I met with him about it a few weeks ago and I can guarantee that he isn't going to talk to anyone about you or anything else."

"Still, you have no reason to release me. It's all risk and no reward. Why are you toying with me? You don't seem like the type, and you know full well that none of this was personal. If you want something from me, tell me what it is. If you don't, then a quick death isn't too much to ask for."

He grinned. "It isn't?"

"No. It isn't."

"What if instead of me killing you, we were to talk about a job."

"I don't understand."

"I have someone I'd like dead, but I'm not really in a position to do the work myself. It occurs to me that we could both come out on top here."

"You're saying that if I take a contract, you'll just let me go?"

"Yes."

"Then I accept."

"Not so fast. You haven't heard the target."

"Does it matter?"

"It might."

"Who then?"

"Anthony Cook."

"The president of the United States?"

"So, you've heard of him."

Her brow furrowed in exactly the way he'd hoped. It was an expression he'd seen many times before. Hell, he'd seen it in the mirror. She was calculating. Trying to figure out if she could pull it off. When she spoke again, it was as though she'd completely forgotten she was taped to a weight bench.

"I don't follow politics, but it seems like I've read he's cut back on his personal appearances and increased his security. Because of some ISIS threat, if I remember right. They caught one of the men involved, no?"

"All fabricated. It's really me he's afraid of."

"That's why you have an American team watching you."

"Me and my people. The minute any of us drop off the radar, they stuff Cook in a bunker and surround him with a hundred Secret Service guys."

"It's something I'd consider. But I can't speak for Nasrin and Yasmin."

"How bad do they want to keep you alive?"

"I honestly don't know."

"Terms?"

She didn't hesitate. "Five million euros up front, another five when the job's done."

"I thought your fee was two million?"

"This is a different kind of job with different secrecy protocols. More risk to me and likely extremely costly. We cover our expenses from our fee."

"Still, ten million seems steep. I assume that comes with a guarantee?"

"I won't take another job until this one's done or I'm dead. That's the best I can do."

"And you'll do it in a way that won't blow back against me."

"Absolutely. Against either of us."

"One last question."

"Okay."

"Did you once kill a guy by getting his own cows to trample him?"

"Yes."

He nodded appreciatively and pulled her cell phone from his pocket. "What do you say we find out if your friends are taking your calls?"

CHAPTER 41

RAPP backed the SUV through the outbuilding's bay doors and then got out to close them. Cyrah was sitting at his workbench wearing a loose-fitting skirt and sweater. Most of her head was hidden by a knit hat topped with a white pompom that flopped back and forth as she devoured a ham and cheese croissant. A pair of Claudia's sunglasses would eventually complete the ensemble, but for now they were lying next to her plate.

When she was done eating, he'd drive her to Cape Town and drop her somewhere out of sight of the American surveillance team. After that, it would be time to get rid of the other two women in his life. One of Nicholas Ward's private jets was on its way to a remote strip three hours to the north and it would take both back to the United States—Bebe to the relative calm of her life in Maryland and Sadie to New York and whatever the hell it was she did there.

He couldn't fight off a smile at the thought of never laying eyes on Sadie Hansen again. While there was no question that he wouldn't have been able to pull this off without her, enough was enough. He wanted her out of his house, out of South Africa, and out of his hemisphere.

"So, you're really just going to let me go?" Cyrah said through a half-full mouth.

He thumbed toward the SUV. "Your chariot awaits."

She spun around on the stool, examining him for a moment. "Can I ask you a question?"

"Sure."

"What's your real name?"

"What's it matter as long as my check clears?"

She didn't seem inclined to let the subject go that easily. "I don't normally start my client relationships this way."

"Taped to a weight bench?"

"I was referring to the fact that you know who I am. It seems like that should go both ways."

"I disagree."

"You know my identity, Mitch. You know the identities of my team. And you have a way of making contact. It puts us in significant danger. If you were to make a mistake, we could be exposed. If you get into trouble, you could use us as a bargaining chip with the authorities."

"How does my name change any of that?"

She slid off the stool, testing her balance in an overly large pair of Claudia's boots. "You defeated a ten-man hit squad here. You managed to find Gustavo Marroqui—something no one has been able to do—and use what appears to be a military weapon to kill him. Then you were able to capture me. Finally, you've made a personal enemy of the president of the United States. Not very many people fit that profile."

"Do you have a point?"

"Is your real last name Rapp? Because if it is, it would make me more comfortable. Mitch Rapp isn't in the business of making mistakes. And he would never give us up."

There was an undercurrent of excitement in her voice. Barely perceptible, but undoubtedly there. She was dying to take out the president of the United States. And why not? If she pulled it off in her normal anonymous way, it would be hard to argue against her being the best private contractor in history. A status she appeared to really, really want.

The positive side of that was that he trusted her to actually take on the job as opposed to disappearing with his down payment. The women she referred to as her sisters had been more reticent—*pissed* might be a better word—but also more anxious to keep Cyrah alive than she'd expected. The three of them had been through a lot together and they didn't want her to end up under Claudia's bougainvillea.

To the negative, it wasn't going to be a quick operation and he was going to have to disappear for it. Cook would be getting reports about what was happening, and it wouldn't take him and his lapdog Darren Hargrave long to figure out that Legion had been neutralized. When they did, they'd come after him with everything they had.

He opened the gate to the SUV and pointed. "Let's just say I'm taking the Fifth on the subject."

"Dinner's going to be a little late," Sadie said when he entered the kitchen two hours later. "I was having problems with the oven again. I think the upper heating element might have gotten nicked by a bullet."

She was wearing Claudia's apron, holding her chef's knife, and speaking with her accent again. Pots and pans were strewn everywhere, and the air was heavy with something that admittedly smelled pretty good.

"It can't be too late," Rapp said. "I don't want to leave that plane on the tarmac for any longer than I have to. We need to be out of here inside a couple hours. Are you packed?"

"Are we going to get Anna?" she said, sounding confused.

Rapp kept his expression impassive but behind it he was starting to worry. Letting her back in the kitchen had been a mistake.

"No, back home," he said finally.

Her confusion deepened. "To Virginia?"

"No, Sadie. You're going back to New York."

She stepped back, a combination of shock and betrayal crossing her unlined face. “Are you blaming me for this, Mitch? Because you knew I had enemies before we got together. And it’s not like you don’t have the same. If anything, Anna and I are the ones taking a risk being around *you*.”

Rapp just stood there, unsure what to do.

“I deposited half a million dollars in your Swiss account,” he said, realizing too late how off point the statement sounded. In retrospect, sleeping through abnormal psych in college hadn’t been one of his best moves.

“Swiss account? What are you talking about?”

“Sadie, I really appreciate you coming here and *pretending* to be Claudia. It was dangerous as hell, but you pulled it off. We caught Legion and now you can get back to your life.”

“So, let me get this straight. You’re not just leaving me. You’re kicking me out?” Her voice rose to a scream. “Of my own house? This is *my* home, Mitch! Mine and Anna’s. Not yours. If you want to go back to Virginia, do it. We don’t need you. We *never* needed you.”

He took a hesitant step forward. “Sadie, listen to me. This isn’t your home. Anna isn’t your daughter. You have a life in New—”

After everything he’d seen over the course of his lifetime, it wasn’t easy to surprise him. But she managed to do just that when she charged. He didn’t want to inflict damage, but an angry Sadie Hansen with a chef’s knife was not a situation to be taken lightly.

But she didn’t come at him as Sadie Hansen. She came at him as Claudia Gould. Slow, straight on, with the blade held high overhead. He grabbed her wrist, spun her around, and brought her hand up behind her back. Not sure what else to do, he clenched a fist and hit her in the back of the head about half force. Her knees crumpled and he lowered her to the floor before kicking the knife away. Behind him, he heard the creak of the kitchen door.

“I told you so,” Bebe Kincaid said.

“That’s really helpful, Bebe. Thanks. Now go out to the shed and find me a roll of duct tape.”

• • •

The sound of muffled squeals and thrashing coming from the SUV's cargo area increased as Rapp slowed. His headlights washed over a line of scrubby trees and then illuminated the turn he was looking for. Just a few more minutes and it'd all be over.

The gravel road climbed steadily, finally dead-ending into an airstrip with a new Gulfstream G700 on it. Through the windscreen, he saw one of the pilots stand and disappear into the back. By the time Rapp pulled up next to the aircraft, the man had the door open and was coming down the stairs.

"Do you have any luggage, sir?" he asked as Rapp got out and went around to the back of the vehicle.

"Not exactly," he said, opening the tailgate. The pilot's eyes widened when he saw the cargo, but he managed not to comment. The fact that Sadie was liberally wound with duct tape didn't prevent her from attempting to kick Rapp in the groin as he tried to get hold of her. It took some effort, but he finally managed to get her over his shoulder and carry her to the plane.

Once inside, he dumped her in a seat and fastened the seat belt over her lap. She continued to thrash, rocking back and forth in an attempt to escape and tear his throat out. Bebe had opted to skip the private jet ride in favor of a cab to the airport. It was hard to blame her.

Sadie's left contact lens had fallen out and she was staring up at him with one ice-blue eye and one softer brown one. Her hair was stuck haphazardly across her sweating face, and a thin line of snot was running down the silver tape over her mouth. It was hard to ignore the *Silence of the Lambs* vibe.

"I'm sorry it ended like this," Rapp said sincerely. The sound of his voice seemed to calm her a bit. Or maybe she was just getting tired. "You put yourself on the line for me and I won't forget it."

Another dangerous debt, he reflected as he turned toward the pilots standing near the cockpit.

"Under no circumstances are you to let her loose on this plane," he said, handing one of them a box cutter. "When you get to the airstrip in New York, drag her onto the tarmac and leave her the knife. Then immediately take off. Understood?"

They nodded numbly.

"That's not's good enough," Rapp said. "Listen to me. She's going to fight. And probably cry. And if you take the tape off her mouth—which I recommend against—she's going to tell you she has to take a piss or that she's having chest pains or something. But what are you *not* going to do?"

"Let her go," one of them said after a long pause.

"But . . ." the other one stammered. "This is a long flight, sir. She probably really *will* have to use the bathroom."

"A little wet leather isn't going to be the end of the world. What will be, though, is her free in a small aircraft over the ocean. Particularly if she gets her hands on that box cutter. So, I'm asking you again. Am I understood?"

This time their nods were a bit more energetic.

"I didn't hear you."

"We understand, sir."

"Then have a good flight."

He escaped through the open door and instead of going back to the SUV, walked a hundred yards down the dirt road. The stars were a blanket above and a cold wind cut through his sweatshirt like it wasn't there. Still, he didn't move again until the jet's wheels left the ground.

CHAPTER 42

THE WHITE HOUSE
WASHINGTON, DC
USA

THE fact that Darren Hargrave had been directed to the Oval Office suggested he wasn't going to get the one-on-one audience with the president that he'd requested. After a quick knock on the door, he passed through and confirmed that suspicion.

Anthony was sitting behind his desk and his wife had taken one of the two chairs in front. Hargrave had managed to wrestle a significant amount of power away from her, but nowhere near enough. Particularly now that he had no choice but to hand her a weapon. The question was, how much strength did she have left to wield it?

"What's so important that it couldn't wait for morning?" Cook said, neither standing nor offering him a seat.

"I have information on Mitch Rapp and Legion."

Far too much information, in fact. He'd spent the drive there trying to find some way to spin the situation in his favor. Unfortunately, the more he thought about it, the more disastrous it became.

"Is Claudia Gould dead?" Catherine asked.

"No," Hargrave responded, digging a series of eight-by-ten photos from his portfolio. "But we believe that Legion made an attempt on her."

"And?" Cook said.

"It appears to have failed."

Catherine was staring at him from her position to his right and he was pretty sure the bitch was smiling. Just a hint at the corners of her mouth.

He put one stack on the president's desk and reluctantly gave another to the first lady. She didn't seem to have much interest in it, though. The fact that he'd failed was all that would be important to her. Details were of no consequence.

"The first photo shows an ambulance entering Claudia Gould's property and was taken early this morning South African time. Shortly thereafter, it left for a local hospital. Both Rapp and the woman we believed to be Claudia Gould were on it. Bebe Kincaid followed shortly thereafter."

"The woman you *believed* to be Claudia Gould?" Catherine said.

"If you'll wait, I'll get to that," Hargrave said, concentrating on keeping his tone even.

"I look forward to it."

"They were both admitted to the hospital with suspected food poisoning. Not long after, they disappeared, and another ambulance arrived at their house. It reversed up to the outbuilding where Rapp keeps his exercise equipment and was there for less than five minutes before being returned to the hospital by Kincaid. Rapp and the woman we believed to be Claudia Gould went to the house for about an hour and then returned to the outbuilding, where they stayed for about fifteen minutes. They then went back into the house for approximately forty-five minutes."

"Is this going to go on for much longer?" Catherine asked, her husband seemingly content to let her speak for him. "Because I'm still not hearing about the woman you *believed* to be Claudia Gould."

"Please let me finish describing the series of events and then we can discuss what's behind them."

"My apologies," she said with a hint of sarcasm. "By all means continue."

"After that, Rapp returned to the shed and stayed for about thirty minutes. Finally, he backed up to the outbuilding in his SUV, drove to a mall, parked in the underground lot, and went inside to buy a few things. After that, he went home. Bebe Kincaid took a cab to the airport and got on a commercial flight back to the US but is currently laid over in Frankfurt. Rapp drove the woman we believed to be Claudia Gould to a remote airstrip north of Cape Town. Our people weren't able to follow him all the way to the strip without being spotted, so they hung back. He was there for about fifteen minutes and then returned home. A private jet registered to one of Nicholas Ward's companies flew to an airstrip in upstate New York, where they dropped a bound woman on the tarmac."

He watched Cook flip through the photos, finally finding the one depicting a woman using a box cutter to free herself from a significant amount of duct tape.

"And this isn't Claudia?" the president said.

"No, sir. We tracked her back to an apartment in Manhattan. Her real name is Sadie Hansen. She's done various contract jobs for the CIA in the past. Obviously, she also has more than a passing resemblance to Claudia Go—"

"So, Rapp was using her to draw Legion in without putting Claudia in danger," Catherine interrupted.

"That's our conclusion."

"Did it work?" the president asked.

"We believe so. It seems likely that Legion somehow managed to get tainted food to them and then was going to finish the job at the hospital."

"But Rapp played them," Catherine said. "He captured their operative and used an ambulance to bring him back to the house for interrogation."

"That's the most logical conclusion," Hargrave admitted. "But there wouldn't be anything to learn. The way Legion operates creates a veil of secrecy that goes both ways."

"It doesn't really matter," Catherine said. "Legion is likely buried under Rapp's shed. We're now at war with a man who's no longer distracted by trying to protect his partner. What do you think, Darren? Should we dredge up another enemy from her past? One that Rapp hasn't already killed, intimidated, or recruited? Third time's the charm, right? Isn't that what they say?"

"I don't—"

"Where is Rapp now?" Cook said, cutting him off.

"On a commercial aircraft. He'll be landing at the Entebbe airport in Uganda in less than an hour."

"Can we get to him there?"

"No, sir. We don't have sufficient assets on the ground and because of everything he's done for the Ugandan government, he's extremely well protected there. If the past is any indication, he'll be escorted through passport control by the military and taken to a waiting helicopter that will then fly him to Nicholas Ward's compound."

"Where we're even less likely to be able to get to him."

"That's correct, sir."

"Then let's get a back channel going to the Ugandan president. Ward can throw a lot of money around, but he's not the United States. What does he want? Weapons? Access to world markets? Help making his political rivals disappear? There's got to be something."

"We'll start working on him, sir."

Hargrave felt a pang of desperation as Cook turned toward his wife.

"Thoughts?"

She raised an arm and pointed directly at Hargrave. "All of this was about one man. Darren. He needed Mitch Rapp to be a threat in order to push me out. To make you reliant on him. To make you love him. You've known who and what he is since we first met him. And despite that, you let him turn the tables on you. You went from being manipulator to the one being manipulated. At the first sign of a problem, you panicked. You allowed yourself to be led into an all-or-nothing scenario and you ended up with noth—"

"Manipulator?" Hargrave said. "What possible incentive do I have? All I've ever done is work to help Tony get to this place. And not for myself. For him! I don't want to be president. Can you say the same?"

"Darren . . ." the president cautioned.

"No!" he shouted back, startling both of them. Catherine thought the man might physically attack her, but her husband didn't seem to share her concern. Or he didn't care.

"If Rapp succeeds, what do you care?" Hargrave continued. "You'll be out of the White House for a few years and then you'll ride Tony's memory right back in. If he doesn't get reelected, though, you have problems, don't you? If I keep him safe inside these walls and he loses, you're done. You'll never sit behind that desk."

"Safe inside these walls?" she shot back. "If he doesn't get reelected three years from now, what happens then? He walks out the gate with a couple of token guards. He'll be lucky to make it back to California. And even if he does, what happens to you, Darren? Have you thought about that? What will you have when Tony retires to the golf course? When he has no more use for you?"

"Enough!" Cook shouted, slamming both hands down on his desk and leaping to his feet. "I want answers and I want options. From both of you." He sat again. "Now get out."

Hargrave gave a jerky nod and hurried for the door while Catherine watched. When she returned her attention to her husband, he was staring directly at her.

"I meant both of you."

CHAPTER 43

ABOVE SOUTHWESTERN UGANDA

RAPP put a jacket on but refused to retreat farther inside the chopper. He remained in his favored spot on the floor, legs hanging through the open door and taking a beating from rotor wash. To the west he could see the mountaintop that was home to Nicholas Ward's compound, but for now, he ignored it. Instead he looked toward Lake Edward and the scattered clouds beyond.

This would likely be his last visit to Uganda for a long time. Maybe forever. At this point it was hard to predict what his future held. In Washington, the shit was unquestionably hitting the fan. By now that prick Darren Hargrave would be offering the president of Uganda economic aid, cutting-edge military equipment, and maybe even his daughters in order to get the man to betray Nick Ward. And when that was done, he'd offer the same and more to MI6, the Mossad, SVR, and any other intelligence agency willing to join the hunt.

On the brighter side, Cyrah Jafari seemed equally dedicated to making herself the undisputed heavyweight champion of the assassination game. He was looking forward to hearing what crazy scheme she dreamed up almost as much as he was looking forward to seeing Anthony Cook dead.

Until that magnificent day, though, he needed to get lost. A little educational trip for Anna to the far corners of the world. Maybe check out the lemurs in Madagascar. Then to the Seychelles for some diving. Ulaanbaatar. Istanbul. Machu Picchu.

The chopper swung around Ward's compound and set down. Claudia—the real one, finally—was waiting near a stand of trees, using both hands to keep her hat from being swept away.

He jogged clear of the aircraft, wrapped his arms around her, and lifted her off the ground. She laughed and kissed him, keeping one hand on her hat.

"Wow! Look who's in a good mood! Can I assume that Legion's dead? Was it just one person or was it a team like we thought?"

"It was a team," he said, starting toward their cabin. "Three people. And not dead exactly. But no longer a threat."

Her brow furrowed, but she sensed that she should let the story evolve at its own pace. "And no one was hurt? Bebe?"

"Not a scratch. She's on her way home. Maybe even there by now."

"Sadie?"

"Safely back in New York."

"And how did that go? I mean working with her."

Rapp decided to have a little fun. "I have to admit that I was wrong about her. She's not just stunningly beautiful, she's got serious game."

Claudia's jaw clenched despite the fact that he hadn't yet delivered the coup de grâce. "And the amazing thing? She's an incredible cook. I'm trying to get her to send you some recipes."

Predictably, Claudia looked like she wanted to carve his heart out with whatever blunt instrument was at hand. Before she could get a hold of one, he laughed.

"She's a complete psycho, Claudia. Bebe and I had to wind her in duct tape to get her on the plane. I told the pilots to dump her on the tarmac in New York with a box cutter."

Her expression softened. “We owe her, though. For what she did for us.”

“Yeah. And that terrifies me. My hope is to never lay eyes on Sadie Hansen again. Now what’s our situation here? Have you arranged our exit?”

“Of course.”

“How soon can we go?”

“Not tomorrow morning. Maybe afternoon if we push.”

“Then push. I want to be miles away from here before the Cooks can get a cruise missile teed up.”

“Okay. I’ll get on it. Why don’t you tell Anna? She dying to see you and I think she’ll be excited to be moving on. It’s getting a little slow here for her.”

“No problem.”

“Before that, though, you should probably go see Irene. She’ll want a full report on what’s happened.”

“She’s here?”

Claudia nodded. “Waiting on Nick. He’s due tomorrow.”

Not a conversation he was looking forward to. In light of that, a little procrastination was in order.

Rapp swept his toe under the soccer ball and sent it arcing gently into the air. “Use your head!”

Anna sprinted across the patch of grass in front of Nicholas Ward’s house, but wasn’t quite fast enough.

“Scott’s better than you!” she pointed out. “He can get it all the way to me. But he had to leave. He said he had to work. I don’t know where. He has lots of jobs. I wonder if he went to see Joe? Do you think he’s going to come back soon?”

“I dunno,” Rapp said, trapping the ball when she kicked it back to him. “But we’re leaving, too.”

Her eyes widened. “Are we going home? Is the house all fixed? ’Cause—”

"Not home," Claudia called from her position near the pool. "We're going to go have some fun."

"Where? Are we going to get to fly on the helicopter? Because—"

"Not the helicopter," Rapp said. "We're going out by ground."

He tapped the ball back toward the girl, but she let it go right by. "We can't go out on the ground. There aren't any roads that come here."

"We don't need roads. We're not driving."

Anna thought about that for a moment, seeming to seize on the most incredible possibility of her short life. "Are we going to ride horses?"

He frowned dramatically. "Why ride a horse when you can ride an elephant?"

She was momentarily speechless. A rare occurrence. "Are you serious?"

"I never joke about large pachyderms."

Her excitement turned to confusion, forcing her mother to come to the rescue. "He's one hundred percent serious, sweetie. In fact, you get your very own. It's a baby one."

That prompted a flood of questions, from its name to how old it was to whether she could keep it. Rapp went to retrieve the ball while Claudia tried to provide satisfactory responses. He hoped the young girl's excitement would hold up. In truth, it was going to be a tough trip. Unavoidable if they wanted to be certain they weren't tracked, but hard. The first three miles were straight down the side of the mountain on foot. Nothing but slick roots, mud, and humidity. Then there would be another four miles on flat terrain before they got to camp.

The elephants would be their main mode of transportation the next day but, in his experience, the fantasy was better than the reality. While it beat walking, they weren't creatures that gave a lot of thought to what branches, trees, and rock outcroppings their passengers collided with. Then one more night outside, one more day on foot, and finally the Land Cruiser Claudia had waiting for them.

It'd be fine, he told himself. Anna would rise to the occasion because she was tough and there was no other choice. It wasn't like the journey would have been a hardship for a local girl her age. It was never too soon to learn that either life kicked the shit out of you, or you kicked the shit out of it. Particularly when you were unlucky enough to be a member of this family.

As he was dribbling the ball back toward the pool, Irene Kennedy appeared from the trees. Claudia immediately turned her attention to Anna. "Do you want to go for a swim? Why don't you go back to the bungalow and grab our suits. Then we can talk more about the elephants."

"But—"

"Now, Anna."

Recognizing her mother's tone, she ran off, exchanging a short greeting with Kennedy as they passed.

"I thought I heard the chopper."

She was dressed in a pair of jeans and a white blouse, more tanned than Rapp had ever seen her, but not exactly relaxed. And he was about to make that worse. Much worse.

"We're taking off tomorrow. I was coming by to see you but I needed to break the news to Anna first."

"I see," she said, pointing to Nicholas Ward's terrace. He and Claudia followed her onto it and she used a remote to open the louvered walls. At the same time, a large panel rose and created an open doorway shaded by a lattice. She went inside, crossing to the kitchen and opening the refrigerator. "Drink?"

"I'd take a beer," Rapp said.

Claudia just shook her head.

Kennedy pulled out a bottle for him and poured herself a glass of white wine.

"You seem comfortable here," he observed, dropping onto a stool in front of the kitchen island.

"Do I?"

"I take it you've decided to get in bed with Nick?"

She smiled. "Intentional?"

"I was being clever."

"It's complicated. Do I want to have a professional relationship with Nick or a personal one? I don't think both is workable."

"Are you sure?" Claudia said. "It can be, you know. There's such a thing as too much caution where relationships are concerned."

"You're probably right but I've lived my life by the philosophy that there's no such thing as too much caution."

"I'm with Claudia," Rapp said. "You're retired now. What better time to close your eyes and leap?"

"Old habits die hard," Kennedy said, taking a sip from her glass. "For instance, being able to overlook the fact that you're both avoiding the subject of Legion."

He picked up the beer but didn't drink. "They're taken care of and Bebe and Sadie are fine."

Kennedy sat, keeping the island between them. Her unwavering gaze suggested that she expected a more detailed explanation. Claudia was the first to fold under its intensity.

"Legion is made up of three women trained by the Iranians to infiltrate Israel. The program got canceled when the new government came in and they escaped."

"Mitch, you said they were taken care of, but you didn't say they were dead. Could you clarify?"

"I caught the woman who handles the operations end, but there was no way to use her to find her people. She didn't know where they were."

"I still don't have a clear picture of what happened," Kennedy pointed out.

"There didn't seem to be any reason to kill her."

"Really? Because I can think of quite a few."

Claudia commandeered his beer and took a nervous sip.

"You're probably right. But if I'd killed her, I wouldn't have been able to hire her to take out Anthony Cook."

Kennedy's face went blank. It was something he'd only seen a handful of times in their long relationship. Basically, she was so pissed that she couldn't conjure up a cover expression and just went with nothing.

"You did what?"

"It seemed fair. And the vice president is a little soft, but not too bad for a politician."

She fell silent for a long time. Probably a good minute with no sound at all other than the breeze coming through the louvers and the hum of the pool motor.

"Do you have a way of contacting them?"

"Sure. They've dropped their normal secrecy protocols."

"Then you have the ability to call them off."

"I suppose. But I'm not going to."

Kennedy spun her glass on the granite countertop, staring into it. "I'm furious, too, Mitch. And not just about the Cooks' behavior toward you. I blame them for what happened to Mike. They lit a fuse and when he discovered he couldn't put it out, he was forced to try to minimize the damage. Sometimes there's no way to win. The only thing you can do is manage your losses."

"Then we're in agreement," Rapp said. "We sit back and let Legion do what they do."

"No. We're not in agreement. As bad as Cook is for the country, his death could be worse. America's too fragile right now. Too divided. If he were to die, the conspiracy theories that he rode into the White House would explode. I'm not exaggerating when I say I think we could be dragged into another civil war. But even if we aren't, the unrest would cause our allies to turn away from us and look for leadership in places like China. I believe in America, just like you do. I think we're a little lost right now but given time, we'll find our way back."

"Nice speech, Irene, but a little too lofty for my current mood. I'm not living my life on the run because people will throw a fit on Facebook if something happens to him. I want him dead. And the sooner the better."

"What if I can guarantee your safety?"

"You're a magician, Irene. You've proved that more times than I can count. But some things can't be fixed."

"But what if I *can* fix it? Would you let me?"

He didn't answer, instead taking a pull from his beer.

"I'm not asking this for the Cooks, Mitch. Or even for America. This is for me. I'm asking you for a personal favor."

"Are you really going to play that card?"

"Yes."

"Okay. Fine. If you can fix this and *convince* me it's fixed, then I'll call off Legion."

Kennedy gave him a grateful nod. "Thank you."

"How," Claudia said, breaking her silence. "How are you going to do it?"

Kennedy lifted her glass to her mouth. "I have absolutely no idea."

CHAPTER 44

SOUTHWESTERN UGANDA

IRENE Kennedy started up a set of earthen steps that climbed the compound's defensive wall. When she reached the top, she gazed silently over the forest rolling out in front of her. Mitch, Claudia, and Anna had left less than an hour ago. They'd literally headed off into the sunset with nothing but a machete and the packs on their backs. No ticker-tape parade. No eternal gratitude from the country he'd sacrificed so much for. Not even her well wishes for whatever his future held.

She felt shame at that last one, but she'd been angry. Enough so that she'd let it overwhelm her judgment. Not a common occurrence in her life and because of that a difficult one to analyze. Maybe some things weren't meant to be studied. They were just meant to be felt.

There was no question that her old friend had started the timer on a bomb that could destroy everything in its considerable range. A successful attempt on the president—even if it didn't look like an assassination—had the potential to send America spinning out of control. Even worse would be an unsuccessful attempt. Cook could use it to reinforce his narrative of an America beset by enemies that only he can vanquish. It would be another massive step toward gathering the power necessary to collapse America's democracy. History was full of men like him and the sad lesson was that they often succeeded.

But the source of her anger went deeper than that. As appealing as it was to lay all this at Cook's and Rapp's feet, it was also a deflection. She had been in a leadership position for much of her adult life and had been so focused on external threats that she'd blinded herself to what was happening to her own countrymen. The purposelessness. The amorphous rage. The desperate search for identity and an enemy to battle. For something to believe in. And the Cooks had taken advantage of that blindness.

She thought back on her life honing the Central Intelligence Agency into perhaps the most advanced weapon in the history of the world. Aimed outward, it had great power to defend the country she loved. Turned inward by Darren Hargrave, though, it had the potential to bring down the delicate experiment that the country's founding fathers had started so long ago.

The sun finally dipped below distant mountains, painting the horizon a deep orange. She wrapped her arms around her torso against the sudden cold and started back down the steps.

"Where've you been?" Nicholas Ward was standing at the edge of his deck watching her approach.

"Enjoying the sunset."

"Really?" he said, not bothering to hide his skepticism.

"No."

"Do you know if they're okay?"

Kennedy shook her head and followed him to a sectional sofa bathed in the glow of the pool. "Mitch will have all their electronics disabled. He needs to disappear."

"Even from you?"

"Especially from me. I'll be the first stop for anyone trying to find him."

She accepted a glass of wine before sitting. It all seemed so civilized. So calm. As though nothing beyond the walls surrounding them existed. The seductiveness of that illusion was so strong, she found herself having to actively fight it.

"Are you going to try again?" he asked, grabbing some cheese from a silver tray and taking a seat next to her. She could feel the heat of his body, adding to the things she had to fight.

"You mean to reach Catherine Cook? Yes."

He clicked a remote control and a line of gas flames sprang from the coffee table in front of them. "Why don't I try? The Cooks and I have our differences but a trillion dollars makes me hard to ignore."

It was tempting. She'd already left the first lady three increasingly urgent messages. The assumption was that they were being received but it was impossible to know for sure.

"Thank you, but no. This isn't something I want to get you involved in."

"What isn't something you want me to get involved in?"

"You don't want to know."

"Are you sure? I might not be as squeamish as you think."

She smiled and took a sip of what turned out to be a spectacular chardonnay. "There's a war brewing, Nick. And there's no reason for you to be part of it. It could only weaken you and I don't think that's in anyone's best interest right now."

He nodded slowly. "This is your world, not mine. I'm here if you or Mitch need me."

"I know. And I appreciate it. We both do."

He stood and pointed to her glass. "I'm going to go check on dinner. Can I freshen that up first?"

"I'm fine, thanks."

She watched him retreat into the house, admiring his trim physique and the way the light picked up the gray in his hair. Even the dull snap of his ubiquitous flip-flops was becoming increasingly endearing.

One disaster at a time, she reminded herself.

A personal relationship between her and the world's wealthiest man would push her back into a limelight that she very much needed to avoid. And worse, it would increase the size of the already expansive target on his back.

She let out a long sigh and set down her glass in favor of a satellite phone. The number in question was at the top of her history and she dialed it, listening to the now-familiar ring before the voice of Catherine Cook's assistant came on.

"Hello, Dr. Kennedy."

"Hello, Susan. I still haven't heard back from Mrs. Cook. Is she available?"

"I'm afraid not, ma'am. It's been a little chaotic around here over the past few days. Can I put you into her voice mail?"

Kennedy watched Ward pull something out of the oven. In addition to being unimaginably wealthy, brilliant, and good-looking, he was an excellent cook. If her mother were still alive, she'd undoubtedly be hinting that this probably wasn't the time to play hard to get.

"Dr. Kennedy?" Susan prompted.

"I'm sorry. No. I don't think so. Could you write a message for me instead?"

"Of course."

"I find myself in a life-or-death situation," Kennedy said, speaking deliberately. "But it's not my life or death that's in play. And as such, this is the last time I'm going to contact you." She used her free hand to reach for her wine. "Did you get that?"

"Yes, ma'am."

"Please read it back to me."

She did. Hesitantly, but word for word.

"Thank you, Susan."

Kennedy disconnected the call as Ward put their dinner back in the oven and set a timer on his phone. It'd be interesting to see Catherine's reaction to the message. Not just the wording, but the fact that it hadn't come by way of private voice mail. Now her assistant was aware that the former director of the CIA was issuing dire warnings. Not something that would be easy to keep quiet.

Ward sat just as she was putting the phone back in her pocket. "Did you get her?"

"Who?"

"Catherine."

"No, I wasn't calling the White House. Things don't look like they're going well in there and I was ordering Chinese."

He laughed. "In about half an hour, you're going to eat those words along with the best spanakopita you've ever had."

"Well?"

It really was the best spanakopita she'd ever had.

"I don't want you to get overconfident."

He grinned. "It's fun, isn't it?"

She stabbed her fork into some greens that he'd picked himself only an hour ago. "What?"

"Having dinner. Making small talk. Pretending we're normal."

"Just two average people having a bite to eat on a private mountaintop compound in Uganda."

"It requires a little suspension of disbelief," he conceded. "And a few glasses of wine don't hurt, either."

She was about to respond when her phone started to ring. Probably her son, who had postponed their weekly call because of a girl he'd become obsessed with. When she looked at the screen, though, an unknown number was flashing on it.

"Catherine?" Ward said.

"I think it might be. Would you excuse me for a moment?"

"Don't be long. It gets soggy on the bottom when it sits."

"Less than five minutes," she promised as she crossed the deck toward a set of stairs.

"Hello?"

"What do you want, Irene?"

"Your husband's made some errors lately. But I don't think you had anything to do with them."

"And?"

"Payment for those errors is coming due."

"That's all very dramatic and cryptic, Irene. But what do you want me to do with it?"

"I want you to meet with me face-to-face to see if we can fix this before it gets out of control."

"So, I'm supposed to believe that you want to help us. That you suddenly have Tony's best interests at heart."

"Let's just say that right now I see him as the lesser of the evils."

There was a short silence over the line. "If we're going to do this, we need to do it quietly. Next week, I'm reading to some kids at a kindergarten in Maryland. You can meet me there and we can drive back to DC together. Coordinate with Susan."

The line went dead, and Kennedy started back toward the house.

CHAPTER 45

SOUTH OF SWAKOPMUND
NAMIBIA

"QUIT it."

Rapp decided to ignore the advice and used his index finger to poke Anna in the back again.

"Quit it!"

They were halfway up a massive sand dune outside of Swakopmund, climbing in the glare of the relentless African sun. Like him, Anna was carrying a snowboard on her back and squinting through dark sunglasses. The scent of the coconut sunscreen she was bathed in mixed pleasantly with the more familiar dust and sweat.

He glanced back downslope and saw Claudia in the distance. She was sitting in a beach chair set up alongside the Land Cruiser. A cooler rested next to her and he could see the glint of a water bottle perched on it. She gave a brief wave and then went back to the book in her lap.

They'd made it out of Uganda two weeks ago on Latvian passports provided by friends of Scott Coleman. After crossing the border into Tanzania, they'd taken a leisurely route through Zambia before dipping down into Botswana and heading west. Now they were staying in a nice two-bedroom Airbnb that they were seriously considering extending. Namibia was a beautiful country and one not yet bristling with artificially intelligent cameras.

"If we go any slower, all the sand's going to blow away before we get to the top," Rapp said.

"You have bigger legs!"

"Pick it up, shorty."

Twenty more minutes, a few more nudges, and a lot of panting finally brought them to the summit. He helped her get the board attached to her feet and stood her up, pushing her to the edge of the slope.

"All right. You were definitely starting to get the rhythm at the bottom of the last run. Remember, your track should look like mine. A nice smooth squiggle that goes more or less straight down the face."

She screwed up her face and gave a short nod, focused entirely on the steep slope in front of her. He released her and she tipped over the edge, letting gravity take control. The first couple of turns looked solid. She'd inherited her father's athletic ability, but also his tendency toward cockiness. About a quarter of the way down, she was already carrying too much speed.

"Carve a little harder!" he shouted. "Squiggles, not lines!"

He thought she'd taken his advice when she arced right, but quickly realized his error. Someone had built a plywood jump in the middle of the slope and she was lining up on it.

"Stay away from that!" he shouted. "Go back left! Left!"

She ignored him, locking in on the ramp and crouching into something resembling a tuck. The hollow thud of her hitting it was loud enough for him to wince and for her mother to look up from her book. Anna stayed airborne for an excruciatingly long time, finally coming down into what at first appeared to be a decent landing.

Then things took a turn for the worse. The pink of her T-shirt was suddenly replaced by the black of the base of her board, then the blond of her hair. Pink, black, blond. Pink, black, blond . . .

He scooped up his own board and went after her, descending in long leaps as the sand collapsed beneath him. When he finally reached her, he thought she was crying, but the sobs turned out to be guffaws.

"Did you see that?" she said, spitting out sand as she spoke. "I was like fifty feet in the air!"

"At least," he said, checking her for injuries but finding nothing more than a few abrasions. Finally, he pulled her upright. "Are you okay?"

"Yeah. Sure. I can do it next time, though. I just sunk in the front. That's all."

"Why don't we just spend the day getting your board under you and then next time we'll set up a smaller jump. Sometimes it's better to work up."

"Did you see me?" Anna said as they leaned their boards against the Land Cruiser. "Mitch says I was at least fifty feet in the air."

Claudia frowned. "What did I tell you before I agreed to this?"

"That I needed to be careful 'cause we don't even know where the hospital is yet."

"And was that careful?"

"It's, like, really soft. It's just sand, you know."

"Which you now have *everywhere*."

"We can fix that," Rapp said, grabbing the girl, flipping her over, and shaking her up and down by her ankles. She giggled while an improbable amount of sand poured from her clothing. When the flood became a trickle, he flipped her back over and dropped her on her feet.

"Are you ready for your sandwiches?" Claudia asked.

"Definitely! Are you hungry, Mitch?"

"Starving," he said, digging their lunches from the cooler. He sat with his back against the vehicle, while Anna knelt and used the top of the cooler as a table.

"Are we done for the day?" Claudia asked.

Anna shook her head. "We want to do a couple more runs. Then I can get better so we can build a jump next time."

"A jump?"

"Mitch says we can make one a little smaller. Then I can work up to the big one."

He tuned out the ensuing argument, finishing his food and washing it down with an icy Coke. How long could they safely stay there? Two weeks seemed reasonable. Then maybe they could move on to Walvis Bay for another couple before leaving the country for . . . Where?

Anna wolfed down the rest of her sandwich and then guzzled the bottle of water her mother had given her. After that, she was immediately back on her feet. "You ready, Mitch?"

"I've got to make a quick phone call. Why don't you start up by yourself. I'll catch up."

"By herself?" Claudia said skeptically.

He pointed to the empty, wide-open dune. "It's not like she can get lost."

Anna inched toward her board.

"Okay, but go slow," Claudia said. "It's getting really hot."

"Yeah, it's pretty hard. You know, 'cause the sand's soft and you, like, slide back every step. You know what would make it easier, Mitch?"

He glanced up from the phone in his hand. "What?"

They answered in unison. "Elephants."

Rapp grimaced. "You're never going to let me live that down, are you?"

The consensus seemed to be that they would not.

Claudia watched her trudge back toward the slope, waiting to speak until she was out of earshot. "I'm nervous."

"She'll be fine."

"Not about her. About your call. At some point, Anna's going to have to learn more than how to sandboard and why zebras have stripes. That's going to mean figuring out homeschooling. And we're going to have to find a way for her to be around kids her age. She can't just socialize with us."

"The first one's doable, but you know as well as I do that the second one's not. She's a smart kid, but we can't expect her to keep quiet about her past. And the stories she'd tell are going to attract attention."

"I know," Claudia said miserably. "It's just the uncertainty. Is this going to be a few months? A few years? Our whole lives? If I just had some sense, I could make peace with it."

He installed a battery in the phone and powered it up. There was barely time for it to acquire a satellite before a proprietary app created by Legion prompted him to join a call.

"Go ahead," he said, picking up.

"It's not going to be easy."

Cyrah Jafari sounded natural, but not like herself. In addition to the secure sat link and encryption, there was also a voice-altering algorithm built into both ends. Where anonymity was concerned, Legion believed there was no such thing as overkill. It was a philosophy he wholeheartedly agreed with.

"You thought it would be?"

"No. But with you gone to ground, he's not going to be doing many events. And to the degree he does, they'll be like the last one but even more secure and with an audience that's even more loyal."

"Your point?"

"If you stay hidden, it's likely he won't win the next time. After that, things become quite a bit easier."

Rapp shook his head. Anna would be ten by the time Cook lost the White House—assuming he even did. There was only so much of her childhood he was willing to steal from her.

"That's what you're charging ten million for? Unacceptable. And it doesn't get you what you want, either. Not much glory in taking out a civilian with minimal security."

There was a long pause over the phone before she spoke again. "I assumed that would be your reaction. And we actually do have an idea."

"I'm listening."

"Like I said, it looks like he'll still be doing the mixed virtual events—"

"With a limited and well-vetted audience."

"Correct. But a lot of the people he chose for the last event were more than followers. They were more like disciples. Based on social media accounts we've been able to access, some seem borderline unbalanced. They speak about him like he's a kind of messiah."

"Doesn't surprise me," Rapp said, unsure where she was going with this. "Those kinds of followers make for good optics, particularly when you're limiting crowd size."

"Exactly. But unbalanced people tend to be easily knocked off course. They want desperately to be part of something but aren't really that particular about what it is. After some cursory research, we've already found four candidates that fit the psychological profile we've developed. Men who are angry, lonely, and desperate for belonging."

He smiled. "In other words, men who might be easily swayed by a beautiful young Persian woman who suddenly starts paying attention to them."

"Exactly. Love and hate are just two sides of the same coin. If their energy could be redirected, they might do our job for us."

Difficult but plausible. Turn Cook from saint to demon in the eyes of some basement dweller, get him into an event with an undetectable weapon, and let the sparks fly. Rapp had to hand it to her. She was one sneaky bitch. Sadie Hansen was lucky to be alive.

"That's a lot of art and not much science," Rapp commented. "Do you think you can do it?"

"I'm not looking forward to spending my foreseeable future sleeping with multiple . . ." Her voice faded for a moment. "What's the word I'm looking for?"

"I'm going with basement dweller."

"Yes. Basement dwellers. But based on what we've learned so far, it's a promising plan."

"But not a short-term one."

"No. And that's what I want to make clear. We're probably looking at a year. Maybe a bit more."

He glanced over at Claudia, held up a single finger, and mouthed *one year.*

Her brow furrowed for a moment, but the number wouldn't come as a surprise. She'd been the brains behind some pretty convoluted assassinations herself. Still, it was a hard thing to face—a year slinking around the edges of the world with a seven-year-old. Despite that reality, she gave a resolute nod.

Rapp returned his attention to the phone. "You continue to live up to your reputation. Keep me posted."

After disconnecting the call, he smashed the handset on the Land Cruiser's bumper.

"Can she do it?" Claudia asked as Rapp picked up his board in order to chase down Anna.

"It's hard to say for sure, but I can tell you this: I wouldn't want to be Anthony Cook right now."

CHAPTER 46

GREENBELT
MARYLAND
USA

IRENE Kennedy sat watching the rain accumulate on her windshield. Beyond was a sparsely populated parking lot surrounding a series of office buildings. There was a strange serenity to the scene that she couldn't draw from. To the contrary, it seemed to mock her.

The situation had gotten so bad that her only course of action was to risk everything. And even if she came out on top, it was uncertain that anything would be resolved. Democracy was a messy, frustrating compromise that never seemed to last. The American people did it better than anyone, but would that continue? If they stayed on their current trajectory, probably not. But perhaps she could provide the nudge necessary to put them back on track. Back on the path that had made the United States the most successful country in modern history.

If she failed, the consequences would be unimaginably dire. She'd find herself in a very similar position to the one that had killed Mike

Nash: cornered, alone, and with the blood of those closest to her on her hands.

Kennedy saw a limousine enter the lot and followed it in the rearview mirror until it pulled alongside. A quick tug on the door handle and she was out, crossing through the rain and sliding into the luxurious backseat before it could drench her. She stayed to the right, using the angle to examine the face of the driver. The fact that he was unfamiliar wasn't particularly surprising. His Eastern European accent was somewhat more so.

"Good afternoon, Dr. Kennedy."

A mercenary that the Cooks could be absolutely certain she had no connection to? Someone willing to transport her to a black site from which she would never emerge? At this point, it didn't much matter. The only thing to do was enjoy the ride.

"This is a backup limousine," the unnamed driver continued. "The one that took Mrs. Cook to her event will have a mechanical issue and we'll pull in shortly before she's finished. When we arrive, make sure you've moved to the seat directly behind me. That will ensure that the press can't see you when the door opens. The window tint will handle the rest."

"I understand," Kennedy said simply.

As expected, their arrival was timed to perfection. They'd barely glided to a stop when Catherine Cook appeared on the steps, followed by a swarm of teachers and schoolchildren. Her security detail spoke brusquely into their radios as they controlled the press and scanned for threats.

Through the window, Kennedy could see that Catherine had made real strides in her ability to feign emotion and warmth. Her smile was broad as she shook hands, doled out a few hugs to the children, and finally retreated. A Secret Service agent followed with an umbrella, opening the vehicle's door just enough for her to slip inside.

The first lady stared straight ahead, her smile fading as the door was slammed shut and a wall of glass rose to separate the driver. She didn't speak, waiting for the motorcade to pull away before acknowledging Kennedy's presence.

"I'm told we have twenty minutes. So, make your accusations quickly."

"I think we're well beyond that," Kennedy said, pointing to the side of Catherine's head. "May I?"

The woman gave a short nod and Kennedy searched her hair and collar for any kind of listening device. Finding none, she scooted close enough that her lips brushed the woman's ear. "Let's speak in whispers, shall we?"

Another nod.

"Legion has been neutralized."

The fact that her words got no reaction was a good sign. It suggested that the first lady was there to talk seriously instead of to feign ignorance or innocence.

"But not killed. Redirected toward a new target. One you're familiar with."

The woman's throat moved as she swallowed.

"Your husband started a war that I suspect you advised him against. Now the tide has turned against him. Even with all your resources, you won't find Mitch. And he's confident that Legion will succeed."

"What's your interest in this, Irene?"

"As much as I despise everything you and your husband stand for, I don't think his death will serve America or democracy. And, frankly, when I look at my friend's life going forward, I don't like what I see. He deserves better than to spend the next thirty years hiding in caves and watching the sky for drones. His country *owes* him better."

"What do you propose?"

"That we find a way to reinstate the truce between the two foolish men in our lives."

"A tall order, no?"

"I think it can be done. But first we'll have to trust each other."

"An even taller order."

"In this narrow band, we have similar interests."

Catherine shook her head slowly. "You're wrong, Irene."

"How so?"

"The band isn't narrow. Look at what you've done to this country and the world. Look at what the weak presidents you admire have done. How much longer can we survive with a political class and media that benefits from hysteria? American democracy worked for a while but now it's becoming chaos. And you want me to believe that the great Irene Kennedy can't see it? If you think the American people are going to find their reason again, you're deluding yourself. And self-delusion isn't something women like us can afford."

"We don't have much time and I think we're wandering a bit off topic. Our—"

"Come back to us, Irene."

Kennedy wasn't often caught off guard, but this was one of those times.

"We aren't the destroyer of worlds," Catherine continued. "We're not Hitler or Stalin or Caesar, and we don't aspire to be. But the American people have become a mob that's tearing itself apart. For nothing. Entertainment. Boredom. Casual cruelty and momentary glimpses of what they think is power. Darren Hargrave is an idiot and a cretin. He can't help us save this country. You can. Accept my offer and have a seat at the table."

Kennedy leaned back in the leather seat. "Is that what you offered Mike?"

"Yes. And he was smart enough to take it. To put himself in a position to help you and shape policy going forward."

Kennedy nodded thoughtfully. "And Mitch?"

"He has to go, and you know it. But you'll be in the position to protect the others. Scott and his people. Claudia and Anna—"

"Have you ever thought about why?"

"Why what?" Catherine said.

"Why you've spent your life pursuing something that you don't need? You're wealthy. You're powerful. You feel no sense of gratitude to the country that allowed you to succeed in the way you have. You're completely insulated from the chaos you say you're so concerned about. Why not just serve your time in the White House and leave like the others before you?"

"Why do you think, Irene?"

"I suspect it's not complicated. The problem is that it'll never be enough. In my experience, the more power people like you get, the more you crave. And what good is power unless you wield it in the most visceral way possible? You say you just want to bring order to the mess we've made, but you'll get bored with that pretty quickly. Then you'll want to grind your heel into people's throats. To make them kneel."

"Absolute power corrupts absolutely," Catherine said.

"Is it that? Or is it that the people who seek it are corrupt by nature?"

Catherine laughed. "Then take my offer, Irene. Be the angel on our shoulder. Use that incredible mind and your decades of experience to manage us. Manipulate us. Maybe even destroy us. What kind of patriot would you be if you sold out your country for one man?"

CHAPTER 47

DAAN VILJOEN GAME PARK
NEAR WINDHOEK
NAMIBIA

RAPP dodged an enormous web containing a softball-sized spider and began climbing a trail to his right. It felt good to be alone in the wilderness again. The crunch of his running shoes against the ground, the scolding beep of his heart rate monitor as he pushed himself too hard. Morning temperatures were holding just below eighty, but it wouldn't last. At this point, speed was the better part of valor. The small handheld water bottles he'd selected would run dry pretty quickly in the full heat of the day.

He glanced at his watch about halfway up the climb, ignoring the flashing training data in favor of the time. Two more minutes. Probably not a bad idea to find some shade.

It appeared in the form of a concave cliff band to his right. A quick bushwhack through ragged trees and a few more prehistoric arachnids brought him to the base. Rangers had assured him that there were no predators in the park but the acrid stench of urine made him wonder.

Yet another reason to make this quick. He pulled a satphone from his pack and installed the battery. At ten a.m. on the dot, it started to vibrate.

"How's the fishing?" Rapp said, picking up.

"A little slow this morning," Scott Coleman replied. "But it'll get better. I'm feeling lucky."

The former SEAL was floating off the coast of the Greek island he called his second home. Living the good life and offering Rapp an assist with his communications.

The ring of a phone on Coleman's end became audible, followed by some expected crackling. The call was coming from Irene Kennedy on yet another anonymous satphone. Coleman would pick up, tape the two handsets together, and then put them in a soundproof box—likely his beer cooler. The air gap would add another layer of protection against the NSA using the call to locate Rapp in Namibia. Decades of tracking terrorists had made him an expert on the weaknesses of electronic surveillance. Ironic—and a little bit depressing—that he was relying on the same tricks that al-Qaeda and ISIS used against him.

"Irene?"

"I'm here. Are you doing all right?"

"We're fine. Can I assume you've come up with something?"

"I met with Catherine and she's agreed to help try to build a better rapport between you and the president."

"Why would I be interested in that? It didn't work the first time."

"Because we're both going to make the appropriate . . . let's say, gestures."

"When you say 'we' does that mean me?"

"Yes."

"And what are these gestures, exactly?"

"I can get you within striking distance of the president."

"Really? Where?"

"The White House."

He laughed as he moved to a better place to watch the approach to his position. What he didn't need was a cat slinking up on him. The spiders were bad enough. "So, your deal with her is that she's going to let me into a building full of operators with orders to kill me on sight? I think your negotiating skills are starting to slip, Irene. If you don't mind, I'll just stay on vacation for a while and let Legion make my problems disappear."

"I think you're downplaying the risk he's taking, Mitch. There's a long list of people you've killed under conditions that everyone thought were impossible."

"That may be true, but I don't *have* to risk my ass this time. I can just sit by the pool and wait. For once, time's on my side."

"So, Cook dies, the vice president serves for a few years with no real mandate, and then Catherine wins the White House."

"Not a problem for me. And you know why? Because she's your evil twin. She's going to calculate that coming after me doesn't do anything to move the needle in her direction. She'll be fully locked in on installing herself as a dictator and if the American people allow that, it's on them. Like I said before, it's not my job to save them from themselves."

"I know you better than that."

"Are you sure?"

"I think you're taking this position because you don't see it as a real possibility. You think she'll serve eight years and leave the country damaged but fundamentally unchanged."

"You don't?"

"If Anthony Cook dies over the course of the next year, I think that there's a good chance that America's democracy will fail. I think we'll see an explosion of political violence, states attempting to break away from constitutional mandates, and eventually a shattered country with a government that isn't much different than Russia's or Venezuela's."

"That seems kind of alarmist to me."

"It's not."

He swore quietly under his breath. An entire life spent trying to keep the world at a slow boil and the Cooks were blowing the lid off.

"What are you saying I should do about it?" he said finally.

"Deliver our terms."

"Send a letter."

"What I have to say can't be done in writing or over a phone line. And frankly, it can't come from me. As you well know, threats have to come from a position of confidence and strength. They're something you make eye to eye, not from hiding."

He didn't respond.

"Mitch? Are you still there?"

"Yeah, I'm still here."

"Will you do it?"

"I honestly don't know, Irene. They could be luring me in there to put a bullet in my head. And I wouldn't be able to do anything about it. Even if I got my hands on a weapon, who would I shoot at? Those aren't a bunch of terrorists protecting him. They're Secret Service. You're not just asking me to go in there and potentially die. You're asking me to go in there and potentially die on my knees."

CHAPTER 48

OUTSIDE THE WHITE HOUSE
WASHINGTON, DC
USA

MITCH Rapp looked through the limousine's open window and saw something that resembled a checkpoint in an active war zone. In this case, though, the war zone was sunny Pennsylvania Avenue. Barricades and combat vehicles had been positioned to divert traffic away from the White House and the Secret Service had been augmented by operators on loan from the armed forces. Barbed wire, dogs, and lazily camouflaged antiaircraft systems added to the disruption.

He had been aware that the president was afraid of him, but seeing the result of that fear firsthand was a bit disorienting. It looked like America was under siege. And maybe it was, but by him? When had he gone from defending the gates to standing outside them with a Molotov cocktail?

The driver eased to a stop and Rapp held out an item that hadn't gotten much action over the years: his real passport. A camo-clad soldier flipped through the largely empty pages and then compared the photo to the man in front of him. Finally, he handed it back.

"Thank you, sir. Have a nice day."

And then they were off again. Rapp closed the window and his thoughts went to the knock-down, drag-out fight he'd had with Claudia over this operation. Even worse than her anger with him, though, was her fury at Kennedy. The former CIA director was lucky that the security protocols they'd set up made it impossible for Claudia to call her. She'd have learned every swear word in the French language before suffering a burst eardrum.

Coleman and the guys tended to side with Claudia. In fact, they'd started an office pool as to how long Rapp would survive after clearing the White House's gate. Thirty-eight minutes was the longest anyone had been willing to put money on. Rapp had thought that was a little optimistic and bet fifty bucks on eleven minutes, fifteen seconds.

But while this was likely the stupidest thing he'd ever done—a high bar based on his career so far—what choice did he have? While he wasn't convinced Kennedy's plan to get America to step back from the brink was going to work, he owed her his life. And not just his survival. His *life*. The man he'd become. The things he'd accomplished. The lifelong friendships he'd made. Where would the young, angry Mitch Rapp have ended up without her? Probably dead or in prison.

They weaved through a set of concrete barriers designed to slow approaching vehicles and then submitted to a third bomb check. After that, they finally entered the White House grounds. Security was even heavier inside and included a blast-proof structure that was clearly a kill box. Was it just part of the recent upgrades or had it been constructed specifically for him?

Rapp stepped from the limo, stopping to allow a dog to give him a good sniff. Shooters had been distributed in a way that was as innocuous as possible, but he could still feel their scopes on him.

Once the beagle was satisfied, he submitted to his second and most thorough frisking before being led to the kill box. When the door behind him closed, he half-expected to be cut to pieces by automatic fire. But it didn't happen. Not yet.

"Please strip and put your clothes on the shelf in front of you," a disembodied voice said. "Then put on the jumpsuit on the shelf behind you."

He did as he was told, ending up in a bright orange prison uniform and a pair of socks that would make it difficult to run on any surface other than carpet.

"Please move to your left and stand on the yellow footprints."

When he arrived at the indicated position, a different voice boomed in the tight space. "Look straight ahead and raise your arms out from your sides."

He let the sensors probe him as he stared at a blank wall.

"You can drop your arms," the voice said after about twenty seconds. "You'll see a pair of handcuffs hanging by the door to your left. Please put them on with your hands behind your back."

Again, Rapp complied.

"Show them to the camera."

He turned so they could zoom in.

Apparently they were satisfied, because the door opened and a man wearing fatigues and a flak jacket entered. He had a tube of superglue in one hand and a bottle of accelerator in the other. After taking a position behind Rapp, he tightened the cuffs to the point of discomfort and then sealed the keyholes.

"Now the only way to get these off is to cut them off," he whispered in Rapp's ear. "Or maybe we'll just bury you in them."

Not Secret Service. Foreign accent. It'd be interesting to know if they had some history together that Rapp couldn't remember.

He was surrounded by five more men and led to the Presidential Emergency Operations Center—a secure structure beneath the East Wing. Years ago, Rapp had saved the life of a former president who had holed up in a similar bunker not far from there. In many ways, it had been the operation that made him who he was. Would this be where it all ended, too?

The room hadn't changed much since the last time he'd seen it. The main difference was that all of the furniture had been removed, with the exception of two chairs. The one near the door looked like it had been taken from the now-missing conference table. The other was on the far side of the room, constructed of heavy steel and anchored to the floor. Not surprisingly, he was led to that one. After sitting, his handcuffs were padlocked to a chain on the back and the glue ceremony was repeated. Then he was left alone.

Rapp figured he'd have to wait a while for Cook to show up but it turned out to be less than five minutes. Apparently, the situation was weighing on the president enough that he couldn't bring himself to exercise that particular display of self-importance. Even more interesting was that after entering, he immediately closed the door behind him.

"Where's the wife?"

"She has her place," Cook responded, looking down at him from across the room. "This isn't it."

Rapp suppressed a smile. Leaving his smarter half out of this was a mistake. So far, things were going even better than Kennedy and her crystal ball had predicted.

"There are no microphones in here, but there are cameras," Cook said, taking a seat that preserved the distance between them. "One wrong move and there'll be armed guards in here before you even stand. So, don't try it. My men have been training for this and even you're not that fast. No one is. Not even close."

The fact that he wouldn't shut up about it suggested he wasn't as convinced as he wanted to sound. He should have been, though. There was no way out of the cuffs and even at a full sprint, it would take a good second and a half to get to him. But that's not why Rapp was there.

"So where do we start?" the president said.

"I thought a little history. To be sure we're on the same page."

"By all means. Go ahead."

"You and I agreed to a truce. I would leave the country for as long as you were in power, stay in plain sight to the degree possible, make no moves against you. In return, you'd leave me alone."

Cook nodded, so Rapp continued.

"Instead, you sent a dossier about Claudia to her enemies. That caused Gustavo Marroqui to attack us in South Africa and ended with Enzo Ruiz hiring Legion to kill her. I captured Legion and changed their target."

Cook gave another slow nod before speaking. "While I agree in principle with what you've laid out, I have to take your word for the fact that you planned to honor our agreement. Typically, when you bury the hatchet, it's in the skulls of people you consider to be your enemy."

"I do what I say I'm going to."

"Promises are kept until they become inconvenient."

"Spoken like a true politician."

Cook smiled thinly at the insult. "So that's where we've been, Mitch. The question that Catherine and Irene want us to resolve is, where are we going? They seem to think that putting us in the same room is the first step to building trust between us. You've allowed yourself to be handcuffed to a chair inside my defenses and I've agreed to get within a few feet of you alone. I suppose the idea is that we reaffirm our commitment to our imperfect little agreement. And that this time everyone abides by it."

"Is that what you're here to do?"

Cook leaned back and crossed his legs. In his way, he really was impressive. The good looks, the charisma, the sense of quiet strength that oozed from every pore as long as Rapp's handcuffs held. It wasn't hard to see why people were so anxious to follow him. Why anyone would trust him, though, was another matter.

"So, your problem is easy to summarize," the president said finally. "You're handcuffed to a chair surrounded by a hundred armed men sworn to defend me. Mine, though, is a little more complicated.

First, Legion is now coming for me. And second, your men have disappeared."

All true. A few hours before Rapp arrived in DC, his people had gone up in smoke. Coleman had jumped over the side of his boat with some scuba gear and never returned. Wick had disappeared into his backyard—also known as Wyoming. Bruno had lost himself in New Zealand, and Maslick had disappeared down a manhole in Northern Virginia.

"That about covers it," Rapp said.

"So, if I agree to go back to our truce, you'll make your men reappear and call off Legion. Is that what I'm to believe? That you'll forgo any retaliation and just let me continue with my presidency?"

"You seem skeptical."

"You could just say you've called off Legion, but actually do nothing. Then, one day I end up dead. And if Legion fails, you and your men can disappear again and make your own attempt."

"My guys have nothing to do with this. And I wouldn't need them anyway."

"Why not?"

"Because you're not going to have all this security after you resign."

Cook stared at him for a moment and then broke into laughter. A little nervous, to be sure, but it seemed heartfelt.

"Did I say something funny?"

"So many things, really. First that you believe you're in a position to ask for my resignation. But second that you think I'd consider it. You just said it yourself. You'd be able to pick me off any time you wanted."

"I already can."

"Really?" Cook responded incredulously.

Rapp motioned with his head, since his hands were out of commission. "Do you really believe that any of this crap is anything more than a waste of tax money? Let me tell you from decades of experience that anyone you can find, you can kill. And in about a thousand different ways."

"I'm on the edge of my seat. How would you do it, Mitch? How would you kill me?"

"Hard to say, because I've been too busy to give it much thought. Your meeting with that group of African leaders a few weeks from now is interesting, though."

"Is it?"

"Did you know that one of those men—the president of the DRC—got Ebola a couple of years back and recovered? So, he can still get it but would be fairly resistant to becoming symptomatic. Why not pay one of his people to infect him right before he comes? One day you're shaking hands with him and the next you're bleeding from your eyeballs. But again, I'm just spitballing. And let's face it, I'm kind of a Cro-Magnon. My idea of an exotic hit is shooting someone with a SIG instead of a Glock. Legion's a whole different animal. Did you know they once got a guy stampeded by his own cattle? And another one of their targets got hit by a bolt of lightning that multiple reliable witnesses swear to seeing. The bottom line is that when it comes to security, there are always flaws."

In truth, he was downplaying what the Secret Service had accomplished, but it seemed to be working. The overhead lights were starting to pick up a glimmer of sweat on Cook's forehead.

"You're not making a very good case for your survival, Mitch."

"No? I thought I was doing great. Like I said, I live up to my agreements. Plus, I'm not in the habit of killing for revenge. I kill to neutralize threats and without the Oval Office, you're not one."

"I don't believe you," Cook said simply.

"Then we're both dead, Mr. President. Me today and you over the next year or so."

"I'm not so sure," he said thoughtfully. "The CIA seems to think it can bend the odds in my favor."

"The CIA?" Rapp responded. "You mean Darren Hargrave? If my life was on the line, he wouldn't be my go-to."

"Darren's not my only CIA source."

"If you say so."

He pointed at Rapp. "It occurs to me that if I was privy to everything in that head of yours, I'd have quite an advantage. You know everything about your men—how they were trained, where they would run, how they finance their operations. And while you aren't as familiar with Legion, I doubt you're so hands-off that you're completely ignorant about them. I'll concede that you probably don't know *where* they are, but I think you know who they are and probably have some sense of how they're going to come at me. And while I agree that none of that's a sure thing, it's better than walking out of the White House and putting myself at the mercy of a man who famously has none."

"Or maybe not," Rapp said. "I've been interrogated more times than I care to remember, and I've never broken. Plus, I know the people you'd want to use and they'll refuse—some because we're friends and others because they're too smart to risk catching a bullet from Scott."

"I think you forgot someone," Cook said, a hint of smugness creeping onto his expression.

"Who's that?"

"Jane Hornig."

Rapp kept his expression neutral. Dr. Jane Hornig had advanced degrees in both neurology and biochemistry, as well as having written extensively on the psychology of pain. She'd also produced a thousand-plus-page tome called *The Comprehensive Guide to Ancient Torture: Techniques and Devices*. Rapp had received a signed copy of the first edition hot off the presses and immediately thrown it away.

Charlie Wicker once remarked that the woman wasn't just destined for hell, she was destined to run the place. Rapp didn't disagree but had to admit that she'd never failed to deliver the intel they'd needed—even from the most hardened foreign agents and terrorists.

He'd stopped using her years ago when he'd decided that both she and her methods crossed even his line. After that, he'd forgotten all about her. Or, more accurately, purposely erased their brief association from his mind.

"Interesting woman," Cook continued, uncrossing his legs and leaning forward. "Not only does she seem to be completely unafraid, but she actually wants to talk with you. I don't know if it's to suggest that you tell me everything you know so she doesn't have to turn your brain into Jell-O or if it's because she's excited about the challenge of breaking a man like you. If I had to guess, though, I'd say it was the latter."

Rapp agreed. This was a woman who had twice been accused of torturing animals in her basement when they finally cut her loose. The truth was that with the right amount of drugs, suffering, and electrical probes drilled into his brain, she could probably get whatever she wanted.

Cook pulled a phone from his pocket. "No reason to speculate. Let's see what she has to say."

He seemed to be enjoying himself as he scrolled through his contacts. And why not? The way he saw it, the tide of their meeting had just turned violently in his favor.

Cook put his cell on speaker and the superior acoustics of the room carried the ringtone with near-perfect clarity. When the call was picked up, though, it wasn't by a woman.

"You still alive, asshole?"

"Afraid so, Mas."

"Dammit! I had a hundred bucks on sixteen minutes, fifteen seconds."

"Can't win 'em all."

While it was true that Rapp had forgotten about Hornig, Irene Kennedy's memory was a bit sharper. Joe Maslick had snatched the woman from her Fairfax Station home just before Rapp landed in the United States. Cook was probably regretting releasing the man from jail about now.

"How've you been, Jane?" Rapp said.

"I've been fine."

It had been a long time since he'd heard that voice, but it still made him want to take a shower.

"We're playing Scrabble," Maslick said. "Should we finish the game?"

An unspoken second clause hung in the air. *Or should I put a plastic bag over her head and bury her in the woods?*

"Sure. I think you've got time."

The call disconnected but Cook just kept staring down at the screen. Not surprisingly, the smugness in his expression had disappeared.

"If I ran for president," Rapp said, "do you think I could beat you?"

Cook looked up, dazed. "What?"

"You heard me."

"Beat me? No . . . Of course not."

"Would you even give me a second thought?"

His confusion deepened. "Why would I?"

"Exactly. Why would you? You're the best in the world at what you do. The very idea that I could beat you and your team at the thing you've dedicated your lives to is a joke. Politics is your wheelhouse, and you could destroy me in a thousand different ways that I've never even thought about." Rapp paused for a moment. "Welcome to my wheelhouse, Tony."

CHAPTER 49

CATHERINE Cook stopped in front of the closed door to the study. Her husband was inside, but beyond that she knew almost nothing. Only that Rapp had arrived as agreed and that she'd been excluded from the meeting at the last minute.

Why? While her husband no longer seemed to trust her, surely he still understood that he needed her. They were still far greater than the sum of their parts and he was free to ignore whatever advice she offered if he chose to do so. In fact, it was his disregard for her counsel that had gotten them in this situation in the first place.

What had he and Rapp discussed? What had been conserved and what had been negotiated away? But most of all, had they been able to create a framework of assurances that could lead to a lasting détente?

If so, her husband would return to the world and almost certainly walk away with the next election. After that, she would follow for another two terms. At the end of that sixteen-year reign, they would have an unbreakable grip on the country. Everything they'd dreamed of, everything they'd worked for, would fall into place.

If, on the other hand, Rapp was simply trying to lure her husband out from behind his security, the calculus changed. While the White House would be well within her reach, the time and skills required to take permanent control would be lacking. Not quite the prize she'd sought, but a very attractive consolation.

Catherine recognized that she should feel more deeply about her husband's predicament, but it wasn't her nature. Particularly when the wounds in question were entirely self-inflicted. The truth was that he appealed to the fools who worshipped him because, in many ways, he was one of them.

Finally, she stepped inside and closed the door behind her. He was sitting at a small table with a lunch tray in front of him. It was untouched, and instead he was focused on the glass of whiskey in his hand. The image was enough to make sweat break across her forehead.

"Your meeting went well?" she said, managing to conjure a little optimism.

No answer. Instead, he continued to stare into the glass with an expression that was a subtle mix of rage, fear, and impotence.

"Tony? What happened?"

He turned slowly in her direction but seemed to look through her. "Rapp told me that if I resigned, he'd call off Legion and back away."

"What?" she said, confused. That wasn't what she and Kennedy had spoken about. Catherine stood frozen. Or had they? What exactly was said in their short time together? Only that the truce needed to be rebuilt. Not its terms.

"Where is he, Tony? Where is he now?"

Cook shrugged.

"You let him go?"

"Why wouldn't I?" he said, returning his attention to the glass. "If I held him or killed him, it wouldn't stop Legion. It wouldn't stop Kennedy or his men. They'd just keep coming until I'm dead."

"You're in the most secure place on the planet!" she shouted. "And it gets more secure every day. If we'd held him, at the very least we could use him to complicate the situation. To split their focus."

"If you believe all that, why don't you go after him, Cathy? Call him up. Tell him I've backed off but you're not going to. Put *your* life on the line."

"Why, Tony? Why would I do that? This is your mess, not mine. You let Darren get you into a war that you didn't know how to win. *You*. Not me."

He took a long pull on his whiskey, swirling it in his mouth for a moment before swallowing. "I'll concede the point, but it doesn't matter. I'm not going to die so you can build a campaign around my corpse."

"He's playing you," she said, though she didn't really believe it. "He's trying to get you out from behind your security."

Her husband saw through the sudden change in attitude. In truth, it had sounded desperate, even to her. He was the seductive liar in this partnership, not her.

"He gave me his word, Cathy. Aren't you the one who keeps telling me he can be trusted to keep it?"

She'd always considered it a rather banal cliché, but suddenly the walls really did feel like they were closing in on her. They'd devoted everything to this. Every decision, every friendship, every conversation. Their lives didn't exist beyond the momentum they'd built to get them there. It couldn't end like this. Not because of a meaningless former CIA operative.

Her mind began sifting options. A resignation was fatal. Of that, there was no doubt. Once someone walked away from power, there was no getting it back. A divorce? Could she turn him into the enemy and run *against* his legacy? Impossible. She didn't have that kind of support in the party nor the gifts necessary to acquire it. Could she get to Rapp? To Legion? No. Even if it was possible, her husband wouldn't allow it. The office of the first lady was powerless without his support.

She realized that he was staring directly at her, interpreting the emotions unconsciously playing across her face. When he raised his glass again, the rattle of the ice cubes seemed almost deafening.

"Checkmate, Catherine."

EPILOGUE

Outside of Swakopmund
Namibia

"The dishwasher's full," Anna said from her position in the kitchen doorway.

Claudia didn't immediately respond, instead squeezing onto the sofa near Rapp's feet. He moved them to her lap.

"Are there still dirty dishes?"

"Some. But just a few. I put them in the sink."

"Why don't you hand-wash them? We don't want to get any more of those bugs."

"Because there are too many! We can put them in the dishwasher tonight. There aren't *that* many bugs."

"March back in there and don't come out until they're all clean."

"I can't reach the faucet."

"There's a stepstool in the pantry. Any other problems I can help you with?"

"Mitch said he wanted to do them."

He grabbed a decorative pillow and lobbed it, missing her by inches. "You'd already be done with them by now if you just stopped whining."

"You said you were going to be gone for two days and it was like a week! I had to do them the whole time! It's your turn."

It was true that it had taken longer than expected to slip back into Namibia without being tracked. The fact that Cook had just let him go without saying a word about the ultimatum he'd been presented was a little worrying. While it could mean that he was going to take the deal, it could just as easily be a temporary retreat to regroup. And if that was the case, Rapp was likely being targeted by the combined forces of Homeland Security, the American military, and a significant number of US allies. In light of that, a week seemed pretty respectable.

"Anna . . ." Claudia cautioned.

"Fine!" she said before disappearing back into the kitchen. A few moments later the angry crash of dishes became audible.

Claudia sighed. "It could be a very long year."

"We'll work it out."

"I know we will. But if the president doesn't take your offer, we're going to need to sketch out some more concrete plans. We can't just spend the next year throwing darts at a world map and going where they land. Anna needs more structure than that. She's a handful as it is. We don't want her turning feral."

A disturbing silence descended on the kitchen and Rapp was about to get up to investigate when the phone on the coffee table rang. They both froze. The only person with the number was Irene Kennedy and it was single use. If she was calling, it was about something important.

Claudia licked her lips, staring down at the piece of vibrating plastic like it held the secrets of the universe. Finally, she nodded and he reached for it.

"Go ahead."

He heard a familiar clattering as someone taped the phone she'd called to another one in order to create an air gap similar to the one Coleman had helped with two weeks before.

"Mitch?" she said. "Are you there?"

"I'm here."

"My sources say that the president is about to hold an emergency press conference. He goes on in five minutes."

"Any word on what it's about?"

"No. But the networks are all scrambling to run it live. Do you have a way to watch where you are?"

"Yeah."

"Then good luck. To all of us."

She cut the call off. Even with all the security, shorter was better.

Claudia looked at him and let out a nervous laugh. "It's a little like opening a box at Christmas that could be the greatest gift you ever got—"

"Or a half kilo of plastique wired to the flap," Rapp said, finishing her thought.

"Exactly."

He used a remote to turn on the TV and surf through the satellite channels. Finally, he found a news service with a feed of the empty lectern in the White House briefing room. A commentator was speculating endlessly about what the conference could be about, but Rapp suspected that she wasn't even close. There could be only two reasons for the president to be speaking on that particular morning. The first was to announce that Mitch Rapp had threatened to assassinate him and a worldwide manhunt was in the offing. The second was to resign. Which it would be was a coin toss at this point.

The clattering of dishes started in the kitchen again, but they ignored it, remaining glued to the unmoving image on-screen. A few minutes later, President Anthony Cook strode out. No notes, meticulously groomed, and an expression that gave nothing away.

"Thank you all for coming," he said, making eye contact with the reporters lined up in front of him. "I'll make this brief and I'm not taking questions. I've recently been diagnosed with a serious illness. After discussing it at length with my doctor, the first lady, and the vice president, I've come to the conclusion that I can no longer carry out the duties of the presidency at the level that the American people deserve. Because of this, I will be resigning as soon as we can develop a plan to ensure a smooth transition. While my time in the Oval Office has been short, it's been the greatest honor of my life. I thank you all for your confidence and God bless America."

None of the reporters made so much as a sound as he nodded in their direction and walked out. Whether that was out of respect or a stunned silence was hard to say. Once Cook was gone, though, the announcer seemed to remember she had a microphone and began babbling into it.

Rapp used the remote to turn off the television and let his head fall back on the arm of the sofa. He felt Claudia squeeze his leg, but neither of them spoke. Kennedy's bat-shit crazy plan had worked. He had walked unarmed into the White House, threatened a sitting president, and walked out not only alive but the victor. It was over. They had their lives back. His guys had their lives back.

Everyone was going home.